PRAISE

GRANVILLE WYCHE BURGESS

and

THE LAST AT-BAT OF SHOELESS JOE

"*The Last At-Bat of Shoeless Joe* brilliantly bakes wish fulfillment into a period piece. A gripping story that is both illuminating and emotional, it'll hook you early and won't let go. Great for baseball fans, and even true-crime enthusiasts, of all ages."

> — Ken Davidoff, baseball columnist for *The New York Post*

"In Granville Wyche Burgess' new novel, Shoeless Joe Jackson of Black Sox fame comes alive in a most ingenious way. He becomes involved in a struggle between good and evil, and in the end you root for him to become the hero he might have become had dark forces not ended his baseball career. If you love baseball, you'll love this book. If you love books with satisfying endings, you'll give Joe (and Granville) a standing ovation."

> — Peter Golenbock, *New York Times*-bestselling author of *Dynasty*, *The Bronx Zoo* (with Sparkly Lyle), *Number 1* (with Billy Martin) and *Idiot* (with Johnny Damon)

"Joseph Jefferson 'Shoeless Joe' Jackson passed away in December 1951, three decades after he was laid low by the Black Sox scandal. But the mystique of Shoeless Joe has never left us…. [H]e is now the subject of a remarkable new novel by Granville Wyche Burgess. With a grand slam plot wrapped in lyrical and whimsical prose, Burgess gives us the grit and glory of old time baseball, poignantly reviving the spirit of a fallen hero."

> — Raymond Arsenault, author of *Freedom Riders, The Sound of Freedom,* and *Arthur Ashe, A Life*

"Granville Wyche Burgess is such an amazing talent."
— Patzi Gil, nationally syndicated radio host, *Joy on Paper*

"No baseball player has ever been as mistreated as Joe Jackson, but now, on this 100th anniversary of his downfall, he's finally found his champion in Granville Wyche Burgess, a writer with a heart the size of South Carolina. Somewhere, the old slugger is crying tears of joy. I love Shoeless Joe, and I love this book."
— Alon Preiss, author, *In Love With Alice*

THE LAST AT-BAT OF SHOELESS JOE

A Novel

Granville Wyche Burgess

ISBN 978-1-7329139-1-2

Front cover illustration and book design by Scribe Freelance

Chickadee Prince Logo by Garrett Gilchrist

Visit us at www.ChickadeePrince. com

First Printing

GRANVILLE WYCHE BURGESS

THE LAST AT-BAT OF SHOELESS JOE

A Novel

GRANVILLE WYCHE BURGESS received an Emmy nomination for his writing on the soap opera, *Capitol*. He has received awards from the CBS/Foundation for the Dramatist Guild, the National Endowment for the Humanities, the U.S. Department of Education, and the Pennsylvania Council on the Arts, among others. He was President of the Princeton Triangle Club and has an MFA in Directing from The Catholic University of America.

He has also written for the television series *Tales from the Darkside* and for PBS. His musical, *Conrack*, based on the Pat Conroy memoir *The Water Is Wide*, had a sold-out run at Ford's Theatre and was attended by President George H.W. Bush and the first lady, Barbara Bush. Mr. Burgess's plays and musicals have been performed throughout the United States. He was Director of the Walnut Street Theatre School, teaching playwriting, screenwriting, directing and acting. He is Co-Founder and CEO of Quill Entertainment, a charitable company whose mission is "Teaching America's Heritage Through Story and Song."

His bestselling *Rebecca Zook* novels are also available from Chickadee Prince Books.

He lives in Connecticut with his wife, Reba.

THE LAST AT-BAT OF SHOELESS JOE

A Novel

Chickadee Prince Books
New York

For my brother, Frank,
who taught me to love the game

God knows I gave my best in baseball,
and no one can truthfully judge me otherwise.

Joe Jackson

Just keep in mind that, regardless of the verdict of
juries, baseball is competent to protect itself against
crooks, both inside and outside the game.

Kennesaw Mountain Landis

CHAPTER 1

The wail of the mill whistle split the early morning air like the scream of some tortured creature, then suddenly stopped, leaving the air still and lifeless.

Lying in bed, Jimmy Roberts slowly opened his eyes. He didn't need to look at the alarm clock to know what time it was. In fact, he didn't even own one. You always knew what time it was in a mill village. The whistle made sure of that. Six a.m.

He stretched his lanky frame. Five feet, eleven inches. *Not tall enough*, he thought. *But maybe I ain't through growin'. I'm only seventeen.* He raised his left arm and looked at his hand. Large. He flexed his fingers. Long. Slowly he curled them into the grip on an imaginary baseball. Two fingers down the seam. Fastball. He closed his eyes and pictured himself on the mound, winding up, bringing his arm as far back as it would stretch, pushing hard off the rubber, whipping his arm toward the plate. He saw the ball smack into the catcher's mitt. Strike!

He smiled and sat up. Today was the day. A little more practice and he'd be ready. Ten a.m. tryout. The Greenville *Spinners*. Named after one of the soul-less jobs performed in a textile mill in 1951. Spinning, doffing, carding, sweeping, drawing, weaving, loom fixing. Different names, but, as far as Jimmy was concerned, they all stood for the same thing: life sucked out by monotonous repetition. A lifeless existence. The kind of existence Jimmy was determined to avoid.

He stood on the heart pine floor and ambled to a corner of his tiny room. He yawned and stretched. It felt good. Squatting down, he looked at a cardboard box opened up on both sides. It was a replica of Comiskey Park, home of the Chicago White Sox. Or at least as good a replica as Jimmy could manage. He'd outlined the stands down both foul lines and in center field. But instead of putting people in the stands, Jimmy had taped up various newspaper headlines. He didn't bother looking at them. He'd read them hundreds of times. But he did glance at the yellowing picture of a baseball player behind what would have been home plate.

The player was at bat, hitting left-handed. His front foot was slightly lifted off the ground. His stance was wide. His arms were cocked, ready to swing forward. Poised across the front of the jersey, his right arm partially obscured a large "S," for "Sox." Seen in profile was a large nose and square jaw. Jimmy couldn't really see the eyes. They would reveal, he had no doubt, an intense focus, something to emulate. Jimmy couldn't emulate the swing. He was a pitcher, not a hitter. But he could emulate the attitude, he could emulate the purpose, he could emulate the desire. Most importantly, he could emulate the will. *The will to get off the hill* was the little rhyme Jimmy had made up for himself. That's why he had built this shrine to his hero. He had gotten off mill hill, and Jimmy was determined to follow in his footsteps.

He moved to the small wooden chair where he had draped the clothes he'd worn yesterday. He pulled on the rumpled jeans, picked up the slightly dirty short-sleeve shirt, glanced at the small bureau along the wall next to his shrine, and decided to wear yesterday's shirt. Didn't want to make more work for his mother. *Maybe I'll change before the try-out*, he thought, but for now he just wanted to get going.

He reached beside the shrine, grabbed a croker sack full of baseballs, picked up his glove from the top of the bureau, and headed for the kitchen.

On the table was a bowl of grits, growing cold. His mother, Thelma, had made them before heading out for her six a.m. shift at the mill. Jimmy put down the burlap sack, tried a bite, and grimaced. *Nothin' worse than cold grits.* He carried the bowl to the sink and noticed a note from his mother. "Did you talk to him yet?" was lettered in her small, neat hand. Jimmy knew his answer wouldn't please her, but that was for later. Now, he had to get ready, ready for his try-out with a real professional baseball team.

Jimmy hurried from the kitchen and through the front door, paused for a moment on the small porch, and looked to the top of the hill. There sat the object of his hatred. The four-story red brick colossus stretched some seventy-five yards, with at least a thousand windows on all four sides. It was reputed to be the largest textile mill in the world under one roof. The chimney belched black smoke. The faintest hum filled the air, a low-volume reminder of the deafening roar inside. A billboard sign on top proclaimed "Woodside Mill." Jimmy hopped off the porch, turned his back on the mill, and headed in the opposite direction.

He walked briskly down Third Street. It could have been named any other number, and it would have looked exactly like every other street in the mill village. Each house was a flat wooden box, one story in height, raised above the ground on small piles of bricks at the corners. Each consisted of four small rooms around a central fireplace. Many of the dull-red tin roofs were warped with age, and most of the houses sported the same peeling white paint. All of them had porches with railings sitting atop concrete blocks. Some mill workers tried to distinguish their house by having a picket rail instead of a solid porch rail, or by painting a green trim on the house. But to Jimmy, they all looked exactly the same.

Even though it was early, newly washed clothes hung on lines in several yards. They wouldn't dry quickly. It was only mid-May, but the humidity was already settling in. Greenville, South Carolina, may have been situated at the foot of the Blue Ridge Mountains, but that didn't prevent ninety-plus degree temperatures in spring and summer, late afternoon thunderstorms, and humidity so dense it fogged glasses and soaked shirts.

Jimmy quickened his stride. He noticed a few cardboard signs hung on several porches. One or two said "Do not disturb!" hung there by people on the night shift who needed to sleep most of the day. Other signs had numbers, telling the iceman how many pounds of ice to leave in the icebox inside the house. No one locked his door, of course. There was little to steal. More than that, however, mill people lived like next-of-kin, even if they weren't. "Like a family" was the phrase they sometimes used to describe their way of life in the mill village. Neighbors spent the evenings talking across the porches, waiting until it was cool enough to go inside. Jimmy sometimes just sat on the porch steps, closed his eyes, and let the constant buzz of words lilting through the air lull him into pleasant reveries. He liked that part of mill life. But not enough to want to stay there.

At last, he reached the southern edge of the mill village, which abutted the Negro section, called Free Town. Across the barely paved street stood an abandoned barn. Several boards were missing from one side, and the tin roof was crumpled in one corner, but it served Jimmy's purpose well. He crossed the street and entered. Tossing his sack of baseballs to one side, he walked toward an old peach basket nailed to the back wall and adjusted it. Then he retraced his steps to the croker sack, reached in, and withdrew his baseball glove. An old Rawlings, so worn and flexible from use Jimmy could bend the fingers all the way back. He dumped the rest of the contents onto the dirt floor. A dozen or so baseballs spilled out. Some were in pretty decent shape. Some had been used so often they needed tape to make them round again. Jimmy selected one of the taped balls. He liked to work his way up to the best balls, as a kind of reward.

He tossed his glove on top of the small mound of dirt he had built, then began to loosen up. First, he wind-milled his left arm several times, then his right. Next, a few deep knee bends, then touching his toes while bending from the waist. After rolling his head a few times, he stepped onto the mound, easily slid his right hand into the glove, slammed the ball into it a couple of times, and looked down at the peach basket. He was ready to pitch.

An hour or so later, Jimmy stepped outside the barn, satisfied. He had pitched well, his fastball humming, hitting the basket more times than not. His curve hadn't had that much bite, but it was getting better. Besides, players his age weren't expected to have a great curve ball. That's what getting into the minor leagues was for, to develop your stuff. That's what today's tryout was all about. Showing his stuff to the *Spinners'* manager, making the team, working his way up, year by year, step by step — A ball, AA ball, AAA ball, then … the Bigs.

Jimmy wiped the sweat from his brow, hitched up his pants, and set off for Meadowbrook Park, home of the Greenville *Spinners*. He could have taken one of the trackless trolleys that still plied the streets, but he wanted to walk. It would take a little longer, but it wasn't that far, maybe half a mile. He went down Main Street until he reached Birnie Street, following it along the railroad tracks until he came to a small pedestrian bridge. He took the walkway over the tracks and looked at the sign above the front entrance to the stadium. "Welcome to Meadowbrook Park, Home of the Greenville *Spinners*."

For a brief moment, Jimmy thought about not going in. He took a deep breath. *I gotta do it.* He had waited too long, practiced too much, dreamed too sweetly of the results. It was just pitching. He knew how to do that. He'd thrown thousands of pitches. The mound would be a little bigger than he was used to, but it was still the same sixty feet six inches to home plate; home plate still had the same five sides coming to a point in the rear; and the baseball had the same nine-inch circumference. Of course, it was probably a lot newer than the balls Jimmy was used to, but that should make it easier to throw, not harder. This was it. His chance to escape the mill. *Gotta do it* he repeated to himself under his breath.

A guard nodded Jimmy's way inside. He took the first aisle on the right, as instructed, walked up the ramp, and emerged into the early morning sunshine. The sight before him stunned Jimmy. Green grass so healthy it looked painted. The dirt infield raked to perfection. White chalk down the foul lines, the open-ended rectangles of the coach's boxes, the familiar fat-T outline of the batter's box, the pitcher's mound rising like a sacred mountain from the middle of the infield. He'd seen it before, of course, from the knothole in the outfield fence. Since they couldn't afford a ticket, he and his friends sometimes watched the *Spinners* game through the knothole. They even had a name for themselves: The Knothole Gang. But this was different. Now he was on the other side of the fence. He was on a baseball diamond! Not like the scruffy diamonds of the Textile League ballparks, but a magical, mystical arena designed for heroic feats and dreams-come-true. Jimmy almost gasped. This was heaven. This was it!

In the stands along the first-base side, a group of some fifteen young men listened to the manager address them from beyond the stands. Some were his age, many were older, some looking to be almost thirty. Short, tall, fat, thin, they all had the same dream. Jimmy hurried to join them. Walking had taken longer than he'd thought.

"That's it," the manager was saying. "All you gotta do is pitch, and keep pitching till I tell you to stop."

"How will we know how we did?" a scrawny kid in a Judson Mill uniform asked. "Will you send us a letter or something?"

Everyone laughed. "No letter," the manager answered. "If you've got a phone, you'll hear from me. If not, and I want you bad enough, you'll find me on your doorstep. You, there, go pitch." The manager pointed at Jimmy.

"Me?" Jimmy asked. "But I just got here."

"Serves you right for bein' late," the manager replied, spitting tobacco juice into the dirt. "Hurry up. Ain't got all day."

Some of the other hopefuls turned and looked at Jimmy. Others stared at their feet, thanking their lucky stars they hadn't been picked first. Jimmy gulped. No time to settle in, no time to think through what he wanted to do, just up and at 'em. He grabbed his glove, walked down the aisle, and hopped over the small wall onto the field. The manager moved off towards home plate, calling out, "Corky!" A portly catcher emerged from the dugout and headed for his spot behind the plate. Jimmy felt the eyes of all the other pitching candidates on him and he trudged towards the mound. Once there, he pulled his baseball cap down lower, kicked at the dirt around the rubber, and looked toward home plate.

"Do I get to warm up?" he asked.

"Not on my time," the manager snapped. "Get him the ball, Corky."

Corky fired a baseball at Jimmy, who snagged it with his glove. It stung, but Jimmy was not about to flinch. Instead, he tucked his glove under his left arm, taking out the ball and rubbing it vigorously, trying to still the butterflies in his stomach. After a moment, the manager yelled out, "Let's go!"

Jimmy put the Rawlings on his right hand and stepped on the rubber. He watched as Corky squatted behind home plate and popped his fist into his mitt a couple of times, then held it out as a target. Jimmy moved the ball in the pocket of his glove with his left hand, searching for a good grip. He closed his eyes for a moment in silent prayer. *Lord, let me throw strikes.* The moment he had worked so hard for was here. Would he, finally, be up to the challenge? There was only one way to find out. He went into his windup, rocked back, and let fly as hard as he could.

The ball was about a foot wide of the plate, nowhere near the strike zone. Corky had to stretch to catch it, then wasted no time in whipping the ball back to Jimmy. Standing near the plate, the manager spat tobacco juice dismissively. Jimmy caught the returned ball, and turned his back to stare at the outfield. Not a good start. A Burma Shave sign in center field promised a close shave. *I'll settle for a close pitch,* thought Jimmy. *Come on!* He turned back, gripped the ball, and threw another pitch.

Another ball, this one low and in the dirt. Jimmy hung his head. Corky just lobbed back the ball this time, his energy seemingly deflated by Jimmy's poor performance. What had happened, he threw just fine in the barn? "Show me your curve," shouted the manager, wanting to get Jimmy off the mound and move on to a candidate who might exhibit more promise.

Just two pitches and now I've got to throw a curve? Jimmy turned away from the plate and again rubbed the baseball. *They don't waste any time.* He glanced at the sky, now a hazy blue through the humidity. He looked at the other men, waiting their turn in the seats behind first base. Did they feel sorry for him? Probably not. They wanted to make the team, and so anyone who made it ahead of them was trouble. Finally, he turned and looked towards home plate. The manager stood with his arms crossed, waiting impatiently. Jimmy experienced an overwhelming desire to be anywhere but here. But here he was, needing to throw a curve ball with what felt like the whole world watching. For the first time ever, he regretted his dream.

Jimmy gripped the baseball along one of the seams with his first two fingers and got set to throw his curve. He drew back his arm and brought it forward, snapping his wrist at the last moment. The ball curved all right, curved so much it bounced in front of the plate. Corky made a stab at it, but the ball bounced off his glove towards the third-base dugout. "Goddamn!" the manager croaked. "One more chance. Smitty!" he yelled toward the dugout.

A large man, who must have weighed two hundred and fifty pounds, emerged from the dugout, slowly waving a big bat, and walked lazily to the plate. Jimmy had never seen anyone that big. Mill folks worked too hard to ever grow that large. He certainly had never seen anyone that big in a batter's box, purposefully swinging a bat in his direction. Smitty had been transformed, once he stepped inside that box. He seemed to shed pounds and grow muscle. His eyes narrowed into a hard stare. He looked downright menacing — there was no other word for it. Jimmy turned his back. His hand had begun to sweat. He wiped it on his pants and looked out towards the outfield fence. The Burma Shave ad was slightly out of focus. He blinked a couple of times. *Just pretend he isn't there. Pretend nobody's here. Just pitch to the peach basket.*

With a deep breath, Jimmy turned back to face Smitty, who most definitely *was* there — an ogre with a club, to Jimmy's way of thinking. Jimmy tried to imagine the peach basket, but he all he saw was Corky's mitt. *Just focus on that. Forget about Smitty. Focus on the mitt!* He tried to swallow, but his mouth was too dry. There was nothing to do but throw the baseball.

From the moment the ball left his hand, Jimmy knew something was wrong. He hadn't really completed his motion fully, and the ball flew wide. Wide and high. About as high as Smitty's head. Jimmy watched helplessly as the ball sped towards the batter. Time slowed down. He could see the ball perfectly, rising little by little, slowly approaching Smitty. Only it wasn't going slowly in real time. It was Jimmy's fastball and it was going at least eighty miles per hour.

At the plate, Smitty's eyes widened in surprise, and then he flung his body to the ground. He moved pretty fast, for a big man. Luckily so, for the ball barely missed his left temple. Corky lunged to catch it, but the ball glanced off his glove, ricocheting right into the manager, standing a few feet behind Corky. It slammed into his gut, causing him to double over. He managed a feeble "Goddammit!" before clutching his stomach.

Without hesitation, Smitty scrambled to his feet and started running at Jimmy on the mound. For a half second, Jimmy couldn't believe what was happening. How did he get here, on a pitcher's mound, with a maniac running straight at him, shouting a string of expletives Jimmy couldn't make out but knew came from a deep well of unmitigated anger? From the corner of one eye, he saw the other candidates rise in their seats, as if witnessing a home run. From the corner of his other, he saw the manager begin running towards the mound, joined belatedly by Corky. Three large men running pell-mell towards Jimmy, bent on revenge of a physical nature.

Jimmy decided to run, too. He didn't know what else to do. He turned and sprinted towards dead center field and the Burma Shave sign.

If he could just keep it in focus, give himself a goal, maybe he could escape with his own close shave. He wasn't sure what he'd do when he reached the sign, but he didn't have time to think. He only had time to run like hell.

As he crossed second base, he began to hear things more clearly. "You better run!" yelled the manager. "Hit my best player? I'm gonna murder your ass!" "Come back here, you little punk!" Smitty screamed. "I'm gonna stuff that glove down your throat!" Lacking sufficient vocabulary, Corky could only shout "Yiiiiiiiiii!" But Jimmy didn't need words for motivation. What little imagination he mustered, as he ran harder than he'd ever run before, convinced him that having these three large, angry men pile onto him was not an option.

When he reached the outfield wall, Jimmy had a sudden shock. The wall was a lot higher than he'd thought. He couldn't just jump over it; he'd have to climb it. But the wall was flat. *Maybe there's another way.* Jimmy turned around. Smitty and Company were bearing down on him. If he tried to reverse field, and run around them back towards home plate, they might be able to chase him down. And who knew, maybe the other candidates would pour from the stands and tackle him, trying to score points with the manager. He turned back towards the outfield wall. Then he remembered. *The knothole!*

Jimmy began running towards the hole. His pursuers immediately changed direction to follow him. "I'm gonna rip your arm out," Smitty yelled. That was all the final motivation Jimmy needed. He backed up a few feet, ran towards the wall, leapt as high as he could, placed his right foot in the knothole and launched himself. His hands grabbed the top of the fence, he hoisted himself up and over, and dropped to the ground. On the other side, he could hear the manager yelling. "You son of a bitch, don't ever let me see you around here again!" As he raced towards the dirt parking lot and freedom, the shouting continued. "What's your name? What's your name?" When he reached the lot, Jimmy stopped and began laughing giddily. *Thank God I got here too late to fill out the information slip with my name an' address on it!*

CHAPTER 2

Inside Jackson's Liquor Store, 1262 Pendleton Street, in the commercial district just outside the Brandon mill village, a tall, lanky man, sixty-three, six-foot-one and still near his playing weight of 200 pounds, sat behind his cluttered desk, staring blankly at the wall of liquor bottles opposite him. He had the large face and big ears of a typical country farmer. But this was no farmer. This was Joseph Jefferson Wofford Jackson, whom some called the greatest baseball player of all time, known to most of the world by his moniker, Shoeless Joe. That is, to most of the world who remembered him, for Shoeless Joe's prime had been the years between 1908 and 1919. That final year, his team, the Chicago White Sox, had lost the World Series, and Shoeless Joe and seven other players had been accused of throwing the series for money. That had been the last year of professional baseball for Shoeless, who was banned from the game forever in 1920. Thirty-one years ago. Plenty of time for people to have forgotten. Plenty of time for people to have even stopped wondering "Whatever happened to Shoeless Joe?" Plenty of time for everyone except the big-boned, stoop-shouldered man slouched in the wooden desk chair in the mid-morning heat of a Carolina summer day. He would never forget.

Joe roused himself and crossed to the calendar nailed to the wall. He tore off the page saying "May 16," crumpled it, and tossed it nonchalantly towards the trash basket next to his desk. He made it without even trying. The greatest natural athlete of all time was another thing people called Joe Jackson. Crossing to the windows looking out onto Pendleton Street, he rolled up the shades of the shop. People had to know he was open, even if not too many folks bought booze in the morning. A few local alcoholics and one or two bums who had managed to scrape together enough for a bottle of cheap wine. Truth to tell, Joe could probably wait until after lunch to open the store. But then again, what else would he do?

Once the shades were rolled up, he crossed to a corner and lifted the cover off a large birdcage. "Feed me, you sonofabitch!" squawked an obviously well-fed parrot from his perch. His red, blue, and green feathers seemed as bright as ever. Maybe the yellow ones had faded a little. This was the way the parrot, Pee Wee, greeted him every day.

His previous owner had taught him how to curse, so Joe thought he'd improve matters by teaching Pee Wee baseball words. He'd started with his least-favorite umpire. "You're blind, ump!" Joe said.

"You're lousy, O'Laughlin!" Pee Wee replied.

Joe dribbled some birdseed into Pee Wee's small cup and re-locked the cage door. He used to let him fly around the shop, till Pee Wee had landed on a customer's head and begun pecking. It was a woman with a bountiful head of red hair, styled into an attractive perm. At least, it had been attractive to Pee Wee. Perhaps it stirred some primordial instinct, from jungle days, of a nice place to perch. The woman had threatened to sue, but a free bottle of Smirnoff had convinced her otherwise. Nevertheless, Shoeless had decided then that Pee Wee had to stay caged. He couldn't afford to be giving away free liquor all the time.

Liquor. How had he gotten into this business? He didn't even like to drink that much, probably a good thing, surrounded by alcohol as he was. But how had his life become the sorting and shelving of gins, vodkas, whiskeys and cheap wine? Joe looked around the room. So many kinds of booze. He shook his head in disbelief. Some people probably drank just to get happy, but Joe didn't think many. He thought most people drank to pacify some ultimately unassailable ache, pain, injury — something that needed smothering or smoothing-over, some rush of feeling that had to be rejected and repulsed. Given what he'd been through, Joe sometimes thought, it was amazing that demon rum had not devoured him.

Walking back to his desk, he stopped and looked at the floor. A brown bobby pin lay resting on its side. Joe hesitated. From force of habit, he looked around. Seeing no one, he bent down and picked up the bobby pin. He turned it over in his palm and stared at it. And remembered.

Connie Mack Stadium, Philadelphia, September 11, 1908. Twenty-year-old Joe Jackson trotted up the dugout steps with Black Betsy in his hands. When he was a teenager, Ol' Cap'n Martin, who drove one of the first street cars in Greenville, had given the bat to him. Said he'd whittled it from a hickory tree, which may have explained the crook in the bat. Betsy measured 36 inches and weighed 48 ounces. Not many baseball bats of the time were black. And surely this was the only one that had gained its color by the countless coats of tobacco juice young Joe had assiduously applied to it over the years. Joe loved to hit with the crook facing the pitcher, which made the contact sound like he'd hit the ball with a brick bat.

On his way to the plate, Joe paused, bent down, and picked up a bobby pin. He smiled and stuffed it into his back pocket. Frankie Lavagetto called to him from the bench. "Hey, Jackson, why in hell do you pick up those things?"

Joe didn't want to respond, but he knew if he didn't answer, Frankie would just keep after him, and he needed to concentrate. He'd only been with the Philadelphia Athletics for a week. That is, if you didn't count the two days he'd played with them a month ago. Last August, his teammates had harassed him so much he'd simply gotten on a train and gone back to Greenville. They'd called him a dumb hick, a hillbilly, and a lot worse. But it was the trick they'd played on him in the hotel dining room that did it for Joe. He'd innocently asked why there was water in the small bowl in front of his plate. Frankie, a well-built Italian from Philadelphia and a local hero, had told him it was drinking water.

"Why don't they put it in a glass?" Joe asked.

"It's special water," Frankie replied. "Comes from the mountains of Pennsylvania. It's kinda rare. Hotel saves it just for us. Try it, you'll like it."

"Some folks claim it improves your sex life," George Harding volunteered. "It's a ... What's that called, Professor?"

He looked towards Larry King, whom everybody considered the smartest man on the team because he'd gone to college. "An aphrodisiac," Larry answered.

"Can you say 'aphrodisiac,' Joe?" George asked.

"Apherdisiac."

"Close enough!" George's riposte brought gales of laughter from the other teammates.

"Come on, Jackson, drink up!" Frankie urged. "It'll do you good."

Joe was no different from any other rookie. He wanted to be liked. He wanted to fit in. He wanted to be part of the team. He lifted the bowl somewhat awkwardly, placed it to his lips, and took a swallow.

If the laughter had been loud before, now it was raucous. "That's a finger bowl, you dumb rube," Frankie cried between laughs. "You clean your fingers in it!"

"How was it, Jackson?" another player asked. "Sweaty?"

"Here, Joe, have some of mine!" someone else offered. "Mine, too!" another player shouted, holding up his finger bowl. "For your sex life!" a third player chimed in.

By that time Joe had risen red-faced from his chair and was walking out of the dining room. The taunts continued behind him, but he was determined not to hear them. He was determined never to hear these so-called teammates again. Because Joe was different from most rookies.

He didn't need baseball. The next morning, without a word, he got on a train and went back to Greenville.

Once home, his mother had persuaded him to return. The Greenville News *was reporting that if he didn't return, he might be blacklisted from baseball forever. Connie Mack, the owner and manager of the Athletics, telegrammed him a terse "Report at once!" But what probably changed Joe's mind was that some people were calling him a coward. Because the team he was to face next was the Detroit Tigers. The team of Ty Cobb, the Georgia Peach, the most-feared batter in the American League. They said Joe was scared to play against him.*

So Joe had returned to Philadelphia. But the torment from his teammates had continued, and Joe had a terrible week at the plate. In the first game of the double-header against the Washington Senators, he'd gone 0 for 4 against Walter Johnson. He'd made outs his first two at-bats in the second game. You'd think his teammates might have let up, hoping his bat would propel them to a win. But they were more interested in harassing Joe than beating Washington.

Rookies were supposed to be harassed, of course; it was part of the culture, and it was mostly done in good fun. But the baiting and mocking also had a darker purpose. The rookies were there, ultimately, to take the jobs of the veterans. Survival of the fittest. If the veterans could keep the rookies from taking batting practice or even make them go home, it was all for the best, as far as the vets were concerned. And so here was Frankie Lavagetto, the Philadelphia Athletics left fielder, taunting Shoeless Joe Jackson, the rookie whose position just happened to be left field.

"I said, why the bobby pins, Joe? You keeping the field clean?" Frankie's latest volley caused a ripple of laughter to spread down the bench.

"I pick 'em up fer luck," Joe finally said. He smiled, to indicate that he knew it was kind of silly, but lots of players had superstitions.

Joe, however, wasn't lots of players. He was Shoeless Joe Jackson, The Carolina Confection. The Carolina Crashsmith. Homerun Joe. The Pride of Brandon. "You sure you don't bring 'em out at night to practice your counting?" Frankie fired back.

"Hell, no, Frankie," Willie Sutton joined in. "He puts 'em in his hair. That's why it stands up so purty!" More laughter.

"Country-cured!" added a teammate, to more giggles.

"Get on up there, Shoeless," Connie Mack finally said. "Don't listen to these knuckleheads. Knock it outta here."

Joe walked to the plate, took a couple of practice swings, and stepped in to hit. But he had listened to those knuckleheads. He couldn't focus on the pitcher, could hardly see the baseball as the first pitch split the plate. Ordinarily Joe would have hammered it. The pitcher had made a mistake, left the ball over the middle. But Joe didn't even swing. The bobby pin in his back pocket didn't feel like "luck" at all. It felt incongruously heavy, weighing him down. "Stee-rike!" called the umpire.

He called "strike" two more times before Joe turned and headed back to the dugout. He hung his head. "Better luck next time, Jackson!" Frankie yelled. "Look for another bobby pin." His teammates laughed. Joe reached into his back pocket and pulled out the bobby pin. He flung it down the first-base line, as far as he could. The next morning he took another train back to Greenville, and this time he didn't return.

Back in his liquor store, Joe continued to stare at the bobby pin he'd just found. A simple thing, a bobby pin. How could it carry all that weight? For a moment, Joe was tempted to fling it away again. Instead, he dropped it into the trash basket and sat down at his desk.

The door opened cautiously. Joe didn't even bother to look up. He knew who his first customer was every day. "Git," he blurted out.

In the doorway, Willie Jones, a ten-year-old colored boy, held his ground, though a bit hesitantly. He never knew what kind of mood Shoeless Joe would be in when he came with his daily request. There were days when Joe felt sorry for him, or was in a good mood for some reason, or just didn't care enough, and he let Willie have the Southern Comfort. It was to comfort Willie's daddy, at least for a while. But having to come get it for him caused a great deal of discomfort in Willie.

"Please, Mr. Shoeless," Willie intoned.

"I told you not to call me that," Joe responded. "Use my first name."

"I did."

"*Joe* is my first name, Willie. Not 'Shoeless.' Got that?" Joe asked sharply.

"Yessuh, Mr. Shoeless," Willie replied. He could tell this was not going to be one of those good-mood days for Joe.

"Tell yer father to git his own sorry self over here," Joe continued, looking at Willie. He saw a scrawny boy with very dark skin, dressed in a dirty pair of cotton shorts with an even dirtier tee shirt to match. Barefoot. But with what Shoeless used to call "Happy Eyes," eyes that seemed bright no matter the circumstances of their owner. Some people had that ability to stay positive no matter what. Willie was one. Joe's wife, Katie, was another.

"You know I cain't wake him, Mr. Shoeless," said Willie. "He don't get up this early, but he sure likes his Comfort when he do."

"You're too young to be buying booze." Shoeless rose from his desk and walked over to Willie. His six-foot-three frame towered over the small boy.

"You done sold it to me yesterday," Willie argued.

"That was yesterday," Joe replied.

"You know what Daddy'll do to me if I don't bring him his Comfort," Willie pleaded.

"Jes' stay away from him till he gets it some other way, then he'll leave you alone," Shoeless responded. He knew Willie's father wasn't a bad man, he just needed alcohol to make him feel right. Willie was lucky. Some people got violent on booze. Willie's dad got nicer.

"Yessuh, Mr. Shoeless," Willie said, softly, eyes downcast.

Despite himself, Shoeless felt sorry for the boy. It wasn't easy growing up poor in South Carolina. It was even harder if you were Negro. Playing ball in northern cities, Joe hardly ever mixed with colored people. Down south, they were an every day part of life. A familiarity often existed between Negroes and whites that would have astonished a northerner. Sometimes even a fondness. Like what Shoeless Joe felt for Willie right then. "Come on over and say 'hello' to Pee Wee, Willie."

Willie's happy eyes turned happier. He scurried across the room. "Hiya, Pee Wee! What's the score?"

Joe always worried what might come out of Pee Wee's mouth, but this time he kept it clean. "Three to two, three to two," squawked the parrot. It was always the same score.

"What inning, Pee Wee?"

"Bottom ninth," Pee Wee answered. It was always the same inning. Shoeless liked tight ball games. He liked imagining himself coming to bat with the game on the line. He liked imagining hitting a towering home run. At least, he had liked imagining it when he'd taught Pee Wee certain words and phrases years ago. Not so much now. But once you teach a parrot something, he knows it forever.

"An' Shoeless Joe Jackson comin' to the plate," Willie cried excitedly. He really didn't know that much about Joe's past. He knew he had once been famous for being a great ballplayer. And he'd heard about some sort of scandal that had caused him to be kicked out of professional baseball. But actually, people didn't really care that much about Shoeless any more, even in his hometown of Greenville. A lot of people didn't even know he lived there. The greatest hitter of all-time, right there, and all the boys in Little League and Pony League and all the hundreds of ballplayers around the Piedmont area probably didn't even know it. There might be an occasional article in the newspaper, but for the most part, Shoeless was a forgotten man. And that's the way he liked it.

"Bottom ninth," Pee Wee repeated. Shoeless hadn't bothered to teach him the outcome of the game. With Joe Jackson at the plate, it was a foregone conclusion.

The door opened again and Katie Jackson walked briskly inside, closing it after her. "Lawdy, it's hot," she said by way of introduction. "Hey, Willie, how're you doin'?"

"Fine, Miz Jackson," Willie replied.

"Willie was jes' tellin' me he might look like he's ten, but actually he's twenty-one, old enough to buy liquor," Joe teased.

"How 'bout I give the money to Miz Jackson, she'll buy it, then give it to me," Willie suggested.

"Oh, no, don't get me in the middle of all this," Katie objected. "I just keep the books. But I can go out back if you've got business to transact," she added with a smile.

"We don't," said Joe, firmly. "Now git on home, Willie. An' tell your daddy to come get his own liquor from now on."

"Yessuh, Mr. Shoeless," Willie responded, moving towards the door. "Sure will." They all three knew he wouldn't, and that it wouldn't do any good if he did. "Y'all goin' to the baseball game tomorrow? Brandon versus Woodside, oughta be a good 'un."

"Got better things to do, Willie," Shoeless replied icily. Katie let a small sigh escape. *Like waste all day in a liquor store?* But she held her tongue. Willie shouted a quick good-bye on his way out the door.

Katie Jackson was typical of older mill women of the time. She'd been thin when Joe married her in 1915, and she was still thin at age fifty-eight. She was quite pretty, her brown hair stylishly cut in a pageboy, with a pleasantly oval face and smiling brown eyes. Katie had been to college. She could read and write, neither of which her husband could do, a lack that bothered him no end. But Joe, like most young boys, had gone into the mill early. He had worked off and on, beginning when he was six, and had started a full-time shift when he was twelve. How he had snagged a woman as beautiful and smart as Katie continued to amaze him, but there was no doubt about the genuine love between them.

"Why don't we go to the game tomorrow, Joe?" Katie asked.

"Gotta keep the store open," Joe responded.

"You know nobody comes in during the game. Everybody's there."

"That's impossible, Katie. Not everybody's nuts about baseball aroun' here. What if somebody drives through town?"

"I'll mind the store, then. You go."

"I don't wanna go."

"You'd rather mope around here?" she asked, not sharply, but not shyly, either.

"Who's mopin'?" Joe said. To prove his point, he walked briskly back to his desk and pulled out a drawer or two, as if looking for something important. Katie smiled and crossed to the desk. She put her hands on his, stilling them. They were huge hands. Back when he'd played baseball, the tiny mitts of those years had barely covered them. His wife's small hands barely covered them, too.

"All right, Joe," she said with a smile. "You don't have to pretend to be busy. I won't make you go to the game. I might go, though," she finished, with a twinkle in her eye.

"I need you here, Katie," Joe said forcefully.

Katie smiled at him. "Guess I'd better stay here, then. So, what shall we do while we wait for all the customers to storm our door? Inventory?"

"Sure," Joe said. Rising from his chair, he heard the door begin to open. "See there, Katie. A customer!" But when he turned to see who had entered, another boy, this one older than Willie, stood in the doorway. "May I help you, good buddy?" he asked. Joe called most every male "good buddy" when he didn't know his name.

"Sorry to bother you, Mr. Jackson. I'm Jimmy Roberts. May I come in?" Jimmy asked, timidly.

"Sure. Cain't sell you no liquor, though," Joe said, "Lessen you can prove you're of age."

"That's not what I want," Jimmy said. He looked at Katie and nodded. "Hello."

"Hello," she said. "I'm Joe's wife."

"What can we do for you?" Joe asked.

"Well, sir," Jimmy began slowly. "I wanted to ask you somethin'." He hesitated, not knowing exactly how to proceed. Joe waited impatiently. Jimmy began again. "I'm a ballplayer. Play for Woodside Mill in the Textile League." He paused. Shoeless Joe waited. "It's about baseball." Joe could wait no longer.

"What about it?" he demanded. "Spit it out, boy."

Jimmy spoke before he lost his courage. "I wanted to know if you wanted to play it again."

"How do you mean?"

"Well, not play, exactly, but teach me to play. I mean, I know how to play, 'course, but teach me to play better."

"I ain't no teacher," Joe said firmly.

Jimmy swallowed hard and plunged ahead. "Mr. Jackson, if I could get good as you was, well maybe not that good, but, you know, better, good enough so's they'd start writin' 'bout me in the paper the way they done you, then maybe I'd get noticed like you did, by a scout or somebody, an' then maybe I could make it to the big leagues or at least the minor leagues, maybe play for the *Spinners*, anywhere, play anywhere, just get out of the mill, get out of the mill by playin' ball like you done." Jimmy paused, out of breath. He'd stated his dream as best he could.

A quiet filled the store, then Joe said softly, "I think you'd better go."

But once started, Jimmy was determined to give it his all. "Please, Mr. Jackson, you don't have to join a team or anything, just coach me, give me advice."

"My advice is to stay away from professional baseball."

"I know they done you wrong, Mr. Jackson, an' I'm sorry about that, but that don't mean it'll happen to me. Please, I cain't stay in the mill the rest of my life!"

Jimmy's desperation was palpable. But Joe was determined to ignore it. Ignore it and the baseball dream that caused it. "That ain't no concern of mine. Plenty of people are happy in the mill."

"But not me!" Jimmy cried. "An' not you, neither!"

"That was a long time ago. And baseball failed to keep faith with me. Now I run a liquor store." To emphasize the point, Joe turned his back on Jimmy and prepared to resume working.

"But you're still Shoeless Joe Jackson!" Jimmy almost shouted.

Shoeless Joe turned back to Jimmy, shouting himself. *"Was*, kid, *was!* Now I'm Joe Jackson, liquor store owner. An' you're too young to buy booze, so why don't you skedaddle?"

Katie interrupted. "Joe, don't you at least want to talk about it?"

"There's nothin' to talk about!" Joe marched to the door and held it open.

Jimmy looked at Katie, but all she could do was smile sympathetically. He looked at Shoeless Joe, standing impatiently at the door. Finally, he dropped his head and walked slowly out.

Joe slammed the door after him. "Don't start!" he cut off Katie. "I'm goin' out back an' begin the inventory."

When he had disappeared out the rear door, Katie sighed and walked over to Pee Wee. "Stubborn, isn't he, Pee Wee?"

"You're out!" squawked the bird.

"But the game's not over," Katie said determinedly.

CHAPTER 3

As the noonday sun baked the unshaded grass outside, Howard Stone managed to stay reasonably cool in his large, columned house on West Avondale Avenue, where some of Greenville's wealthier residents lived. He had fans whirring in every room, and all the floor-to-ceiling windows open, and still it was hot as Hades, as his father used to say. It was his father who was responsible for Howard being stuck in this hellhole in the first place. He had passed on Woodside Mill to Howard in his will. His father had owned a mill in Sarasota, New York, where Howard grew up, but during the Depression he'd decided to sell the Sarasota mill and buy Woodside, because in South Carolina labor was cheap and he wouldn't have to fight the union. Southern textile mills were filled with farmers and other people who had come down from the mountains in search of a steady paycheck. They held on to many of their customs and traditions, and — most importantly, as far as Howard's father was concerned — their strong independence. Mill workers often thought of themselves as family, but that sense of family definitely did not extend to joining a labor union.

Fortunately, Howard had mostly avoided living in the south at the time, since he'd been in college at Cornell when the family had moved. He spent one awful summer in Greenville after his junior year, and that had been enough to convince him that he did not want to spend the rest of his life with those "yokels," as he called them. After college, his employment had kept him largely in the northeast. His father, of course, never dignified what Howard did as "employment," and he never hesitated to let him know. For Howard had pursued his dream of playing professional baseball. "In the midst of a depression you're going to try to make money playing a game?" his father had screamed at him. "Life is not a game, young man! It looks like I wasted my money on educating a fool!"

Howard had struggled hard to prove his father wrong. For a year he played for the Wheeling Stogies, a Class C team in the Yankees farm system. If a summer in South Carolina had begun Howard's irritation with the South, a summer in West Virginia turned it into full-scale contempt. Saying Howard didn't like living in the South was akin to saying elephants don't like living in trees. It was an environment totally unsuited to his personality. The disconnect was almost metabolic: Howard simply moved to a faster rhythm than most southerners. The way they drawled their speech, their ambling way of walking, their snail-paced eating — for Howard, everything in the South was so s-l-o-w, and slow to him meant lazy, stupid, and irredeemably boring.

Luckily, he had escaped after one season back to New York and the Class A Binghamton Triplets. The name made Howard wince — what did triplets have to do with baseball? — but the locale was very much to his liking. He would have stayed, but after two seasons, the team let him go. And so, in the midst of the Depression, Howard had made the hardest decision of his life. He'd asked his father if he could come to work for him at Woodside Mill. True to form, his father waxed triumphant. "Tail between your legs, huh? Okay, let's put that education to work. You can start in the weaving room."

Howard hated life inside the mill — the heat, the lint, the unceasing, pounding noise — and his resentment at his father grew with every spindle doffed. Then the inevitable had happened. Five years ago his father had died, leaving the mill to Howard. He would have sold the mill right away, except mill life had one redeeming feature for Howard: baseball. Each mill had its own team. And if he couldn't play, at least, as team owner, Howard could immerse himself in the game in other ways — discussing personnel with the manager, poring over team statistics, even sprucing up the ballpark to be the best in the Western Carolina League. Owning the Woodside Wolves gave Howard something to care about for six months of the year, something to make the other six months, if not tolerable, at least survivable. And something to dream about. Howard had long hoped that he could somehow translate his ownership of a Textile League team into ownership of a professional baseball team, one most definitely *not* in the South. And now it looked as if his dream might actually happen. An opportunity to buy his old team, the Binghamton Triplets, had come up. An opportunity with a large "IF" attached to it: he needed to win the championship of the Western Carolina League that summer.

That morning, Howard was excited about a recent move he'd made to ensure the Woodside victory, and he was anxious to capitalize on that move. But first there was the little matter of growing rumors about a union on the part of his mill's workers, which is why Howard now sat opposite the Reverend Robert Nally, pastor of the Woodside Baptist Church — Rev Bob to everyone but Howard, who drew the line at casual intimacy. "Lord, it's hot," Rev Bob said, taking out a red bandanna and wiping his brow. Howard smirked to himself. Even the preachers down here had no class.

"Go ahead and stand in front of the fan if it helps you any, Reverend Nally," Howard said.

"Don't mind if I do," replied the Reverend, waddling his two hundred and fifty pounds closer to the biggest fan in the room.

Howard wanted to get back to business and send the Reverend on his way. "As I said, Reverend, I'll be glad to supply a bus for your gospel choir to attend the choir competition at Furman University next month," he said. "Would a school bus be all right?"

"Fine, fine, Howard," Rev Bob intoned in his deepest baritone.

"You think you might win?" inquired Howard.

"Oh, we just have a good time, it don't much matter who wins," Rev Bob replied genially.

"It matters to me," Howard said firmly. "Tell you what. You win and you'll find an extra fifty dollars in your collection plate. Unless you'd rather I give it to you personally."

"Sure thing. I'll just add it to the plate," Rev Bob promised. Howard knew that was about as likely as Rev Bob passing up fried chicken at a church social. But now that the Reverend could see how generous Howard could be, it was time for a little *quid pro quo.*

"I've been wondering, Reverend Nally, is there anything in the Bible about unions?" Howard asked innocently.

"Unions? I don't think so."

"Well, something about the spirit behind wanting to join a union, then."

"Why?"

"I heard they were trying to organize Cannon mills up in Charlotte, which means they'll be heading our way soon," Howard said pointedly.

"I see." Rev Bob thought for a moment. "Well, unions are about brotherhood. I believe there's a good deal about brotherhood in the Bible."

God, these crackers are dumb, thought Howard. *I'll have to lead him to it.* "I was thinking more along the lines of a sense of betrayal," he said. "A sense of becoming an outcast, maybe even a sense of sin."

"A sin to join the union?" asked Rev Bob, somewhat doubtfully.

"Isn't it?" Howard asked. "Who were the outcasts in the Bible, Reverend? Lepers?"

"Yes, but I don't think our brethren are gonna be persuaded to think of themselves as lepers. 'Course, there's the money-lenders Jesus threw out of the temple."

"*I'm* a money-lender, Reverend Nally," Howard snapped. "I don't think that's a good idea."

"No, no, of course, not, I was just thinkin' out loud," Rev Bob said quickly.

"Isn't there something about some mark of the beast somewhere," Howard prompted. "What's that about?"

"Yes, yes, Revelations. About people who worship the beast. They get this mark on their forehead."

"A mark? I like that. Something you can see. What could union sympathizers be worshipping, Reverend?"

"I don't rightly know."

"Why don't you give it some thought, see what you come up with?" Howard suggested. *Next, I'll be writing the damn sermon myself!* "So we have us a deal. Bus for you, sermon for...." Howard smiled. "All of us."

"Sure thing, Howard. Down here we say, 'Let's lick thumbs' to seal the deal." To demonstrate, he licked his thumb and marked the air with a slight downward movement. "Now you do it."

Howard barely managed to keep the scorn out of his voice, as he answered, "No thank you, Reverend. Now, you practice that choir, and work on that sermon about unions, and I'll work on finding us a bus to take you to the competition," Howard said, rising from his chair and showing Reverend Nally the door. "Hope you don't mind if I don't walk with you outside, but I'm trying to stay as cool as I can."

"Not a'tall, not a'tall, Howard," Rev Bob said.

"Let me know when that sermon's going to be, I might want to drop by to hear it," Howard said. "And don't wait too long."

"No, no, next couple of weeks, for certain," Rev Bob answered.

They shook hands and Rev Bob proceeded through the front door and onto the veranda. He plopped his hat on his head and stepped off the porch and into the searing southern heat.

Howard watched him go. He looked towards the skies. It was a habit he had developed, a habit he loathed, as if he were asking for his father's opinion, or, worse, for his approval. *He's been dead five years, what the hell am I doing?* he chastised himself. But he couldn't seem to stop. His father had dominated him his whole life, always told him what to do, what to think. Worst of all, Howard knew his father thought of him as a loser. It hadn't helped when he'd failed to make it in professional baseball. But now Howard had a chance to erase that moniker forever. He smiled as he remembered how the sunshine had first peeked through the gloom of his life with that unexpected phone call last February.

"Howard, this is Socks." The voice on the other end was older, but Howard recognized it instantly. *Socks Singleton, the shortstop on the*

Triplets, his partner on the best double-play combination in the Eastern League when Howard had played second base. That had been the happiest part of Howard's baseball experience, his one unqualified success. He couldn't hit, but he could field, and with Socks grabbing every grounder in sight, he had turned his fielding into a superb display of athletic prowess. Running off the field after an inning-ending double-play, Socks popping him on the butt with his glove and shouting "Attaway!", his teammates slapping his back when he entered the dugout, Howard experienced in those fleeting moments what it might have been like to have succeeded at playing pro ball.

"Socks!" Howard shouted into the phone. "How are you?"

"Fine, fine."

"What a wonderful surprise!" Talking with Socks, Howard felt as if he were twenty-five again, instead of forty-one. He'd thought recently how old he was beginning to look. His hair was still dark, cropped short in the style of the day. But a hint of sallowness had begun to appear in his cheeks. His brown eyes had definitely lost the luster they'd had just a few years back, and he was slowly beginning to spread around the middle. Worst of all, he felt smaller these days. At five feet, eight inches he'd always been on the short side, but he had compensated by feeling bigger inside than he looked outside. Not any longer. That's why this phone call was a jolt of joy. "It's so good to hear your voice!"

"I know, I know, it's been a long time," Socks continued.

"How did you find me?" Howard asked.

"Simple. When you left Binghamton, you said you were going to work for your father in his textile mill. As I recall, you weren't too happy about the prospect. How's it working out?"

For a moment, Howard was tempted to tell Socks the truth. After all, they had been great friends those two summers in Binghamton, sharing everything — hopes and dreams, triumphs on the field and off, long late-night conversations in their boarding house bedroom, each in his single bed staring at the tin-plated ceiling. But Howard knew that when he had been let go from the Triplets, Socks had signed a contract with the Yankees Double-A team, moving up when Howard had been moving out. Now his pride wouldn't let him answer Socks honestly. "Good, good, Socks. Running a mill's not as bad as I thought it'd be. We've got a baseball team, you know, Textile League."

"I know. Matter of fact, baseball's what I called about. Remember what I told you when you helped me out that time?"

Howard assumed he was referring to the money he'd given Socks to help cover some gambling debts he'd accrued betting on the ponies at the Sarasota racetrack. When he'd asked him for the loan, Howard could see the actual fear in Socks' eyes. Apparently, his creditors were not the kind of men who would wait patiently to be paid or refrain from violence in the event of a default on a debt. "They'll really hurt me, Howie, ruin my baseball career!" Socks had said, the desperation clear in his urgent voice. So Howard had given him the three hundred dollars he'd saved from off-season work in a local hardware store. It was all the money he'd had at the time. Socks had been very grateful, but Howard hadn't remembered that he'd said anything in particular.

"I remember you were grateful," Howard replied. "But you paid me back over time."

"That's nothing," Socks answered. "What I said was, 'I'll never forget this. I owe you more than just the money.'"

"I remember now. So what?"

"Well, in those late-night talks you used to say that, if you couldn't make it as a professional ball player, you'd like to own a professional team someday. So I'm calling to tell you that the Binghamton Triplets will be up for sale after the coming season, and I can help you get the inside track."

Howard was stunned. Was Socks offering him a way to escape the South and have his dream too? He didn't understand. "How can you help, Socks?"

"Because I ended up being Director of Scouting for the New York Yankees. I know the current owners of the Triplets. I know they are tired of owning a losing team. That's the other important part of this deal, Howard. You'll have a much better chance of getting the team if you come in as a winner."

"Why would the owners care, they're selling the team?"

"It's the Yankees who care. The Triplets are a Yankees farm club. The Yankees like winners. All things being equal, Yankee management will encourage the Triplets owners to sell it to someone who has proven he knows how to win. That could be you. How's your team gonna be this summer, Howie?"

Howard paused. The Woodside Wolves were always one of the better teams in the league, but, in Howard's time as their owner, they had yet to win the championship. At that moment, however, Howard experienced a clarity of purpose that ran through his body like an electric current. "They're great," he told Socks. "They're gonna win the championship."

"Glad to hear it," Socks said. "So let's keep in touch during the season, anything I can do for you, you let me know. Meantime, I'll mention

*you to the owners, and when you win that championship, I'll set up a
meeting in New York."*

"I don't know what to say, Socks."

*"You sure you're interested? I know you said running a mill's not
as bad as you thought."*

"Socks, it's hell!" Howard blurted out.

*Socks laughed, and so did Howard. "I thought that might be the
case, Howie. Well, good to hear your voice. Looks like I'll be hearing it
again, and it would be great to have you back in the professional game.
Keep in touch."*

"I will, Socks, I will. And thank you!"

*"Howard, you saved me when I needed saving. Maybe this can
save you, too. Take care of yourself."*

Back in his office, Howard felt energized by the memory of the phone call.
He had worked hard at making sure the Woodside Wolves had been ready
when the season had opened, and now he had landed the ballplayer that
would guarantee the championship.

He pulled car keys from his pocket and headed outside. As soon
as he stepped through the door, the heat blasted him, reminding him in an
instant why he so desperately wanted to leave the South. The humidity
must have been around ninety per cent. By the time he reached his car,
Howard was perspiring enough to begin to soak through his white cotton
shirt. He hurried to start the engine and get moving so at least some airflow
might cool him a little.

Howard felt the usual thrill when the Cadillac's V-8 engine roared
to life. One-hundred-sixty horse power! The whole car spoke of power,
from the cast-iron block to its126-inch chassis to the tailfins inspired by
wartime aircraft. He loved its look, too. White sidewall tires, rear fender
skirts, the egg-crate grille that resembled the open mouth of a large shark.
Power windows, the new Hydra-Matic drive, and chrome everywhere
possible. Best of all, it was a convertible. Hot when the roof was down,
but cool with the wind whipping through the opened interior. Howard felt
a rush every time he slipped behind the wheel.

He turned it around, drove left out of his driveway, and headed for
the Riverside Hotel, beside the Reedy River. Greenville called itself "The
Textile Center of the World." The enormous Textile Hall housed
exhibitions of textile machinery and served as an auditorium for sports
teams and entertainment. Some eighteen mills were scattered about
Greenville County alone, with many more dotting the landscape in
surrounding counties. *The Greenville News* referred to them as the Textile

Crescent. A thriving commercial district boasted banks, department stores, and two first-class hotels, the Ottaray and the Poinsett, for the city's 58,000 residents.

Driving down Main Street, Howard passed the Ottaray, with its grand, curved porch, small shops like Sutton's shoes and Hale's Jewelers, and large department stores like Ivey's and Myers-Arnold. The First National Bank, solid in its massive stone structure, sat across the street from the magnificent seventeen-storied Woodside Building, the tallest building in town. Greenville wasn't really that backwards a town, but it was a far cry from the teeming city that Howard longed to live in. He finally turned off Main Street and drove to the hotel, parked his car, and crossed the street to the lobby.

The Riverside Hotel did not cater to the usual guest. A few prostitutes milled around the front porch, but none of them bothered to call out to Howard. They knew he wouldn't be interested. This was hardly his first visit to the establishment, and they knew he came for one reason only: to place a bet with his favorite bookie, Jellycakes Jones.

Jellycakes was a Negro man of some thirty-three years, small and wiry, only five-feet seven or so. His was the deep, dark black of the son of a farmer who was only a few generations removed from slavery. His father had come to work in the mills in the picker room, where workers opened the cotton from bales. This was the worst job in the mill, and it was reserved for men of color only. Dirt and dust filled the basement room where the cotton arrived. Seeing his father cough and spit blood his whole life had convinced Jellycakes that he'd rather do anything than work in the mill. So he'd left. There weren't that many jobs for a Negro man in the South before the war. Jellycakes had survived on the streets, been arrested a few times for misdemeanors, fathered Willie, and turned to making book to support himself and his son. It had been a pretty good living, especially after the war, when soldiers returned home with a few bucks in their pockets.

At first, Howard had found it unusual, given the segregation of southern society, to find a colored man running his "business" from a white establishment. Of course, the Riverside was not a first-class hotel by any means. But as he became more familiar with the South, Howard noticed the easy familiarity that often existed between white and colored. They knew how to "lick thumbs," as Rev Bob had called it. White teens, who had a yen for some liquor, for instance, knew they couldn't buy it in any of the liquor stores like Joe Jackson's. But they knew they could go out to the colored neighborhood on White Horse Road to Uncle Frank's shack and buy a pint or two of rum to mix with their Cokes. Whites and

Negroes found a way to get along that was mutually beneficial. Of course, blacks were the people who did most of the compromising to make this easy co-existence work. They compromised because they had no choice.

Howard found Jellycakes in his favorite chair in a corner of the lobby. He rose to greet Howard with his usual enthusiasm. It didn't pay for a bookie ever to be gloomy, no matter how his recent bets had turned out. "Well, how 'do, Mr. Howard, suh. I had a feelin' I might be seein' you today. How you been?"

"Hot!" Howard replied.

Jellycakes chuckled. "Yessuh, mighty warm, mighty warm. Could use us a thunderstorm to cool things off."

"Long as it doesn't storm tomorrow," Howard said.

"Yessuh, got that big game tomorrow! You bettin' your usual?" Jellycakes gestured and Howard sat down in the nearby chair, Jellycakes following suit.

"A little more than usual, Jellycakes," Howard said, pulling out his wallet. He counted out three hundreds and handed them to Jellycakes.

"Oo-ee! You that confident Woodside gonna whup Brandon?" Jellycakes stuffed the money into his pocket and made a notation in the small book beside his chair.

"It's practically a sure thing," Howard replied with a smile. "What's the spread?"

"Four and a half runs," Jellycakes responded. "I figure your team gonna win by at least that. They do, and you got yourself a nice piece of change. How come you so confident?"

"A new player I'm adding to the Woodside lineup. Bought him off Charlotte, just this week."

"An' who might that be, if you don't mind me askin'?"

"Crusher Goodlett," Howard answered with a small smile.

"Crusher? Lord, Mr. Howard, I'm glad you told me. I got to increase the spread."

"But mine stays the same," Howard reminded him.

"Oh, yessuh, you still got the four-run spread on Woodside. But I believe I'll make it five from now on, bet lots of people will pick Brandon to beat that spread. Lots of people who don't know Crusher Goodlett'll be in Woodside's lineup, that is!" Jellycakes smiled broadly at Howard. "I sure do thank you for the news, Mr. Howard."

Howard got up and turned to go, when he saw a familiar face enter the lobby. "Yancey?" he called out. "Is that you?"

Yancey Dickerson, the suave Speaker of the state's House of Representatives, quickly disengaged himself from the company of the busty platinum blonde with whom he'd entered and walked towards Howard.

"Hello, Howard. Fancy meetin' you here."

"Might say the same, Yancey."

"Well, Friday's the day I collect the rent. Usually send somebody down from my office, but sometimes I pick it up myself, if I'm in the neighborhood," Yancey replied. He had a mellifluous drawl that lazed out his lips in the beautiful melody that epitomized southern gentility. Yancey was the scion of one of the most powerful families in the state. He was some fifteen years older than Howard, but hardly looked it. Lots of golf and tennis saw to that. That, and other "sports" that required great exertion. A head full of silver hair completed the picture of southern aristocracy. Even in the heat and humidity of the day, it was perfectly coifed.

"I see," Howard replied, evenly. He looked at Yancey, who could tell that Howard did, indeed, "see." But Yancey's "rent-collecting" was safe with Howard. As one of Yancey's biggest contributors, he wasn't about to start a scandal. "How about a bite to eat?"

"Thank ye kindly, Howard, but I'd better get back to the office with this rent. Plus, I'm workin' on a little project that might interest you, bein' as how you love baseball so much."

"And what might that be?"

"Think I'll keep it a secret a bit longer. But you'll know soon enough, I reckon."

"Got a little secret myself," Howard said. "But since you're my good friend, and since Jellycakes happens to be right here to make it convenient for you, I'll tell you. I've hired Crusher Goodlett away from Cannon Mills to come play ball for us. He'll be in the lineup for tomorrow's game against Brandon."

"Crusher Goodlett! My-oh-my!" Yancey said. "That's quite a coup."

"Not really. I've found that coups happen quite often, if you have the cash."

Yancey laughed. "That they do, Howard, that they do. Well, then, you're right. I believe I ought to visit our little friend in his 'office.' If you'll excuse me, Howard."

Howard nodded farewell and started for the door, as Yancey ambled over to Jellycakes in the corner. He heard Yancey inquire as to the spread on tomorrow's game, and he couldn't help smiling as he heard Jellycakes answer, "Five and a half runs, Senator. I was you, I'd bet on Brandon to beat that spread."

        Back in the street, Howard got inside his convertible. He wondered what Yancey's little secret was. Howard didn't like secrets, except the ones he kept. With a silent prayer that Crusher Goodlett would be his ticket out of this backwater hellhole, he fired up the Caddy and raced back toward home and the albatross of Woodside Mill.

Inside that mill, Thelma Roberts, Jimmy's mom, paused briefly from her job watching two dozen mechanical looms weave yarn into cloth. She had time for a quick mop of her brow before returning to her vigil. If any one of the hundreds of threads on each loom broke, as often happened, she had to retie the ends with a weaver's knot. It took delicate fingers to draw the threads through the looms, and quick ones to tie the knot before too much thread could spill onto the floor. A counter on top of each loom counted the picks — the number of times the loom's warp threads shifted and the shuttle flew across. Since she was paid by the pick, Thelma was diligent in monitoring the looms. Even with the inside temperature at one hundred degrees, Thelma actually preferred days with high humidity, like today. It kept the threads moist. Dry threads tended to break more easily, and a break in the thread could happen at any moment, and that meant less pay. By the end of her shift, her clothes would be completely soaked, her feet would ache from standing on trembling floor boards for eight hours straight, and her ears would be ringing from the incessant screeching and clacking of a hundred looms. The noise was so deafening that supervisors used a series of blinking lights to communicate things like the end of a shift, a fire drill, or anything else workers needed to know at the same time.

        Woodside Mills made mainly towels, sheets, and bolt cloth. Manufacturing began in the opening room, where Negro men opened the bales of raw cotton. A vacuum system carried the cotton through a giant tube to the picker room, where card hands fed sheets into carding machines, whose sharp, metal teeth finished the cleaning process and converted the mass into a continuous sliver that was coiled into cans. Workers directed the slivers onto drawing frames, spinning machines wound them round each other onto bobbins, doffers replaced the full bobbins with empty ones, and the process began all over again.

        In the weaving room, where Thelma worked, yarn was dipped into a bath of hot starch and oil, dried over steam-heated drums, and wound onto a giant spool. Drawing-in girls laced each thread through individual eyes in the loom harness. Once drawing-in was completed, weavers put the beam and harness on the loom, and the weaving process began. At the end, women in the finishing room inspected the cloth for defects, then other women folded the textiles for shipping.

Inside the mill, cotton lint floated everywhere, covering everything in the cavernous room — man, floor, clock — like fine snow. It was worse in the spinning room, where Thelma had previously worked. She'd coughed a lot in those days. It was not uncommon for mill workers to vomit balls of cotton. Thank goodness the superintendent, Waddy Benson, had taken pity on her and moved her to the weaving room. He liked Thelma. She was beginning to suspect that perhaps Waddy liked her too much. His eyes followed her everywhere. She didn't mind eyes. She was used to it. Thelma had always been good looking, and her body was still firm for a woman in her late thirties. Her rear was especially enticing, even in the loose dress she wore to work. She could handle Waddy. She could handle anything that got her out of the spinning room.

Thelma had worked hard her whole life. She'd begun at the mill at age twelve and knew she'd probably never leave the mill. But like many mill parents, she worked and saved as much as she could in hopes that her child might escape. She understood that baseball might be Jimmy's ticket out, though she also understood that the odds of that happening were pretty steep. Still, she'd do anything to help Jimmy leave. That's why she had been pressuring him to go ask Joe Jackson for help. After all, here was one of the greatest players in the history of the game, right there in their back yard — Woodside Mill was a short walk from the Brandon Mill area where Shoeless lived. Jimmy had resisted. He didn't want to bother Shoeless. The last time he'd argued back at her, Thelma had dragged Jimmy to the front porch, pointed up at the mill, and said quite strongly, "There's the bother, Jimmy!" Maybe it had made a difference. Time would tell.

Thelma glanced at the clock on the wall. She could barely make out the time, for all the lint that covered the clock's face. One-fifty. Only ten more minutes and she could walk out the door, greet Jimmy coming in to work the afternoon shift, and find out how his try-out had gone. Wouldn't it be wonderful if the Spinners manager liked his pitching! Would that mean they'd hire him right away? Would they send him to another team to develop him? Could her son actually be on his way to the big leagues?

These daydreams were interrupted by Jenny Hart's shout from nearby. "Supe wants to see you, Thelma!"

Thelma didn't understand her right away. Jenny was a replacement worker. She took a worker's place when she went on their ten-minute break. They got two ten-minute breaks and one twenty-minute break per shift. Replacement workers tended to be older, and their voices were softened by years of having to shout to be heard. Given the noise level inside the mill, everyone had to shout. Thelma walked closer to Jenny and yelled "What?"

"Waddy wants to see you in his office," Jenny said. "I'll replace you."

"What about?" Thelma asked.

"Didn't say," Jenny shouted and began walking between the rows of looms, checking for broken threads or other malfunctions.

Thelma walked to the door of the superintendent's office in the far corner of the noisy room and knocked. "Come in!" Waddy shouted from within.

Thelma entered the windowless office and saw Waddy seated behind his desk, smoking a Lucky. Various textile manuals were stacked on top, but Waddy had a car manual opened at the moment. He had a car manual opened whenever possible. Waddy lived and breathed automobiles, when he wasn't breathing lint. Actually, the lint wasn't too bad in his office, since it had no windows. A large fan circulated the hot air, but gave little respite. Like most people in the mills, however, Waddy had long ago accepted that a hot, windowless office was just the way things were and had adjusted.

"Hey, Sugar," Waddy began.

Thelma cringed inwardly. "Sugar" was not her favorite nickname, especially when used by Waddy. "Hi, Waddy," she replied. "What can I do for you?"

"It's more like what I can do for you. Or what we can do for each other, more like it. Rest your bottom," he said. Thelma sat down. She was tired and her feet hurt, so any chance to sit was welcomed. "Ready for the big game tomorrow?"

"Sure, but I ain't the one playin'."

"Jimmy, then. How's he doin'?" Waddy blew out a couple of smoke rings from his latest drag on the Lucky. They hung in the air until the fan turned and blew them apart.

"Says his fastball's hoppin'," Thelma said.

"Good, good." Waddy smiled. His crooked teeth were stained with tobacco. Waddy wasn't too bad-looking for fifty. His arm muscles rippled, thanks to all the work he did on or under cars, and he wasn't so fond of beer that his stomach had begun to pouch. Blue eyes shone from a tan face, eyes that could look quite kind, if they didn't reflect other things on Waddy's mind. "'Course, Brandon ain't worth shucks, I doubt our boys'll have much trouble tomorrow."

"Probly not." Thelma stretched her arms over her head, which caused her breasts to rise and press against her damp blouse. This sight gave Waddy the encouragement he needed to go on.

"Thelma," he began. "You know I've always had a fondness for you. Always tried to look out for you when I could, look out for your best interests, you might say."

"I 'preciate that, Waddy," Thelma said noncommittally.

"That's why I wanted to let you know that a floor manager position's opening up soon in the weaving room. I was wonderin' if you'd like to be considered?"

"Heck, yeah, Waddy, that'd be great. Me an' Jimmy could use the money. I ain't lyin', it's been kinda tough since Earle left."

"Why that dummie'd run out on a gal good-lookin' as you is beyond me," Waddy said.

"Some men need more'n one woman, I reckon," Thelma replied without rancor. She'd worked hard on getting over Earle since he left for good seven years ago and had succeeded pretty well. Jimmy was another matter.

"An' they end up with none." Waddy knew. He was one of those men. That fact didn't lead him to appreciate the irony of what he was about to propose, however. Irony wasn't Waddy's strong suit. "So, okay, good, I'll consider you. An' maybe you'd consider givin' me a little consideration in return, Thelma." Waddy smiled at her suggestively.

Thelma played dumb. "Sure, Waddy, Jimmy an' me'd love to have you over to dinner some night."

"I was thinkin' more of another direction," Waddy said.

"In what direction would that be, Waddy?" She looked directly at him, hoping somehow to ward off his interest. But Waddy had come too far to back off now.

"In the direction of 'you scratch my back, I'll scratch yours,' honey." Waddy returned her gaze. "Only my back ain't the itch I'm referrin' to."

Thelma didn't answer right away. She'd love to have the floor manager's job. She wouldn't have to spend eight hours on her feet, she could rest from time to time, spend her days talkin' to folks, makin' rounds every now and then, taking care of any problems. She'd make more money. A mill worker's wages were low, so money was a big consideration. But it wasn't consideration enough for scratching the kind of itch Waddy had.

"Waddy, you're gonna have to find some other gal to do that for you. Or scratch it yourself." Thelma got up and gave Waddy a smile. "But

I 'preciate the consideration, all the same." She turned and walked toward the door. Because she knew Waddy would be staring at her behind, she swayed it a little side to side, just to let him know what he'd be missing. When she'd closed the door behind her, Waddy stubbed out his cigarette with a hard jab. "Damn!" he exhaled, shaking his head in a combination of appreciation and loss.

The whistle blew and the lights blinked just as Thelma left the office. In a second, what had been a shattering noise so loud it made your ears ring became instant silence, as workers turned off six hundred machines at once. The silence was then replaced by the sound of hot, sweaty, bone-tired people shuffling towards the exit, mumbling few words, too exhausted to speak.

When Thelma came out of the building, she searched for Jimmy in the line of those waiting to come in for their shift. She spotted him just outside the gate. "Jimmy!" she yelled, and moved quickly towards him. "How'd it go, son?"

"It didn't," Jimmy replied glumly, continuing to shuffle along the line.

"What do you mean? You pitched, didn't you?"

"Four pitches, Mama. Three balls, an' I hit the batter with the last pitch. They ran me outta the place."

"Ran you out of the — ? Will you stop walkin' an' tell me what happened?" Losing patience, she pulled Jimmy from the line.

"Nothin' happened, that's all. I was stupid to think somethin' would!" Jimmy said angrily. "I pitched terrible. When I hit that batter, he started runnin' at me. The manager too. They chased me clear out to the outfield. I had to scramble up the wall to escape them, Mama. How's that for a dream come true?"

Thelma saw the pain in her son's eyes. "I'm so sorry, Jimmy," she consoled. "You'll get 'em next time, when you're better."

"Oh, yeah, that's what happened to another dream, Mama," Jimmy continued bitterly. "I did what you've been buggin' me to do to try to get better."

"You went to see Mr. Jackson?" Thelma asked excitedly. "What happened?"

"Nothin'." Jimmy began to head toward the entrance again.

"He musta said somethin', Jimmy."

Jimmy stopped. "Yeah. He said he wasn't Shoeless Joe Jackson, famous baseball player. He said he was Joe Jackson, liquor salesman. He's become nothin', too!" Jimmy turned and hurried through the gate. The whistle let out its long piercing shriek. Next shift.

Thelma watched him disappear inside. Her heart sank a little. If baseball couldn't get Jimmy out of the mill, what could?

CHAPTER 4

Textile baseball's glory days had come and gone by the summer of 1951. In the Thirties and Forties as many as four thousand fans would cheer their local teams. Folks came to the game to forget hard times and enjoy each other's company. It didn't hurt that the mills closed at 2 p.m. on Saturday, game day. Owners recognized the need to provide some measure of enjoyment to compensate for the daily drudgery of mill work, and a few hours of shut-down in the summer months was a small price to pay for the round-the-clock labor they demanded the rest of the year. A small price indeed, considering the wages they paid. True, they rented mill homes to their employees for only five dollars a week, but considering the highest wage paid was only fifty dollars a week for supervisors, and most workers earned in the thirties, owners knew they were getting a bargain. So they scheduled no Saturday deliveries, shut down the machines, and encouraged their workers to attend the games by making admission free.

But change had come. The post-war boom had given workers — even mill workers — more choices for their leisure time, and interest in baseball had waned. However, in the summer of 1951, at least in mills like Brandon and Woodside, baseball was still a big draw. And when Jimmy Roberts was scheduled to pitch, fans knew they'd be witnessing a stellar performance.

That's what Waddy Benson was explaining to Crusher Goodlett inside his office that Saturday morning. He'd gotten Crusher settled into his new home, a mill house like everybody else's. And he'd summoned him to his office to talk about his job. But first Waddy wanted to talk to him about the real reason Crusher was now working for Howard Stone.

"Got a mean fastball, Crusher," Waddy was saying about Jimmy's best pitch. "I bet even you might have trouble keepin' up with it."

"The hell you say!" Crusher oozed confidence. He was a big man, six-foot-two and some two-hundred-forty pounds, most of it muscle. His hair was cut short, which only accentuated his large head. Big nose, big eyes, big ears — everything about Crusher Goodlett was big. Including his ego. "Nobody beats me inside. Outside neither. So this Roberts fellow's the team star, huh?"

"I reckon you might say that. But we don't talk about stars here."

"You will." Crusher looked around for a place to spit his tobacco juice, fired some at the trashcan near Waddy's desk, made most of it and the rest oozed down the side and onto the floor. "What kind of work you got lined up for me?"

"Mr. Stone said to take good care of you," Waddy answered, handing over a hammer and screwdriver. "You can make repairs on the mill houses."

"In this heat?" Crusher asked, not bothering to take the tools. He let the silence settle between them.

Waddy retreated. "Well, just walk down a street or two, then come on back inside. We can set you to work fixin' machines in here," Waddy countered. Goodlett's size cowed him, so he could imagine what it did to opposing pitchers.

"As long as it ain't really work." Crusher took the tools and stuffed them in his pants. "I come here to play ball."

"I understand that. Folks are gonna be mighty excited to see you on that field today. I'm sorry the game's over at Brandon, 'stead of here. We got us a real stadium, not that cow shed they call a ball park."

"Long as they got a fence I can hit it over. Goin' for a cigarette." Crusher stood up, paused for a minute to tower over Waddy for effect, then made his way out the office door.

He ambled to the smoking circle in the center of the room. With the incessant racket from the looms pounding his ears, he thought maybe working outside pretending to fix houses might not be so bad after all. *Too bad I gotta work, period!* Mr. Stone had said that if things worked out like he wanted 'em to, Crusher might get a shot at the Yankee farm system. "Just play so people'll notice," Stone had said. To Crusher, that meant play like a star. And there could be room for only one star on the Woodside Wolves, as far as Crusher was concerned.

He introduced himself around to the three or four other men enjoying a cigarette, then lit up a Pall Mall from the pack he kept in the sleeve of his rolled up tee shirt. There wasn't much conversation, since you had to shout to be heard, and most men tried to save their voices so they wouldn't go hoarse. A wiry man with a cigarette dangling from his mouth did shout out to a worker passing by, "You get 'em today, Jimmy! How's the arm?"

Jimmy circled his thumb and forefinger in an "A-OK" sign and kept walking. But Crusher called out, "Roberts? You Jimmy Roberts?" He broke out of the circle and approached Jimmy. "I'm Charlie Goodlett. People call me Crusher. I'll be playin' shortstop for you today."

"Nice to meet you," Jimmy said, putting his hand out to Crusher, who gave it a strong shake.

"Mr. Stone brought me down from Charlotte yestiddy. I hear you're a pretty good pitcher." The words came out more as a challenge than a question.

"Sometimes."

"Well, you won't have to be today. I'll get you plenty of runs, don't you fret none about that." Crusher tossed his cigarette to the floor and stomped it out.

"I won't," Jimmy shouted. "I just worry batter to batter. Welcome to Woodside, Charlie."

"Crusher! Call me Crusher!" Crusher demanded. At that moment, the whistle sounded and the lights blinked, announcing the end of the shift. Jimmy nodded and moved off. Various people shouted to him as he passed. "Ten strike-outs today, Jimmy!" "No, fifteen, I got money on it!" "Look sharp, Jimmy, look sharp!" Crusher watched him go. One day soon they'd be shouting at him instead, he determined.

In the Brandon Park outfield that afternoon, players from both teams shagged fly balls. There was an intimacy in textile league ball not found at other levels. After all, these men from opposing teams might be cousins or uncles or in-laws. Their uniforms — white for Woodside, gray for Brandon — were wool and so were the caps — hot, but, in the South, heat was a fact of life. The pants came below the knees, and then a stirrup-type stocking descended to the black leather, cleated shoe. "Brandon" was stitched across the Braves uniforms in dark yellow, "Woodside" across the Wolves' in orange. Jimmy loved being in uniform. He loved how it made him feel special and, looking around at the other Brandon uniforms, how it made him feel part of a team.

Fans were allowed along the foul lines, and they'd shout from time to time at a favorite player. Or, as in the case of Jerry Brownell, they'd shout for other reasons. "Hey, Piggy!" Brownell called to an overweight player nearby. Piggy Simpson tried to ignore him, but Brownell was hard to ignore. He had a voice louder than a trolley clanghorn and he loved to use it, especially in favor of his favorite team, Woodside. Brownell was known as a "leather-lunger," because his lungs never seemed to wear out. "Piggy, look here! Look here!" Brownell waved his arms for emphasis.

Piggy's weight was a rarity on mill hill. Most people worked too hard to put on much weight, even if they did have a lot to eat, which most of them didn't. But Piggy couldn't take it off. His real name was Steve, but he'd been called Piggy as long as anybody could remember. At first, he tried to ignore the name and not answer, but he soon realized that if he wanted to talk to people, he'd have to answer to his hated nickname.

"What you want, Jerry? I got a game to play."

"That's what I know," Brownell answered. "Just wanted to show you what I'm carryin'. Might use it if you start catchin' too many fly balls today." Brownell pulled up his shirt and revealed a pistol tucked into his belt. He patted the gun. Piggy took a step back in surprise and shock. He knew textile ball wasn't as regulated as the professional leagues. He'd even heard the stories of how umpires had to carry guns in times past to control fans. But this was the first time he'd ever been threatened for playing a game. Just then, a fly ball landed at his feet. Piggy flinched, and jumped backwards. "Thattaway, Piggy! Let 'em drop if you know what's good for you!"

Piggy wandered nearer the foul line, where Jimmy was warming up. "What's the matter, Steve?" Jimmy inquired. "You look nervous or somethin'."

"Brownell just threatened me with a gun!" Piggy exclaimed.

"What?"

"Yeah, he showed it to me, said I'd better not catch any fly balls." Piggy looked uneasily over his shoulder at Brownell, who smiled and patted his belt.

"Aw, he's just teasin' you, Steve," Jimmy said. He had refused to call Piggy by his nickname ever since they'd met in eighth grade at Parker High School, which all the mill children attended. And Piggy had been grateful. Through the years, they had become good friends, playing on the same baseball teams, attending the same classes. But then Jimmy had dropped out of school and gone to work in the mill, playing for Woodside. Piggy had graduated, but then he, too, had gone to work in Brandon Mill.

"Hope so," Piggy responded unsurely.

"I'll try to help you out today if I can," Jimmy said. If it wouldn't cost his team, Jimmy sometimes threw Piggy a pitch he could hit. He knew Piggy was barely staying on the team. He wasn't much of a hitter, and not much of a fielder, either. In fact, Piggy was afraid of fly balls, always had been, despite Jimmy's efforts to convince him that a baseball couldn't really hurt him that much. "Now get on back out there, Steve, an' forget about Brownell. And good luck today!" They shook hands and Piggy moved cautiously back onto the field.

The trolley arrived in back of right field, disgorging fans from around the Greenville area. They had to pick their way through a small herd of cows lazily chewing grass near the right field fence. The fence was in need of repair, much of the lumber having peeled and splintered from a lightning bolt that had hit the fence last week. Toby Gower, the owner of Brandon Mill, hadn't had the time or the interest to repair the fence in time for today's game. Since his team wasn't doing very well, Toby wasn't inclined to spend money where he didn't have to. So he'd had some rope strung from the remainder of the fence to the right-field foul pole. He hadn't counted on the herd of cattle from the farm next door wandering over, but in textile league ball, you never knew what the field would be like. You could probably count on lots of rocks and small stones in the infield. Players who liked to steal bases had numerous cuts and bruises as tokens.

A pretty young blonde, wearing a straw hat to keep out the sun, walked past the colored fans seated on ramshackle benches along the right field foul line. Their bleachers were separated from the rest of the park, and they had the worst view of the game, but the stands were packed. Negro fans were just as enthusiastic as white ones, and just as thankful for an entertaining diversion from their daily lives. Standing along the bottom of the stands was Jellycakes, doing a brisk betting business, much of which involved how many home runs Crusher Goodlett would hit that day, now that the word had gotten out that he'd be playing for Woodside. On the grass, Willie and a group of other Negro boys were throwing a taped-up baseball to each other. None of them had a glove, but they fired the ball pretty hard anyway.

When the girl crossed the small space separating the black bleachers from the other ones lining the right field foul line, Thelma called to her from the stands. "Rhoda! Over here, Rhoda!"

Rhoda looked over and waved. She began moving towards Thelma, her walk an easy saunter. Dark, warm brown eyes peeked beneath the hat and her smooth, tanned skin glistened in the sun. She had the big hands and robust cheeks of a mountain girl. Nearing Thelma, Rhoda broke into a smile. "Hi!" she called, drawing out the vowel to an unnatural length. "Ain't this excitin'?"

"You never been to a ball game before?"

"Uh-hunh. We don't play ball up in the mountains."

"Well, welcome to civi-li-zation!" Thelma joked. "How's work?"

"Lots different from farmin', that's for sure. I worked hard on Daddy's farm, but I didn't have to concentrate like I do in the spinnin' room. Tell you what I do like, though. That paycheck at the end of the week. I ain't never had that before."

"Try not to spend it all in the company store," Thelma advised. "Not that I've been able to follow my advice much."

"Well, you got a mouth to feed an' no husband to help. But you know, Thelma, there's another thing I like besides bein' paid. I like bein' around all these people. I never knowed how lonesome I was in the mountains till I come down here. It's nice to have somebody to talk to on your break. An' the church choir! Thank you so much for suggestin' that to me."

"When I heard you singin' those hymns first day you come to church, I knew the Lord had done sent us a singin' angel!" Thelma rejoiced.

"I doubt the angel part, not with my mouth. Now, where's your son at?"

"Over there throwin' near third base." Thelma pointed across the field to Jimmy. They both watched him wind up and throw to the catcher.

"Oh, he really throws it hard!" Rhoda exclaimed.

"He's purty good, if you'll excuse a mama's pride."

"Baseball!" Rhoda exclaimed, savoring the word. "This is gonna be fun! Now you'll have to explain all the rules an' everythin', Thelma."

As Thelma bent to her assignment, Frankie Thompson, the umpire, signaled for the managers to meet him behind home plate with their lineup cards. Juber Lee Morgan of Brandon and Rusty Peters of Woodside shook hands. "What're we gonna do about them cows out beyond right field?" Rusty asked the umpire.

"'Long as they stay outside the fence, they won't matter," Frankie asserted.

"Fence? A couple of pieces of rope strung across that openin'. An' what're we gonna do about all them cow patties in the outfield?"

"If a ball goes in a cow patty," Frankie answered, "Tough shit!" He laughed a deep laugh, joined by Juber Lee.

"Dang cow park!" Rusty muttered.

"You gonna quit complainin' an' play ball?" Frankie asked. Rusty shook his head in dismay, shook Juber Lee's hand, and both managers returned to their dugouts.

Halfway up the seats behind home plate, Toby Gower sat next to his rival owner, Howard Stone. Both men wore white shirts, but Howard sported a tie. Toby had a black felt hat placed firmly on his head, but Howard was hatless. "You gonna choke in that tie, Howard," Toby said.

"Got to keep up appearances," Howard replied.

"Not at a ball game. An' your head. You need a hat to protect you."

"No, you need a hat," Howard shot back. "I've got hair!" Toby laughed at the gentle ribbing. He doffed his hat and held it in front of

Howard. "I'll need it to collect all the money you'll owe me after the game."

"I believe it'll be the other way around, Toby. And you may not pay me in Confederate dollars!"

Everyone rose as a scrawny young woman named Velma Love made her way to home plate. Velma was the chief beautician at Velma's Waves. The Brandon band began the familiar melody, and Velma started singing. Unfortunately, she was better at shaping hair than shaping notes. After a few measures, it was painfully obvious that to call what emitted from her mouth "singing" was to defile the generally accepted definition of the word. People began by wincing, and by the time she reached "the rocket's red glare," many of them had moved their hands from over their hearts to over their ears. In the seats along first-base, Rhoda and Thelma gritted their teeth in anxious anticipation of the high note on "land of the FREE!" Velma didn't disappoint, letting out a note that even had the cows outside right field raising their heads. The pain over, Frankie called "Play ball!"

Despite his disappointment at his poor tryout for the Spinners the day before, Jimmy was ready to pitch. He'd gotten in his usual practice with the peach basket in the shed before his shift at the mill. His conversation with Shoeless Joe disturbed him more than his tryout. With Thelma's enthusiasm about the idea, he had begun to believe that maybe the famous Joe Jackson might, indeed, agree to teach him. Looking at his shrine when he'd picked up the croker sack of balls that morning, Jimmy had been tempted to rip it down, especially when he'd glanced at the headline that read "LEGENDARY 'SHOELESS' JOE OPENS LOCAL STORE." But he'd resisted and had instead used his disappointment to fuel his pitches, imagining bottles of booze inside the peach basket, his fastball shattering them to pieces. "Booze over ball!" Jimmy had muttered to himself in disgust. By the time he'd finished practicing, Jimmy felt purged. And prepared. He struck out the side in the top of the first inning.

Brandon went down in order and Crusher Goodlett led off the second inning. He wasted no time showing the fans why Howard Stone had paid such a high price to bring him to Woodside. The "thwack" of his bat boomed so loudly that the left fielder didn't even bother taking a step. He just watched the ball sail over his head and out of the park.

Willie Jones did more than watch, however. As soon as Crusher had come to the plate, he'd positioned himself along the chalk line in the corner of right field, and at the crack of the bat, he took off after the homer. Willie raced behind center field, out-running the one or two other black boys who'd also given chase. When he reached the street behind left field, he had to guess which way the ball had bounced. Picking out what he thought might be the right direction, Willie raced over a dirt yard. Sure enough, there was the baseball, lying near the house. Willie ran to it, picked it up, and was about to race back to his seat when he saw someone from the corner of his eye. "Mr. Shoeless!" he shouted, seeing the familiar figure standing next to a small tree, holding a pair of binoculars.

Joe didn't greet Willie. Nor did he offer to explain why he was standing there. Instead, he simply said, "You didn't see me here, Willie."

That was enough for Willie. "Yessuh," he replied, and beat a hasty retreat. What did he care why Shoeless Joe was there? He had an almost new baseball in his hands!

Joe watched him go. He'd told Katie he was going for a walk that afternoon, would she mind watching the store? In truth, something about his encounter with Jimmy the day before had disturbed him. His passion had reminded Joe of his own deep love of baseball when he was young, before that love had soured. He'd decided to see for himself what the kid was made of.

Crusher finished his home run trot and returned to the dugout. His jubilant teammates clapped him on the back, shook his hand, and babbled their praise in over-lapping excitement. "Attaway, Crusher!" "You killed it!" "You murdered that apple!" "Tore the cover off it, Crusher!" "Never seen a ball hit so hard!" Crusher soaked it up. At the far end of the bench, Jimmy stuck out his hand. "Nice poke!" he said.

"Poke? Like to see you poke one that far, Roberts."

"I didn't mean nothin' by it, Crusher. I appreciate the lead."

"An' I ain't finished!"

Up in the stands, Toby was impressed. "Who in heck is that?" he asked Howard.

Howard smiled broadly. "My ticket to freedom. Hold on to your wallets, boys!"

As the game progressed, Jimmy continued his masterful pitching, holding Brandon scoreless. Crusher smashed another home run, this time with a man on base, in the fifth. So when Jimmy stepped to the plate in the seventh, he had a comfortable 4-0 lead over Brandon.

Things on the field had changed imperceptibly, to everyone but Jimmy. Willie had dislodged the rope keeping the cows outside the playing area when he'd chased Crusher's second home run, and as he looked down the right field line, Jimmy noticed that two or three cows were wandering onto the playing field, one of them pausing to deposit a fresh patty in the grass. Jimmy decided to try and have a little fun with the Brandon right fielder.

Batting left-handed, Jimmy hoped for a pitch on the inside corner he could pull towards right. Sure enough, the pitcher threw a curve that broke inside and Jimmy pounced on it, driving the ball far into the outfield. The right fielder chased it and might have caught it, but for an unexpected obstacle. He slammed into a cow full-speed, and the animal let out a painful yelp and ran off, the other cows following her. Not back towards right field, however, but towards the infield. The right fielder bounced off the cow and onto the ground, and Jimmy's hit landed safely a few feet away and rolled towards what used to be the fence.

Jimmy was rounding first base when the right fielder picked himself up and began chasing the ball. He managed to grab it just as Jimmy went past second and headed to third. With a good throw, the fielder could at least hold him to a triple.

The fans were on their feet, screaming. Some urged Jimmy onward, others yelled "Get those damn cows off the field!" "Time out, ump, time out!" shouted Juber Lee from the Brandon dugout. "Run, Jimmy, run!" Thelma called out from the opposite side of the field. And Rhoda proved what a salty tongue she'd developed growing up with her brothers in the mountains. "Move your butt, Jimmy, move your butt!" she screamed. Thelma looked at her for a moment, before abandoning propriety. "Yeah, move your butt, son!" she shouted.

Jimmy did his best to oblige. The third base coach, noticing the right fielder raring back to throw, put his hands up to stop Jimmy from trying to score, but, as it turned out, he had no cause for concern. Pushing off his back foot to throw, the fielder slipped on a freshly minted cow patty and fell on his backside. Glancing over his shoulder, Jimmy couldn't help but laugh as he slowed to a trot and crossed home plate. His teammates ran out to greet him, all of them laughing more than cheering.

Brandon's manager protested, of course. "You cain't call that a run, Frankie," Juber Lee yelled. "That's interference!"

"I don't know no rule 'bout interference by a cow, Juber Lee," Frankie offered.

"Shit-fire!" Juber Lee swore, kicking up dirt.

"You got half of it right!" Frankie responded, breaking into laughter himself.

In the stands, people were laughing and guffawing. Howard Stone couldn't believe it. "You call this baseball?" he asked disgustedly.

"Heck, yeah!" Toby answered. "What do you care, it favored your team."

"I care about the integrity of the game."

"This is integrity, textile-style!"

Others got in the spirit of what had just happened. "Cow turds cain't help a team of cow turds!" Brownell, the leather-lunger, screamed from behind third base. Frankie Thompson had the final word. "This goes down as an error on the cow!" he chortled.

Some of the Brandon players shooed the cows back beyond right field and replaced the rope. Play finally resumed and the rest of the game proceeded without incident until Jimmy found himself leading five to nothing in the bottom of the ninth inning. With two outs and a man on second base, Jimmy suddenly realized he was on the verge of pitching a shutout, his first of the season.

"A hundred dollars says Roberts doesn't get the shutout," Toby Gower offered from his perch behind home plate.

"What?" Howard answered. "You've already lost a hundred on the game."

"Tryin' to get my money back, is all. Jack Washington is one of my best hitters. I doubt he'll strike out, so if he puts the ball in play, who knows what might happen. Hit, error — I'll take my chances. Will you?" Toby smiled. He knew the answer.

"You're on," Howard was already confident he'd win his bet with Jellycakes, comfortable that Woodside's five run lead would hold and beat the four-run spread the bookie had given him. Why not add to his winnings?

Crusher approached Jimmy on the mound from his shortstop position. "Let's pick him off."

"What for? We're one out away from a win, with a four-run lead."

"Jes' for the fun of it. You're gonna win the game. No way the runner'll be expectin' a pickoff. It'll be like practice, easy."

"But I've got a — " Jimmy stopped. He didn't want to jinx his shutout by talking about it.

"What's the matter, ain't you got no pickoff move?"

That stung. Jimmy was proud of his pickoff moves. He'd worked hard on them, and he'd picked runners off second base several times before. Crusher was right, the runner wouldn't be paying much attention. Jimmy could get his third out, and he wouldn't even have to face the batter, who'd already gotten two hits off him that day. "Okay. First pitch. You cover." Crusher nodded and returned to shortstop.

Jimmy looked in for the sign. He shook off the first one, just to convince the runner he was focused on home plate. Behind him, the base runner took a modest lead off second. Goodlett moved a small step towards the bag. Jimmy nodded at the next sign, using the half-windup customary with a runner on base, then whirled and fired the ball towards second base, where Crusher would be waiting to put the tag on the runner.

Only Crusher wasn't there. Crusher hadn't moved. The ball rocketed into center field. A surprised "Oh!" rang out from the stands. Howard Stone dropped the cigar he had taken out in anticipation of his victory and his winnings. The runner, after a stunned moment's hesitation while his brain registered that the pitcher had just thrown the ball into the outfield, took off. The center fielder ran to the ball and fired it to Goodlett, who had come out to take the throw. Goodlett whipped the ball towards home plate as fast as he could. But it was no use. The runner crossed the plate without even having to slide.

"What in the hell?" Howard screamed into the air. Toby whooped and hollered and slapped him on the back.

"Now we're all square, Howard," he gleamed. Howard grunted. He should have had two hundred dollars of Toby Gower's money in his pocket instead of none. What's worse, he hadn't beaten the spread, so he'd just lost his bet to Jellycakes, another three hundred dollars. Five hundred dollars, all because of Jimmy Roberts' bonehead play.

Jimmy looked around at his teammates. Some looked back in puzzlement, others pawed at the dirt to avoid looking at him. Crusher stared back as if nothing had happened. Jimmy wasn't puzzled. He knew what was up. "You got lint for brains!" shouted the leather-lunger. *No*, thought Jimmy. *Just a teammate who's not about the team.*

Jimmy returned to the job at hand, but his thoughts were with Crusher. *Why would he deliberately make me look dumb? What did I do to him? Should I ask him about it, or just ignore it?* Distracted, he walked Washington, but then settled down and got the next batter to pop up for the third out, ending the game. As his teammates trotted past Jimmy walking slowly towards the dugout, they slapped him on the butt or patted him on the back with their gloves, saying "Great game, Jimmy!" "Way to pitch!" "Never forget that homer of yours!" Only Crusher trotted past without a word.

Thelma bid Rhoda good-bye. "See you in church tomorrow?"

"Dang straight," Rhoda said. "Gotta pray to forgive all them swear words I used today." Thelma laughed. "Thanks for invitin' me, Thelma, it was funner than bein' nekkid in a rainstorm." She moved off. Thelma looked at her son in the dugout and decided the best thing to do was to go home and talk to him about the game there.

As the players packed up their gear, Rusty came over to Jimmy. "What the hell was that play, Roberts?"

"Just wasn't thinkin', coach," Jimmy responded. He wasn't going to complain about how Goodlett had set him up. That'd be whining. It'd also make him look foolish.

"Well, forget it. You pitched a great game, go home an' get some rest, I'll see you Monday at the mill." Rusty went to congratulate Crusher, who was surrounded by teammates extolling his hitting. Watching Crusher enjoying all the attention, Jimmy knew Rusty was right about one thing. He needed to go home and rest his arm. But he also knew he was wrong about another. Jimmy would never "forget it."

CHAPTER 5

Jimmy didn't go to church much lately. He'd rather be practicing his pitching. Thelma didn't like it, but she didn't usually force the issue anymore. After all, Jimmy was old enough to start making his own decisions. Today however, she had insisted. So there he sat, watching the sun's rays through the stained glass, half-listening to Rev Bob's sermon, and still trying to puzzle out just why Crusher had set him up to fail in that pickoff move yesterday. Jimmy hadn't done anything to Crusher, he'd only been nice. That comment about "poking" one out of the park? That didn't make sense. A lot of people used "poke" when talking about hitting a baseball. He was still angry at Goodlett for tricking him that way. Earlier in the service, during the Lord's Prayer, when he'd mumbled to himself "as we forgive those who trespass against us," Jimmy knew he didn't want to forgive Crusher. Instead, he really wanted to smash him in the face and knock some teeth out.

Rev Bob's sermon was on the sin of pride. He had decided to fulfill his promise to Howard Stone with a series of sermons about the seven deadly sins, and he had started out with the one acknowledged to be the mother of them all. He was now approaching his climax. "It's dangerous territory, that place between righteousness and self-righteousness." Rev Bob's deep voice echoed through the sanctuary. "Yes, the Lord wants you to be *proud* of your achievements. He wants you to be *proud* of your work, *proud* of the part you play in turning out a beautiful towel or a crisp, new sheet. But not too proud!" He began to build to his climax. "Not *braggin'* proud-uh! Not *'I'm better 'n' everybody else'* proud-uh! Not so *proud-uh* you think you deserve more than you're gettin'!" He paused to make sure his next line sank in. "That you *demand* more than you're gettin'. That's the kind of *proud-uh* that'll have you broken on the wheel, my brothers an' sisters, *torn apart* on the *wheel* of God's *justice*! So watch out! Don't be too *proud-uh*!"

The word "proud" penetrated Jimmy's brain. Had he been too proud? Or was Goodlett so proud that he wasn't going to let anyone else on the team have a moment of glory that might detract from his own? Whatever the answer, being teammates with Crusher Goodlett was probably not going to be much fun.

Rev Bob announced the final hymn. "*Do Lord*!" he shouted. He didn't even bother with the hymn number. No one would need to look at the words to sing this one. A rush of excited anticipation flashed through the congregation. *"Do Lord!"* Carrie Robinson boomed out the introductory chords on the tiny pipe organ. In the choir stalls to the right of the pulpit, Jimmy saw his mother rise. He also saw the pretty girl seated next to her rise, too. He'd noticed her at yesterday's game with his mother. Who was she? And why did he care? He'd never given girls much thought, never even had a girlfriend. No time. Even when textile league ball finished for the season, there were always pickup games. And practice with the peach basket. One reason his mother had divorced his father had been the latter's interest in "other women." Jimmy didn't want to be anything like his father. And that included his interest in women.

"Do Lord! Oh do Lord! Oh do remember me!" the congregation began. Rhoda threw in an *"Oh Lordy!"* at the end of the first line. *"Do Lord! Oh do Lord! Oh do remember me!"* She added an *"Allelujah!"* after this line. *"Do Lord! Oh do Lord! Oh do remember Me! Look a-way beyond the blue."* Rhoda started clapping. She might be new to the choir, but she wasn't shy about taking a lead in the singing.

Soon the little church was rocking with their love of singing, their love of the Lord, and their rejoicing in a Sunday that might bring them a picnic, a walk, a long talk with a neighbor, perhaps a little tidying up around the house, but no mill. *"I Got A Home In Glory Land That Outshines The Sun."* It was thoughts like these that helped make mill life tolerable. Singing and clapping with friends and neighbors on a beautiful Sunday morning might even make it enjoyable, at least for short periods.

After the service, Jimmy waited outside the church for his mother to change her robe and emerge. He chatted with a few neighbors. All praised his pitching the day before and no one asked about his failed pickoff move. Thelma finally came out in the company of the girl from the choir. Jimmy couldn't help noticing that up close, in her blue dress dotted with yellow sunflowers, she looked even prettier.

"Jimmy, I'd like you to meet Rhoda Dawson," Thelma said. "She works over at Brandon Mill, but they ain't got much of a choir, so she's joined ours."

"Hey," Jimmy said, giving her a nod.

"How do?" Rhoda responded.

"She's got a voice like an angel, doesn't she, Jimmy?"

"'Specially when I call the hogs. 'Sooeeeeeee!' " Rhoda sang out, loud enough to turn the heads of those standing in the churchyard. She laughed a hearty laugh. *She ain't shy!* Jimmy thought.

"Yep, that ain't no angel voice." Thelma laughed. "I asked Rhoda to have lunch with us," she began, "But she's gotta eat with her family.

She said she'd love to come some other time, though. Wouldn't that be nice?" It was not intended as a rhetorical question, but when Jimmy treated it as one, Thelma said "Why don't you walk Rhoda back home to Brandon, Jimmy?"

"Oh, that's all right, Mrs. Roberts, it's not a fer piece."

"Jimmy don't mind, do you, son?" Thelma smiled sweetly at him, but he knew the meaning behind that smile.

"No, ma'am."

"If you're sure you don't mind," Rhoda said to Jimmy.

Jimmy usually practiced pitching after church while his mother prepared lunch. But seeing Rhoda's warm brown eyes and beautiful smile, he had the sudden thought that maybe walking her home would be a duty he wouldn't mind so much. "Sure," he said.

"See you in church next week, Mrs. Roberts," Rhoda said brightly.

"If not before, honey," Thelma smiled back at her.

Jimmy and Rhoda set off down the block, turned left, and moved towards the edge of Woodside's mill village. "Thank you for doin' this, Jimmy."

"Ain't no never mind."

Rhoda waited for him to continue, but when he didn't, she just walked beside him, hurrying to keep up with his long strides. They passed a woman sweeping her dirt yard. She waved at Rhoda. Rhoda paused and called to her, "Hot 'nuff to fry spit!"

The woman stopped to wipe her forehead with the back of her hand. "Amen!"

Jimmy hadn't slowed and Rhoda had to run to catch up. "We could follow the train tracks if you wanna. That'd be quicker," he said.

"Okay."

He led the way up a small slope to the tracks and they set off in the direction of Brandon Mill. He walked on the track ties while Rhoda walked outside the rail. He set a brisk pace. "What's your hurry?" she asked.

"I need to practice my pitchin'."

"Even on Sunday?"

"Every day."

They walked along in silence for a few minutes. "You ain't much for jaw-flappin', are you?" Rhoda asked.

"Jaw-flappin'?"

"You know, talkin'."

"Oh."

"Well?"

"What do you want to talk about?"

"How 'bout baseball. I ain't never seed a game before. I really liked it. But I didn't understand how come you all of a sudden turned around an' threw the ball into the outfield that one time? Were you trying to hit that runner? Is that another way to get him ... what do you say, get him out?"

Everyone after the game and at church had studiously avoided talking about that play with Jimmy. Rhoda's directness disarmed him, but he knew from her tone of voice that she intended no harm. He recognized in her calm eyes a genuine curiosity.

"No, you cain't hit runners to get them out, that's illegal. I was tryin' what's called a 'pickoff move,' where you try to tag the runner out before he can get back the base safe."

"But no one was there to tag him."

"There was supposed to be. The shortstop was supposed to cover the bag." Jimmy couldn't disguise the anger he still felt about having been duped.

"Why didn't he?"

"I don't know, Rhoda. Crusher — that's the shortstop — called the play himself, an' then he didn't follow through on his part."

"A flat-out liar," she said definitively. "He's as low-down as a snake in a wagon track. He does that to you again, you let me know."

"What would you do?" Jimmy asked, surprised.

"I don't know, but sumpin'." The way Rhoda said it, Jimmy was pretty sure he wouldn't care to be on the receiving end of Rhoda's "sumpin'."

In the trees along the tracks, a bird sang. Rhoda suddenly mimicked its song, calling *purdy, purdy, purdy.... whoit... whoit... whoit.* Jimmy stopped. "What are you doin'?"

"That's a cardinal. Look, see, there it is." She pointed to a small oak tree, on one of whose branches a bright red bird perched and sang. *Purdy, purdy, purdy.*

Purdy, purdy, purdy! Rhoda sang back.

"How'd you learn to do that?"

"Practice. Jes' like you an' your pitchin'. You know anything about cardinals?"

"The St. Louis Cardinals," Jimmy said.

"What kind of cardinal is that?"

Jimmy laughed. "The baseball kind."

"Huh?"

"It's the name of a baseball team, in St. Louis, Missouri. Got one of my favorite players on it: Stan 'The Man' Musial."

"Everything's baseball to you, idn' it?"

"Pretty much."

"Ain't that kind of limitin'?"

"I ain't found much else to interest me."

Rhoda thought for a minute. "How 'bout bird calls?"

"Bird calls?"

"Yeah. I'll teach you the cardinal call."

"No, thanks."

"What's wrong, skeered to learn sumpin' new?" She stopped and stared at him, hands on hips.

Jimmy looked at her. Why in the world would he want to learn a bird song? On the other hand, with this pretty, strong-minded teacher in front of him.... "All right, show me."

"We'll work on the 'purdy' part first." She demonstrated: "*Purdy, purdy, purdy.* Now you."

Jimmy tried to imitate her, but it sounded more like *party, party, party.*

She laughed. "Pooch out your lips more."

"Huh?"

"Pooch 'em. Like this." Rhoda took Jimmy's lips in her fingers and formed them to resemble fish lips. She held them there and said, "Now say it." Jimmy tried again. "Better. But sing it more, Jimmy." He tried again, and it sounded almost like a cardinal. "Good! Now practice that, an' the next time I see you, I'll teach you the *whoit, whoit, whoit* part."

She walked on down the tracks. For a second, Jimmy just watched her go. Had a girl just been teaching him to sing like a cardinal, standing on the railroad tracks outside Brandon village? He ran up beside her. "Where 'bouts you from, Rhoda?"

"Up past Pumpkintown, near Sugarlikker Lake, on the way to Caesar's Head."

"Caesar's Head? How come they call it that?"

"Well, there's this big ol' rock, an' it's got this bumpy part stickin' out — that must be the nose. An' underneath's a small cave cut in the rock, shallow, just big enough to sit in. That's the mouth. I like to sit in there."

"You like to sit in Caesar's mouth?"

She laughed. "It sounds kinda silly when you say it like that, but it's true, I do. You get a view of the whole valley from there. I can see all the way to Greenville."

"How do they know it looks like Caesar? Wadn' he some Roman emperor or somethin'?"

"Yeah. We learned 'bout him in school, didn't you?"

"Reckon not. I had to leave at fifteen to work in the mill. I learned about him in the Bible."

"Anyway, it probably dudn' look like Caesar, they just wanted to make it somebody famous so it'd be more impressive." Rhoda thought for a moment. "Maybe they should have called it 'Jimmy's Head!' "

"No! Rhoda's!" Jimmy shot back.

"No, no, it's gotta be somebody famous." She arced her hands across the sky, announcing "Napoleon's Head."

"Doesn't sound right."

"Well, come on, then, who else? Think!"

Jimmy puzzled his eyebrows. "I cain't think of anybody."

"I got it! I got it!" She made a broad, sweeping gesture in the air and proclaimed, "Stan 'The Man's' Head!"

Jimmy laughed. "Stan 'The Man's' Head!" he sang out.

The loud blare of a train whistle rent the air. Jimmy looked down the tracks to see the bright headlights of a Southern Railway freight train headed their way. "Off the tracks, Rhoda!" he called and jumped to one side. Rhoda jumped to the other and the train rumbled between them.

Jimmy watched the cars blur by, *clackety-clacking* coal and bales of cotton somewhere south. He found himself imagining Rhoda on the other side of the tracks, her soft, round face, big, brown eyes, the sun-bleached blonde of her hair. He found himself wishing the train would hurry by so he could see her again. And, from out of nowhere, came a twinge of anxiety that maybe she wouldn't be there, that maybe she would have disappeared with the passing train.

But when the train's caboose finally passed by, there she stood, a huge smile on her face. She sprang onto the tracks, her face aglow. "That was incredible! We ain't got no trains in the mountains! The air on my face, blowin' my hair back, all that noise! Shoot me for a billy goat, I cain't wait to do that again!"

They resumed walking down the tracks, a little more slowly this time. Jimmy marveled at Rhoda's enthusiasm. A passing freight train? He'd experienced that a thousand times, but he'd never considered it a thrill. But Rhoda had. She seemed to find joy and meaning in practically everything.

"What in tarnation is that?" She pointed to the top of a small hill, where two boys stood next to a metal contraption of some sort.

"An iron wagon," Jimmy replied.

"Where do you get it?"

"You make it. From old machine parts from the mill. It goes purty fast, considerin'." Just then, the boys began pushing the wagon, then one of them jumped in. The wagon picked up speed as it moved down the hill.

"He'd better put on the brakes," Rhoda shouted.

"Ain't none."

"How's he gonna stop?"

The answer came as the driver steered the iron wagon towards a clump of weeds growing at the bottom of the hill. He pitched himself into the weeds and the wagon slowed to a stop a few yards away. The other boy ran down the hill, shouting "My turn! My turn!"

"That looks like fun!" Rhoda smiled. "There sure is lots to do in a mill village."

Lots to do? Jimmy thought. *There's baseball an' doffin' the spools of thread at work. There's eatin' an' talkin' an' maybe goin' to church an' goin' to the Christmas parade in Greenville once a year. There's Mama an' my teammates. Lots to do?*

"There's my street," Rhoda said. She jumped off the tracks and ran down the hill. Jimmy followed. "Thanks for walkin' me home. Maybe I'll see you in church next week."

"I don't go to church much."

"Why not? You could come sing in the choir with your mama an' me."

"No thanks."

Rhoda looked at him for a moment. "Suit yourself. Like I said, thanks." She smiled, turned, and walked down the street. Jimmy watched her mount the porch of her home, wave, and disappear inside. He climbed the hill back up to the tracks. Once there, he looked carefully around. The two boys had gone off with their iron wagon. No one was around. Jimmy slowly brought his hand to his lips and pooched them out like a fish. *Purdy, purdy, purdy*, he sang.

CHAPTER 6

"Fire him? Are you sure?" Rusty Peters pulled out the blue bandanna from the back pocket of his dungarees and wiped the sweat from around his neck. It was Monday morning, and Rusty had enjoyed his Sunday off, basking in the 5-1 victory over Brandon on Saturday and thinking about what a fun season it was going to be with Crusher Goodlett to manage. That's what he thought Howard Stone wanted to talk about when he was summoned from his job as foreman of spinning at Woodside Mill to Howard's office inside the mansion on the hill. It was the highest paid job in the plant, so Rusty could have been forgiven for feeling a little superior, but there was no need for forgiveness in Rusty's case. He was as down-home modest as they come, a true team player. His spinners loved working under his tolerant eye, and his baseball players loved playing under his enthusiastic management. If hand clapping had been an Olympic event, Rusty would have won the gold. But there was nothing to clap about the news Howard had just delivered.

"I'm always sure, Rusty," Howard said evenly.

"I know, Mr. Stone, I didn't mean to question your judgment, it's just that Jimmy Roberts is our best pitcher. He's a team leader, too." Rusty liked Jimmy. Everybody did. Except, apparently, Howard Stone.

"We've got Crusher to lead the team now," Howard replied. He stood up from behind his desk to at least get a little air circulating. *If it's this damn hot at ten a.m....* he thought. "I assume you're happy with the trade I made?"

"Oh, yessir," Rusty said quickly. "It's gonna be great to have him on the team. That home run he hit...." Both men paused a moment to remember the ball Goodlett had "crushed" over the left field fence.

"Then let's not worry about a little pitcher, okay?" Howard asked with a friendly smile.

"Only Jimmy's not a 'little pitcher,' " Rusty said. "He's 6 and 1 already, he's got the best ERA on the team — "

"And he made one of the dumbest plays I've ever seen on a ball field," Howard said. He didn't bother to mention that the play had cost him five hundred dollars — the side bet with Toby Gower plus losing to Jellycakes on the spread. One thing for sure, Howard Stone did not like people who cost him money. "Even if we lose every game Jimmy would have started, which I doubt will happen, but let's say it does," he continued. "He only pitches every other week. We're in first place by six games. I am not worried about firing Jimmy Roberts costing us the pennant."

Rusty looked at Howard and knew further protest was useless. Howard wasn't "one of them." You couldn't talk to him like you could other folks. Howard was, in the end, a Yankee. He didn't understand mill folks or mill life or Southerners. He was ruthless in a way southerners seldom were. Oh, southerners could be ruthless, no doubt about it. But they weren't so obvious about it. The steel fist inside the velvet glove. But Howard Stone wore no glove. "Nothin's wrong with it, Mr. Stone," Rusty answered. "I'm sure we can win the pennant without Jimmy. I just hope no other team picks him up."

"I wouldn't worry about that, Rusty," Howard said. "We owners tend to stick together, respect each other's wishes, if you know what I mean."

Rusty knew what he meant. "I'll tell him when he comes in today."

"I'll have Waddy tell him."

"I'm the manager, I should tell him he's off the team."

"And Waddy's the Super. He should tell him he's out of the mill."

Rusty was so shocked he rose from his chair. "You're firing him from the mill?!"

"No need to be upset, Rusty. It's actually none of your business, is it?" Howard stared at Rusty, who meekly lowered his eyes.

"No, sir."

"Jimmy's just a doffer. I can replace him in a heartbeat. But he embarrassed me, Rusty, and I don't like being embarrassed. Now, you're not going to embarrass me by not winning this championship, are you?"

The consequences if he did were suddenly crystal clear to Rusty. "No, sir!" he answered firmly.

"Good. Then go out and do it."

Rusty walked swiftly out the door, sad for Jimmy, but happy to escape the poisonous air that seemed to surround his vengeful boss.

After Rusty left, Howard had a moment's hesitation. He was firing his best pitcher, was this really the right thing to do? "You're always over-reacting!" His father's words wormed their way inside his head. He'd spent a lifetime building walls to try to keep them out, but there they were again. "Don't think with your heart! You're a businessman, goddammit, think with your head!" *But this is business,* Howard insisted to himself. *What if Roberts makes a stupid mistake in a crucial game? And I've got*

Crusher now, Daddy! Howard winced. Why did he still call him "Daddy" at his age? *Dead five years!* Sometimes Howard thought he'd never die. Sometimes he knew it. But if his plan worked, he'd bury his "daddy" for good.

Coming to work for his Monday afternoon shift, Jimmy felt fine. A couple of nights' rest had lessened his embarrassment about the aborted pickoff move. After all, he'd pitched a good game, one of his best. He still didn't understand what had happened with Goodlett, but the best thing was to let it go. He could play with Crusher. He was, Jimmy had to admit, a great addition to the team. They were sure to win the championship now.

"Hi, Mama!" he called to Thelma as she passed through the gate.

"Hi, Jimmy! Did you sleep all right?"

"Great!" Jimmy replied. Thelma smiled to herself. Her son, usually so quiet and intense, had been extremely chatty last night. He'd sat on the porch for quite a while, talking to neighbors. He'd even played pickup ball with some of the younger boys in the street. Winning games he'd pitched always put Jimmy in a good mood, but, Thelma had noticed, there had seemed an extra sparkle in him last night. Thelma was pretty sure she knew the reason why. And she was relieved. Much as she wanted Jimmy to escape the mill, she also knew it was high time Jimmy showed some interest in girls as well as baseball. "See you tonight, Mama!" Jimmy called, as he disappeared inside the building.

Waddy Benson was waiting for him at his post in the seventh row of looms. "See you a minute in my office, Jimmy?" he said, turning towards the door before Jimmy could answer. The whistle sounded, the lights blinked, and the looms sprang to clattering life as Jimmy followed.

Inside the office, the sound of the machines shrank to a dull roar as Waddy motioned Jimmy to a chair. He took his own chair behind his desk. "Jimmy, there ain't no good way to put this, so I'll just get it over with. We gotta let you go."

"Let me go? What do you mean?" Jimmy straightened in his chair. "From the team?"

"Yeah, well, that has to happen, too. But, no, I mean from the mill. You're fired."

Jimmy rose quickly from his chair. "Fired? What do you mean? What for?"

"For tryin' that dumb pickoff move."

"What?"

"Now take it easy, Jimmy. It don't make no sense to me, neither. But that's what Mr. Stone wants."

"But why?" Jimmy pleaded. "We won the game!"

"I know we did."

"Are you sure?" Jimmy took a step towards Waddy, who rose from his chair. For a minute, he half-expected Jimmy to take a swing at him.

Waddy held his hands out, palms down, to calm him. "Believe me, Jimmy, when Howard Stone tells you somethin', you're sure."

Jimmy sat back down. He didn't know what to say. Fired from the mill? Even though he didn't like it, the mill was his life. And the money! How were they going to live on just his mother's pay? And the team? Jimmy shoulders sagged.

"I'm sorry, Jimmy," Waddy said. "Tell you what, I got me an idea. When you get home, tell your mama I wanna see her."

"Mama? What for?"

"Just tell her I still got that itch that needs scratchin'."

"What the heck's that mean, Waddy?"

"She'll know."

Jimmy was too devastated to argue. "All right," he mumbled. He looked at Waddy, who stared back, saying nothing. There was nothing to say. Mill owners owned more than the mill. They owned your whole life.

When Jimmy opened the door to Waddy's office, the sound of the mill hit him full force. It was excruciatingly loud — pounding, pounding, pounding. As he walked between the machinery, some of his co-workers looked up. They could see that Jimmy wasn't walking at his usual brisk pace. They could see that he kept his eyes on the floor. And they could see that he walked past his workplace behind looms 7-12 and right on out the door.

Outside, Jimmy didn't know where to go or what to do. He'd always wanted to leave the mill, but not this way. He didn't want to go home. His mother was there, and he couldn't face her now. He considered going down to the baseball diamond, just to see who might be there. But he was no longer on the team. Did that mean he couldn't throw the ball around, or practice his hitting? Was baseball no longer a part of his life? Jimmy shook his head violently, trying to drive away the horrible thought. No, he definitely couldn't go to the baseball field. For a moment, he contemplated taking the bus to the library to look up Julius Caesar. Where did that crazy idea come from? As he reached the gated entrance to the mill, he heard the mill humming behind him. But he didn't turn around. He took a deep breath and stepped through the gate.

Half a mile away, Katie Jackson was excitedly reading *The Greenville News* to her husband in his liquor store. "In introducing his resolution to the House of Representatives, Speaker Yancey Dickerson said, 'Fact and fancy have been so confused that today it is still not known what actually took place in the 1919 World Series. Thirty-two years is too long for any man to be penalized for an act when there was strong evidence that he was no party to the conspiracy. What *is* known is that the ex-star shouldn't suffer life-long ignominy. That is why I offer the following resolution: *We, the people of South Carolina, through our State Representatives, do hereby humbly request that the Commissioner of Major League Baseball immediately reinstate Joseph Jefferson Jackson to full status as a professional baseball player.'* " Katie put down the paper. "Oh, Joe, can you believe it?" she cried. "They want to reinstate you!"

Joe sat stoically behind his desk. "Stirrin' ashes," he said evenly. His dull voice contrasted sharply with that of his wife.

"They need to be stirred!" Katie replied hotly. "Things need to be set right."

"They won't let you set things right, Katie. Who knows that better 'n us?" Joe's voice was no longer calm, but filled with anger. "I tried to set things right, remember? Went to Kid Gleason when I heard the rumors about a fix, asked him to bench me, take me out of the series, Katie. An' he wouldn't do it! Said Mr. Comiskey would fire him from managin'. So much for tryin' to set things right."

"But this is a state representative makin' this resolution, Joe! What if the House agrees, endorses it? How can Commissioner Chandler deny them?"

"Because the Commissioner of Baseball can do anything he damn well pleases! Like kick me out of baseball even though a jury said I was innocent. Baseball hadn' kept faith with me and I don't intend to ask any favors of it. Why do you want to stir things up?

"Because you deserve to be in the Hall of Fame!"

"Stop it, Katie, stop it! Let it be!" Joe rose from behind his desk. His six-foot-one frame towered over his smaller wife. "I've spent thirty years gettin' over what baseball done to me, an' I ain't about to get my hopes up an' let 'em do it to me again!"

"What are you goin' to do, Joe? The resolution's been introduced. You cain't stop it."

"But I don't have to support it," Joe shot back. "An' I don't have to read about it — or, rather, have my wife read it to me. An' that's another thing that'll happen. They'll start talkin' all over again 'bout how I cain't read or write, 'bout how the dumb ol' hick got tricked into cheatin'." Joe stomped towards the front door. "I'm goin' for a cigarette."

Katie sighed. She understood, of course. It had been painful for Joe, for both of them. She had hated seeing her husband slandered and mocked. Somehow they had managed to live a good life — a life without baseball, except for Joe's one attempt at managing mill teams back in the Thirties. Joe had made it to sixty-three years, by denying himself the thing he loved more than anything in life. Or having it denied to him. It wasn't right. It needed fixing. This resolution just might be the answer. It might finally bring a measure of justice. Joe might not support it, but she surely would. She strolled over to Pee Wee. "Got any advice?"

"Go to hell!" the parrot cawed. Katie laughed despite herself.

At that moment, the door to the store opened. It was Jimmy. He had turned left outside the mill gate and, head down, had mindlessly begun placing one foot in front of the other. At one point, he had looked up and seen Brandon Mill outlined against the sky. Surprised, he had thought about turning back toward Woodside. But then, where would he go and what would he do? But why was he here now, in Brandon? And then it came to him.

"Hello," Katie called from the back of the shop. She came forward. "Oh, it's you. Nice to see you again. Jimmy, isn't it?"

"Yes, ma'am," Jimmy replied, standing in the doorway.

"Come in, come in, keep the heat out." Jimmy shut the door and turned back towards Katie. "What can I do for you, Jimmy?" He looked around. "Joe's not here at the moment."

"Oh." He turned back towards the door.

"But he should be right back," Katie said quickly. "You wanna wait for him?"

"I ... I guess so," Jimmy was still a little surprised to be back in the store after his last reception. But a lot had changed since then. Then he had been a young kid trying to get some help with his dream. Now he was an unemployed mill worker with no time for dreaming any more.

Katie noticed Jimmy's reluctance and pulled out a chair from behind a counter. "Here, sit down." She placed another chair nearby. "I'll join you." Jimmy moved slowly to the chair and sat. Katie sat facing him. "I'm sorry I cain't offer you anything to drink. I could run next door to the house...."

"Oh, no, thank you. I really don't know why I'm here."

"Well, that makes two of us. Maybe if we talk about it, we can figure it out." She smiled. Jimmy wriggled uncomfortably in his chair.

Katie guessed he wasn't the one to start a conversation. "Have you heard the big news?"

"No ma'am."

"Speaker Yancey Dickerson has introduced a resolution in the State House of Representatives tellin' the South Carolina legislature to ask the Commissioner of Baseball to reinstate Joe into baseball. Joe might can get back into the game!"

"I don't understand."

"The Commissioner can do anything he wants. Commissioner Landis threw Joe out, now maybe Commissioner Chandler will let him back in. That means his records an' everythin' will count! He's a shoe-in for the Hall of Fame!" Katie was delighted at her unintended pun. "Hey, that's a good 'un! Wait'll I tell Joe." Jimmy sat silently. "Aren't you happy for him?"

"Well, yes ma'am, I guess so," he managed. "If he's happy."

"Well, he ain't. That's why it's up to folks like us to make sure that resolution passes. For folks like Joe, folks who've had a big hurt laid on 'em in life, sometimes you gotta *make* them happy. Will you help me, Jimmy?"

"Do what?"

"Well, I don't rightly know yet. Keep the pressure on them politicians somehow. They're mostly a chicken-hearted group, far as I can tell, so you gotta show 'em the way to courage. You got any ideas?"

"No, ma'am," Jimmy mumbled.

Katie paused. "Are you all right?"

"Yes ma'am. Why?"

"I thought you'd be a little more excited about the news, that's all."

"Oh, well ... I just got other things on my mind, is all."

"Anything I can help with?"

Jimmy looked at Katie. He knew she was kind, and he could use a friend. Truth to tell, he was a little afraid of Joe. Since his dad had left him when he was only ten, he didn't really know how to talk to older men. Maybe he could warm up by talking to Katie. He definitely needed to talk to someone. "I need a job," he finally blurted out.

"What? Why?"

"I got fired."

"Fired? From the mill?" Jimmy nodded. "What for?"

"For makin' a stupid baseball play." Saying it out loud made the reason seem all the sillier. But that didn't change anything. "In yesterday's game. I tried a pick-off at second base, an' I ended up throwin' the ball into center field. I guess I embarrassed Mr. Stone or somethin'."

"That's ridiculous! He fired you for that?"

"That's what the supervisor said." Jimmy left it there. The facts were the facts, whatever the reason. Something the wife of Shoeless Joe Jackson surely understood.

Katie softened. "I'm sorry, Jimmy, I really am. Have you told your mama?"

Jimmy shook his head. "She's at work. Besides, I wanted to see 'bout somethin' else first."

"What, Jimmy?"

Jimmy swallowed. He couldn't summon the courage to look at Katie. He looked at the floor and said quietly, "I wanted to see if Mr. Jackson would give me a job."

Katie was surprised. And then delighted. "Here in the liquor store? Why, that's a wonderful idea! I'm sure Joe will like it."

It was Jimmy's turn to be surprised. "You are?"

"Sure! Why wouldn't he? You could help me with the books, too. You any good at arithmetic?"

"I was purty good till I had to leave school."

"Oh, it'll come back quick. An' you can help sweep — won't mind givin' up that job! Oh, there's lots of things we can think of for you to do here." Jimmy looked at Katie. She smiled confidently back at him. For the first time since he'd been summoned to Waddy's office, he felt a little better.

The door swung open and Jimmy got up from his seat as Joe walked in. Joe looked at Jimmy sternly. "What do you want?"

When Jimmy didn't answer right away — or couldn't — Katie stepped in. "Jimmy has somethin' important to ask you, Joe."

"If it's about baseball, I don't wanna hear it."

"It's not." Jimmy paused.

"Well?" Shoeless said, closing the door and approaching Jimmy.

Jimmy swallowed hard. He looked at Katie, who smiled encouragingly. "I need a job, Mr. Jackson. I just got fired from the mill."

"What for?"

"Because the owner felt like it, that's why," Katie chimed in. "Jimmy maybe made a playin' mistake in Saturday's game, an' the owner fired him. It idn' right!"

For a moment, Joe said nothing. He knew how tough it was for mill families, even when everyone was working. "I'm sorry to hear that, son. But I don't see how I can help you."

"He wants a job here," Katie said.

"Here?" Joe asked. He looked at them both. Had Katie put Jimmy up to this, to ease him back into caring about baseball? "I'm sorry, but we don't need any help." He moved towards his desk. "If I hear of anythin', I'll let you know."

"He could help me with the books an' carrying crates — your back isn't that strong any more, Joe," Katie pleaded. "I'm sure we could think of things for Jimmy to do."

"Might could. Except we ain't in the charity business. I run a small liquor store. An' I bet first thing he'll be doin' is askin' me to teach him ball."

"No, sir," Jimmy said strongly. "I'm through with baseball." The words surprised him.

"Probly a wise decision. It's just a game, an' you cain't play a game your whole life. Best you learn that now."

"Cain't we at least try him out for a while?" Katie asked.

"That's all right, Mrs. Jackson," Jimmy said, starting for the door.

Joe felt bad, but what could he do? Why should he spend good money hiring someone he didn't need? "I'm sure you'll find a job in another mill, son."

Jimmy opened the door, then suddenly stopped and turned. "How can you say that, Mr. Jackson?"

"Say what?"

"Talk about workin' in the mill, spendin' my whole life in there?" Jimmy's voice rose. "You lived that life once. How can you wish it on anybody?" He ran out the door, slamming it behind him.

"Jimmy! — " Katie quickly opened the door and looked down the street, only to see Jimmy running away. She closed the door and turned to look at her husband.

"I'm sorry, Katie. But we don't need the help."

"No, Joe. But Jimmy does."

"It's a dream, him wantin' to leave the mill. I ain't in the dream business."

"You were once," Katie replied evenly, then opened the door and left.

She didn't return to the store and Joe worked alone. Somehow he made it through the rest of the day and closed up. Somehow he made it through a mostly silent supper. And somehow, when Katie had gone off early to bed and had closed the door firmly behind her, Joe found himself sitting in a small cane chair in his dimly lit basement, staring at the contents of an old cedar chest. It had been many years since he had opened it, but Jimmy's cry for help had penetrated the wall Joe had built to hide his own pain. It reminded him of something, something he now felt compelled to remember.

He reached into the chest and pulled out a weathered telegram, dated September 28, 1920. Joe stared at it for a long while. He couldn't read it, but he knew what it said. It was from his old boss, Charles Comiskey, owner of the Chicago White Sox.

> YOU AND EACH OF YOU ARE HEREBY NOTIFIED OF YOUR INDEFINITE SUSPENSION OF THE CHICAGO AMERICAN LEAGUE BASEBALL CLUB. YOUR SUSPENSION IS BROUGHT ABOUT BY INFORMATION WHICH HAS JUST COME TO ME, DIRECTLY INVOLVING YOU (AND EACH OF YOU) IN THE BASEBALL SCANDAL NOW BEING INVESTIGATED BY THE (PRESENT) GRAND JURY OF COOK COUNTY, RESULTING FROM THE WORLD SERIES OF 1919. IF YOU ARE INNOCENT OF ANY WRONGDOING, YOU AND EACH OF YOU WILL BE REINSTATED; IF YOU ARE GUILTY, YOU WILL BE RETIRED FROM ORGANIZED BASEBALL FOR THE REST OF YOUR LIVES IF I CAN ACCOMPLISH IT.
>
> UNTIL THERE IS A FINALITY TO THIS INVESTIGATION, IT IS DUE TO THE PUBLIC THAT I TAKE THIS ACTION EVEN THOUGH IT COSTS CHICAGO THE PENNANT.

Joe let the telegram fall listlessly back into the chest. He remembered the day he'd received it, a muggy Wednesday in Chicago. He was preparing for the team's trip to St. Louis for a three-game series against the Browns to end the season. The game before, Joe had gone 1 for 3 against the Tigers, moving the White Sox to within a half-game of Cleveland for first place. He had had a great 1920 season, batting .384, second behind George Sisler of the Browns. He was third in slugging, total bases, doubles, and triples, fourth in runs batted in, and had slammed twelve home runs.

And then the baseball world had been shocked by a headline in the *Philadelphia North-American* that Monday which quickly spread over the wires: "GAMBLERS PROMISED WHITE SOX $100,000 TO LOSE". Comiskey had sent the telegram on Tuesday, the day the Chicago Grand Jury had issued an indictment against Joe and seven of his teammates. Joe had received it the next day, ending his season and, as it turned out, his baseball career.

Joe placed both hands on the side of the chest and stared down at the mementoes of his life. How could it all have gone so wrong?

October 4, 1919. Lexington Hotel, Chicago, Illinois. Shoeless Joe sat numbly in a chair in his hotel room, his un-eaten dinner on a tray beside him. That afternoon, his White Sox team had lost to the Cincinnati Reds, 2-0, putting them behind in the Series 3 games to 1. How had the White Sox lost? Joe was afraid he knew the answer. But what should he do about it?

A knock on the door interrupted his thoughts. When Joe opened it, there stood Lefty Williams, one of the Chicago pitchers. He had two envelopes in his hand. "Here."

"What is it, Lefty?"

"Money." Joe could smell that Lefty had been drinking. "Five thousand clams."

"I don't want your money."

"It's yours," slurred Lefty.

"No, it's not," Joe shot back.

"Sure it is. Here's mine." Lefty held up the other envelope.

"Keep all of it!"

"But, Joe, you earned it — "

"I did not! I played hard, you know that! Get out!" He tried to shut the door, but Lefty pushed past him into the room.

"I ain't leaving till you take this! You knew the fix was in."

"I did not! Chick came to me in Boston, asked me if I'd take ten grand to 'frame up something', an' I told him 'No!' Back in Chicago, he tried to get me to go in for $20,000, I told him 'no' again."

"And he told you he'd already told the gamblers you were in."

"Without my permission!"

"Permission or not, that's what the gamblers believed! That's what the rest of us believed. And if this ever comes out, that's what the Commissioner will believe."

"I tried to tell Comiskey about this before the series. Asked Kid to bench me! He said he wouldn't, so I played. Played knowin' I'd told Gandil 'no!' "

"Like I say, Joe, that ain't what Chick told the gamblers. Just take it." Lefty looked around. "You got anything to drink?"

"Don't do this, Lefty," Joe implored. "I'm havin' a great series. You've lost a game, sure, but you can win the next one. We can win this thing!"

"It won't work, Joe. The fix is in. Chick's been keepin' us informed. You gotta have something to drink around here." He moved towards a cabinet, searching.

Joe grabbed him by the lapels. "Forget about the damn booze for once, will ya'? Sure, Gandil's been talkin', but I ain't been listenin'. I don't wanna know. I just wanna play ball. I wanna win the World Series!"

"You think them gamblers care what you want? What do you think's gonna happen if we don't follow through on what Gandil said we'd agreed to? These men are rough. We both got wives, Joe. We gotta think about our families."

"If they want to have me knocked off, let them do it!"

"You stupid son of a bitch!"

"Don't call me 'stupid!' " Joe cocked his hand. Lefty flinched. But Joe suddenly stopped himself, and turned to leave the room.

"Where are you going?"

"I'm talkin' to Comiskey in the morning!" Joe answered over his shoulder.

"Don't do it, Joe!" Lefty called after him. But Joe was gone. "Dumb cracker!" He opened the drawers to the cabinet, but found nothing to drink. Lefty looked at the envelopes in his hand. "He'd better not," he said, threw Joe's money on the hotel room floor, and walked out.

When Joe returned that evening, the envelope was still on the floor. He put it in the cabinet. He'd known about the fix, that's why he'd tried to take himself out of the series. But Comiskey had refused. Gandil or Williams would report on meetings they'd had with the gamblers, but Joe had always turned away, trying not to listen. He'd refused the money twice. And he was playing as hard as he could. But had he done enough? If he could just get Comiskey to listen, then he'd know what to do. He was his boss. It was his team. He had to learn what was going on.

After a sleepless night, Joe knocked on Comiskey's office door the next morning. Comiskey always kept the office locked, so if you wanted to talk to him, you had to ask through a shutter on the door. That way, it was easier for Comiskey to avoid unpleasant topics, even if he were inside. Harry Grabiner raised the shutter. Harry was Comiskey's secretary. Everybody reported to Comiskey through Harry.

"Whattaya want, Joe?" he asked.

"Harry, I gotta see Mr. Comiskey right away."

"He's busy."

"But I've got something important he should know about!"

"What?"

"This" Joe thrust the envelope with the money into Harry's face.

"What is it?" asked Harry, without much curiosity.

"Money. I want Mr. Comiskey to have it."

"He doesn't want your money, Joe."

"He will when he knows where it came from. I got it from Lefty Williams. He gave it to me because —"

"Get out of here, Jackson. We know."

"You know?"

Harry slammed closed the shutter. "Harry!" Joe called, banging on the shutter. "Harry, let me in! Please, I gotta talk to Mr. Comiskey! He needs to tell me what to do! Harry!"

Silence. Joe looked at the shutter. Shut out. Just like in baseball, when a team scores no runs. Like last night, when Cincinnati had shut out Chicago. Eddie Cicotte had pitched. Poorly. And Joe knew why. But apparently Mr. Comiskey didn't want to know. Or he already knew, as Harry had suggested. He knew about the fix and he didn't care? How could that be? It was the World Series. His team was favored to win it. Joe looked at the envelope of money in his hand. No one would take it. No one would even listen to his story. What could he do? The only thing he knew how to do. Play baseball. And play it hard.

But it hadn't been enough. Joe had hit better than anybody on either team. He'd made no errors and had thrown out five runners. He'd batted in six runs, scored five himself, slugged a .563 percentage, and hit the only home run. All to no avail. Cincinnati had won the series, five games to three. And Shoeless Joe Jackson had returned to South Carolina a few days afterwards with the five thousand dollars in his pocket. He hadn't known what else to do.

Back in his basement in Greenville, Joe looked into the chest, then pulled out a small book. It had a page marked and he turned to it. He knew what it said, too: "Joe Jackson, while trying to throw the Series of 1919, made 12 hits and batted .375. His average led both teams and his twelve hits set a World Series record." Joe tossed the book back into the cedar chest. *Ripley's Believe It or Not.*

A rumble of anger stirred in Joe's gut, the anger he had tried to shut out all these years. He recognized the pain behind the rumble, and then he knew what had driven him to his basement chest. Jimmy was feeling that same pain, the pain that made you shout inside, *It ain't fair! It ain't right!*

CHAPTER 7

Jimmy lay in bed Tuesday morning trying to think of a reason to get up. He heard his mother in the kitchen, preparing his grits, getting ready for work. Work. Somethin' Jimmy didn't have to do that day. Just like he didn't have to get up that morning. He'd have a whole day to do whatever he wanted; yet all he wanted was to do what he'd always done. And there was no point looking for work in another mill, at least not yet. Mill owners stuck together. Howard Stone would make sure no other mill would hire him.

When he'd told Thelma about the firing after she'd come home from work yesterday, she'd been outraged. "That son of a bitch!" she'd shouted, stunning Jimmy, since his mother seldom swore. She'd immediately changed gears, given him a big hug, and told him he could find another job, that things would work out fine. Jimmy hadn't told her about asking Shoeless for a job and being turned down. But he had told her that Waddy had an "itch" he needed scratching. "What's that mean, Mama?"

Thelma hadn't answered right away. Her face darkened and she'd looked at Jimmy for a long moment. Then her entire countenance seemed to brighten. "It means maybe Waddy can help us out."

"How?"

"I don't know, maybe I can get some extra work or somethin'. But don't you worry, Jimmy, God will see us through this."

God. As far as Jimmy could see, God hadn't been particularly helpful so far. God had put him in a mill home and Howard Stone in a mansion. God had sent him a father who drank too much and then ran away. God had given him talent and then denied him the use of it. Jimmy didn't know who would see them through this, but he was pretty sure it wasn't God.

He finally struggled out of bed and went into the kitchen. "Oh, hey!" Thelma said, surprised. "You didn't have to get up."

"Couldn't sleep."

"I know, son, but try not to worry. I just know somethin' good'll come out of all this. If God takes somethin' away, he usually gives you somethin' else."

"I thought 'God helps them who help themselves.' "

"That, too. Well, you're in luck. For once your grits won't be cold." She slid the bowl across the table.

"I ain't hungry." He sat down and pushed the bowl of grits aside.

"Jimmy," Thelma said, sitting next to him. "I know you feel bad, an' I feel bad for you. It hurts to be fired. When your daddy — " Jimmy gave her a look and she stopped herself. "The point is, you're gonna feel bad for a while, so just let yourself be. There's no sin in feelin' bad. But it'll help if you still do the things that make you feel good. You cain't play on a team, fine. But that dudn' mean you cain't still practice your pitchin'. For the time when you get another job an' you can play on a team again. We ain't destined for the po' house tomorrow. I'm still workin'. We still got our friends an' neighbors, people who care about us."

Thelma placed her hands over Jimmy's. "Don't stay in here an' mope all day, all right? Get outside. Enjoy the sunshine. Heck, enjoy your freedom! You been workin' since you were fifteen years old, ain't no shame in takin' a little holiday." She kissed him on the cheek. "I gotta go. There's stuff for your lunch in the icebox. I'll see you about two, if you're still here. Which I hope you won't be." With a final ruffle of Jimmy's hair, Thelma left the kitchen.

Jimmy heard the screen door open and close. Then he heard nothing, nothing but the low hum of the mill in the already-muggy silence of a Carolina summer morning. He tried a spoonful of grits. They did taste better warm, but he had no energy for eating. He dragged himself up from his chair and trudged back into his bedroom. In the corner was the Shoeless shrine. Jimmy knelt on the floor and looked at the various headlines taped to the outfield wall. "GREENVILLE BOY MAKING GOOD" read one from *The Greenville News*. He read the first sentence. "Joe Jackson of Brandon Mill is tearing up the major league playing for the Cleveland Indians. There have been several players from the mill teams who've played in the big leagues, but none has piled up the numbers of Shoeless Joe. He is a proud representative of our neck of the woods."

He had always dreamed someone would write a headline like that about him some day. For a long moment he hung his head. Who was he? A nobody. Just another linthead stuck in a dead-end life. Making good? He no longer even had a team to play on! He reached up and tore the headline off the wall, crumpled it, and threw it across the room.

Inside Brandon Mill, Thelma spent her entire shift worrying about her son and about what she was thinking of doing. It was true when she'd said they weren't destined for the poor house tomorrow, but they might not survive too many tomorrows without some drastic changes in their lives. She'd never told Jimmy, but when his father had left, he'd taken what little savings they had with him. She'd saved as much as she could since then, but the wages of a mill worker didn't allow for much. She couldn't see any other way out. The way the owners stuck together, it would be almost impossible for Jimmy to get a job in another mill. Maybe sometime in the future, when baseball season was over and things had settled down, some other mill might hire him. And maybe, if Woodside won the pennant, Mr. Stone might even give him his job back. Maybe, but not likely. The truth was, it would be hard getting by on just one salary. Jimmy might find a job somewhere else in Greenville, but then he'd be away, out of her sight, and who knows what trouble he might get into. No, she'd rather have him home in the mill village.

But at what cost? Her honor? She laughed. Whatever that was, she'd lost it a long time ago, when she'd first slept with Jimmy's father before they were married. A "bad" act, some would say, but look what had come from it. Jimmy. A good result, a wonderful result. If that act had produced Jimmy, who knew what this one might produce? Oh, not another child, Thelma would take care of that. But somethin' good, surely somethin' good would come of it. Watching the shuttle pass back and forth on the loom, Thelma worked hard to convince herself that what she was about to do was all right. Sometimes life in the mills made you choose between two bad things, and Thelma had decided this was one of those times. She tried to pray, but the mill was too noisy and she was too distracted. God would just have to look in her heart to know why she was doing it.

She saved her ten-minute break until just before the end of her shift. She knocked on Waddy's office door at 1:50 p.m. "Come in," Waddy called. Thelma opened the door and stepped inside. Waddy looked up, surprised. "Well, hey, there, Sugar, what's on your mind?"

Thelma closed the door. She turned to face Waddy. He smiled at her eagerly. Thelma took a deep breath and said, "Scratchin' your itch."

Waddy's smile broadened into a huge grin. "Well, all right! Take a seat, darling,' an' let's discuss the best medicine, whattaya say?"

On the other side of the mill village, the Woodside baseball field baked in the afternoon sun. It was empty, except for one very drunk young man.

After his mother had left that morning, Jimmy had tried to fall back to sleep, but he was too restless. If he went out, what if he met somebody from the mill village? Would the word have somehow gotten out? How would he explain it? He even worried what Rhoda would think. Rhoda, he barely knew her, why was he thinking about her? Finally, he'd dragged himself out of bed, eaten as much of the cold grits as he could stomach, taken his mother's advice, and set out for the barn with his croker sack of balls. But his pitching stank. His fastball had no pop, and his curve wouldn't bite. And he couldn't concentrate. What was the point? Why get better? Where would he play ball anyway?

He wasn't sure what compelled him to put the balls back in the croker sack, grab a bat he kept in the barn, and walk to the nearest liquor store. Maybe some inherited gene from his father to seek comfort in alcohol. Maybe a desire to try what many of his friends had already tried. It hadn't been too hard to find a kind stranger and ask him to buy some whiskey for him. He always kept a few dollars in the bottom of the croker sack for emergencies. This certainly qualified. So, croker sack and bat in hand and a half-pint of bourbon in his back pocket, Jimmy had slowly walked to the nearby Woodside diamond.

The first few swallows had been hard. After all, he wasn't used to it. Then, with the booze warming his stomach, it had become easier. He didn't feel like pitching; he needed to hit something. To let out his anger and frustration, to exhaust himself, maybe even to get baseball out of his system for good. So he stood at home plate and hit all the balls in his sack as far as he could. Then he walked to the outfield, gathered them all together, and hit them back towards home plate. He repeated this routine a couple of times, swigging bourbon in between swings, until he was too drunk to hit the ball hard — or even to hit it at all. So he sat down on home plate, stuck the bottle of bourbon between his legs, and stared.

The symmetry of the baseball diamond always brought him a kind of peace. The foul lines receding perfectly away to the outfield. The fence curving around, enclosing this sacred place, protecting it from reality. The bases standing guard at the corners and up the middle, each a perfect ninety feet apart. The pitcher's mound, rising in the exact center of the infield. Standing on the mound, Jimmy often imagined himself atop some impregnable fortress, hurling stones down at his victims. And home plate, with its unique design, a square with a triangle on top. Home. The ultimate objective of every effort. Each player striving to get home. Safe! Would he ever be safe at home again?

The thought disturbed Jimmy so much that he struggled to his feet and began to jog towards first base. Halfway down the line, he increased his speed to a trot, then, after rounding the bag, he broke into a full-out run. He raced past second base and kicked his legs into a higher gear, reaching third and then heading for home. His eyes were wide with effort, his arms pumped mercilessly. Home, he was almost there!

And then he was there, stomping on the plate with his right foot as he sped past. But instead of stopping, Jimmy swung towards first base. He lowered his head for more speed. His white cotton shirt was now soaked and sticking to his body. Second base, third base, then home again. And again not stopping, but continuing on, running, churning, striving for home. Around the bases Jimmy ran. His head was pounding now, his legs ached, the sweat poured into his eyes until he could hardly see. Three, four, five times he ran around the infield, his stride finally slowing, his steps staggering this way and that, his arms hanging at his side, too tired to raise. There it was, home! Ten feet away, he stumbled, sank to his knees, reached out his arms, and fell across the plate.

He lay there, breathing heavily, dirt on his face, in his mouth, the smell of sweat and earth in his nostrils. His heart pounded, echoing in his ears. He felt the warm sun on his neck. Slowly his breathing eased, his fists unclenched. He took a final, deep breath. And slept.

A few hours later, Jimmy walked through the front door to find his mother in the kitchen, making supper. She turned and looked at him with shock. "What in the world happened to you?"

The sleep had lessened the effects of the bourbon, but Jimmy was still groggy. "I've been playin' baseball," he said softly.

"Who with?"

"Myself."

"Huh?"

"Just myself, that's all. I went out to Woodside Park an' I just...." Jimmy let the thought die. How could he explain the strange compulsion that had come over him? What had made him do it? Anger? Despair? A sense of doom? Whatever it was, it had worked. Jimmy felt better. Deadly tired, but somehow with the strength to go on. "Just by myself," he finished, and started towards his bedroom.

"Well, you look like you been wrestlin' a pig," Thelma shouted after him. "Drag the tub into your bedroom an' take a bath while I finish makin' supper. Then I got somethin' to tell you."

Jimmy did as his mother suggested and when he sat down at the table half an hour later, he felt restored. "Ham?" he asked, surprised, when he saw what was on his plate.

"Bought some this afternoon. An' collards an' cornbread. An' puddin' for dessert. We're celebratin'."

"Celebratin' what?"

"My new job."

"What?"

"You're lookin' at the new floor manager of the Woodside Mill weavin' room, complete with longer breaks an' a higher salary! How 'bout them apples?" Thelma did a little dance and finished with a small bow.

"I don't understand, Mama."

"I told you Waddy was considerin' me for the position, since Rosa Lee done left to go back to the mountains. Well, he considered some more an' came to the right conclusion!" Thelma sat down and continued excitedly. "An' that's not all. I got to change shifts to the afternoon. Now I won't have to get up so gol-danged early an' you an' me can have us a leisurely breakfast an' I can tend the garden better an' who knows what all. I told you somethin' good would come from all this."

"I don't know what to say."

"You can start with 'congratulations!'

"Of course, mama, that's great. I'm so happy for you." Jimmy smiled for the first time since he'd gone into work the day before.

"Happy for *us*! Now you can take your time lookin' for work, see what happens, maybe get you back to work at Woodside, or maybe find you a place in another mill. Eat your ham. It's salted!"

Jimmy cut into the thick slice of ham, put the piece in his mouth, and chewed eagerly. Thelma watched him contentedly, happy to see her son enjoying himself. She'd have to pay for that enjoyment, but, for now, it was worth it.

Later, Thelma was straightening up Jimmy's room as he lay in bed before sleep. "Mama," he said. "You know what I did today? I got drunk."

Thelma looked at him, concerned. "Drunk?"

"Don't worry, I didn't like it."

"Thank the Lord!"

"Is that why Daddy drank? Because he felt bad?"

Thelma sat on the edge of the bed. "I don't think it started out that way, Jimmy. Your daddy was like most teenagers, just tryin' out things, pretendin' to be like older folks, gettin' as much thrill out of defyin' the rules as out of what they was defyin' 'em for. An' he got to like the liquor, I reckon."

"I don't see how. It tastes awful." Jimmy wiped his hand across his mouth, remembering the bitter sting. "At least, at first."

Thelma let out a small laugh. "You get used to it, that's for sure. I was lucky, I reckon. Earle didn't get mean when he was drunk, he got happy. Got too happy, was what it was. Got to wantin' to party all the time, which is all right, maybe, when it was just him an' me. But when you came along, an' I started gettin' on him 'bout helpin' out more around the house so's I could sleep some, the responsibility just got too much for him, I reckon. He tried. Tried real hard for a time, while you were growin' up. But, then, I don't know, I probly started lookin' older, an' other women started lookin' younger, an' bein' happy started feelin' less like tuckin' your son in at night an' more like...." Thelma paused. "Well, anyway. After lettin' him run aroun' for a while, hopin' he'd change, I found I was gettin' more an' more unhappy, an' I didn't want to turn to drink, so I just ... kicked him out." She looked at her son. "I'm sorry, Jimmy."

"Mama, you did the right thing."

"But for you not to have had a daddy all these years...." She felt the familiar surge of sadness.

"It's fine, Mama. I've had you."

Thelma felt she might cry. Instead, she leaned down and hugged her son. She was grateful beyond measure to have him in her life. She loved him so much, she'd do anything for him. *Anything.*

Later that night, after Jimmy had fallen asleep, Thelma came into his bedroom to look at him. It had been a long, hard day. Waddy had promised he'd "treat her nice," but, still, she felt agitated about the whole thing, uneasy, maybe even fearful. She'd distracted herself by shopping at the Kash 'N' Karry, with its famous motto — "Prices Are Born Here, Raised Elsewhere" — then cooking, then enjoying being home with Jimmy. But now, it was time.

Thelma sneaked out of the house, walked down Third Street, turned, and continued away from the mill rumbling on the hill. After a few blocks, she saw the car up ahead in the shadows, idling, saw the outline of the man waiting for her. Could she go through with it? *Should* she go through with it? She thought of her son, sleeping peacefully at home. Their home, a home that would now be secure. She raised her head, threw back her shoulders, and set off to do anything for her son.

CHAPTER 8

The next week was the longest of Jimmy's life. He may have hated working in the mill, but at least it gave him something to do. Those eight hours of work — day after day, week after week, month after month — gave a structure to his life he had never really appreciated until he didn't have it any more. He would get up to have breakfast with his mother, and then the day stretched out before him like a distant horizon he had no chance of reaching. The mornings weren't too bad, because his mother was home before her afternoon shift began. He enjoyed having breakfast with her, and she was sensitive enough to avoid painful topics like baseball or getting a job. She didn't seem all that anxious about his getting work, which puzzled Jimmy a little. Her newfound fondness for occasional late-evening walks puzzled him some, too. She never asked him to come with her, although they had gotten into the habit of walking around the village in the mornings together. Jimmy would help with the wash. He finally repaired the fence that had fallen apart over the years. He weeded the garden. He did what he could to help out. But when the whistle blew, calling his mother to the mill, Jimmy's heart always jumped a little. And he came to want something that he never thought he'd want: he wanted the whistle to call him, too.

On Sunday, his mother said, "I'm sorry I didn't make you go to church today, Jimmy. Rhoda sang a solo. Beautiful! Made me feel like, I don't know, like a sunset: glorious. I think that's what they mean by that word, glorious!" She sighed at the memory. "Rhoda asked about you."

"She did?" His words came out louder than he'd expected, and his voice contained the tiniest touch of excitement.

"Yes. She's concerned about you, wanted to know how you're feelin'. Everybody's concerned, Jimmy. People here love you."

"What'd you say to Rhoda 'bout how I'm feelin'?"

"Sad."

"Ah, mama, why'd you tell her that?"

"It's the truth, isn't it?"

"I just don't want Rhoda feelin' sorry for me."

"What should I tell her — I mean, if she ever asks again?"

"Tell her — " Jimmy hesitated. What should she tell her? It was just Rhoda. She lived in another mill village. Only time he'd see her was at church, unless he made a special effort. And he wasn't going to make any special effort. "Tell her whatever you want," he finally said, ending the conversation by taking his dishes to the sink.

The next day, Jimmy decided to practice his pitching after his mother left for work. What else could he do? Most of his friends were on the baseball team, and he didn't feel like hanging around them. He planned to go looking for work in another mill, but it was too early for that, things had to settle down a little. The owners would still be abiding by the unwritten code that you didn't hire someone who'd been fired from another mill. He could always look for a job in Greenville, but doing what? Digging ditches? He had no skills that weren't related to working in the mills. His only real talent was baseball, as far as he was concerned. But he couldn't take another day of sitting on the front porch staring at the mill, so he grabbed his sack of balls and walked to the shed.

He hadn't enjoyed his night's rest. Well, he had, and he hadn't. He'd kept thinking about Rhoda. She'd asked about him. Was she interested in him? What kind of interested, just friendly, or more? More what? He'd tried to think of something else, and would succeed for a moment, but then suddenly an image of Rhoda would pop into his head. Like her lips when she was imitating that bird call. How they pursed, so round, and full. *Why am I thinkin' about her lips?* And her laugh, when she'd made up that silly game. Stan The Man's head! And Caesar's mouth. Jimmy had laughed a small laugh, there in his bed in the middle of the night, thinking about Rhoda sitting inside someone's mouth! *Why am I thinkin' these crazy things?* He was glad when the mill whistle had awakened him from his restlessness. And now he could concentrate on pitching and forget about Rhoda.

Only he couldn't concentrate on pitching for long. After he'd thrown for about half-an-hour, he fired one more fastball and was startled by a voice he never thought he'd hear in his secret barn. "I'd a-hit that one out of the park," said the voice, and Jimmy turned to find Shoeless Joe Jackson standing there, a pair of binoculars draped around his neck, a baseball bat in his hand. For a moment, Jimmy just stared, trying to comprehend. "Ain't you gon' say nothin'?" Shoeless asked.

"Hello, Mr. Jackson," Jimmy finally managed. "What are you doin' here?"

"I came to see you."

"Me?"

"You see anybody else aroun' here?" Joe asked bluntly.

"But why?" Jimmy took off his glove and mopped his brow with the back of his hand.

"Didn't you ask if I would teach you ball?" Jimmy nodded, uncertainly. "Well, here I am."

"Gosh, Mr. Jackson!" Jimmy spluttered. "How'd you know I was here?"

"I followed you." He stared at Jimmy, hands on his hips. "Well?"

"Well, what?"

"You want me to teach you or not?"

"Yes, sir!" He put his glove back on his hand and reached for a ball.

"I ain't talkin' 'bout pitchin'."

"Huh?"

"I'm here to teach you hittin'."

"But I'm a pitcher," Jimmy protested.

"You got hitter's instincts."

"What's 'hitter's instincts'?"

"You notice things. Like that game when the cows started driftin' onto the field, you noticed that. An' you took advantage. That's what hitters do: take advantage."

"You were watchin'?" Jimmy's eyes widened in amazement.

"These are powerful binoculars," Shoeless said dismissively. He took them off and put them on a ledge.

"But why?"

"Felt like it!" Shoeless responded testily. "Now, you gonna jaw all day or you gonna learn some things?"

"You really think I'm a hitter?"

Shoeless held out the bat. "Wanna find out?"

Jimmy looked at him, the greatest natural hitter of all time, offering to teach him how to hit. He liked hitting, he just thought his chances of making it to the big leagues were better as a pitcher. But that was before Shoeless Joe Jackson held out a bat to him. He grabbed it.

"Now pick up them balls, we're goin' over to Brandon Park."

Fifteen minutes later Jimmy found himself standing at home plate in scruffy Brandon Park. "Let me see how you bunt," Shoeless said.

"Buntin'?"

"Gotta start with the basics. Show me." Jimmy squared around to bunt. Shoeless looked at him for a minute. "Don't hold the bat so tight with your right hand. An' you better move them fingers back or you might break one." Jimmy adjusted his hands. Shoeless looked carefully. "Good," he said, and retreated to the mound with the croker sack full of balls.

Shoeless pitched and Jimmy bunted. He bunted down the third base line. He dragged the ball down the first base line. Then he did it all again. Once in a while Shoeless would come down from the mound and show Jimmy how to adjust the bat angle, depending on whether the pitch was a fastball or a curve. After a half hour or so, Jimmy blurted out, "Mr. Jackson, you said you'd teach me how to hit. Buntin' ain't hittin'."

"Ever heard of Ty Cobb?"

"Of course. He was a great hitter. You played against him, didn't you?"

"Yep. And Ty was also a great bunter. You never know when buntin's gonna be the perfect hit. But you'll know it if you know the situation."

"The situation?"

"Them instincts of yours I was talkin' 'bout. Say there's a runner on third base, one out, tight ball game. It's a squeeze play situation. But everybody knows you might be buntin', so how're you gonna keep the third baseman back near the bag? Play third," Joe said. Jimmy trotted out to third base, Shoeless stood at home plate. "Okay, okay, I square around to bunt, you're gonna come runnin' in with the pitch. Come on, run in to field a bunt." Jimmy started towards home plate. "But what if I — " Shoeless tosses up a ball and smacks a liner right at Jimmy, who has to dive to the ground to avoid being beaned.

"Hey! You said you were gonna bunt!"

"I said the situation called for a bunt. An' I might bunt next pitch. But I needed to keep you back, an' my guess is you're gonna charge a bunt a mite more carefully next time, which might give me the step or two I need to beat it out. Know the situation." Shoeless spat in the grass, between his teeth. He hadn't done that in a long time. There was something about baseball and spitting, they just went together. "Nine o'clock in the mornin', I got a liquor store to run." He moved off towards home.

"But we didn't hit!"

Shoeless turned. "What's the situation?"

"Huh?"

"The situation is, I'm the teacher, you're the student, an' it's hot as hell." He spat again, adjusted his Panama hat, and marched off through the outfield towards home.

True to his word, the next morning Shoeless Joe began teaching Jimmy what he knew about hitting. They both batted left-handed, so that helped. But Shoeless found it quite difficult to communicate his knowledge. He'd never really thought about it much, he just swung the bat. Hitting came as naturally to him as breathing. But not for Jimmy. He'd focused most of his efforts on pitching. That had been his dream. And now Joe was trying to change that dream. Not too much: the goal was still to make it to the majors. But the path would be different.

Shoeless threw and Jimmy swung. "You're still steppin' in the bucket," he called out to Jimmy from the pitcher's mound. "Lemme see you stride." Jimmy got set at the plate and stepped toward Joe. "That's good, that's steppin' towards me, not towards first base. Now do it when I pitch it." Shoeless wound up and threw towards the plate. Jimmy strode towards the pitch with his right leg, swung, and dribbled the ball foul of third base. "Bucket!" Shoeless shouted. Jimmy slammed the end of the bat into the ground. "Batter up!" Shoeless called, and Jimmy got set to try to hit the next pitch. This time he swung and missed.

Jimmy screamed at the sky. "Arrrrrrrrrgghhh! I wanna pitch!"

"Why?"

"Pitchers control the game. Everything starts with the pitch."

"An' ends with the bat. Hitters got the last word." Shoeless threw, and Jimmy swung and missed again. "No, the ump does: 'you're out!' " Shoeless smiled. He was enjoying himself. But he could tell that Jimmy wasn't. "Wanna quit?"

"Throw me another curve ball."

"I got a better idea. You're havin' trouble hittin' the curve ball. I gotta teach you 'bout seein' things true."

"What's that mean?"

"Let's meet at my house tomorrow an' I'll show you. You know where I live?"

"Yes, sir."

"You do!?"

"I been watchin' you sometimes, too." He looked at Shoeless, who considered him a moment, spat, and turned toward home. Jimmy allowed himself a small smile, grabbed the sack, and began picking up the baseballs scattered over the field.

At nine the next morning, Jimmy knocked on the white frame door of the small brick cottage tucked neatly behind a white picket fence at 113 E. Wilburn Street. Joe let him in and Jimmy followed him into the front parlor. A large stuffed chair stuck out into the room, a standing ashtray beside it, and a table with a radio on top in one corner. A small, brick fireplace, with a gas heater inside it, dominated one wall. A television set was in the corner. Jimmy had never seen one before. He was surprised at how tiny the room was. The living room of his mill home was not much bigger. If Shoeless had made a lot of money, his house certainly didn't reflect it. Jimmy noticed a small card table in the middle of the room, with two metal chairs behind it. On the table was a six-inch candle in a holder. "Have a seat," Shoeless said.

Jimmy sat down in one chair and Shoeless sat in the other. "Jimmy, I don't know how much I can teach you about your swing. We're kinda born with the swing we got. I can help you make improvements here an' there, but I've decided the best thing I can teach you is what I call 'seein' things true'." He shoved the candle towards Jimmy. "I trained my eyes so that I could see the spin on the ball better'n anybody else. I knew if the pitcher threw me a curve, or a fastball, or even a spitter. I trained 'em with a candle."

"How?"

"By coverin' one eye at a time an' starin' at it." Shoeless lit the candle, then got up and pulled down the shades on the windows. The room darkened. "Start starin'," Joe instructed and moved towards the door to the kitchen.

"How long, Mr. Jackson?"

"Fifteen minutes one eye, then move to the other, then repeat."

"Repeat how many — ?" Jimmy started to ask, but Shoeless had already disappeared. Jimmy looked at the candle, sighed, and covered his left eye. He stared. The candle slowly flickered. The small, yellow flame moved slowly back and forth.

At first, Jimmy was afraid he would fall asleep, but his head filled with thoughts. He wondered what his mother was doing at home, all alone. She had seemed different this past week, but Jimmy wasn't sure how. He just sensed a small increase in the energy of her words, of her movements, as if she was afraid of slowing down too much. Most nights she would talk to him or to the neighbors from the front porch, as usual. She was tired after working all day and would go to bed around nine. But a couple of nights, she'd made herself a cup of coffee and gone out for a walk.

"Fifteen minutes!" Shoeless shouted through the door. Jimmy took his hand down and blinked. The candle had burned down only an inch. He sighed. This was definitely not what he had in mind when Shoeless Joe Jackson had said he was going to teach him all he knew about hitting a baseball. Staring at a candle with one eye closed in a hot, stuffy room? Jimmy switched hands and covered his right eye with his right hand. His mind filled with flickering thoughts, like the candle.

Candle.... Mama.... Candle.... Flame.... Flicker.... Shoeless.... Bunt.... Stupid... Situation... Bunt... Shoeless Joe... Candle... Tired... Focus..!. Stare...! Rhoda... Rhoda...? Wonder what she's doin'....

Focus.... Hand's tired. Wanna shake it.... Stupid...! Trust him.... Trust him.... He knows baseball.... Stare...! Stare...! Mouth's dry.... Water.... How much time's passed...? Tired.... Head's heavy.... Focus.... Just a little rest.... I'll open my eye in a minute.... In a second....

A shade snapped open with a loud whack. Jimmy's head popped up from the table, where it had rested ever since he'd fallen asleep. Shoeless raised the other shades until sunlight flooded the room. "Sorry," Jimmy muttered. Shoeless didn't say anything, he just blew out the candle. "Did you really used to do this?"

"Every day. But it helps if you stay awake."

"Can I try again, Mr. Jackson? Please?"

Shoeless looked at Jimmy. He remembered wanting to get good, then wanting to get better. Silently, he took another candle out of the drawer, placed it in the holder, lit it, pulled all the shades down, and left the room. Jimmy slapped his face with his hands a couple of times to make sure he was wide awake, then covered one eye and began to stare.

That was the routine for the next few days. They'd start out with batting practice. Shoeless worked on making sure Jimmy stepped towards the pitcher when he swung. "Try to take my head off," he'd say. Then he'd throw Jimmy a curve, Jimmy would miss, then he'd really want to hit the ball straight at Shoe's head. "Don't try so hard. Take the emotion out of the situation."

"Whattaya mean?"

"Don't get mad at yourself. If you gotta be mad at somethin', be mad at the baseball. You're gonna make outs. You're gonna make mistakes. The best hitters only hit safe about a third of the time. Don't worry about why you make an out, worry about *how*. What'd you do wrong? An' sometimes you didn't do nothin' wrong, the pitcher was just better'n you on that pitch. An' when you hit it, think about what you did right. Remember: baseball is a game of inches, and the most important six inches in the game are right here." He tapped Jimmy on the head. "Between your ears." Shoeless looked at Jimmy's determined face, his focused eyes, the set line of his lips as he followed Shoeless's every word. *He's tryin' so hard! Just like me.* He had a sudden urge to reach out and tousle Jimmy's hair. Instead, he retreated back towards the mound. "Let's try it again."

After an hour or so of hitting, and talking about the situation — "You're in left field, ahead 6-1, bottom of the fifth, runners on first an' second, lined ball to you, where do you throw?" "Home." "Second base. Forget the run, you're way ahead. Stop the big inning." — they would walk over to the house for an hour of "candle-watchin'," Jimmy began to call it. Then they'd sit around the kitchen table and drink the lemonade Katie had left for them.

At first, Shoeless didn't talk much. But after the first week or so, he began to reminisce. He told Jimmy about the race for the batting title he'd had with Ty Cobb in 1911, how Cobb had feigned an injury so he wouldn't have to play the final games, that way he wouldn't risk lowering his league-leading average. "Wormy," Shoeless called him. "An' meaner'n a cornered rattlesnake." He told how, when he played in the textile league, he used to throw the ball from deep center field all the way over the backstop behind home plate.

"Wow! How far is that?"

"They tole me it was over four hundred feet. Fans used to clamor for it. Called it a 'showout.' Didn' bother me none, I was happy to please 'em." These moments with both of them sitting around the table, shirts clammy from dried sweat, were Jimmy's favorite. Shoeless had begun to look forward to them, too.

One morning Shoeless didn't have time for the candle-watching, he had an appointment, so Jimmy wandered over to the Brandon company store after batting practice to get himself something to drink. He yanked a Coca-Cola out of the icebox, set it on the counter, and pulled out his coupon book. "Sorry, son," said the clerk. "Woodside coupons don't work in a Brandon store. You got any money?"

"No, sir."

"Then I'm afraid I cain't help you."

"I can," said a voice behind Jimmy. He turned and saw Rhoda, holding a coupon book. "I got Brandon coupons."

"That's all right," Jimmy said.

"Don't tell me you're gonna be one of them stubborn types. I could use a Coke myself." She tore a couple of coupons from her book and plunked them on the counter.

"Thank you."

She went over to the icebox, took out a Coke, and popped the cap off in the bottle opener. "Cheers," she said, raising her Coke. "Ain't that what they say?"

"I reckon." He popped his own cap, tapped Rhoda's bottle with his own, and they both took long drinks.

"Oo-ee, it's thick in here. Let's get some air." She walked past Jimmy and out onto the sidewalk, Jimmy following. "Better."

For a minute, they stood there, silently swigging their Coca-Colas. A few automobiles lumbered by. Even the cars seemed to move more slowly in the oppressive heat. A dog lay in the dirt in front of the store. A man in overalls exited the store, snapped his fingers, the dog raised himself lazily up, and they moved off towards the mill village. "We could use a belly washer, that's for sure," Rhoda said.

Not sure what she meant, Jimmy offered feebly. "We got a tub at our house."

Rhoda laughed. "I'm not talkin' 'bout us! I mean a lotta rain, enough to reach your belly."

"That's stupid. Who'd want that much rain? An' why'd you use it to wash your belly?"

Rhoda whooped. "Oh, law'! Cleanin' your belly with rain!" she gasped, which caused another outburst of laughter. Jimmy just stood there, embarrassed. He wasn't used to being laughed at, especially by a girl. "I'm sorry," Rhoda finally said. "I didn't mean to laugh at you." She smiled at Jimmy. Her white teeth shone, her brown eyes warmed.

Jimmy couldn't help but smile back. "That's all right."

"Walk me home?"

"Sure."

They finished their Cokes, returned the bottles inside the store, and set off towards the mill village. After a moment, Rhoda asked, "How come you never come to church?"

"Don't like it."

"How come?"

She paused. He didn't like talking about God, but something about Rhoda made him want her to know how he felt. "I don't understand a God who puts the mill owner in a mansion on a hill an' the rest of us down here."

"Maybe up there's hell, down here's heaven."

"Then God ain't never worked in a textile mill."

"I kinda' like it."

"Workin' in the mill?"

"Uh-huh. I work in the cloth room, an' when I hold up the towel, I don't know, it makes me kinda proud."

"It's just a towel, Rhoda."

"But I helped make it."

They walked in silence for a bit. At a cross street, Jimmy asked, "Which way?"

"Left. We go down Sixth Street, turn left on Third Avenue, I live in the middle of the block."

"That's what I hate about mill villages, they name all the streets with numbers. Why cain't they give 'em real names?" Jimmy said with some heat. "I wanna live on a street with a real name."

"Then change it."

"Huh?"

"Change the name. Call it somethin' else."

"Then how will folks know where I live if I tell 'em my address? That's stupid."

"You think a lot of things are stupid, don't you? Well, I might be from the mountains, but I ain't dumb." She stopped at the next corner and looked up at the street sign. Third Avenue. "Okay, here's my street ... Bird Avenue!" she said defiantly. "Thanks for the walk," she added, and moved off down the street.

Jimmy called after her. "Hey, Rhoda!" She stopped and turned towards him. "Thanks for the Coke. I'll pay you back."

"Durn straight!" she said, and turned towards her house. Jimmy watched her go. He looked up at the street sign. "Bird Avenue," he muttered, then smiled, despite himself.

"We need to build you some muscle," Shoeless announced, the next time they met at Brandon Park. "Do this." He held the bat by the handle, fat end towards the ground, arm out straight. Then he handed the bat to Jimmy, who did the same.

"Now what?"

"Just hold it."

"How long?"

"You're a durn one for time, ain't you?"

"Reckon it's livin' all my life by the mill whistle."

"Might be," Shoeless conceded. "Just do it till your arm's tired, then switch arms."

"You do this?"

"*Did*," Shoeless said, and smiled. He took out his tobacco pouch and stuffed a chew into his cheek. Then he retired to the shade of the dugout, leaving Jimmy standing at home plate, arm outstretched.

Jimmy was surprised how short a time he could hold the bat out straight until his arm felt weak. He switched arms, but his right arm was naturally weaker than his left, so he was able to hold the bat an even shorter length of time. When he lowered the bat to rest, Shoeless hollered out, "Other arm!" Jimmy switched back to his left arm, raised the bat, and held it out.

He tried to think of things to distract himself. Rhoda. Was she mad at him? He hadn't meant to call her stupid. He actually thought she was kinda smart, despite those dumb expressions. *There I go again. Okay, maybe they aren't dumb. Maybe they're just ... different.* Different. That certainly summed up Rhoda. Jimmy hadn't thought much about girls. Of course, he'd thought about them, the way most teenage boys think about them, but they hadn't really interested him. Nothing much had interested him except baseball. But Rhoda interested him. He wanted to know more about her. What she liked, what she didn't like. Maybe even whether she liked him.

"Ten minutes, that's good, better switch," Shoeless called from the dugout. Jimmy blinked. He had forgotten he was holding the bat. He switched arms.

After a half-hour of bat-holding, Shoeless emerged from the dugout. "Let's hit." On his way to the pitcher's mound, he stopped. He kicked something in the dirt with the toe of his shoe, then stooped to pick it up. "What's that?" Jimmy asked.

"Bobby pin," Shoeless answered.

"What do you want with a bobby pin?"

"Always used to pick 'em up for luck." Shoeless looked at the bobby pin for a moment, then pocketed it.

"That's just a superstition."

"Reckon it is," Shoeless replied and headed for the pitcher's mound. "Ain't you got no superstitions?"

"No, superstitions are stupid!" Jimmy tried to stop himself, but it was too late.

Shoeless stopped and looked hard at Jimmy. "Don't you never call me 'stupid!' " he said fiercely. He spat some tobacco juice, turned, and strode purposefully towards the outfield and home.

"Mr. Jackson, I'm sorry!" Jimmy yelled, but Shoeless kept walking. Jimmy ran after him. "Mr. Jackson! Mr. Jackson!" He caught up with Shoeless. "Mr. Jackson, please, I'm sorry, I'm sorry. I don't think you're stupid." Jimmy had to run alongside Shoeless, who never broke stride. "You're one of the smartest men I know, 'specially when it comes to baseball. Please forgive me!" Shoeless stopped and looked at Jimmy. "Please!" he begged. "I'm so grateful for all you've done for me. You've taught me so much. Just takin' the time to teach me, you don't know how much that means to me. I ain't never had nobody take time for me, besides Mama. I don't know how I'll ever repay you, but I'm gonna try. Please, don't go, Mr. Jackson!"

Shoeless saw the desperation in Jimmy's eyes. "Here's how you can repay me, kid."

"How?"

"See things true. That applies to baseballs an' to people."

"Yes, sir. I will."

They returned to their positions, Shoeless on the mound, Jimmy at the plate. He swung and dribbled a pitch to the left of third, then another, then another barely inside the line. His arms were tired, but he wasn't about to say so. He wiped the sweat from his eyes. If he could just see the ball better, it wouldn't matter how tired his arms were. Shoeless threw the next pitch, Jimmy swung the bat, and he missed. Shoeless came down from the mound to Jimmy at home plate.

"Let's try somethin'," he said. He took the bat from Jimmy's hands. "I don't want you to try to imitate me, you got your own swing. But there's somethin' we might try. I used to hold the bat different from most folks. Never saw no one hold it this way." He placed his hands on the bat, right hand just above the handle. "Used to move my little finger 'roun' the handle like this." Joe curled his finger around the knob of the handle. "Somehow it felt comfortable for me. Maybe it will for you." He handed the bat to Jimmy.

Jimmy grabbed the bat and placed his hands around it, little finger on the knob. "It feels — " He stopped himself. "A little funny, but let me try it."

Shoeless went back to the mound and Jimmy took his place in the batter's box. He tried a couple of practice swings. At first, his finger slipped off the knob, so he held it tighter. Shoeless threw him a fastball. Jimmy swung. He made contact. The ball shot back towards the mound, straight at Shoeless's head. Joe ducked, as the ball whistled past. When he straightened up and looked towards home plate, he saw Jimmy grinning. He got set to throw another pitch, a curve this time. Jimmy wobbled the bat behind his head, narrowing his eyes. Shoeless cocked his arm, strode forwards, and snapped his wrist, imparting a hard spin to the ball.

Standing at home plate, Jimmy saw Shoeless release the ball. He saw it spin off Joe's hand and head towards the plate. What was it, fastball? Curve? And then he knew! He saw the pitch! Curve! Jimmy swung at the pitch confidently. The ball cracked off the bat and launched towards deepest center field. Shoeless turned and watched it soar overhead. Jimmy finished his swing and watched it, too. The ball flew over the fence.

"I saw it! I saw it!" Jimmy yelled from home plate. "It was a curve, Mr. Jackson! I saw it spinnin'! I saw it! I saw it true!" He jumped up and down.

Shoeless Joe Jackson stood on the mound, Jimmy's excited shouts ringing in his ears. He looked far away to where the baseball finally came to a rest. And smiled.

CHAPTER 9

Woodside, Piedmont, Mills Mill, Monaghan, Conestee, Poe, Judson, Brandon, Camperdown, Pelzer, Liberty, Poinsett, Pelzer. Over the next week or so, Jimmy spent his afternoons looking for work in a textile mill. He even rode the bus to Victor Mill, twelve miles away in Greer, and Easley Mill in nearby Easley. He swallowed his pride and applied for jobs in mills that didn't even field a baseball team. But the result was always the same: "No spots"; "Don't need ya' "; "Full up." Sometimes he didn't even get in to see the superintendent, just got word back from a messenger that there were no openings. When he did see a super, he could tell by the way he looked at him that the super had gotten the word from Woodside: don't hire him.

The constant rejection was beginning to weigh heavily on Jimmy. Although he loved working with Shoeless most mornings, and although he was diligent about strengthening his arm muscles and training his eyes with the candle, Jimmy was beginning to get discouraged. He didn't see any point, if he couldn't find a team to play on. He thought about asking Shoeless to help out, but he'd already asked him for a job and been refused, so he decided just to be grateful Shoeless was taking an interest in his baseball talent and leave it at that.

Even a neglectful mother would have noticed the change in her son's behavior, and Thelma was far from neglectful. When Jimmy returned from his trip to Easley and barely said hello before retreating to his bedroom, Thelma called him into the kitchen for a glass of sweet tea. "No luck, huh?" she began when they were seated at the table.

"No, ma'am."

She smiled. At least he hadn't forgotten his manners. "Well, how are things goin' with Mr. Jackson?"

"Fine."

Thelma paused. Talkin' baseball wasn't goin' to help this time. But there weren't too many other subjects that stirred her son's interest. She thought about just letting it go, just making dinner, not talking much. But she knew what would be going through her son's mind. Awful thoughts, self-loathing thoughts, thoughts about how worthless he was. So she tried another tack. "Ever run into Rhoda when you're over to Brandon?"

"Once."

"How's she doin'?"

"Fine."

"What'd she have to say?"

"Nothin'. She loaned me some coupons so I could buy a Coke."
Jimmy began drumming his fingers on the table distractedly.

"She's a nice girl, isn't she?"

"I reckon."

Thelma decided to start supper, make it seem less like Jimmy was
on the witness stand. She opened a cabinet door and removed a large pot
for boiling water. "Did ya'll talk 'bout anything in particular?"

"No'm. I walked her home."

Thelma muffled her delight. "Really?" She began shucking the
corn into a bowl.

"Yeah." Jimmy stopped drumming, sat back in his chair.

"Where's she live?"

"On Sixth Street."

"Nice house?" Thelma placed a cleaned ear of corn on the counter.

"I didn't see it."

Thelma stopped her shucking. "Why not?"

"Didn't get that far." He paused. Did he really want to talk to his
mother about Rhoda? But she was a woman. Maybe she'd have some
advice. "I think Rhoda's mad at me."

"What'd you do?"

"Called her 'stupid.' " Thelma's eyebrows shot up. "I didn't mean
to. I was talkin' 'bout how I wish I could live on a street with real name,
not just a number, an' she made a kind of joke or somethin,' said I could
just change the name if I wanted to, an', I don't know, it just seemed like
a dumb idea an' I said so. Don't you think it's dumb?"

Thelma proceeded cautiously. "What's dumb to some people
might not be dumb to others. What'd Rhoda do?"

"She walked off by herself. It's just an expression, I didn' mean
nothin' by it. What's 'stupid' is gettin' all huffy about it."

Thelma put the corn aside. "Words mean different things to
different people. 'Stupid's a pretty strong word. Maybe use another one.
Like 'silly.' Or 'crazy.' People know you don't really mean 'insane' when
you say somethin's 'crazy.' "

"Or maybe don't say nothin'." Jimmy remembered Shoeless's
reaction when he'd called his superstition "stupid."

"Knowin' when to keep your mouth shut is one of life's most
valuable lessons, honey." Thelma smiled at him. "Words are powerful
things. Fortunately, they can be just as powerful the other way."

"What do you mean?"

"Well, there's nothin' more powerful than sayin' 'I'm sorry.' There's just somethin' about them two words. You hear 'em an' your heart kinda softens, your body relaxes. I think that's why Jesus talked about forgiveness so much. He was the Prince of Peace, an' he knew the best road to peace is forgiveness." Thelma looked at her son. His eyes dropped down, his brows furrowed the tiniest bit, thinking over what she'd said. She decided it was time to follow her own advice about knowing when to keep quiet. "Now, how 'bout helpin' me shuck the rest of this corn?" Jimmy got up from his chair. He was glad to have something to do while he wrestled with what his mother had said.

Thelma wasn't the only person to notice how discouraged Jimmy was becoming. He had made great progress as a hitter, Shoeless could tell that. He was rapping the ball hard, hitting to different fields. All the time spent holding the bat out straight from his side was beginning to develop some strong arm muscles. He was capable of hitting a home run any time at bat now. But the routine was getting stale for Jimmy. Shoeless, too. You could only spend so much time practicing. At some point you needed to play, needed game situations, needed the thrill of throwing a runner out at the plate, the satisfaction of seeing your teammates turn a nifty double-play, the whoop and holler of a home run celebration. Joe never thought he'd be feeling those urges again. They had crept up on him while he was busy teaching Jimmy how to hit, how to field, how to know the situation. But there they were, gnawing in his gut. If he was hungry to play, Joe could only imagine how starved Jimmy was feeling.

A recent article in the sports section of *The Greenville News* had given Joe an idea. The reporter, Charlie Deerhart, had called the Brandon Braves an "embarrassment" after their latest loss, a 14-0 snoozer. Katie had read it to him, and Joe had decided to keep the paper under the counter in the liquor store. He knew he could use it soon.

"How much, Joe?" Toby asked, plunking down a bottle of Johnny Walker Red. As expected, he'd stopped by for his usual order.

"Yes, sir, Mr. Gower." Joe reached under the counter to pull out an account book and tucked the newspaper under it. He pretended to look up the number. "How are you today, sir?"

"Been better."

"Things all right at the mill?"

"Oh, yeah, oh, yeah, folks'll always need things to dry off with. That is, if they bother to wash!" Joe responded with a hearty laugh. As he did so, he lifted up the account book, exposing the newspaper article underneath. "I see you been readin' the paper," Toby noticed. "Never seen such a bunch of losers. I cain't hardly stand to see Howard Stone any more, the way he lords it over me."

Joe smiled sympathetically. "Yes, sir," he said, putting away the account book. "That'll be $4.98."

Toby reached for his wallet. "Stone's been gettin' his hand in here, too," he said, gesturing with the wallet.

"That's no good."

"No, it idn'. I tell you, Shoeless, I wouldn't mind half so much if Stone weren't a dang Yankee. Stirs my blood."

Toby placed a ten-dollar bill on the counter and Shoeless rang him up. He knew what Mr. Gower meant. All the time he'd spent up north, he still had never felt comfortable. Yankees were just different, to Joe's way of thinking, just not folks you enjoyed being around much, folks you could relax with. That's why he'd started drinking too much up north, trying to relax. Once he'd come back home, Joe had cut way back on the booze.

The part about stirring Toby's blood made sense, too. Maybe it was the residue from the War Between the States, but something about Yankee's desire to always win, no matter what, rankled Shoeless. Joe had wanted to win when he played, no question about that, but it hadn't been life and death, the way it often seemed with the northerners on the teams he'd played for. And it hadn't been about the money for Joe, the way it seemed to be with a lot of Yankees. They were just so dang smug about winning. Yes, Shoeless knew exactly how Toby Gower felt about losing to Howard Stone.

"You know, Mr. Gower, there's a fella might be able to help you start winnin'," Joe began.

"Who's that?"

"Jimmy Roberts."

"That pitcher from Woodside? I heard Stone fired him from the mill."

"Yes, sir, he did. Which means he's available," Joe continued carefully.

"Don't need another pitcher. Pitchin' idn' my problem."

Shoeless pounced. "Jimmy's a hitter now."

"A hitter? How do you know?"

"I been coachin' him."

Toby's jaw dropped. "Whattaya mean?"

"Just that. We've been workin' every mornin' for weeks. Been teachin' Jimmy all I know 'bout baseball." Shoeless put the change in Toby's hand, but he let it rest there.

"All you know...." Toby digested that for a moment. He noticed the change in his hand and pocketed it. "Is he learnin' good?"

"Durn good." Shoeless looked straight at Toby. He allowed himself a small smile.

Toby began to grin back. "Stone wouldn't like it."

"No, sir, he wouldn't." Shoeless paused to allow time for that thought to do its work. "Want me to send him around to see you?"

Toby nodded. "Why don't you just do that, Joe? Right quick!"

"Will do."

"Thank ye kindly," Toby said, picked up the Scotch, and headed for the door.

"Mr. Gower, just a minute." Joe went over to the shelf and brought down another bottle of Johnny Walker Red. He walked to Toby at the door and held it towards him. "Two for one today. Mill owner's special."

Toby took the bottle and considered Joe. "Why're you takin' such an interest in Jimmy Roberts, Shoeless?"

"Let's just say I know how it feels."

Toby nodded. He understood just what Joe meant. As Toby walked out the door, Shoeless walked over to Pee Wee, who was standing on the perch in his cage. Forgetting what the previous owner had taught him, he reached up to stroke Pee Wee's feathers.

"Keep your damn hands off me!" the parrot squawked. Joe laughed. He couldn't wait to tell Katie about Jimmy.

Two days later, Jimmy was exiting Brandon Mill after the night shift when he saw Rhoda walking his way. He stayed by the gate until she saw him and stopped. "Jimmy!" she cried in surprise.

"Hello, Rhoda."

"What are you doin' here?"

"Gettin' off work, same as you."

"Huh?"

"I'm workin' at Brandon Mill now."

"You are?"

"Mr. Jackson got me an interview with Mr. Gower, an' he hired me."

"I see he gave you the worst shift."

"I asked for it."

Rhoda was surprised. "The graveyard shift?"

"Gimme a lot of daylight hours to play baseball."

"Well, welcome to Brandon."

She stepped through the gate and started toward home.

"Rhoda, wait!" She stopped. "I, uh ... I wondered if you'd be comin' to the game tomorrow. Brandon's playin' Mills Mill. Won't be much of a game, we're terrible, but, well, Mama's gonna be there, so I thought you might wanna come sit with her." He paused. "Or somethin'."

Rhoda considered Jimmy's request. "I might," she said finally, and began walking away.

"Wait!" Jimmy called again. "I got somethin' for you." He reached into his pocket and pulled out a coupon book. He tore out one coupon and gave it to Rhoda. "For the Coke."

Rhoda looked at the coupon for a second, then took it. "Thanks. Now we're even."

"Not really. I still owe you somethin'." He paused, then said deliberately. "Rhoda, I'm sorry I called you 'stupid.' I didn't mean it. I was just ... bein' careless with words. Fact is, I think you're right smart." He straightened. "Anyway, like I say, I didn't mean it an' I hope you'll forgive me." He looked at Rhoda and forced himself to hold her gaze.

Her face softened into a smile. "Well I'll be hog-tied! Sure, I'll forgive you, Jimmy. On one condition."

"What's that?"

"You buy me a Co-Cola after the baseball game tomorrow."

"I'd like that, Rhoda," Jimmy beamed.

She smiled back. "See ya' then," she said, and walked down the street. Jimmy watched her go. Pieces of lint wafted off her clothes as she walked along. He had the strange urge to go pick one up and keep it.

At the game the next day, it was soon obvious that Jimmy had been right about one thing: the Brandon Braves were a terrible baseball team. Jimmy felt like he'd joined a clown act. The manager, Juber Lee, put him in center field, and the very first ball hit his way, the right fielder, his friend, Piggy Simpson, waved him off. "I got it! I got it!" Piggy cried. So Jimmy moved behind him to back him up. All of a sudden Piggy stopped and put his hands over his head as the ball hit the ground behind him. Jimmy scooped up the ball and fired it into the infield, managing to hold the batter to a double. Piggy gave him a sheepish grin. "Thanks."

"Still afraid of 'em, huh, Steve?"

"Guess so."

"Well, maybe we can work on it."

"Yeah, great! It's really good to be playin' with you again, Jimmy. I never liked bein' on a different team from you, an' now we're not!' Piggy trotted back to his position in right field, telling himself that he'd be sure not to wave Jimmy off on the next ball hit their way.

The next batter for Mills Mill bunted. Johnny "Red" Roe, the pitcher, charged the ball, and so did the third baseman, Bill White, whom everybody called Whitey. He and Red arrived at the ball simultaneously. As they struggled back and forth over who was going to field it, the runner from second ran all the way home. Jimmy rolled his eyes. There was worse to come.

In the fifth inning, with Brandon down only by a score of 4-0, Mills Mill had runners on first and second base. If Red could get out of this inning with no runs across, Brandon might be able to score and get back in the game. Things looked good when the batter popped the ball up to the first baseman, Jack Washington. Jack tapped his glove a couple of times, neatly caught the ball, then jogged towards the dugout. Red began screaming at him. So did everybody on the team, it seemed, except Jimmy. He simply stared in disbelief. When Jack reached the dugout, Juber Lee yanked off his hat, threw it at him, and yelled, "There's only two outs, you stupid linthead!" Jack turned to see the lead runner heading for home and the other runner pulling into third base. He was too shocked to even attempt a throw.

After that, the fight went out of Brandon and Mills Mill piled up the runs. The final insult came when Piggy hit a towering drive down the left field foul line and took off running. Once he got up a good head of steam, his fat body propelled him forward. Legs pumping, arms churning, head down, Piggy rumbled past second base, where the umpire shouted at him to stop. He didn't, barreling towards third. The Mills Mill third baseman, a bemused look on his face, stepped aside as Piggy rounded the bag and charged for home. Now the whole Brandon team was yelling at him, but Piggy couldn't hear what they were saying. He crossed home plate and fell to the ground, exhausted. The umpire yelled, "Foul ball, you idiot!" Piggy's teammates turned away from him, but Jimmy stuck out a hand and pulled Piggy to his feet. "Hey, don't worry about it," he said. "It wasn't foul by much."

Jimmy managed to get three hits, all of them singles, all of them hit hard. He was seeing the ball well. The candle exercise was paying off. He felt good about that. And he felt good about seeing Rhoda sitting with Thelma behind first base, close enough so he could hear her yelling when he came to bat. "All right, Jimmy, mash it! Womp it! Knock the stuffin' outta that ball!" And, when he was standing safely on first base: "Jimmy, Jimmy, Jimmyyyyyyyyyyyyy!" She pumped her fist at him. *Lord, she's loud*, Jimmy thought. But he liked hearing her yell his name.

When the game ended, Thelma and Rhoda hopped out of the stands. "You played good, Jimmy," Thelma said, giving him a hug.

"I was 'bout the only one. Ten-to-nothin', can you believe it?"

"Least you're on a team again," Rhoda added.

"Ain't much of one."

Rhoda gave him a look. "Well, I ain't interested in standin' here in the broilin' sun listenin' to you bellyache. But I am interested in collectin' my Coke."

"Coke?" Thelma asked.

"Your son promised to buy me one after the game. You want one, too?"

"No, thanks. I'm goin' home an' sit in front of the fan."

"Take this with you, okay, Mama?" And Jimmy handed her his glove.

"Ooo, eee, look at them hands, Jimmy!" Thelma said. "You 'least got to wash up some if you gon' go squirin' 'roun folks purty as Rhoda Dawson."

"Miz Roberts!" Rhoda blushed.

"I will, Mama. There's a spigot right outside the store."

"All right, then," Thelma said.

They turned and walked off through the outfield. Thelma watched them go. She allowed herself a small smile. Jimmy was seventeen. It was about time he found himself a gal and got married. *Now, Thelma, don't get ahead of yourself!* But it was a nice dream, all the same.

She turned back towards the stands. There was Waddy, waiting. She hadn't wanted to meet him today, especially not here, where everybody could see. So far, she thought none of her neighbors knew. She had kept most of their meetings to night times, and they had gone to the Riverside Hotel, where she was confident nobody she knew would ever be. And Jimmy? What if he ever found out? She'd have to stop this soon, but not yet. Sure, Jimmy had a job now, but he'd just started. Best to let things stay the same for a while.

Waddy nodded at her, then turned and headed for the parking lot. Thelma would walk out of the village and he'd pick her up. Reality was back.

RHODA PROPOSED THEY DRINK THEIR COKES down by the reedy river. "No, thanks!" Jimmy said.

"Why not?"

"We call it the river the nose knows."

"Huh?"

"It's full of all the stuff the mills dump in it. You can tell what day of the week it is by the color of the Reedy River. If the water's purple, it's Thursday. Kinda yellow, Tuesday."

"That's terrible. We got the Saluda River up in the mountains, it's so clear. An' cold. Lordy, what I wouldn't give to be standin' there right this minute."

Jimmy set off and they started walking aimlessly. "You miss the mountains?"

"Yeah, I do. 'Specially the rhododendron."

"What's that?"

"It's a bush that's got these beautiful flowers. You ain't never seen no rhododendron?"

"We ain't got a lot of flowers in Woodside. What do they look like?"

"Tiny, white petals, an' loads of 'em, growin' on these dark, green bushes. 'Bout this time of year the mountains are full of 'em, so thick you cain't hardly walk through 'em. You know how at night you can look up at the sky an' see all them stars, thousands of 'em. Well, sometimes a whole mountainside will feel like that, like a universe of stars."

"I'd like to see that."

"I'd like to show you."

Suddenly a thought struck Jimmy. "That why you're named Rhoda? After the flower?"

"Yeah. My pa's idea. Said I was purty as a rhododendron. I didn't used to like my name, nobody's named Rhoda 'roun these parts, but I guess maybe it's growin' on me." Seeing her in profile, her hair swept behind her ear, the flush of her cheek, her sturdy nose just a touch turned up, Jimmy felt inclined to agree with Rhoda's father, even though he'd never seen a rhododendron.

They had reached a creek that ran through Brandon, called Longbranch. Rhoda stooped to put her hands in the water. "Nice an' cool!" she said.

"You got any sisters, Rhoda?" Jimmy asked. He stooped down and put his own hands in the water.

"Nope, just my brother. You?"

"Nope, I'm the only one. My ma an' pa weren't even 'sposed to have me."

"How can you not be 'sposed to have a baby?"

"I just meant they weren't married then."

"Oh! My pa an' ma' ate supper before they said grace, too."

"What has food got to do with it, Rhoda? What in tarnation are you talkin' 'bout?"

"Well, just think about it a minute, Jimmy. What if you was real hungry, an' you sat down an' there was a plate full of fried chicken a-settin' in front of you, an' it was lookin' so fat an' juicy, an' you just couldn't wait for grace to be said, you just dug in?"

Jimmy thought for a minute. "Fried chicken...?" he puzzled.

"An you're in a hurry...." Rhoda prompted.

"Oh!" he shouted, and burst into laughter. "You cain't wait for grace, you gotta get to it!"

"Put on the feed bag!"

"That musta been some fried chicken!"

"Deep fried!" Rhoda whooped, setting off more laughter.

On their way back to the store for more Cokes, they passed the Branwood Theatre. Rhoda read the name of the film showing there. "A Streetcar Named Desire."

"What kinda stupid title is that?" Jimmy scoffed. "Can you imagine one of our trolleys named 'Desire?' "

"I like it. Oh, look, it's got Vivien Leigh in it."

"Who's that?" asked Jimmy.

"She starred in *Gone With The Wind*."

"How come you know so much 'bout movies?"

"I read about 'em in magazines. Now that I'm a big-city girl, I can actually go see one!"

"Maybe I'll go with you." The words were out of his mouth before he knew what he was saying. *Did I just ask her for a date?*

"May be," Rhoda said with a coy smile. "Hey, let's go to Tucker's for our Cokes, it's right around the corner."

Tucker's was a soda shop in West Greenville. Jimmy had never been there, since he was just getting to know the Brandon area. *A soda shop? This really is sounding like a date.* "Okay," he agreed.

Rhoda ordered a cherry Coke so Jimmy did the same, and they sat in a booth and sipped them. Rhoda told Jimmy more about life in the mountains, about deer and raccoons, deep forests and craggy rocks, even about the year it snowed. "Sounds kinda magical," Jimmy said.

"I reckon. Magic's where you make it. I'll show you what I mean some time."

"All right." He looked forward to finding out what she meant, thinking how Rhoda was full of surprises.

"Wanna come for supper?" Rhoda asked.

Oh my gosh, now I'm meetin' her parents! Jimmy thought. But he found he didn't care. "Sure. Lemme call Mama an' ask if it's okay."

The Dawsons didn't have a phone, so Rhoda took Jimmy to the next-door neighbors so he could borrow theirs. She waited outside in the yard. "What'd she say?" she asked when Jimmy returned.

"She wasn't home. Funny, she always makes supper on Saturday nights for us. Wonder where she's at?"

"Probly at a neighbor's."

"Jaw-flappin'!" Jimmy joked.

"Yeah! Let's go eat. My stomach's doin' a organ recital."

Jimmy enjoyed Rhoda's parents, whose strange accent and unusual expressions only heightened his feeling that the mountains were a different and mysterious place. Rhoda's baby brother, Bobby, was just learning to play baseball and made Jimmy promise to play catch with him some time. When Rhoda's mother served fried chicken, Rhoda shot Jimmy a huge smile and he had to restrain himself from laughing out loud. And when her pa said, "Let say grace," they both couldn't help but giggle.

"What's so funny?" Bobby asked.

"Nothin'," Rhoda told him. All during the short prayer, Jimmy thought how much fun it was to share a secret with Rhoda.

After supper, Rhoda told Jimmy she wanted to show him something, so, when he'd thanked the Dawsons for the meal and made a date with Bobby to play catch, they set off through the mill village and wound their way around to the backside of Brandon Mill. "It's always funny to see the mill settin' quiet," Jimmy observed.

"The machinery's restin' up for the comin' week, too. All them looms an' pulleys, an' shutttles an' cables, an' motors an' pipes, they're all storin' up the clang an' clatter for Monday mornin'."

Jimmy shook his head and smiled. "Rhoda, you're a wonder."

"Whattaya mean?"

"Just the way you think about things."

"See what happens when everything's not baseball?" she teased. "But come on, I'll show you a real wonder."

She led the way into a small wooded area that abutted the mill's chain link fence and stopped at the base of a tall pine tree. "Like to climb?" she asked, and shinnied up the trunk, then looked down at him. "Come on!"

Raising his eyes, Jimmy could see Rhoda's strong, tan legs spread apart bracing on the limb, underneath her skirt. When she reached up to hold onto the branch above her head, her skirt lifted, and he could see the flesh of her thighs, and the barest glimpse of her underwear. The sight aroused him and left him slightly dizzy. It was a feeling he'd never had before.

He hoisted himself up into the tree as Rhoda climbed onto the limb above her, then sat with the branch between her legs and began to scoot forward. It was a big limb and it stretched out over the fence. When she reached the end, she grabbed the limb with her hands, swung herself down to dangle some ten feet above the ground, and then dropped to the earth. She looked back at Jimmy and motioned him to follow.

He tried to understand what was happening, as he climbed onto the limb and scooted out. What was he doing here with this mountain girl, following her onto the mill's private property? Where could she possibly be taking him? As he reached the end of the limb and lowered himself over it, hanging on with his hands, he realized he hadn't done anything like this for a very long time. How dull his life had become. The same mill, the same people, even the same baseball. His life had become like a shuttle, back and forth, back and forth, movement without meaning. As he let go of the limb and fell to the ground, he knew at once that, with Rhoda, his life would never be the same.

She took his hand and pulled him excitedly along towards the water tower, looming round and dark against a sky already turning soft with scattered streaks of orange and yellow. "Hurry!" Rhoda whispered, "Or we'll miss it!" When they reached the stairs that circled around the tower to the top, Rhoda released the latch that kept the last few steps raised off the ground, expertly lowering this final part of the staircase into place, and began climbing. Following, Jimmy once again had the pleasing sight of her legs drawing him onward.

The stairs made one long loop around the entire tower, and then they were standing on the top. Rhoda rushed to one side. "Isn't it amazin'?" she gasped. Jimmy followed. They were high up, some hundred feet above the ground. Spread out below them was all of Greenville. Jimmy could see the Woodside Building rising from downtown. To the west, Jimmy saw the small business district with Joe's liquor store on a corner. *Shoeless Joe Jackson, my coach!* The thought made him smile.

Further west, he could make out Woodside Mill and its village. His mother was there somewhere. *My home,* Jimmy thought. With Rhoda by his side, it didn't seem so bad all of a sudden.

"Look!" Rhoda shouted, pointing to the far distance. "The mountains! See, Jimmy? That's my home!" Jimmy looked at the outline of the distant hills. They resembled their name: a blue ridge. The sun had almost disappeared behind them now, only half of its orange disc visible. Streaks of light painted the strands of clouds pink and purple. Slowly, slowly the sun disappeared. All the world seemed to glow with its vanished light. "See, Jimmy. Magic!" Rhoda said, squeezing his hand. "It's beautiful!"

He pulled her to him. "Purdy as a rhododendron," he whispered, and kissed her.

A mile or so away, Thelma dragged the galvanized tin tub into her kitchen and began filling it with water. She stripped off her dress and pulled the bra over her head. She looked down at her breasts. *Her* breasts, to do with as she wanted. No, not wanted. Needed. She'd needed to strike the deal with Waddy, hadn't she? She peeled off her panties, sticky with humidity and sweat, and tossed them on top of the bra and dress, stepping quickly into the tub. The water was warm. What Thelma wouldn't have given then for a cool shower, one where she could stand and watch the water gurgle down the drain, taking her shame with it. No, she wouldn't be ashamed! She'd done what she had to do. She reached for the bar of soap and began scrubbing herself vigorously. Unlike her son, there'd been no magic in Thelma's night.

CHAPTER 10

As Jimmy and Rhoda were embracing at the top of the Brandon Mill water tower, Shoeless Joe was in the basement of his house somewhere below them, looking at the opened cedar chest containing his memories. If Jimmy and Rhoda were feeling buoyant at the beginning of a new relationship, Shoeless was staring at the painful reminder of an old one: the business card of Alfred Austrian, senior partner in one of Chicago's most prestigious law firms in 1920, and lawyer for Charles Comiskey and the Chicago White Sox.

Joe remembered the day he'd received the card. It was September 28, 1920, the day after the news of the betting fix had broken. When Joe had heard the news, he'd immediately set out for Comiskey's office, thinking that Comiskey, as Joe's boss, would know what Joe should do, how he should handle his impending grand jury testimony the next day. Comiskey had arranged for Joe to meet with Austrian at the courthouse that following morning. What Joe didn't know was that Comiskey had also arranged for Eddie Cicotte to meet with Austrian earlier to advise him as well about his grand jury testimony.

Charles Comiskey had been playing a clever game. Like so many people in the fall of 1919, he had had strong suspicions that the fix was in. Joe himself had told him so. And Comiskey had hired three private investigators, who had also confirmed that the rumors were true. During the spring and summer of 1920, Comiskey had kept his tongue, watching to see how events would play out. But when the grand jury had acted, he had acted, too, by immediately suspending the suspected players. Honest Charles Comiskey would wreck his own baseball team, because it was the honorable thing to do, was how he had shaped the story. Now he had to protect that image by making sure those who testified did not somehow divulge that he had re-hired men he knew to be corrupt and played them for a whole season.

"Come in, Joe, come in," Austrian said, as Shoeless entered the vacant courthouse office. "I'm Alfred Austrian, the White Sox' lawyer. I'm honored to finally meet you." He offered a well-manicured hand, which Joe feebly shook.

"I know who you are, Mr. Austrian. Mr. Comiskey's not here?" Joe asked.

"Busy man, Joe, busy man. He asked me to listen to your story, which I am happy to do. Have a seat." Austrian gestured to a chair at a nearby coffee table. Joe carefully settled his large body into the chair, as Austrian took a chair opposite. A perfectly tailored blue suit fit snugly over his trim body, a red silk tie bulging behind a matching vest. Now that he had reached fifty, Austrian was glad that his hair had finally turned silver, though he still had to dye it here and there to maintain his look. *"Cigarette?"* he asked. *"Drink?"*

"No thank you, sir," Joe answered. He looked around the room.

"There's nobody here but us, Joe," Austrian said smoothly. *"We can talk freely."*

"Yes, sir." Joe tugged at the lapels of his sports jacket. He'd worn a tie for the occasion and wished he could loosen it, but Katie had warned him to keep it on.

"I am so sorry, Shoeless, for this terrible mess," Austrian began sympathetically. *"I can hardly believe it's happening, especially to such a wonderful team as ours. Let me assure you, as the lawyer for your team, I am here to help you in any way I can."*

"Thank you, Mr. Austrian."

"Why don't you tell me what you know, Joe."

"Hasn't Mr. Comiskey told you?"

"I'd like to hear it from you, if you don't mind."

Joe took a deep breath. He'd been hoping he wouldn't have to go over the painful memories. He told Austrian how he'd refused to go along when Chick Gandil had approached him about throwing the series for money. And how he'd asked Mr. Comiskey to take him out of the series and Comiskey, through the manager, Kid Gleason, had refused. How Joe had played his heart out during the games. How he'd refused the money Lefty tried to give him. And about his short conversation with Harry Grabiner, when he'd tried to return the money to Comiskey. He spoke clearly and with enough detail that he was confident that Austrian would see the truth.

When he had finished, Austrian cleared his throat. *"I want to believe you, Joe, I truly do. But I must tell you that it just doesn't add up."*

Joe was shocked. Here was the White Sox lawyer practically calling him a liar. He raised his voice. *"What do you mean?"*

"I mean two people have already named you as a co-conspirator. Billy Maharg and Eddie Cicotte."

"*Maharg's a two-bit gambler tryin' to cash in on that reward Mr. Comiskey offered for hard evidence,*" *Joe replied hotly.* "*He ain't got no evidence! He's just repeatin' what Chick Gandil told him!*"

"*And why did Gandil tell him that?*"

"*I don't know, Mr. Austrian. Like I said, I told Gandil I didn't want no part of it. Is it my fault if he went an' told everybody I was in on the fix?*"

"*I must tell you, Joe, that Eddie Cicotte is down the hall in the Grand Jury room right now naming you as one of the conspirators.*"

"*What?*" *Joe leaned forward in his chair.* "*Why would Eddie say that?*"

"*That's what I'm asking you, Joe.*"

"*I don't know why Eddie'd say that. Probably the same thing: he got it from Gandil!*"

"*Look, Joe, although I find that hard to believe, let's just say it's true, for argument's sake.*" *Austrian's voice took on the tone of a hard-edged attorney.* "*That still doesn't explain why you left Chicago with $5,000 in your pocket.*"

"*I tried to give it back!*" *Joe shouted. He took a breath to calm himself.* "*Look, I know it looks fishy, but it's the truth. I had the money an' I didn't know what to do with it, so I took it back to South Carolina till I could figure somethin' out.*"

"*And did you? Did you figure something out?*" *He looked hard at Joe.* "*Did you put it in a secure bank account? Did you try to send it back by Western Union? Did you take a train to Chicago and try to meet again with Mr. Comiskey?*"

Joe met his gaze, realized what it meant, and hung his head. "*No, sir,*" *he said weakly.* "*I didn't.*"

Austrian paused and switched gears. "*Joe, you can tell your version to the grand jury and see if they buy it. I don't, and I don't think they will either, but you can take your chances. If they don't and it goes to trial, you can see if a jury buys it. Or you can try another approach, one I would recommend.*"

"*What's that?*"

"*Admit it, and say you're sorry.*"

Joe had been slouched in his chair, but now he sat upright. "*Lie?*"

"*It's your best chance, Joe. You know how forgiving the American people are. They just want sinners to say they're sorry. Do you think they want you out of baseball? You're Shoeless Joe Jackson, for God's sake! The fans love you! They'll forgive you for one little mistake.*"

"Mistake...?" Joe tried the idea out. *Taking the money to South Carolina had been a mistake, but that was his only one. Now Austrian wanted him to say he'd made another by cheating.*

"And what about this, Joe?" Austrian continued. *"What about the gamblers. They think you were in on it. And then you tell the world you weren't, that you played your heart out to win? They might take that as a double-cross. And gamblers don't exactly have a reputation for forgiving."*

Joe remembered what Lefty had said about protecting his family. He thought about Katie. He certainly did not want to put her at risk. But what would she say when she found out he'd lied to the Grand Jury? Why wasn't Katie here now so he could ask her? He needed someone he could trust.

As if sensing his thoughts, Austrian said, *"Joe, I'm the lawyer for the Chicago White Sox. Would I want to give you bad advice?"*

"Does that mean you're my lawyer, too?"

"I'm the team's lawyer," Austrian said evasively. He didn't mention that he'd been a friend of Charles Comiskey for twenty years.

"I don't know, Mr. Austrian. I'm confused."

"That's it!" Austrian suddenly shouted.

"What?"

"The linchpin of your story!" Austrian rose and began pacing as he spoke. *"We blame it all on Gandil. I mean, you do. Tell them he talked you into it and then double-crossed you over the money — promised you twenty grand and only forked over five. You were taken in, deceived. Confused, like you said. Give 'em the dumb yokel act, tell 'em you didn't know what the hell you were doing."*

The dumb yokel act. Joe hated it. Yet it was true, that is what a lot of people thought about him. Joe tried out the idea to himself. *Poor boy from South Carolina taken in by northern sharpies. Say how sorry he was. Say he just wanted to play baseball, that's all he'd ever wanted to do. Beg the jurors to just let him play ball. "Do you really think it'll work?"*

"Positive!" Austrian replied. *"Now, go down to that grand jury room and tell them what we've agreed on. Be humble. Be sorry. Put in a good word for Mr. Comiskey, tell 'em what a great boss he's been, how you're so sorry to have let down such an honorable man. Tell 'em how ashamed you feel in front of your wife. Tell 'em you just want to play baseball for the good people of Chicago, bring a World Series Championship back to this great town, they deserve it."* He picked up a piece of paper from his desk and held it out to Joe. *"One other thing."*

"What's that?"

"Nothing. Just a legal matter you need to sign before you testify."

"What's it say?"

"You can read it if you like," Austrian answered, knowing Joe couldn't.

"I cain't read, Mr. Austrian," Joe answered humbly.

"Well, then, I guess you'll have to trust me, huh, Joe. Think you can trust the lawyer for your baseball team?" he said lightly.

"Can I take it to Katie to read?"

"No time, Joe. Who knows when Eddie will be finished testifying, they could call you any minute." Austrian took a gold fountain pen from its holder on the desk, handed it to Joe, and pointed to where he wished him to sign the paper. Joe took the pen and painstakingly drew the letters of his name, the only words he knew how to write.

Austrian took the piece of paper, placed it in a drawer, then came around the desk to offer his hand to Joe. "I'm glad we got to talk, Joe, and, as I said, I'm honored to finally meet you." As he walked him to the office door, Austrian reached into his wallet and pulled out his business card. *"Here,"* he said, handing Joe the card. *"It's got my private number on it. When you've finished testifying, call me up right away. I want to know how it went. Do you promise, Joe?"*

"I promise," Joe said.

"Good," Austrian replied, ushering Joe out the door and closing it firmly after him.

Back in his basement, Joe looked at the card in his hand. It had faded a lot in the intervening thirty-one years. He turned it over and looked at the phone number. He remembered dialing it after his testimony. And dialing it. And dialing it. Alfred Austrian never answered, and Joe never saw him again in his life.

"Whatcha doin', Joe?" Katie asked. She was in her nightgown, standing at the bottom of the basement stairs.

"Nothin'. Go back to bed."

"Not without my man." She padded over to Joe sitting in his chair in front of the opened chest. "What's that?" she asked, pointing at the card.

"The business card of Alfred Austrian."

"Oh. Why would you keep that?"

"I kept everything."

"An' that's the problem. You should throw half of that stuff away."

"What should I keep?"

"The good stuff." She stroked Joe's head gently.

"Like what?"

Katie knelt down in front of the chest and picked up a pile of newspapers. She read some of the headlines out loud. "'Jackson Glove: The Place Where Triples Go To Die.' That's a keeper." She placed it aside and read the next headline. "'Greenville Boy Making Good.' That, too." She smiled up at Joe as she shuffled the papers to produce the next headline. "'Legendary Shoeless Joe Opens Local Store." Remember that, Joe? How happy everybody was when you came back home for good?"

"Yeah, I do." Katie looked at the next headline and then placed it aside. "What's wrong?" Joe asked.

"That's for the throw-away pile."

"What's it say?"

"Never mind."

"What's it say, Katie?" Joe insisted.

Katie reluctantly read, *"Carolina Cracker: Too Dumb For His Own Good.* I told you it was a throw-away." She started to toss the paper aside, but Joe stopped her.

"No! Keep it. An' keep the one that says *Black Sox: Benedict Arnolds of Baseball.* An' the one that says *Joe Jackson Is Ty Cobb From The Neck Down.*"

"You memorized them?" Joe nodded. "Why?"

"'Cause that's who I am."

"No it's not, Joe!" Katie said, jumping up. "Those are just words. Words newspapermen gotta turn out. Words people read. Words people say. Words they mean an' words they don't mean. Words in a so-called confession an' words you tell your wife. Words, words, words! But words are *not* Joe Jackson! This is!" She put out her hand and gently raised Joe from his chair. Then she kissed him, tenderly, lovingly, but with the strength of her conviction vibrating throughout her entire body as she pressed it against him.

"You're the greatest home run of my life," Joe whispered into her hair, holding her tightly.

"An' that's the greatest honor of my life" she whispered back. Katie looked at husband. "Now, your greatest home run wants to know what the heck you're doin' down here in the middle of the night."

"Tryin' to decide somethin'."

"What?"

"I watched the Brandon baseball game today."

"Like always," Katie smiled at him. "You know, you wouldn't have to watch it through binoculars if you'd just go to the game."

Joe was surprised. "You know?"

"For a long time. Why do you think I keep pressin' you to just go?"

"Well, maybe now I will. Brandon stinks. They're pure-tee terrible!"

"Even Jimmy?"

"No, he played good. But that's the problem. I hate to see Jimmy wastin' his talents with that bunch of no-goods."

"Well, that's his team."

"But what if I make it *my* team?" Katie looked at him quizzically. "What if I manage?"

"Manage Brandon?" she gasped.

"I'm not sayin' I can make 'em great — "

"Of course you can!"

"But I might could help 'em improve a little."

"You'll make 'em champions!" Katie shouted. "Oh, Joe!" She hugged him.

"The thing is, they've already got a manager. An' Juber Lee's a friend of mine. I don't want him to think I'm pushin' him aside."

"He'll be thrilled that you want to get back into baseball. Everybody will! Joe, I've waited so long for this!" Her eyes welled with tears, but Joe didn't notice, trying as he was to puzzle out a solution.

"I just cain't take his job. He gets paid to manage, you know."

"Then let him keep his paycheck! Yes, Joe, it's a perfect solution. We don't need the money."

"That might help," Joe pondered. "I reckon Mr. Gower might go for it."

"To have Shoeless Joe Jackson manage the Brandon Braves? You bet he would!"

"You think I should do it?"

"If you don't, I'll give 'em another headline to write: *Wife Clouts Husband With Black Betsy!*" Katie smiled as she slammed down the lid of the chest, took Joe's hand, and let him upstairs, away from old memories and into some new ones.

Howard Stone was feeling good. An afternoon thunderstorm the day before had cooled things off a bit, the humidity had lessened, and, for once, when he'd stepped out of his morning shower, he hadn't immediately felt the need to jump right back in. Woodside Mill was making good money, and even though he didn't like living in the south, he did like the increase in his bank balance. It left him time to dream about what he would do once he moved back north. His plans seemed to be working out. Crusher had provided the spark his Woodside Wolves needed to launch themselves into first place in the Western Carolina League, where they held a comfortable four-game lead over Dunean, with Pelzer in third, Piedmont fourth, and Brandon in the cellar, a full ten games behind. His bets with Jellycakes had been paying off, too, further improving both his bank account and his mood. Howard loved winning, and winning with money on the line was all the sweeter. Yes, it was a fine Monday morning, and for once, Howard actually looked forward to the week ahead.

His breakfast of eggs-over-easy, toast, and jam was interrupted by the phone ringing. *Who the hell's calling me at this hour*, Howard thought, glancing at his watch: 8:37. Anybody who knew Howard knew it had better be urgent to call him at home instead of in his office. His impatient tone said as much, as he picked up the speaker and barked, "Hello."

"Mr. Stone?" a young man's voice on the other end asked.

"Who is this?" Howard demanded.

"Charlie Deerhart, sir, of the *The Greenville News.*"

"Can't this wait until I get to my office?"

"Yes, sir, it can, but I thought you might be interested in this piece of news my editor just received from Toby Gower."

"Gower? What news of his could I possibly be interested in?"

"It's about his baseball team, sir. But I can call you a little later at your office." Charlie knew how to make people want to talk.

"No, no," Howard half-shouted, taking the bait. "Tell me!"

"It's pretty big, I think. It's about Shoeless Joe Jackson. It seems he's decided to get back into baseball. He's decided to manage the Brandon Braves."

"What?" Howard exploded. He prided himself on being able to handle surprises, but this news had stunned him. "Are you sure?"

"Yes, sir, Mr. Stone. Mr. Gower called my editor about it first thing this mornin'. He seems pretty interested in it, wants us to put it right in the paper."

Howard was silent for a moment. Then he asked more calmly, "Why are you telling me this?"

"Well, sir, I thought you might want to make a comment. After all, this might affect Woodside's standing in the League."

"And why might that be, Mr. — what did you say your name was?"

"Charlie Deerhart."

"Mr. Deerhart. Why might Jackson's managing affect my baseball team?"

"He does know his ball, sir."

"*Did*, Mr. Deerhart, *did* know his ball. Who knows what he remembers after, what, about thirty years?"

"You don't think it's all that big a deal, then?"

Howard hated news reporters. They were always trying to get you to put words in your mouth. "I didn't say that," he replied firmly. "I'm just saying that Shoeless made his reputation as a player, and players don't automatically make the best managers."

"Yes, sir," Charlie said encouragingly, trying to get Howard to continue. "You're confident you'll remain in first place, then?"

"Very confident, Mr. Deerhart, very confident. Did Mr. Gower say that Jackson would be a playing manager?"

"He said Jackson told him specifically he would not be playing."

"There you go, then. If Shoeless were playing, it might be cause for a little concern, although I bet he's a bit rusty after all these years. But Peters is a good manager. We've got Crusher Goodlett leading the league in homers and RBI's. And we're in first place, and Brandon's in the cellar. As I said, I'm very confident we'll win the pennant."

"You've got no objection, then, to Shoeless Joe Jackson gettin' back into baseball?"

"You mean, because of his past?" Howard considered for a moment. If he did have any concerns, this might well be why. "He is banned, as you know, Mr. Deerhart. I think I'll see what the other owners say before I answer that question. Thank you for the news, Mr. Deerhart."

"Just one more ques — " Charlie began.

Howard replaced the receiver and allowed himself a smile. Hanging up on a reporter always made him feel good. But his enjoyment was tempered by the knowledge that Joe Jackson would be managing a rival baseball team. Brandon was far behind in the pennant race, and they weren't very good. Even Shoeless Joe Jackson might not be able to make decent players out of that team of misfits and no-accounts. Still, there was something vaguely troubling about the news. Things were going smoothly, and any change might present a problem. And a change of this magnitude might present more than that.

He pushed his food aside and dialed a number he knew by heart. "Yancey Dickerson," Yancey answered in his smooth drawl.

"It's me."

Yancey was surprised. "Well, hello, Howard. What gets you up at the peep of day?"

"Wondered how that resolution to get Joe Jackson reinstated was going."

"We're grindin' corn. We passed it in the House an' sent it to the Senate. They'll probably pass it in the next couple of weeks, then get it over to the governor's office for his signature."

"Do you think it'll matter?"

"What do you mean?"

"I mean, do you think the Commissioner of Baseball might reinstate Jackson because a bunch of yahoos think it's a good idea?"

"Now, Howard, I'm not sure I take kindly to that remark. But I'll overlook it in the interest of our friendship. What makes you so interested in our resolution all of a sudden?"

"Because, all of a sudden, Shoeless Joe Jackson is managing the Brandon Braves."

"Well butter my butt and call me a biscuit!"

"Cut the cornpone, Yancey," Howard said sharply, "This might be serious."

"You sound fit to be tied, Howard." Yancey smiled. He didn't often hear Howard Stone perturbed, and he rather enjoyed it. So much so that he decided to ruffle a few more of his feathers. "Might be good for the league, Howard, bring us a little attention. Aren't you always complain' that nobody up north knows about us? Might help move that resolution along, too."

"I'm not sure I like your resolution, Yancey. And with Jackson getting back into baseball, I might like it even less. I can't quite put my finger on it, but something about this bothers me."

Yancey chuckled. "I can put your finger on it, Howard. You're afraid Shoeless will manage you right out of the pennant."

Howard didn't bite. He was suddenly tired of Yancey's slick talk. "You let me know when that resolution goes over to the governor's office."

"I surely will, Howard, I surely will. An' you let me know if I might join you the next time Woodside plays Brandon. Got a feelin' that might be a heckuva game."

"Good-bye, Yancey," Howard fairly spat into the receiver.

He was surprised at how the news of Joe's managing had affected him. But upon closer examination, he began to realize just why he was disturbed. Growing up he'd developed a passion for baseball and he'd been outraged when he first heard that some players had purposefully lost a World Series. Howard truly loved the game, and he'd taken it as almost a personal affront that anyone would dishonor it, especially in that way. Of course, he had never bothered to check out the complete story, he'd just accepted the consensus that Commissioner Landis would never have banned the greatest natural player ever without good reason.

Howard wondered if he should inform the Commissioner's office about Jackson and the Braves. Shoeless had been banned from professional baseball, but, technically, the textile leagues weren't professional, although they had plenty of players of professional quality playing in them. And they were paid to play — at least some of them. He also thought he'd heard a story that Shoeless had been denied the chance to manage a minor league team back in the Thirties. Maybe he should be denied again. It wasn't worth looking into yet, he decided. Chances were Shoeless wouldn't be able to transform the Brandon Braves from a very bad team into a contender in half a season. Howard decided he liked his odds and went back to his eggs. They were cold, but he ate them anyway. He needed something to chew on.

Early that afternoon, Jimmy waited in the shade of the bleachers for Joe to arrive for practice. The Braves began their sessions at the end of the day shift. That cut down on the time Jimmy could sleep after the graveyard shift and before his session with Shoeless. Today, he was exceptionally tired because he'd spent all day Sunday with Rhoda. Since that night on the water tower, he had wanted to be with her whenever he could. She was constantly in his thoughts. Jimmy had gone to church because she'd sung a solo, and, sitting in his pew, hearing her beautiful voice, seeing her face radiant with song, he had been transported by feelings deeper and more mysterious than any he'd ever known. They had snuck back onto the water tower that night, talking some and kissing a lot. When he'd awakened Monday morning after a night of the sweetest dreams he could remember, all he could think about was when he would get to see her again. For the first time in his life, Jimmy had wished he didn't have any baseball in his day.

When Shoeless strolled onto the diamond at Brandon Park, wearing his Panama hat, white short-sleeved shirt, and tan trousers, he was surprised to see Jimmy sitting in the shade. Usually, no matter the heat, Jimmy would be practicing something, throwing himself fly balls or holding out the baseball bat at arm's length to strengthen his muscles. But today he was just sitting.

"Jimmy!" Joe called out, awakening him from his daydream.

Jimmy jumped up. "Oh, hi, Mr. Jackson."

"Whattaya doin'?"

"Just thinkin'."

"'Bout what?" Shoeless asked, dumping baseballs out of the croker sack.

"'Bout my weekend," Jimmy said happily.

"Had a good 'un, huh?"

"Best weekend ever!" Jimmy answered with a huge smile.

Shoeless was surprised. "Even though you lost the game Saturday?"

"We got killed!" Jimmy said, grinning.

Joe was confused. He thought Jimmy would be upset by the 10-0 loss and by the way his team had played. And here he was, grinning. "An' that didn't bother you?"

"Yes, sir, it did."

"Then why are you so happy?"

Jimmy debated telling him about Rhoda, and decided against it. "At least I'm playin' again. An' if I keep workin' hard, I'll get better — heck, I'm already better, thanks to you. We got more than half the season left. Who knows how good I'll be by the end?"

Joe picked up a baseball, put on his glove, and began tossing the ball with Jimmy to loosen them both up. "An' your team?"

"Yeah, we ain't too good right now. But maybe I can pass on things you teach me to the others, an' they'll get better, too."

Joe and Jimmy threw the ball for a few minutes in silence, enjoying the smack of the ball in their gloves. Shoeless debated waiting until the end of practice to tell Jimmy his news, but, truth to tell, though he did his best to hide it, he was as excited as Jimmy about the events of his weekend, too. "You might not need a translator, Jimmy," he said softly.

"Huh?"

"Teachin' the others. Might not need to do it yourself."

"Who'd do it, then?"

"Maybe I would." Shoeless looked at Jimmy, who stopped his arm in mid-motion and checked his throw.

A puzzled look knitted his brows. "You mean, get the whole team here every day?"

"Y'all practice together at the end of the day shift, don't you? Maybe I'd just show up at practice, do a little coachin' then." Shoeless was enjoying drawing out the good news.

"Well, I guess so, yeah.... Long as Mr. Morgan wouldn't mind."

"He wouldn't."

"How do you know?" Jimmy eyed Shoeless. What was he talking about?

Joe decided to end Jimmy's confusion. "'Cause he's no longer your manager."

"He's not? Who is?"

Shoeless couldn't keep a huge smile from creasing his face. "I am."

Jimmy dropped the baseball from his hand. "You're gonna manage the Brandon Braves?"

"Yup."

"Yeeee-hiiiiiiiiii!" Jimmy let out a yell that would have done a rebel soldier proud. He yanked off his glove and flung it as hard as he could. It spiraled over second base and landed in center field. When he looked back, Shoeless was laughing.

Jimmy started laughing, too, jumping up and down. "You're gonna manage my team!" he shouted. "You're gonna manage my team! Thank you, Mr. Jackson! Thank you!"

"Don't thank me yet, boy. Who knows if I'll be any good?"

"You'll be great! Everybody's gonna love you!"

"I ain't lookin' for love, I'm lookin' for work. Now what say you get that glove you throwed to high heaven an' let's get to it?"

"Yes, sir!" Jimmy shouted and took off running. Shoeless watched him go. He couldn't stop grinning. He was surprised at how good it felt making somebody else feel good.

CHAPTER 11

The baseball arced high in the blue sky and fell towards Piggy Simpson, who awaited it with trembling hands. Just as the ball was about to land in his glove, he flinched. The ball caromed away. Piggy hung his head. "Dagnabbit, Steve, what are you afraid of?" Joe called out from home plate, where he was hitting fungoes to the outfielders. "Just a minute." Joe searched among the balls scattered near home plate, found the softest one he could, and walked into the outfield up to Piggy. "Sit down," he commanded.

Piggy sat in the grass. Shoeless held the ball over his head. "Now, Steve, I promise this won't hurt. Do you believe me?"

Piggy nodded cautiously. Shoeless dropped the ball onto Piggy's head. Piggy flinched again, but he didn't say anything. "Did that hurt?"

"No, sir, not really."

Shoeless picked up the ball and dropped it on him again. "How 'bout that?"

"No, sir."

"Now, I realize a ball comin' down at you outta the sky is gonna land harder, but the idea's the same: you're not really gonna be hurt. An' if you think you are, then the best way of protectin' yourself is to put up your glove an' catch the ball. Does that make sense?"

"Yes, sir."

Shoeless reached down a hand and pulled Piggy to his feet. "Now, this may sound crazy, but I want you to find someone to drop baseballs on your head, okay? An', after a while, maybe stand on the bleachers an' drop 'em from a little higher up. Purty soon, you won't be afraid of 'em. Will you try that, Steve?"

"Yes, sir," Piggy responded, a bit uncertainly.

"I'll help you, Steve," Jimmy said. Piggy smiled gratefully. He knew he could trust Jimmy. And Jimmy might help him trust Shoeless.

They had been practicing for a week. Shoeless was trying to teach the Brandon Braves everything he knew about how the national pastime should be played. It had been hard work. They had started with the basics. Running drills, hitting drills, sliding drills, pickoff drills, bunting drills, throwing drills, stealing drills. Drills, drills, drills. Shoeless had been everywhere on the field, teaching the pitchers how to throw a better curve; showing the shortstop how to back up third base on a ground ball; teaching the whole team the inside-out swing to hit to the opposite field; explaining, demonstrating, cajoling, shouting, whistling, gesturing, clapping. Jimmy hadn't realized how much there was to playing baseball, or, at least, to playing it right. It was exhausting. He wondered if some of his teammates thought it had been too much work. As for himself, he loved it.

It was time for the outfield drills and Jimmy stepped to his place in the line. Now that he was no longer pitching, he'd been playing the outfield again. That's where he'd played when he'd first started baseball. Juber Lee had put him in center, but Shoeless had played left, so that's where Jimmy had asked to play, figuring he'd learn the most if he played the same position. Shoeless lofted a fly ball in his direction. "Run on the balls of your feet, Jimmy. If you run up an' down on your heels, the ball bounces in your vision an' you cain't see it as good." Jimmy ran to his right, running hard on the balls of his feet. Shoeless was right, it was easier to see the ball. He got behind it, caught it running forward, cocked his arm, and fired at the shortstop, Jawbreaker Johnson. Jawbreaker, who got his nickname because of the results of a fight, came out to take the cut-off, leapt high in the air, and just managed to snag Jimmy's throw.

"Throw it at his head, Jimmy!" Shoeless shouted. "That's the only way to give him the option of takin' the throw or lettin' it go. If the cut-off man ducks, you done it right."

"Yes, sir," Jimmy cried happily, as he returned to the end of the line.

"Footwork!" Shoeless called out, and the outfielders stretched out in a horizontal line. Shoeless trotted out from the pitcher's mound into shallow center field, and held a baseball above his head. He moved it left — to the player's right — and they ran in that direction, keeping their eyes on the ball above Joe's head. Then Shoeless switched and moved the ball to the right, and the players had to immediately switch direction. Joe again reversed directions, and the players did, too. Then he pushed his arm forward, and everybody started backpedaling. Except for Piggy, who tripped and fell. The others kept pedaling, but instead of lying there, as he'd done at the beginning of the week, Piggy jumped back up and joined the others.

Jimmy smiled and patted Piggy on the butt. "Good hustle, Steve."

"Damn feet!" Piggy muttered.

"Pig's feet!" Pepper Forrester called out.

"Pickled pig's feet!" shouted Jawbreaker. Piggy joined in the laughter. Having Shoeless Joe as their coach seem to take the edge off a lot of things.

Shoeless called the players to him. "Remember, keep your feet close together when you're in position. Lots of folks like to spread 'em." He spread his feet. "That helps you go left or right." He scooted left and then right. "But it slows you up when you try to go forward or backwards." Joe ran backwards a few yards. He was surprisingly agile for a sixty-one-year-old. "Bucket drill!" he called out.

The infielders took their positions. The catcher, Petie Merritt, brought out a battered tin bucket with twenty balls inside and dumped them at home plate. Whitey took the empty bucket to third, put it just outside the bag, and took his position. Shoeless hit the ball to him, Whitey threw to Jack Washington at first base, Wash threw to Petie at home, who threw back to Whitey at third. Since all the throws were good, Whitey dropped the ball into the bucket. No errors, one for one. Joe hit the next ball to Jawbreaker at short — first, home, and back to third without an error, so Whitey dropped another ball into the bucket. Two for two. Wofford — most of the team called him Whiff because he struck out so often — bobbled the next ball hit to him at second, so they couldn't deposit that one into the third-base bucket. The goal was to get twenty balls in a row into the bucket. Twenty ground balls without an error. Jimmy seriously doubted they'd ever make it, but it was fun to watch them try. He shouted encouragement, "Shake it off, Whiff! Next time, next time!"

Whiff did shake it off. In that Saturday's game against Pelzer, Brandon actually turned a double-play! In the top of the fifth inning, Whitey scooped up a grounder at third and fired to Whiff covering second, Whiff threw it as hard as he could to Wash, and they just nipped the runner at first. The entire infield ran off the field, whooping and hollering and slapping each other as if they'd just won the World Series. The outfield ran in, too, and the bench was alive with chatter: "Attaway, Whiff!" "Good stretch, Wash!" "Tinker to Evers to Chance got nothin' on us!" Brandon lost the game, but it wasn't the usual blowout. And when Shoeless said, "See you at practice Monday — be early!" Jimmy sure would be, and he could tell by the look in his teammates' eyes that several of them would be, too.

After the game, Jimmy took Rhoda for what had become their regular "Coke walk," as they'd named it, down by the creek. She asked him about the game, and Jimmy explained it to her in great detail. He enjoyed talking to her about it. He was just telling her about how he'd aimed for Jawbreaker's head and made a perfect cut-off throw when Rhoda said, "That's enough," and pulled him into a long kiss. Eyes closed, Jimmy reveled in the feel of Rhoda's body pressed against his own. Her lips tasted like Coca-Cola with a little perspiration, sweet and tangy at the same time. They broke apart and Jimmy buried his face in her hair. *How could anything feel this good?* he marveled.

The second week, Joe focused on hitting. "I ain't gonna change your swings much," he told them. "I figure you're pretty much born with the swing that's best for you. Just wanna remind you of a few fundamentals." He stepped into the batter's box. "All right, here's my normal stance. Bat back, off the shoulder, legs shoulder-width apart, knees bent, elbows in. Now...." He stepped forward in the box towards the pitcher's mound. "Why would I move up in the box?"

"Hit a curve before it breaks," Jimmy answered.

Shoeless smiled at Jimmy. "Right. Now why would I move back in the box?" Shoeless backed up as far away from the pitcher as possible.

"Get more time to swing the bat," Whiff Wofford answered.

"You might try that, Whiff," Shoeless said.

"Yeah, Whiff!" Petie shouted.

"Don't make Whiff into a hitter, Mr. Jackson," Pepper called. "Then what'll we call him?"

Joe continued. "Now, when do we want to swing at a pitch we've decided to hit?" The players looked at him, confused. "The pitch is comin' at you, you seen it good as it left the pitcher's hand, when do you swing?"

"When the ball gets to the plate," Jack Washington offered.

"Wrong," Shoeless answered. "You wanna swing *just before* it crosses the plate, otherwise you'll be too late. You'll foul it off or miss it completely. I'd rather see you pull the ball foul than swing too late any day. An' if you find yourself hittin' it foul to the opposite side of the plate, swing earlier. Let's hit some!"

Murph McDowell and Red Roe ran out to the pitcher's mound with the bucket of balls, and the players lined up for batting practice. Shoeless stood near the batter's box, making small adjustments in the swings. He shouted "Now!" as each ball crossed the plate, pushing them to start their swings earlier.

Joe looked around. The whole team was standing nearby, watching each batter hit. Shoeless hated to see ballplayers standing around. "All right, we'll just take three at a time," he told them. "The rest of you go with Jimmy for candle practice."

"What the heck's candle practice, Mr. Jackson?" Pepper asked.

"Jimmy'll explain it," Shoeless replied, and turned his attention back to the batter.

"Into the dugout," Jimmy said, and he trotted over and ducked under the dugout roof. He opened a box of candles Shoeless had bought, stuck one in between the slats on the dugout bench, and lit it with a match.

"What the heck you doin', Roberts?" asked Jawbreaker. "It somebody's birthday?"

"All of ours," Jimmy replied. "The day we're born as better hitters. Mr. Jackson taught me this. It makes your eyes stronger so you can see the ball better when the pitcher throws it. An' it works."

"How do you know?" Petie asked.

"Because I've been tryin' it. Mr. Jackson's been givin' me lessons. He's been coachin' me private-like."

His startled teammates peppered him with questions.

"You're kiddin'?"

"Come on?"

"Since when?"

"How'd you get him to do it?"

"I asked him." A pinch of pride eased its way into his heart. He'd had an idea, had the courage to pursue it, and it had worked out. Not only that, but here he was acting like Shoeless Joe Jackson's assistant, teaching others what Shoeless had taught him. "Here's all you do." He covered one eye and stared at the candle. "That's all, just look at it. Your eye'll get tired, but keep at it. After 'bout ten minutes, I'll switch you to the other eye. Okay, line up, lookin' at the bench, it's darker that way."

Jimmy stuck candles all the way down the bench, positioned his teammates to look at them, instructed them to squat down or sit on the ground so their eyes would be level with the candle, and called out, "Cover your right eye." And ten young men started staring at burning candles in their dugout. When Shoeless glanced over, he couldn't help but smile. *Learnin' folks is kinda fun.*

After everyone had batted, Shoeless lined them up and told them about building up their muscles by holding the bat out straight from their sides for as long as they could, then switching arms, and doing the same thing on the other side. "It's not just about your muscles," he told them. "It's about trainin' your mind to concentrate. You cain't be distracted playin' ball. The minute you start thinkin' 'bout what you gon' eat for supper, or how you're gon' hit that curve the next time up, that's the exact moment somebody'll hit the ball right to you. You'll see, if you start thinkin' 'bout somethin' besides holdin' this bat, the bat'll start to droop, an' you'll have to focus on it to bring it back up again. You got to make your mind behave."

A week of batting practice under the discerning eye of one of the greatest hitters of all time had its intended effect. In Saturday's game against

Monaghan, Brandon scored five runs. And Murph held Monaghan to six runs, so that when Whiff Wofford came to bat in the bottom of the ninth inning, Jimmy and Whitey were on second and third base, and a hit would win the game. What's more, there was only one out, so Jack Washington had a chance to hit if Whiff didn't connect. He swung at the first pitch and missed.

"Back up in the box," Jimmy called from third base.

"You're the man, Whiff!" Whitey called from second base.

Whiff backed up in the batter's box, but the next pitch, a curve, fooled him completely and he swung and missed. In the dugout, Shoeless watched silently, letting Whiff's teammates provide the encouragement. He focused on Whiff, concentrating on his swing. Whiff let the next pitch go by, a ball, and the next, another ball. So the count was two-and-two. Whiff took a couple of hard practice swings. Stepping off third base, Jimmy actually began to believe Whiff might hit it, and Brandon might win!

Whiff did hit the next pitch. He hit it very hard, down the third base line, and Jimmy started running. But Whiff had hit it straight at the third baseman, who caught the ball and stepped on third base, leaving Jimmy staring back at the bag in disbelief. He was out, Whiff was out, double play, game over.

The Coke with Rhoda afterwards didn't taste as good as last week. The walk didn't seem as invigorating. Even the kisses by the creek didn't taste as sweet. "Sad about the loss, huh?" Rhoda asked.

"Yeah. I guess I thought if Mr. Jackson came on board, we'd magically just start winnin'." Jimmy scuffed at some dirt with his shoe.

"Sometimes magic takes a while, I reckon. Practice helps." She took Jimmy's hand. "Fer instance, there wadn' much magic about that kiss you just give me. Nothin' like how I felt last week. So I'd like a little practice." She looked frankly at Jimmy. "Come on, I won't bite you. You practice baseball, don't you? Well, let's practice kissin'."

"You cain't practice kissin'."

"Watch!" She moved her mouth towards Jimmy's and kissed him. Their tongues danced. After a long while, they separated.

Rhoda looked up at Jimmy, her eyes shining.

"What'd you feel?" she whispered.

"Magic," Jimmy whispered back. "Let's practice some more."

WHEN THE TEAM ASSEMBLED on the Brandon diamond Monday and began tossing baseballs to warm up, Shoeless could tell the throws didn't have the same pop. So he called them together. "You fellas look kinda mopey." The players looked down at the ground, out towards the outfield, anywhere but at Shoeless. "What's wrong?"

Jimmy finally answered. "Guess we thought we were finally gonna win one."

"Failin'? Is that what this is about, failin' to win?" He paused and spat some tobacco juice into the dirt. "Lord have mercy, boys, baseball is a game of failure. You play, what, a hundred and fifty-four games in the Big Leagues, and most teams lose more'n half of 'em. Heck, if you bat .333, you're only hittin' safe a third of the time. You wanna learn how to play baseball, you gotta learn how to deal with failure. That's what makes it such a good game for learnin' how to deal with life."

"So how do you deal with failure, Mr. Jackson?" Piggy asked.

Shoeless paused. This really was *the* question, wasn't it? If anyone could have been said to have failed, it was Shoeless Joe Jackson. Born with all that talent, and what had he done with it? Thrown it away. Or been careless with it and let it slip away. Whatever, he hadn't taken care of it as he should have, hadn't nursed it into its full bloom. No, he'd let somebody else's crookedness trip him up. He'd fallen on his face, hard, maybe harder than most. Talk about failure? How about the greatest natural hitter of all time banned from baseball for life?

But this wasn't the time or the place for Joe to deal with all that. These were young men on the threshold of life, looking to him for answers. He looked out at the faces: Petie, Piggy, Wash, Jawbreaker, Murph, Hal, Whitey, Red, Pepper, Jimmy, and the few backups. Eager. Expectant. Well, if he didn't have any answers, if he was still struggling with how to deal with his own failure, he would have to fake it.

He spat some juice. "I like to think of what Babe Ruth used to say. He said, 'Every strikeout gets me closer to my next home run.' You think you strike out a lot, Hal?" Joe asked. "Babe Ruth struck out one thousand, three hundred and thirty times." Hal's eyebrows raised in utter shock. "But he also hit seven hundred and fourteen home runs, which is still the record by a long shot. Might never be broken." Shoeless took his time, looking at them all slowly. "Yeah, we lost our last game. But the way I see it, that just brings us closer to our next win." He spat a final time. "Now let's practice. Wind sprints!"

Joe expected the usual groan. Wind sprints meant running from home plate to the centerfield fence, touching it, then running back to home. With Shoeless shouting at them the whole way, "Hustle! Hustle! Hustle!

Hustle is the name of the game!" But this time no one groaned or complained. They lined up around the plate and, at Joe's "Run!" they took off, full speed.

That week they did everything full out. Bunting, stealing, hitting, fielding, pitching, running. They fired the ball around the infield, each one trying to make his throw pop louder than the last. The outfielders threw at the cutoff man's head so hard most of them ducked and just let the ball go. Lots of times it took one bounce and landed in Petie's mitt at home or Whitey's glove at third. When someone booted a ground ball, instead of the usual "Shake it off!" he was just as likely to hear a teammate shout "Way to fail!" If someone swung and missed, he might hear "One step closer to a hit!" By the end of the week, they had even developed a kind of cheer. "We like to hit, we like to run, but most of all, failure's fun!"

"I'm so proud of them," Joe told Katie after practice that Friday. "They've taken one of life's biggest worries an' made a joke out of it. They don't wanna fail, of course, but they ain't afraid to fail. With that kind of attitude, we might just go out an' win every game left!"

"That just goes to show you the ol' sayin's true," Katie smiled back at him. "You want to learn somethin'? Go teach!"

"Whattaya mean?"

"Maybe you're not afraid to fail again, either."

Joe smiled at his wife. "Smart aleck!"

"Yep!" Katie shot back, with a self-satisfied grin.

That Saturday, Jimmy, as their captain, summoned them into a circle and thrust his hand into the middle. The others followed suit, stacking their hands on top of each other's. When all hands were in, they looked at each other, and a light began to dawn in one man's eyes, then another's, then another's. And then, as if by magic, they all threw their hands in the air and shouted, "Failure!"

The opposing players for Southern Bleachery were confused. "What'd they shout?" they asked each other. "Failure?"

It worked. The Braves played with an abandon that brought new power to their game. They beat out the bunt. They turned the double play. They hit the cutoff man. They lined their singles and hit their run-scoring fly balls. Because they knew it didn't matter if they didn't. No one was going to die. Shoeless wasn't going to yell at them. Their mother wasn't going to refuse to serve them supper that night. They were playing a game, a game they wanted to win for sure, but a game that would be followed by another and another and another, as long as they wanted to play ball.

In the seventh inning, a batter hit a fly ball to Piggy in right. Pepper, in center, ran over and could have caught it, but Piggy waved him off. He settled under the ball, raised his glove, and watched it descend. Then, at the last minute, he ducked, and the ball boinked him on the head. Pepper scooped up the ball and fired it back into the infield, holding the runner at second. Before returning to his position, Piggy said excitedly to Pepper, "Pep, it didn't hurt that much!"

"Way to fail, Piggy!" Pepper shouted to him. The rest of the team picked it up. "Good failure, Pig!" Jawbreaker called out. "Failure! Failure! Failure!" Jimmy shouted from left field. This carefree attitude completely un-nerved the Southern Bleachery team. They played terribly. They were the ones who failed, by the substantial score of 8-1.

After the game, Jimmy leaned back against the willow tree down by Longbranch Creek, Rhoda sitting inside his legs, snuggling against his chest. Her hair caressed his face. He closed his eyes. What a summer it had been. He had a girl in his arms. He was playing for a new team, the Brandon Braves, the worst team in the Western Carolina League. But they were now managed by Shoeless Joe Jackson himself. Who knew, they might turn out to be the best. The test would be the July 4th game next week against his old team, the Woodside Wolves. If they could beat them…. And if they couldn't, well, he was holding a beautiful girl, one who seemed to like him as much as he liked her, a mountain girl, different from any he'd ever known. Jimmy inhaled her hair with a deep breath. He turned her to face him. She looked at him tenderly. And together they practiced their magic.

CHAPTER 12

The morning of July 4, 1951, dawned bright and beautiful in the Carolina Piedmont. Puffy, white clouds bounced along an azure sky in a light breeze. The humidity was tolerable, which meant one could hope to get through the day without completely soaking shirt, pant, or dress. The air smelled cleaner, perhaps because the Reedy River wasn't filled with the detritus of a dozen mills. For once, the mills stood still, their incessant whistle silenced by the holiday.

American flags hung from every porch or window in Brandon village, sometimes accompanied by the Confederate stars and bars. Lemonade stands sprouted in front of several yards, while young boys threw taped baseballs in the street and young girls giggled and told each other secrets. In Brandon Park, the Braves baseball team gathered at home plate. In front of them, the Brandon Mill Concert Band, in white uniforms and sailor hats, stood in formation, awaiting the leader's baton. The slender wand flashed in the sunlight, the band struck up "Dixie," and off they marched towards Woodside Mill for the day's big game.

When they reached First Avenue, they found it lined with hundreds of fans, cheering, shouting, and waving small American flags. The boys cleared out of the street and stood aside, adding their shouts to the growing throng. The girls smoothed their dresses and waved modestly as the players passed. Men and women applauded lustily. The band struck up "Take Me Out to the Ballgame" to the crowd's loud cheers.

Jimmy and Shoeless were leading the team down the street. It had taken some persuading to convince Shoeless to walk with them. He had tried to just meet them at Woodside, but Jimmy had led a minor revolt of the team. "If you don't walk, we don't walk," he'd told Shoeless on behalf of his teammates. So Joe had walked. And now, when Jimmy sneaked a sideways glance at him, he saw Shoeless waving left and right, a big smile on his face.

As he met Jellycakes in his "office" at the Riverside Hotel, Howard called out "Morning, Willie" to the young boy throwing a taped baseball against the wall and catching the rebound.

"Get Mr. Howard a Coke, son," Jellycakes said. "An' quit that racket!"

"That's all right, Willie," Howard said. "I don't need one."

"Suit yourself," Jellycakes said, taking a sip from his own glass of Coca-Cola, which had been liberally sweetened with Southern Comfort. Since he'd started managing, Shoeless had looked a little more kindly on Willie's daily mission for "comfort" for his father. "What you got for me today, Mr. Howard?" Jellycakes asked.

Howard opened his wallet and forked over four $100 bills. "Mmm, mmm, Mr. Howard," Jelllycakes said, "You sho-boys confident today!"

"Hell, Jellycakes, you don't expect me to run scared just because Brandon finally won a game, do you?"

Jellycakes licked the end of his pencil and recorded the bet in his blue spiral notebook. "What about Shoeless, how you think he gon' be as a manager?"

"From what I hear, he's teaching those boys real well. But a manager's only as good as his players, I don't care who he is." Howard glanced around. "Thought I might see Mr. Dickerson here."

"Mr. Yancey done come an' gone."

"Collected his 'rent' already, eh?" Howard smiled.

Jellycakes winked. "Yessuh, the rent's in his pocket." He chuckled. "Said he'd see you at the park."

"Guess I'll see you there, too," Howard said.

"Yessuh, yessuh. Big day at the park, big day! Independence Day," he added wryly.

Howard looked at Jellycakes, nodded his understanding, and adjusted his hat on his head. "All right, see you later."

When Howard had gone, Jellycakes turned to his son. "You know what I mean by Independence Day, dontcha?"

"Yessuh," Willie replied. "That's when we got free from England."

"Whatcha mean, 'we'?"

"Us Americans."

"You free to use that toilet down the hall, or drink from that water fountain outside the door?" Jellycakes asked sharply.

"No, suh."

"That's right. Only the white folks got their so-called independence. The only thing we gonna be celebratin' today is either a Brandon victory or Woodside not makin' the spread." Jellycakes opened the cigar box by his side and deposited Howard's money. He pulled out a dollar bill and handed it to Willie. "Here ya' go, son."

"What's this for, Daddy?"

"Anything you want. You got the *freedom* to choose an' *I'm* the one who give it to you," he said with a wink.

When he arrived at Woodside Park, Howard noticed Yancey and Toby Gower were already in his box in the last rows behind home plate. It wasn't really a box in the usual sense. Howard had set aside a section of some fifteen seats for him and his guests, creating something of a private space separating them from the rest of the crowd. Halfway up the stairs, Howard took a moment to admire his ballpark. It was far-and-away the best in the league. Unlike Brandon, it had a complete outfield fence — no gaps where cows might wander in and disrupt the game. The freight train tracks did run past the fence in right field, which Howard didn't like. He thought it made the park seem rinky-dink and rural. But inside the park, the grass grew green and straight, the foul lines, batter's box, and on-deck circles gleamed white with new lime, there was not a pebble or stone in the infield, and the stands and bleachers still sparkled with new paint. It was a beautiful park, and Howard had spent the money to make it so. His love of the game demanded it.

As he entered his box, the Wolves were just finishing their pre-game warm-up. "How do, Howard?" Yancey greeted him, shaking his hand.

"Hello, Yancey," Howard said. "You're looking fine." Yancey was wearing a blue seersucker suit, white shirt, and red tie. It was July 4, after all, and Yancey was the consummate politician. Next to him, Toby Gower had already taken off his coat. "Hello, Toby." Howard shook Toby's hand and took off his own coat, carefully folding it and placing it flat on the empty seat next to him.

"Hello, Howard. Beautiful day for baseball, isn't it?"

"Couldn't be better. Where's your team?

"Marching here with our band. There they come now." He pointed to the left field fence, where a guard swung open a gate and the band and players marched onto the field to the tune of "Yankee Doodle."

"That's in honor of you, Worthy Opponent."

"I'm touched," Howard replied, placing his hand over his heart.

A sudden cheer rose from the crowd. Shoeless Joe had entered the ballpark. "Reckon some of your fans might be pulled in two directions, Howard," Yancey remarked. "Told you it'd be good for the game to have Shoeless back."

"And I told you to let me know when that resolution gets to the governor's desk," Howard answered back.

"You plannin' on interferin'?" Toby asked.

"Just monitoring." Howard smiled amiably. "I'm looking after the good of the game, and I'm not yet convinced that letting a confessed liar manage your team qualifies."

"As I recall, Shoeless retracted that confession," Toby said.

"After the fact."

"The whole thing's murky, Howard. Pretty clear that some of 'em cheated, but it's less clear that Shoeless did."

"He's still banned, Toby," Howard said.

"From *professional* baseball, which the Western Carolina League most definitely is not," Toby said smugly.

"Boys, boys, let's not spoil this beautiful day by arguin'," Yancey said.

A shapely brunette walked out to home plate as the band lined up behind her. "I love you, Mary Ella!" shouted Brownell, the leather-lunger, from his perch behind third base.

"Who's that?" Toby asked.

"Don't you recognize your own Miss Greenville?" Howard replied. "Beautiful, isn't she?"

"I suggested to Howard that it might add a little class to the game to have Miss Mickel sing," Yancey said.

Toby shook his head. "Lord, you politicians got more ways to get a vote than a dog has fleas!"

The Brandon Mill Concert Band struck up the National Anthem and Mary Ella began to sing. She was definitely a physical improvement over Velma Love, Brandon's singer; but they shared the same vocal defect: neither could carry a tune in a leak-proof bucket. "She'd shut up a screech owl" was the way Rhoda put it to Thelma and Katie in their bleacher seats by first base.

"I got me an idea." Thelma whispered to Katie. "After the ordeal."

Finally, Mary Ella finished torturing the assembled. As she strode off the field to a smattering of applause, the leather-lunger, called out, "I still love you, Mary Ella!"

"What's your idea?" Katie asked.

"Your husband willin' to put in a good word to Mr. Gower for a new singer?"

"Who?

"Rhoda, a' course. She's a regular songbird."

"Joe's always had a weakness for purty women," Katie smiled.

"Purty women who can sing!" Thelma crowed.

The Brandon Braves gathered around Shoeless in a circle. He looked around, spat out some tobacco juice, and began. "Aw right, boys, remember: this is just one game. You've had a bunch before this 'un, an' you'll have a bunch afterwards. Now, if you're battin', I want you to know where you're tryin' to hit the ball, want you to picture that ball line-drivin' over the infielder's head. In the outfield, keep those feet drawed in an' look lively. An' watch me. I don't know all these hitters, but Jimmy does — he pitched to 'em in practice an' seen 'em in games — , an' we done gone over 'em all, so I'll be positionin' you some." Shoeless looked at Jimmy and nodded. A couple of the players slapped their fists into their gloves and shouted, "Attaway, Jimmy, attaway!"

Shoeless shifted his wad of tobacco to the other side of his mouth. "In other words, know the situation. *Know. The. Situation.*" he emphasized. "Y'all done learned a lot these last few weeks. You can whup these boys. You got the talent to do it. More'n' that, you got the *desire*. But win or lose, I want you to go out there an' have fun! 'Cause you're playin' the greatest game there is!" It was here that Shoeless had wanted to stop, but he'd promised Jimmy he'd be part of the ritual. Feeling a little foolish, but feeling more than a little proud, he stuck his right hand into the middle of the circle. The rest of the team crowded round, stuck in theirs, one on top of the other, and, flinging their hands into the air above them, shouted, "Failure!" Then they ran into the dugout, laughing and slapping each other's butts.

"Play ball!" called out the home plate umpire, Frankie Thompson. And Pepper Forrester stepped into to face the Woodside pitcher, Curly Dawes.

He struck out. And so did the entire first-inning lineup. Over in the dugout, Shoeless withdrew a potato from his pocket and began peeling it. It wasn't going to be easy to beat Woodside, that much he knew.

In their half of the inning, Murph pitched well, too, getting the first two batters on weak ground balls. He walked the third one, however, and then Crusher Goodlett came to the plate. The outfielders didn't have to look at Joe to know they should back way up, and they did. "There ain't enough room for you to get far enough back, Roberts!" shouted Brownell from the stands.

Crusher launched a bomb towards Jimmy in left. The runner on first took off. Crusher started trotting down towards first base, convinced he'd hit it out of the park. But Jimmy timed his jump perfectly, and gloved the ball about eight inches above the left field wall. When he came back down, he fired the ball to Jawbreaker and started for the dugout. Crusher had stopped in his tracks halfway to second base. Jimmy gave him a big smile as he ran past.

In the bottom of the second, Jimmy came to bat. He took a few practice swings. He felt good. He felt loose. He looked down at Rhoda in the stands behind first base. She smiled at him, clapped her hands, and yelled, "Knock the crap out of it, Jimmy!" Jimmy ducked his head. He couldn't help but smile. What a mouth on that girl!

On Curly's third pitch, he connected. The ball cleared the right fielder's head and rolled to the wall. As he headed towards second, Jimmy noticed Crusher come over to shallow right to take the cutoff throw. That was usually the second baseman's job. But Jimmy didn't have time to ponder that, he was digging for third, trying for a triple. In shallow right, Crusher took the throw, turned, and fired. Jimmy saw third base about fifteen feet away. He was preparing to slide when he felt the baseball slam into the middle of his back. It stung so much, it knocked him forward. Frankie stepped out in front of the plate, waving his arms and shouting, "Take the bag, you're safe." Jimmy picked himself up and walked over to third base and stood on it. He looked back at Crusher, just taking his place at shortstop again. One look at the smile on his face and Jimmy knew he'd thrown at him on purpose. "Nice throw," he said sarcastically. Crusher tipped his fingers to his cap in a small salute.

As Jack Washington stepped to the plate, Jimmy looked into the dugout. Shoeless was nonchalantly peeling the potato. Wash walked into the batter's box, settled in, and took a called strike on the inside corner. Jimmy trotted back to the bag, touched it, and took his lead off third base for the next pitch. This time Wash swung and missed on a good curve ball. "Come on, Wash," Jimmy called from third. "Be a hitter, be a hitter!" *We gotta score*, he thought. *Me on third, no outs, just hit it to the outfield, Wash, that'll score me."* Jimmy looked over at Shoeless in the dugout. He had put down the potato and was making a series of gestures with his hands. Swiping his right hand across the brim of his hat, wiping the front of his shirt with both hands, two claps — nothing, just using some signals to set up the real sign. Jimmy almost looked back at the batter. *A ground ball to the right side might score me. Fly ball definitely will.* But just as he was turning his gaze back towards home plate, Jimmy saw Shoeless clap firmly twice, then slide the fingers of his two hands in between each other, squeezing them hard, then releasing them and going back to his brim for the meaningless signs. *Are you kiddin' me?* Looking for the sign from home plate, Wash, too, looked surprised. But then he tapped the bat hard on his cleats and stepped into the box.

Curly went into a full windup, ignoring Jimmy at third, concentrating on getting Wash out. As soon as he started his movement towards home plate, Jimmy took off. Curly had tried to waste a pitch inside to the right-handed hitting Wash, thinking he might get lucky and get him to swing at a ball. He might have, too, if Wash had been swinging. But Wash wasn't swinging, he was bunting. A squeeze play. The inside pitch was a batter's dream. He laid his bat on the ball, which dribbled up the third base line. Curly and the third baseman took a moment to realize what had just happened, but it wouldn't have mattered. Jimmy cruised past the ball on his way toward home and scored standing up. Wash beat out Curly's throw to first by a mile.

The Brandon bench erupted in whoops and hollers.

Brandon 1, Woodside 0.

Howard had jumped up from his seat. "Is he crazy?" he shouted at Toby. "Who calls a squeeze play with no outs in the second inning?"

"Shoeless Joe Jackson!" Toby replied with a chuckle. "The best manager in baseball!" Howard gritted his teeth and resumed his seat.

Wash died on first, and both lineups went up and down with no more damage until Crusher came to the plate in the bottom of the fourth. This time he left no room for heroic catches, pounding the ball out of the park in deepest center field. "Cain't catch that one, boys!" boomed out the leather-lunger. To rub it in, Crusher jogged the bases just a little too slowly. Game tied.

It remained that way through the rest of the fourth, the fifth, and the top of the sixth. But when Woodside batted in the bottom of the inning, they put men on second and third with only one out. Shoeless called time and signaled for Petie to come over for a chat. He draped his arm around his catcher and talked earnestly in his ear, walking both of them away from home plate. Then Shoeless slapped Petie's mitt, and turned back to the dugout. Petie resumed his place, squatting behind home plate and signaling Murphy for the next pitch.

When it came — a fastball, outside — Petie rose up, grabbed the pitch, and immediately threw towards third base, attempting to catch the runner napping. The ball sailed over Bill White's head into left field, and both runners took off running. But a baseball wasn't what had sailed over Whitey's head. The baseball rested in Petie's right hand, as he calmly stepped in front of home plate and tagged out the runner from third, then threw down to Whitey, who tagged out the runner coming from second. Two outs, double play, end of inning, game still tied.

The stadium erupted. Players from Woodside poured onto the field, most of them running right at the home plate umpire. "What the hell is goin' on?" screamed Rusty Peters, the Woodside manager.

"Dunno, Rusty," Frankie said calmly. "Your boys started runnin' and Petie tagged 'em out."

"With what?" shouted Rusty?

"With this." Frankie held up the baseball Bill White had tossed him at the end of the inning.

"What in tarnation did Petie throw into left field then?" Rusty asked.

"This," said one of his players, and handed Rusty the object he'd run into the outfield and retrieved.

"A potato?" shouted Rusty. "What's Petie doin' with a potato in his glove?"

Several Woodside players began shouting at Frankie.

"Come on, ump! That ain't baseball!"

"That ain't fair!"

"That's crazy, ump!"

"Don't let 'em cheat, Frankie!" yelled the leather-lunger.

Frankie ignored everyone. "Maybe Petie thought he'd get hungry," he said to Rusty, turning away.

"This ain't funny, Frankie!" Rusty ran in front of him, blocking his way. "You cain't throw a potato onto a ball field!"

"I'm not sure there's a rule about that, Rusty," Frankie said, his voice beginning to rise in anger.

"There sure as hell oughta be! Jackson's behind this, I guaran-damn-tee you! You oughta throw him outta the game."

"I'm gon' throw you out if you don't get out of my way an' get back to playin' baseball," Frankie threatened.

"Me? I ain't the one cheatin'! Throw him out!" screamed Rusty, sticking his face right next to Frankie's.

"Throw him out! Throw him out!" echoed the Woodside players.

By this time, dozens of Woodside fans had wandered onto the field, eager to join the argument. "Throw Jackson out! Throw Jackson out!" they chanted.

Frankie was encircled by an angry, swelling mob. He assessed the situation and decided it was serious. Frankie knew from experience that dangerous situations arose from time to time in textile ball. The fans were passionate, and there were no guards or fences to keep them off the field. A lot of pent-up frustration from their life-sapping jobs could easily translate into violence, if it got out of hand. He had umpired a long time and knew the situation called for action. So he took it, the kind of action umps in professional ball weren't allowed to take, but, then, this wasn't professional baseball.

Frankie reached into his umpire jacket, pulled out a .45 caliber pistol, and fired it three times, twice in the air, and then once in the ground to make Rusty and the fans back up. Back up they did. "Lissen," he said calmly, "There ain't nothin' says a player cain't throw a potato on the field. The inning's over!" He looked at the fans and waved his gun. "Y'all get your butts back in your seats!"

With some grumbling and mumbling, the fans moved back to their seats and the Woodside players took the field for the seventh inning. Frankie threw the baseball out to Curly and play resumed.

Howard Stone was apoplectic. "Was that the potato I saw Jackson peeling?" he shouted at Toby.

"Looked like it," Toby answered, trying not to smile too much.

"This horse-shit league!" Howard shouted again. "You call this baseball?"

"Textile-style," Toby responded matter-of-factly. "But it's still nine men to a team and twenty-seven outs, same as everywhere else."

"It is not the same as everywhere else, Toby!" Howard said. "Not by a long shot. Everywhere else, potatoes aren't baseballs!"

"Same way of keepin' score, too," Toby continued amiably. "One to one, top of the seventh." He sat back down and Howard, still fuming, did so as well.

Jimmy drew a walk his next time up. Clearly, Curly was rattled by what had happened. And Shoeless, like a good manager, decided to take advantage of that discomfort. When Petie made an out without advancing Jimmy to second, he gave Jimmy the steal sign. Taking his lead off first base, Jimmy was confident he could steal second. Jack Washington was batting, and Jimmy knew Jack would swing at a strike and miss on purpose to give Jimmy a little extra time to run to second. When the ball left the pitcher's hand, Jimmy ran flat-out for the base.

Ten feet from the bag he went into his slide. The throw from the catcher was high. Crusher, covering the bag, leapt into the air, caught the ball, and came down to tag Jimmy. Jimmy was safe, his right foot already resting on top of the bag. But when Crusher's foot landed, instead of placing it to the side of the bag, he slammed it into Jimmy's foot. The spikes on his shoe easily tore through the thin leather of Jimmy's. Jimmy felt a stabbing pain and cried out.

"Jimmy!" Thelma gasped.

"You did that on purpose, you sorry piece of pig poop!" Rhoda swore at Crusher.

Jimmy rolled over on his side, holding his foot. "Time!" Shoeless called from the bench, and he and several players ran out to Jimmy at second base.

Jimmy tried not to writhe — he was an athlete, after all, he wasn't supposed to show pain. "You all right?" Shoeless asked, bending over him.

"A little hurt, but it's okay."

Joe looked at the foot. A trickle of blood began to seep from Jimmy's shoe. "See if you can stand on it." He helped Jimmy to his feet. Jimmy winced when he tried to walk.

"Get a band aid from Mama Jackson!" Brownell yelled from the stands.

Frankie approached the group at second base. "How 'bout I get a pinch runner till I see if he can still play?" Shoeless asked him.

"Once he's out, he's out," Crusher Goodlett said from nearby.

Frankie gave him a hard look. "Who made you umpire?" He turned to Jimmy. "You okay, son?" Jimmy nodded. Frankie turned to Shoeless. "All right, Joe, get yourself a runner, tend to his foot, but he's gotta go back into the field to play when your inning's over."

"Thanks, Frankie. Help him," he said to Wash and Piggy. They slung Jimmy's arms around their necks and walked him off the field. Shoeless looked at Crusher, standing with his arms on his hips, a few feet away. He walked slowly up to him and stared him hard in the face. Then he lowered his eyes and spat. The tobacco juice landed squarely on Crusher's left shoe, leaving a brown stain. "Sorry," Shoeless said, then looked Crusher steadily in the eye, raised his head, and walked back to the dugout.

Shoeless told Jimmy to take his shoe off. "No," Jimmy said. "If I do, I might not get it back on."

Shoeless looked at him for a long moment.

"Whiff," he said. "Get some kind of ice from the ice-cream man, put it on his foot. Rest of you fellas, make this the longest inning you can. We gotta rest that foot."

Whiff took off running. Jimmy's teammates tapped him on the shoulder with their gloves. "Hang in there, Jimmy." "Shake it off." "We got 'em!" Piggy slid a bucket under Jimmy's foot to prop it up. "Take your time," he smiled. "We will."

What followed was one of the longest half-innings many had ever seen, especially considering it proceeded without another run scored or even another hit. The runners on first and second base called time-out to tie one shoelace, then called time-out to tie the other. The batters took so long between pitches, Frankie had to order them back into the batter's box or be thrown out of the game. Shoeless suddenly had an urge to talk to his batter, called time-out, spoke lengthily to him, started back to the bench, then had another idea, called time again, and returned for another lengthy conversation. By the time Brandon's next two batters made outs, Jimmy's foot had been packed in ice for a good twenty minutes.

It still hurt when he took his place in left field, but he could walk on it. Running would have been another matter, of course, but Murphy bore down and managed to get Woodside out in the bottom of the seventh with no balls hit Jimmy's way and no runs scored. Jimmy didn't bat in the eighth, so he could ice his foot further, but Woodside pushed across a run in the bottom of the inning. When Jimmy limped off the field for the top of the ninth, Woodside led 2-1.

Shoeless greeted him at the entrance to the dugout. "You cain't hardly walk."

"Long as I don't have to run," Jimmy replied, taking a seat on the bench.

"Well, you're battin' this innin', you might have to," Shoeless said. "I wanna see that foot."

The way he said it, Jimmy knew it would have been useless to protest. He slowly took off his shoe, wincing as he pulled it over the wound. He and Shoeless stared down at the sock where the blood had already hardened. Jimmy was glad he hadn't looked earlier, because the sight showed him just how badly he'd been cut by Crusher's spikes.

"Can you stand?" Shoeless asked him.

"I'd rather not," Jimmy muttered.

"Well, Frankie's a friend of mine, but I don't think our friendship extends to him lettin' you bat from a chair."

Jimmy smiled weakly. "Just wanna rest it until the last minute."

"You ain't gon' get that shoe back on," Shoeless said.

"I know. So I guess I'd better take the other one off, too." Jimmy smiled at him. Shoeless grunted, spat some juice, and turned to Whiff. "Get up there an' show me you don't want that name no more."

Whiff did. He didn't get a hit, but he put all that candle practice to good use, looked over every pitch carefully, and drew a walk. Jawbreaker walked, too, and it looked like Brandon had a good chance to tie or get the lead. But then Petie hit into a double-play, sending Whiff to third. Trotting back to the bench, Petie looked apologetically at Jimmy in the on-deck circle as he passed. "Next time, next time!" Jimmy said.

As Jimmy hobbled to the plate on one good foot, one bloody foot, and no shoes, Rhoda exclaimed, "Katie, he's shoeless!"

"That's bound to be lucky!" Katie enthused.

Brownell filled his lungs. "It ain't the shoes, Roberts, it's who's in 'em — an' who ain't!"

Shoeless trotted out to talk to Jimmy before he stepped in to hit. "What's the situation?"

"I figure I got one good swing."

Shoeless nodded. "Then it better be the first pitch. With Whiff on third, the pitcher'll be real careful not to get behind in the count. Probably throw a strike, and probably come right at you. Figure you'll be too weak to pull the ball; he'll come at you outside. Be a good pitch to hit to the opposite field."

Jimmy gave a quick nod and Shoeless headed for the bench. "Blow it past him!" Crusher urged Curly from shortstop. "No batter! No batter!" Woodside's catcher called out to the mound. Jimmy looked down behind first base. "You can do it, Jimmy!" Rhoda shouted, clapping her hands vigorously. "You the one! You're the one!" his mother cried. Whiff danced off third. "Bring me in, Jimmy!" he yelled.

In their box, Howard, Toby, and Yancey rose to join the rest of the crowd. Everyone sensed that this was *the* moment of the game. "You're lookin' mighty confident," Toby said to Howard.

"I got the lead with a cripple at the plate and two outs," Howard replied. He reached into his pocket and withdrew a long cigar.

"You aren't lightin' that now?" Yancey drawled.

"Why not?" Howard answered.

At the dugout, Shoeless stopped and narrowed his eyes to see the huge flame leap out of Howard's lighter. "Not so soon, Mr. Stone," he muttered. "You just might get bit yet."

"Come on, Jimmy, make me a happy man!" Toby called out.

Getting ready to step into the batter's box, Jimmy heard the shouts, the jeers, the whole cacophony of a baseball park in full volume at a climactic moment. He thought about Shoeless's instructions to hit the first pitch to the opposite field. That was indeed what the situation called for. But then he heard the far-off whistle of the daily freight train that passed by the fence in right. And he remembered a newspaper headline from the shrine to Shoeless Joe in the corner of his bedroom. Maybe there was another situation to consider. Jimmy smiled and stepped in to hit.

He narrowed his eyes. He knew he was going to see the pitch perfectly. He placed his left foot as far back in his side of the box as he could. Thank goodness Goodlett had spiked his right foot; he'd need the left one to push off with power. Striding forward to come down on his right foot would be painful, but Jimmy drove that thought from his mind. He set the bat back behind his shoulder and gripped it around the handle with his little finger, the way Shoeless had taught him. The sound of the cheering grew louder, but, focused as he was, it seemed far away. Curly looked in for the sign. Jimmy heard the faint whistle of the freight train approaching. *Come on, come on, throw it! Throw it now!*

Jimmy saw Whiff start down the line at third, trying to distract Curly. He saw Curly's right arm whip forward past his ear and his hand release the baseball. He saw the barely discernible spin: fastball. Coming towards the outside of the plate, but definitely a strike. And definitely hittable. Jimmy remembered all the hours of practicing to hit the ball *before* it reached the plate. He swung early. He swung with all the strength in his legs, hips, and arms, arms made more powerful by all those excruciating minutes of holding thirty-two ounces of wood straight out from his side. He swung with the accumulated knowledge of all he'd been able to absorb from the greatest natural hitter of all time. And he connected.

From the crack of the bat, Jimmy knew he had hit the ball on the sweet spot of the bat. He knew it was probably over the fence. But he wanted more! When his front foot came in contact with the earth, the pain shot through Jimmy like lightning. He crumpled to the ground. What had been the growing shout of a thousand voices suddenly morphed into a long "Oh!" Jimmy looked up from the ground, watching the right fielder race back towards the fence. When he saw the ball sail over his head, the fielder slowed his pace and just watched. Jimmy's teammates ran out of the dugout and watched. Willie and Jellycakes, Howard, Toby, Yancey, and a thousand fans all watched. And what they saw was one of those cosmic conjunctions of time and space that have the power to make us feel that there is, indeed, a divine spirit guiding our lives, and that it has a delightful sense of humor.

For as Jimmy's home run ball descended to the earth, the engine of freight train #309 sped by, followed by the coal car, followed by an open boxcar full of cotton. And into that boxcar the ball fell like a drop of rain into a pond: softly, barely making a ripple. The engineer, oblivious of the unexpected addition to his train, yanked on his whistle cord in greeting to the assembled fans and carried Jimmy's home run ball on down the tracks and into history.

Jimmy managed to get to his feet, despite the pain. As he limped around first base, he saw Rhoda throwing her arms out to him in ecstasy, and his mother and Katie jumping up and down, holding each other and screaming. As he rounded second, he smiled and touched his fingers to his cap at Crusher. When he looked up, he saw the entire Brandon baseball team lining the foul line from third base to home plate. As he hobbled past them on his way to home plate, they slapped him so hard on his butt, his arm, his back, even his head, that Jimmy stumbled and thought for a minute he might fall down again. But he regained his balance and limped across the plate. Then he was mobbed, the entire Brandon team jumping up and down on him and on each other, screaming and shouting and hollering, and hugging their crippled hero.

Unable to contain himself, Toby began pounding Howard on the back. He knocked the cigar right out of Howard's mouth, then bent down and picked it up. "I'll smoke this, if you don't mind!" he shouted at Howard.

The bottom of the ninth was really a foregone conclusion. Shoeless brought in Red in relief, and he mowed Woodside down, 1-2-3, sealing the Brandon Braves' upset of the Woodside Wolves, 3-2.

Walking home with Rhoda after the game, Jimmy couldn't help chuckling. "Happy 'bout your home run?" she asked.

"Yeah. But mainly I'm happy 'bout what inspired it."

"What's that?"

"'Member I told you 'bout my shrine to Shoeless? Well, there's a headline I got taped there. *Jackson Wins With Longest Home Run Ever.* He hit one way out of the park in Cleveland. But guess what? Mine still ain't hit the ground yet! It's on the way to Atlanta and who knows where else? An' that means I just done hit the longest dang home run ever!" He put his arm around her, pulling her to him. "An' shoeless, to boot!"

CHAPTER 13

Howard Stone was angry. And every time he looked down at the headline in Sunday's *Greenville News*, he got angrier. "BRANDON WINS WITH LONGEST HOME RUN EVER." He read the lead sentence: "Jimmy Roberts hit what is possibly the longest home run in the history of baseball yesterday, launching a rocket that dropped into the lead boxcar of the Southern Railway's freight train #309 and took off for Atlanta and parts unknown." He fumed, reached for the phone on his desk, and dialed. Sunday had been a long day for Howard, as he had waited for Monday to start his response to the humiliating loss his team had suffered on Saturday.

"Sports desk," drawled a hoarse voice on the other end.

"Let me speak to Charlie Deerhart," Howard said.

"Speakin'."

"This is Howard Stone."

"Oh, hey, Mr. Stone," Charlie said, jovially. "Sorry about that loss. Quite a game, though, huh?"

"From the looks of your article, you enjoyed it," Howard said flatly.

Charlie noticed the less-than-friendly tone. "What can I do for you, Mr. Stone?"

"It's not what you can do for me, Charlie. It's what you can do for baseball."

"Huh?"

"I'm talking about the manager for Brandon."

"Shoeless. I thought he managed a great game."

"I'm not questioning his skills, I'm questioning his status."

"Sir?"

Howard hated when southerners called him "sir.' The formality, coming from the mouth of a redneck reporter, sounded absurd. Clearly, he would have to be more direct. "His status as a confirmed cheater. His status as a man banned from baseball. Do we really want someone like "Shoeless" Joe Jackson leading our young men?"

"I don't know, sir, do we?" Howard's line of thought was confusing Charlie. He understood numbers and percentages and wins and losses, but moral questions were not his strong suit.

"No, Charlie, we don't!" Howard shouted into the phone, his exasperation showing.

"I'm not sure what I can do about it, Mr. Stone."

"You can write about it, Charlie. That's what you do, isn't it?"

"Yes, sir." This was firmer ground. "What should I write?"

Howard drew a deep breath before proceeding more calmly. "Write what you know, Charlie. They don't call it the Black Sox *scandal* for nothing, but people might be a little rusty on their facts. Remind them. And remind them of exactly what Commissioner Kennesaw Landis said when he threw Joe Jackson and the others out of baseball *forever*. It's a stirring speech, look it up. And while you're at it, remind yourself that I have some connections in New York City, and if your story should just happen to get the notice of *The New York Times*, who knows where it might take you, but probably further than Greenville, South Carolina." Howard paused. "Is that enough?"

"Yes, sir, Mr. Stone." Charlie now understood. "Thank you for the reminders."

"Just doing my duty as a citizen of this fine state and a life-long fan of baseball," Howard intoned piously.

"Yes, sir. Now about those connections — "

Howard hung up. His next call, to Rev Bob, was easier. A chance at a fire-and-brimstone sermon was an opportunity a preacher like Reverend Nally was not likely to pass up. The challenge, as usual, was to help him find the appropriate subject matter.

"Reverend Nally," Howard said, when Rev Bob had answered his phone. "This is Howard Stone."

"Well, hello, Howard. Got another trip for the choir comin' up this fall. Hope I can talk to you 'bout transportation again."

"You certainly can, Reverend." Howard smiled at his luck. It was trading time again. "And it so happens that you can do me a favor in return, much like the one you did me earlier this summer about the union."

"Glad to, Howard, glad to. I enjoyed givin' that sermon very much."

"I think you'll enjoy this one, too. I suppose you've heard Joe Jackson is managing the Brandon Braves?"

"Yes."

"What do you think about that, Reverend?" Howard asked solicitously.

Rev Bob paused for a moment. He knew what Howard probably thought about it, especially since Shoeless's team had just beaten his last Saturday. And he knew that he'd be better off to align his thoughts about

Joe with Howard Stone's. And he knew, given his earlier "work" for him, that Howard probably had the same kind of idea in mind to counteract Joe Jackson's success. Knowing all that, he answered smoothly, "Why I think it's a dang shame, Howard. A criminal like that, a man thrown out of baseball for cheatin', thinkin' he can waltz right back in an' start managin', just like that. It ain't right." Rev Bob stopped to give Howard his chance to agree.

"Glad to hear you speak like that, Reverend Nally," Howard said soberly. "I couldn't agree with you more."

"Now, mind you, Mr. Jackson's a God-fearin' man. But still, I don't like a man who runs a liquor store runnin' a baseball team full of a bunch of young men with unformed minds, boys who could easily be led astray by a liar an' a cheat." Rev Bob was warming to his topic now.

"We've got to look after our young people," Howard agreed. "Now, I don't want to tell you your business, Reverend, but do you think a sermon from someone as distinguished as yourself might be appropriate, a sermon that reminds people just how they ought to feel about a liar and a cheat in their midst?"

"Why, Howard, I think it would be completely irresponsible of me *not* to deliver such a sermon. An' the sooner the better."

"I'm so glad I called you, Reverend Nally. I feel better already. Why, if I were there, I might just lick thumbs with you!"

Rev Bob laughed. "Let's just say we did it over the phone, Howard."

"Done! Thank you, Reverend."

"No, thank you, Howard, for carin' so much about our community." He hung up, as did Howard, both men relishing how completely they understood each other and how such understanding would help them both.

Satisfied that Rev Bob understood, Howard left and drove to the Woodside building in downtown Greenville and the offices of Dickerson and Bradley, Attorneys-at-Law. Being a state representative did not pay enough to be a full-time job, so Yancey continued in his law practice. Howard parked his Cadillac opposite the Poinsett Hotel, crossed the street, and took the elevator to the seventeenth floor. The receptionist greeted him, buzzed Yancey to let him know Howard Stone was here, then ushered him into the office. Yancey came around from behind his desk. "Mornin', Howard. What brings you out in this heat? Must be somethin' urgent."

"It is," said Howard, placing his hat on the coffee table and taking a seat on Yancey's small couch, where the fan could more easily find his face. He paused for a moment to let his perspiration cool. "How's that resolution about re-instating Jackson going?"

"The Senate passed it," Yancey said proudly. "It's on my desk now, waitin' to go to the governor for his signature."

"Make sure it stays there, Yancey."

"Now, Howard, I know you're none too happy about losing that game last Saturday, but aren't you over-reactin' just a little? Why should you care whether Shoeless gets reinstated into baseball so he might qualify for the Hall of Fame?"

"It's the principle of the thing."

Yancey chuckled. "I never knew you to be a man of principle, Howard."

"My 'principles' pay for your goddamn elections, Yancey!" Howard said hotly. "Or do you want me to stop my donations?"

Yancey paused, surprised. "You really mean it, don't you?" Howard's answer was a firm stare. "Just because he's managing Brandon doesn't necessarily mean they're goin' to win the championship, you know."

"I prefer not to take that chance. Let me be clear, Yancey." Howard rose from the couch and stepped towards him. "I am winning this championship and no dumb-hick linthead and a lying cheat are going to stop me."

Yancey mused, "Gettin' that resolution signed by the governor would make me a mighty popular man."

"Popular enough to win without my money?"

"Which you'll continue to provide even after you leave town?"

"Of course, Yancey," Howard replied cynically. "You stay in this dung-heap as long as you want, but I'm getting the hell out!" Howard gave Yancey a hard look, placed his hat back on his head and marched out the door.

As he rode down the elevator, Howard's countenance softened a little. He enjoyed making demands, a privilege money often afforded him. Especially with politicians, whom he knew to be desperate, weaseling creatures who, in their effort to please anybody who could vote, often left themselves vulnerable to the muscle money provided. Walking through the glass doors and down the steps into the sunshine, Howard felt good about all he had accomplished that morning. But he had one more appointment to make, an appointment he was not looking forward to, so he decided to enter the Poinsett Hotel and treat himself to a shoeshine first.

Howard loved getting his shoes shined. He enjoyed sitting up high above the shoeshine man, like some sort of royalty. He liked the pressure of the shoeblack's fingers through his shoes as he applied the polish in quick, deft strokes. He enjoyed the back-and-forth of the cloth behind his heels, and, especially, the sharp snap when the shoeblack yanked it off the shoe.

Howard sat back and closed his eyes as Henry, the shoeblack, began his magic. After a while, his thoughts drifted to his father. He remembered how, as a boy, he'd watched his father get his shoes shined. "A shoeshine shows success," his father had instructed him. "A businessman with a shine on his shoes is a businessman to be reckoned with."

"I'm a man to be reckoned with, Daddy," Howard muttered out of his daydream.

"What's that, Mr. Stone?" Henry asked. Howard opened his eyes. "Did you say sumpin'?"

"No, Henry." Henry yanked off the cloth with a satisfying snap. "They look good." Howard pulled a five-dollar bill from his wallet and handed it to Henry, who reached into his box for change. "That's all right, keep it."

"Thank you, Mr. Stone!" Henry smiled a toothy smile.

"You're welcome, Henry." Howard enjoyed being a generous tipper, and he recognized that part of his enjoyment was that his father had been such a tightwad.

Howard drove to his least favorite place in Greenville. As he parked his Cadillac, the noise from the mill rumbled in his ears. How he hated that noise and all it represented. How he longed for the salubrious sounds of a northern city. His connections with Socks Singleton just might get him back north, where he belonged. But Socks' admonition rang in his ears. "The Yankees like winners." Howard was determined to be one.

He moved quickly up the stairs to the weaving room and hurried across to Waddy's office. As expected, he found Waddy with his feet up on his desk, doing nothing. He quickly sprang to attention when Howard entered.

"Mr. Stone!"

"Hello, Waddy. Hope I'm not disturbing you."

"No, sir, no, sir," Waddy said, quickly moving some papers on his desk to simulate work. "Nothin' that cain't wait for you, Mr. Stone. Sit down, please." Waddy gestured to a cane chair opposite his desk. Howard closed the door, lowering the noise from the looms to a dull roar, and sat down. Waddy also sat, and waited to hear what had prompted this unusual visit to the inside of the mill.

"It's about Thelma Roberts." Waddy sat forward. Why would Howard Stone want to talk about her? "I understand you and she have become 'friends.' " Howard looked at Waddy, who stared warily back.

"Yes, sir, Thelma's a right-good worker," Waddy offered.

"I'm sure she is. And I'm sure she's good at other things, too." Howard eyed Waddy pointedly, making sure he understood.

Waddy swallowed. How did Howard know about him and Thelma? He had been extremely careful, at her insistence. She hadn't agreed all that many times in the first place. But somehow Howard had found out.

Howard was enjoying watching Waddy squirm. It hadn't been that hard to learn what was going on. When Waddy had told him he was promoting Thelma, Howard naturally had wanted to know why. He hadn't bothered asking Waddy, of course. He was too good a student of human nature to waste his time with that. But a co-worker of Thelma's, one who perhaps had wanted that promotion herself, was only too happy to let Howard know the truth. "Waddy," Howard continued, getting down to business. "What consenting adults do with their spare time is none of my business. But I was just wondering: does Jimmy know?"

Waddy was taken aback. "I ... uh...."

"I didn't think so. Don't you think he should?"

Waddy was stunned. Heck, no, he didn't want Jimmy to know. He'd be really angry, maybe mad enough to come after Waddy. What would be the point of telling the son of the woman he was sleeping with about what his mama was up to? Yet that seemed to *be* the point Howard was making. "Well, now, Mr. Stone, to my way of thinkin,' Jimmy might not take kindly to knowin' what his ma an' me been doin'. Might upset him some."

"Waddy, I believe it might upset him a lot. Might weigh on his mind, distract him, make him not care about things. Things like winning baseball games." Howard let that thought sit there while he looked intently at Waddy.

Waddy leaned back in his chair. So that was it. "I guess Jimmy might find out some way," he said carefully. "But how?"

"That's up to you, Waddy. I'm sure you can figure it out. Telling him's the simplest way, but I understand if you're reluctant to do that, given how upset Jimmy's bound to be. I do know that these kinds of secrets always seem to get known, sooner or later. And I prefer this one be known sooner. Definitely before next Saturday's baseball games." Howard rose, and so did Waddy. "Do we understand each other, Waddy?"

"Yes, sir," Waddy answered submissively.

"I'll see my way out," Howard said and promptly left.

Waddy leaned back in his chair and considered his problem. How do you let the son of the woman you're sleeping with find out you're sleeping with her? And how do you make sure he doesn't come after you once he does?

Back in his office, Howard lit a cigar. He didn't usually like to smoke this early in the day, but he'd accomplished a lot that morning, so he decided to treat himself. He wasn't sure what Jimmy's reaction would be when he heard the news. It might be that he and his mother would talk it out, come to some kind of understanding, and Jimmy would be clearheaded enough to play good baseball come Saturday. But it was a good card to play and it cost him nothing to play it. Besides, he remembered how angry he'd been at his own father when he'd found out about all the women he was running around with. Why wouldn't Jimmy feel the same way?

As he tasted the pungent tobacco in his mouth and let it out in a long, slow gust, Howard felt content about all the disturbances that were about to descend on this sleepy southern town he was forced to call home. *Puppet Master of Greenville,* he thought to himself. He took another pull on his cigar, looked down at his brightly polished shoes, and smiled.

That evening, Shoeless Joe, Jimmy, and Katie sat on the Jackson porch, enjoying some lemonade. Joe had invited Jimmy over after practice to show him something. The "something" turned out to be an old newspaper headline from Cleveland *Plain Dealer*, which touted *Jackson Home Run Longest Ever*. They compared it with the story from that morning's *Greenville News*. "Reckon you done outhit me, Jimmy," Shoeless said.

"Hear, hear!" Katie said, raising her glass of lemonade.

"In honor of my teacher," Jimmy said, raising his own glass.

"Hear, hear!" Katie said again, and they all drank.

"Now tell me true, Jimmy," Shoeless said. "Were you really tryin' to hit it onto that train?"

"Sorta. I knew about your home run." He hesitated, then decided to plunge ahead. "You see, Mr. Jackson, I've got a kind of shrine to you in the corner of my bedroom. Just some articles about you, an' pictures, an' statistics. I don't know, I just like to look at it every day, remind me of my dream."

Katie could tell that Joe was touched. "An' what dream is that, Jimmy?" she asked.

"To make good in the big leagues, like Mr. Jackson," Jimmy replied softly. He quickly changed the subject. "Now, 'bout my home run. I heard the train whistle an' knew it would be passin' by. I had a good guess what the pitch would be. I knew the situation, an' swung!" He took a sip of lemonade. "Now, you tell me something true, Mr. Jackson. What is the real story about how you got your nickname?"

Katie looked at her husband. She knew what he was thinking. She knew that he really didn't like this story, so it would be a test of how fond he'd become of Jimmy if he told it. She waited. Joe's answer, or whether he'd answer at all, would also tell her a lot about how his feelings about baseball might have changed.

"It ain't much of a story," Joe began, and Katie smiled and sat back. "I'd bought myself some new spikes in, what year was it, Katie?"

"1908, Joe. In a game against the Anderson Electricians."

"Long time ago," Joe mused. "Ain't it funny how some things just stick to you?" He swirled the lemonade in his glass around a few times. "Anyway, them spikes were killin' me during the game — I hadn't had time to break 'em in. So I just took 'em off when I came up to bat. Turns out I hit one purty deep to right an' I was tryin' to stretch it to an inside-the-parker, an' some fan yelled at me as I was roundin' third, 'Run you shoeless sonofabitch!' "

Jimmy laughed. "That's how it happened?"

"Well, Scoop Latimer of the *News* picked it up in the paper the next day, that helped it stick."

"It's a great nickname," Jimmy said enthusiastically. Joe's face darkened. "Isn't it?"

"Joe doesn't like it," Katie said.

"Why not?"

Katie looked at Joe. He was the one to explain. "Everybody thinks I got that name because I was too poor to buy shoes," he said. "Or too dumb to wear 'em. Either way, it don't reflect good on me." Jimmy was shocked. He'd always loved the name. Joe's face hardened. "I've made Katie promise they won't put that on my tombstone. You make sure she keeps it," he said to Jimmy.

"No need to, Joe. I know how you feel about it," Katie said slowly.

"An' if she goes first, I'm countin' on you, Jimmy," Joe said.

"Yes, sir," Jimmy vowed solemnly. "I won't let it be on your tombstone, if I can help it."

A silence settled over them. Their jovial mood had disappeared. "More lemonade?" Joe asked, and got up and went to the kitchen before anyone could answer.

"Hope I didn't upset him," Jimmy said.

"He's fine," Katie reassured him. "He likes you, Jimmy. I'm so glad you showed up. You've given Joe somethin' to look forward to every day besides rows and rows of liquor bottles. Thank you." She reached out and placed her hand on top of Jimmy's. He ducked his head in gentle embarrassment.

"I'm the one who's grateful," he replied. He paused. He wanted to ask a question, especially since they'd been talking about Shoeless's past, but he also was afraid to ask. Finally, he said, "Mrs. Jackson, how come they always say Mr. Jackson is a 'confessed liar'? I thought he was declared innocent by a jury."

Katie hesitated. She wanted Jimmy to know the truth, but there was a lot of truth to know. "It's complicated."

"You don't have to tell me if you don't want to," Jimmy said quickly.

"I'd be happy to tell you, Jimmy. But I think I'll leave it up to Joe."

"Oh, I'd never ask him. Besides, it don't matter none. I'm just happy to know him an' happy he's helpin' me learn to play better."

"It might matter some day, Jimmy. An' when it does, Joe'll tell you the truth. One thing he's lousy at is lyin'."

"Yes'm, I know that."

"I want to show you somethin'," she said and popped up from her chair, went inside for a brief moment, and returned holding a newspaper clipping. "Did you happen to see this piece in the paper about a resolution 'bout Joe?"

"Resolution?"

Katie showed him the clipping, which Jimmy read as she explained it to him. "They're tryin' to get Joe back into professional ball. Gonna get the state behind it, get politicians petitionin' for it."

"That's great!"

"I know it. But Joe doesn't want anythin' to do with it."

"He doesn't?"

"He's afraid of stirrin' up the past, of people gettin' all worked up about what they say he did or didn't do, callin' him a liar an' a cheat an' what-not!" Katie had to take a moment to calm herself. The injustice of what had happened to Joe, one of the nicest, most honest people she'd ever known, never failed to rile her. "If Joe would just get behind it, if we could get us some publicity, let people know about this resolution.... See!" she confirmed. "You didn' even know about it." She pointed to the newspaper in Jimmy's hand. "It's just a little announcement. No wonder most people missed it."

He handed the clipping back to her. "I wish I could think of a way to help, Mrs. Jackson."

"I do, too, Jimmy. But that's why I told you. I figure two brains workin' on it are better'n one." She looked at Jimmy, emotion welling in her eyes. "I agree we don't want 'Shoeless' on his tombstone. But it would be awful, simply awful, if he was to go to his Maker draggin' that chain as a cheater."

Jimmy didn't know much about that chain, and he certainly didn't understand all the links involved. But, looking at Katie Jackson, seeing the pain spread over her beautiful face, he knew he had to help. "I'll think on what to do, Mrs. Jackson," he said softly. Her eyes brightened in silent gratitude.

"Here go!" Joe said, coming onto the porch with the pitcher of lemonade. Katie quickly tucked the newspaper clipping into her dress pocket. Joe re-filled everyone's glass and sat down. He had recovered from the sour mood a discussion of his nickname always visited upon him. He picked up the *Plain Dealer* headline, looked at Jimmy, and held it towards him. "You might like this."

"Oh, no, Mr. Jackson, I couldn't," Jimmy protested.

"For your shrine. An' why don't you put this-here one from today's paper alongside it? You an' me up there together. Home run kings!"

Jimmy was shocked. He and Shoeless Joe Jackson ... together? "You sure?"

"He's sure!" Katie answered. She looked at her husband with pride. She was so happy he had found a reason to care about baseball again. She raised her glass. "A toast!" she exclaimed. Joe and Jimmy raised their glasses. "Greenville *boys* makin' good!" They smiled and clinked glasses.

Waddy worried the rest of the week about how to tell Jimmy. What could he possibly say? "Jimmy, your mother an' me have been shackin' up together, just thought you'd like to know." The more he tried to find the right words, the more he realized he couldn't do it himself — at least, not face to face. And then there was the matter of what Jimmy might do to him. Waddy was a big man, he wasn't worried about holding his own in a fist fight. But what if Jimmy "accidentally" got Waddy's arm caught in a loom? What if he loosened the bolts on Waddy's tires? Waddy's imagination conjured up numerous "what if's," creating a strong desire to run. Or at least schedule his vacation now! But that wasn't an option. Not with Howard Stone calling the shots.

The only alternative that made sense, Waddy finally decided, was that he wouldn't tell Jimmy. He'd let him discover the affair for himself. How he'd let him discover it was not a lesson in subtlety, but this wasn't a time for that. Waddy would pay Willie Jones a dollar to give Jimmy a note at the end of baseball practice that Friday. The note would read: "Want to know where your mother goes at night? Try the Riverside Hotel." There was one other problem Waddy had to overcome. Jimmy practiced ball until about 6 p.m, then he was due for his shift at Brandon at 10 p.m. But Thelma worked until 10 p.m. Jimmy couldn't see his mother and Waddy together if she were getting off at the same time he was starting. Waddy, however, had the power to change workers' shifts. So that Friday he'd tell Thelma she'd start work at noon and get off at eight, when he'd meet her at the regular pick-up spot.

On Friday, the two hours between six, when Jimmy got the note, and eight, when Thelma got off, were excruciating for Waddy. Jimmy might storm into the mill and confront his mother, creating a scene. Thelma might name Waddy right then as the author of the note, and then there'd they'd be, looms booming and tempers flaring. From his car, Waddy nervously watched the entrance to the mill. If Jimmy showed up, he'd take off. After all, Howard Stone hadn't said Waddy had to be there, just that Jimmy had to find out. But Jimmy didn't come, so, a little after eight, Waddy picked up Thelma at the edge of Woodside village and they set off for the Riverside Hotel.

Waddy drove cautiously, thinking Jimmy might jump out from behind a car with a crowbar or something. Thelma slouched down in the seat to avoid being seen. "What's wrong with you?" she asked.

"Whattaya mean?" Waddy answered.

"You're usually in a right hurry to get to the hotel."

"Just enjoyin' the summer night," Waddy said. Thelma looked at him curiously. Waddy was not one for enjoying nature.

Her curiosity increased when he parked the car and began hustling her across the street. "Now you're in a hurry!" she remarked.

"'Course," Waddy answered vaguely, looking all around.

"You're a nervous Nellie tonight, Waddy. Fine, then, let's both be in a hurry an' I can get on back home."

A mere forty-five minutes later Waddy dropped Thelma back at Woodside. She'd barely closed her door when he gunned his engine and sped away. Thelma looked after him. *Somethin' ain't right,* she thought.

Jimmy was waitin' when she entered the house. "Shouldn't you be in bed? You oughta lay down some before you haveta work. Big game tomorrow." She tousled Jimmy's hair, but he jerked away. "What's wrong?"

"Where were you tonight, Mama?"

"Round an' about," Thelma answered warily. "It's beautiful out."

"'Round an' about the Riverside Hotel?" He looked at her coldly.

"Why do you ask that, Jimmy?"

"I saw you. I saw you come out with him, Mama." Jimmy began to breathe faster.

"I see." Thelma sat down on the couch and looked at her son.

"You weren't in there all that long." Jimmy's voice was filled with anger.

Thelma ignored the snide remark. "Jimmy, sit next to me an' let's talk about this."

"I don't want to sit next to you!" Jimmy said fiercely.

"Mind if I ask how you found out?"

"I got a note at the ball field after practice." Jimmy handed her the sheet of paper from his pocket.

Thelma looked at it closely. "Waddy," she muttered.

"Why would he want me to know?"

"I have no idea."

"How could you do this, Mama?"

Thelma took a long breath. She knew why she'd done it. When Jimmy had been fired, she'd had no idea how long they might have to live on her salary alone. So she'd found a way to increase it. Life in the mills sometimes forced hard choices on you. She wasn't proud of what she'd done, but she'd done it out of love for her son and concern for their future. She could explain all that to Jimmy, but she knew if she did, she ran the risk of making him feel like it was his fault, like he'd made her do it by being fired. So, praying for God to forgive her, she lied. "I wanted a man," she said simply.

"But you're not married!" Jimmy cried. "It's a sin!"

"I reckon."

"You reckon? You're the one who's always tellin' me to follow the Good Book." Jimmy turned away, running a hand through his hair.

"Don't forget, your daddy an' me weren't married, neither." This stopped Jimmy cold. His shoulders sagged. Thelma immediately regretted her remark. She didn't want to defend herself. She didn't want to argue. She just wanted to hold her son, but she couldn't. Finally, she said, "Jimmy, I cain't defend my actions. Or, I won't."

He turned to face her. "Are you gonna stop?"

Thelma considered for a moment. She liked her new job, but Waddy could demote her any time. Things were different now, though. Jimmy was working, so, as long as she didn't get fired, they'd be all right. For weeks she had been giving Waddy a multitude of excuses, denying him whenever possible. And she'd dealt with her shame by simply ignoring it, pretending that her baths washed it all away. She had always believed that good things could come from bad. If conceiving Jimmy out of wedlock had been bad, look at the good person who had come from it. If it was "bad" that Jimmy had discovered her secret, look at the release it might now bring her. Her spirits actually lifted from the clarity of her answer. "Yes, Jimmy, I'm gonna stop."

Jimmy turned and left the house. Thelma let him go, knowing time and distance were what he needed at that moment.

At work that night, Jimmy tried not to think about it, but his mind wouldn't let him. He remembered the confusion he'd felt on first reading the mysterious note. His mother? The notorious Riverside Hotel? Then fear. Was she in danger? Then anxiously waiting for 8 p.m. That Friday morning, his mother had told him she'd be getting off at eight. Jimmy had proposed a late supper, but his mother had demurred. When he'd received the note, he'd guessed why. Towards the end of his mother's shift, Jimmy had walked to the Riverside and stationed himself across the street, hoping she wouldn't show up. When she had — with Waddy! Her supervisor! The man who'd fired him! — he'd become sick to his stomach. He'd watched the prostitutes lingering outside, seen the men walk up, some hurried and furtive, others calm and commanding, all of them disappearing inside, where his mother was. Finally, overwhelmed with anger, he had raced home. And he'd confronted his mother, only to find she'd done it because she wanted a man!

That night, kneeling beside her bed, Thelma prayed. She could only imagine Jimmy's confusion as he tried to work. She wished he could pray, but Jimmy had basically given up on God when his father left them. Thelma, however, had not. *Dear God, forgive me for lyin' to Jimmy. An' forgive me for what I done. You know what was in my heart when I done it. I'll leave it up to You to judge me. Lord knows, I've judged myself plenty. Only thing is, God, if You can see your way to it, please help Jimmy not to judge me. Please help him to forgive. In Jesus' name I pray, amen.* Thelma climbed into bed. She knew she was in for a restless night.

In his mansion on the other side of town, the man who had set all this anguish in motion slept peacefully, his head filled with nothing but self-satisfied dreams.

CHAPTER 14

Howard Stone's instinct that Jimmy's finding out about his mother and Waddy would cause him to perform poorly in Saturday's game could not have been more accurate. Jimmy showed up yawning. After work, he hadn't wanted to go home, so he'd spent the five hours until game time wandering around Woodside, then Brandon, then walking downtown, then taking the trolley anywhere it would go. "Wake up, Roberts!" Shoeless had barked at him more than once during warm-up.

With the game underway, Jimmy tried not to look behind first base, where he knew his mother, Rhoda, and Mrs. Jackson would be seated. But he couldn't avoid it. And if his eyes weren't drawn there, his mind certainly was.

In the top of the third, Jimmy was on first after drawing a walk. He heard Rhoda cheering him. "Steal the base, steal the base!" He took his strides off the bag. But where was his mother's voice? She wasn't even going to cheer for him? "Get back!" Piggy called from the coach's box. Too late. The Dunean pitcher fired to first, and Jimmy was tagged out before he could take a step.

In the fifth, he misplayed a fly ball into a triple. In the seventh, he overthrew the cutoff man to let in another run. At the plate, he failed to connect with the ball, called out on strikes two times without even swinging. Even so, in the ninth inning, the Braves staged a rally and there was a man on third with a chance to tie when Jimmy came to the plate.

Batting left-handed, he could sense his mother behind his back in her seat near first base. He wondered if Waddy was in the stands. Would she keep her word and break it off? He looked at the dugout and saw Shoeless going through a series of movements with his hands. *He's got big hands,* Jimmy thought. He stepped into the box and watched Jawbreaker dance off third. *Should I go home after the game? I cain't stay away forever.* The pitcher wound up and threw. All of a sudden Jawbreaker broke for home as fast as he could. The pitch crossed the plate, the catcher stepped out with the ball, Jawbreaker tried to stop running and couldn't, and the catcher tagged him out. "Didn't you see the sign?" Jawbreaker shouted. Jimmy stood there, staring blankly. He'd missed the sign for the squeeze play. Brandon's rally was dead. They lost the game, 6-5.

Howard Stone enjoyed reading the sports page of *The Greenville News* immensely that Sunday, certainly compared with how he'd felt reading the same paper a week before. Woodside had won and Brandon had lost. But it was the reality behind the scores that brought a smile to Howard's face, as he sipped black coffee in his well-appointed living room. Howard snapped the paper and folded it in half.

On the top fold of the paper was an article by Charlie Deerhart that couldn't have pleased Howard more if he'd written it himself. Under the headline *What Would Landis Say?* Charlie not only quoted the former commissioner's letter banning the infamous Chicago Eight forever, he laid particular emphasis on the line "a bunch of crooked players and gamblers." He had used it to launch a warning about the possible unhappy consequences of letting a confessed liar like Shoeless Joe Jackson manage "our impressionable young men on the cusp of choosing the straight path or the crooked." *That's almost poetic!* Howard thought, as his smile morphed into a chuckle.

Another article in the sports section also pleased Howard. Under the headline *Shoeless Joe Resolution In Trouble*, Howard read how Yancey was re-assessing his interest in supporting the House of Representatives resolution asking the Commissioner of Baseball to reinstate Shoeless. "I have heard from various constituents that supporting a confessed cheater might not be in the best interests of baseball," Yancey had been quoted as saying. "So I am revisiting the issue with my colleagues and with the governor."

Howard laid the paper aside and turned his thoughts to the other initiative he had put into play. He glanced at the Seth Thomas clock on his marble mantelpiece. Close to 10:30. About the time Rev Bob's sermon would begin at the Brandon Baptist Church. Howard was rather pleased with Reverend Nally. He had dropped by yesterday to give Howard a copy of his sermon and to tell him some good news. Not only would he be delivering a sermon whose reference to Joe Jackson was unmistakable, but he had arranged with his friend, Wendell Manning, pastor of Brandon Baptist, to invite him as a guest preacher that Sunday. So none other than Shoeless Joe Jackson himself would be in the congregation listening to the sermon. Howard almost wished he could be there to see Jackson sitting among his friends and neighbors in public humiliation. But he hadn't set foot inside a church in years.

Joe hadn't paid much attention when Pastor Manning had introduced a "special guest" from the Woodside Baptist. He hadn't even thought much about it when Reverend Nally had started his sermon with a quotation from Proverbs 6 about "the six things doth the Lord hate, chief among them lyin'." But he began paying closer attention when Reverend Nally started talking about the terrible consequences of lying and cheating, as exemplified by the story of Jacob and Esau.

"Jacob deceived Isaac to steal the blessing that Isaac intended to give to Esau," Rev Bob intoned. "Dressed up in goat's skin so his blind father would feel his hands and think they were Esau's. Now that's deception, my friends. Pretendin' to be one thing when actually you're another. An' where did that deception lead, where did that lyin' take Jacob an' his whole family? Down the road to further deception, that's where. Lyin' is the first sin in the Bible. That snake lied to Eve, an' all the rest followed. Revelation 21:8: 'All liars will have part in the second death, the lake of fire.' Yes, sir, lyin' will lead you to that lake of fire just as sure as three strikes will lead to an out!"

Shoeless raised his head. That was a curious comparison, he thought, bringing baseball into the story of Jacob and Esau. And was Reverend Nally looking in Joe's direction as he spoke?

"Let's look at what happened to Jacob," Reverend Nally went on. "Let's look what happened to the cheater. First, he tricks Esau outta his birthright by tradin' him food for it. Then, he tricks him outta receiving Isaac's blessing. Then Jacob's got to leave home for fear Esau might kill him. Had to leave his comfortable home, leave his mother an' his father, an' climb all over the rocky slopes of Canaan. Jacob must have felt pretty lonely when he lay his head down on a stone that night, far from the comforts of home. An' for what? A birthright."

Reverend Nally paused. Joe shifted in his seat. He saw Katie give him a sideways glance. He heard the shuffling of other parishioners as they awaited Rev Bob's message.

"What have we done for a birthright, my brothers an' sisters? What have we coveted so much that we would lie an' cheat to get it? A new job? A little more money? A championship ring?" Joe looked sharply at the pulpit. There was no question Reverend Nally was looking at him now. And he could sense that many in the congregation were beginning to glance his way as well.

Rev Bob lowered his voice to almost a whisper. "An' what was the result of all this mendacity? *More* lies. *More* deception. *More* work of the devil. Jacob thinks he has a deal with Laban to work for seven years and receive Rachel in marriage. But Laban tricks Jacob, switches daughters on him, and Jacob has to work seven more years to wed Rachel. The results of *lyin'*! An' Jacob's offspring, Joseph an' his brothers? They sold him into Egypt, then lied to their father that he'd been killed by a lion? The *lyin'* sin is *spreadin'*!"

The reverend began to raise his voice. "Proverbs 29:12, my friends: 'If a ruler hearken to lies, all his servants are wicked.' That's right, those who lead us must be particularly careful, for their influence is great. Be they ruler, boss, manager, whatever — we all know how a *lie* leads to another *lie* that leads to more *lies!*" Rev Bob raised his voice higher with each repetition. "Until Satan has got a hold of more than just the manager! He's got a hold of the whole team!"

Joe could sit still no longer. He jumped to his feet. Katie stretched out a hand to hold him, but it was no use. He scrambled down the pew and bolted down the aisle and out the church door. The congregation began to murmur. Behind him Reverend Nally thundered on. "Proverbs 101: 'He who works *deceit* shall not dwell within my house. He who tells *lies* shall not continue in my presence!' Thus saith the Lord!"

Outside the church, Joe did not slow down. His mind was a blur. Had he really just heard a sermon aimed directly at him? Had he really just been called a liar and a cheat in front of his neighbors, in front of his wife? All because he was a baseball manager? Baseball! Baseball was ruining his life again!

Panting, Joe tore open his front door, ran to the basement, and opened the cedar chest. He dug down to the bottom and pulled out a worn newspaper article whose headline read, "'SHOELESS" JOE THROWN IN JAIL."

Chicago Courthouse, January, 1924. Joe rose to await the verdict. The jury foreman stood. "We find in favor of the plaintiff, Your Honor, and award him a verdict of $16,000 to be collected for back pay from Mr. Charles Comiskey and the Chicago White Sox."

Joe threw his arms in the air. He hugged his lawyer, then swung Katie around in joy. Pandemonium broke out in the courtroom. But Judge John J. Gregory immediately gaveled for order.

"I believe Mr. Jackson stands self-accused and self-convicted of perjury. Either his testimony here or his testimony given before the Chicago grand jury was false. I therefore set aside the jury's verdict and remand the defendant to jail."

Joe was led away in handcuffs to the county jail. He was fingerprinted, his picture taken, his pockets emptied, and prison jail clothing jammed into his chest, along with a bag for his civilian clothes. The guard pointed to a nearby door, and Joe went in and changed. When he emerged, he was led immediately down the corridor of cells to an empty one at the end. The guard swung open the door, Joe shuffled in, and the cell door slammed shut.

Joe was numb. His breath came quickly. He was almost in a state of shock. He had won a verdict against Charles Comiskey and now he was in jail? He grabbed the bars, cold to his touch, and squeezed them. How had he gotten from the mills of Greenville to this county jail? All he'd ever wanted to do was play baseball. He'd spent a lifetime entertaining people, exciting them by his spectacular throws, his towering home runs, his thrilling base-running. He was a champion, the best of the best. And now here he was....

Joe began to shake the bars as hard as he could. The effort shook the tears from his eyes, the sobs from his throat. Slowly, he lowered himself to the cell floor and curled up like a baby, crying quietly to himself.

And that's the way Katie found him in the basement floor when she came home from church.

Jimmy hadn't gone to church that morning. He had purposefully slept in so he wouldn't see his mother, and he'd stayed out late with Rhoda on Saturday night for the same reason. He realized he couldn't go on avoiding her, but, for now, he needed time to himself. Instead, he had walked over to Brandon to wait for Rhoda to come home from church. They were planning to pack a picnic lunch and spend the afternoon together.

Jimmy saw Piggy outside Brandon Baptist. "Holy mackerel, Jimmy, you should've been in church!" Piggy gushed as he ran up.

"What happened, Steve?"

"Rev Bob preached a sermon 'bout Shoeless!"

"What?"

"Not about him exactly, but everybody knew he was talkin' 'bout Mr. Jackson."

"Why was Rev Bob there?"

"Guest preacher. He gave a sermon 'bout Jacob an' Esau, all about lyin' an' cheatin', an', I swannee, he looked right at Shoeless when he said it." Piggy loosened his tie and yanked it from around his neck.

"What did Mr. Jackson do?"

"Ran outta the church!"

"What?"

"Jumped right up an' skedaddled."

Jimmy thought for a moment. "This ain't good, Steve."

"You're tellin' me."

"Whattaya think he'll do?" Jimmy motioned and they retreated to the shade of an old oak tree.

"Whattaya mean?"

"We barely got Shoeless to agree to manage, an', with this, maybe he won't want to no more."

Jimmy's urgency shocked Piggy. "You think he'd quit?"

"I don't know, but if baseball was the reason people was callin' you a liar, what would you do?"

Piggy began wrapping his tie around one hand. "Wow. That'd be terrible." Neither of them said anything for a few moments, lost in their thoughts about the possibility of Shoeless not managing their team. "Guess we'll know Monday," Piggy finally said.

"If he shows up, Steve, tell the others we've gotta have the best practice ever!"

"I will, Jimmy, I will." They nodded solemnly at each other, and parted.

While he waited for Rhoda, Jimmy sat on a small patch of grass under a scrawny dogwood tree and thought back on the past few days. His world seemed to be coming apart. First his mother, now this. *We gotta make sure he don't quit! We gotta win the championship! I gotta get outta the mill!* His desperation grew with every thought.

"Hey!" Rhoda's loud voice pulled Jimmy from his thoughts. "Why weren't you in church?"

Jimmy got to his feet. Rhoda came up and gave his cheek a peck. "I just wanted to sleep in."

"Well, you missed my solo. But I'll forgive you 'cause that's the kinda gal I am. You shoulda heard everybody goin' on 'bout Mr. Jackson."

"They knew about the sermon already?"

"What sermon?"

Jimmy repeated what Piggy had told him earlier. "Oh, no!" Rhoda moaned. "That's terrible!"

"I guess."

"You guess? How would you like it if somebody gave a sermon 'bout you?"

"I wouldn't. I wouldn't like it at all. I'd want to get as far away from that church an' anybody associated with it as I could. An' that's the problem."

"What is?"

"What if it makes Shoeless quit managin' us?" Rhoda looked harshly at Jimmy, but before she could protest, he went on. "But what were they talkin' 'bout at your church if it wadn' the sermon?"

"That article in the newspaper 'bout the resolution for Mr. Jackson."

"The one that's tryin' to get him reinstated into professional baseball?"

"No, the one from today's paper sayin' they're havin' second thoughts."

"What? Who's havin' second thoughts?"

"Yancey Dickerson, the one who sponsored the resolution. He might not send it to the governor for his signature. Sumpin' 'bout not wantin' to support a confessed liar."

"This makes it a lot worse!" Jimmy paced away a few steps. "First the sermon, an' now this! I finally talked him into gettin' back into baseball, an' then this spotlight shines on him an' he's the center of attention. Bad attention!"

"*You* talked him into it?" Rhoda asked incredulously.

Jimmy didn't hear her, the words rushing out of him like mountain rapids. "If Shoeless quits, I don't know what I'll do! This resolution is the last thing he needs. It just brings up the past all over again. An' what's this liar stuff all about?" He looked at Rhoda, his voice urgent with concern. "What if there's some reason Rev Bob gave that sermon? Do you think Shoeless could be lyin' to me, Rhoda? Do you think he really might be a cheater?"

For a second, Rhoda was too stunned to speak. Then she exploded. "I cain't believe you, Jimmy Roberts! *You* talk poor Shoeless Joe Jackson into getting' back into baseball? *You* might get your nice lil' dream rocked a little when he does? Mr. Jackson's name is dragged through the mud, he's preached at in public, an' all you can think about is how it'll affect *you?*" Her eyes flashed with anger and she yelled right in his face. "Since when did you become Mr. I'm Number One? Who appointed you Most Important Person in the World? What about how all this feels to Mr. Jackson, you selfish — ?" She stopped herself, turned, and stomped away as fast as she could.

"Rhoda, wait!" he called, but she kept going until she had sprung up onto her porch and disappeared inside her house.

That Sunday turned out to be the longest day in Jimmy's life. The hours stretched on, slow and torturous, until he could go to work that night. They stretched even longer as he watched shuttles fly endlessly back and forth across the looms and went through his hypnotic paces with the bobbins: full, replace, empty, full, replace, empty. On the floor above him, Rhoda was spinning yarn into thread. A mile or so away, his mother was probably trying to sleep. He'd hardly seen his mother that weekend. He'd been focused on how angry he was at her, but was she just as angry at him? Was she feeling just as hurt as he was? Rhoda was definitely mad at him. The two most important women in his life had been yanked away. Or had he pushed them away? He kept hearing Rhoda's furious scream. "You selfish — !" Was that really what he was?

And Shoeless. How *was* he feeling? He'd done so much for Jimmy, wasn't there something Jimmy could do for him? He didn't want him to quit managing, there was nothing wrong with feeling that way. But wasn't there something he could do to make him want to stay?

As the hours creaked by, Jimmy thought long and hard about all these questions, and more. But he thought especially about his life in the mill and what might become of it. He watched the loom, watched the threads being added one by one to the fabric, building slowly but ultimately becoming more. More threads, more and more threads. Then, as early morning arrived, as Jimmy imagined the world awakening with new light outside the windowless room, an idea began to take shape. He could build his own fabric, thread by thread by thread. He could make something strong enough to hold them all together, all the people he loved and cared about. And he knew just the person to help him do it.

CHAPTER 15

The next day, Thelma was surprised to see Jimmy stumble sleepily onto the porch in the middle of the morning while she was watering their small vegetable patch. "Hello, honey. Whatcha doin' up at this hour?"

"I meant to be up earlier. I was gonna wait for you to wake up, but I guess I fell asleep." Jimmy yawned.

"Did you want somethin'?" She turned the garden hose from the peppers to the squash.

"Yeah. Could we sit on the porch?"

"'Course." His mother turned off the spigot at the corner of the house, then joined her son on the porch.

Jimmy sat on the swing, his favorite place on the porch. He remembered when he and his father had installed it. His father hadn't left them much, Jimmy sometimes thought, but at least he'd left them that. Thelma sat on a wrought-iron chair nearby and wiped her forehead with the back of her hand. "Whew! It's gonna be a scorcher."

Jimmy began rocking slowly back and forth, trying to decide how to begin. Although he'd rehearsed it many times, now that the moment was here the words weren't coming. Thelma waited patiently. Finally, he put his toes down, stopping the swing. "Mama," he said slowly. "I been thinkin' 'bout you ... and Waddy. An' I reckon I been thinkin' 'bout the Bible, too. What it says about judgin', an' not judgin', an' all." He paused, started to push off with his toes, then stopped the swing again. "I know I said what you done was a sin, but I ain't no preacher. An' I sure ain't God. So I shouldn't go 'round sayin' what's a sin an' what ain't. What I should be sayin', what I wanna be sayin', is ... I'm sorry." He looked at his mother, wondering if he should try to explain what he was sorry about. But her eyes made him realize he didn't need to.

"Thank you, Jimmy," Thelma said after a moment, looking deep into her son's eyes. "That was right-well said. An' I really 'preciate you sayin' it." She smiled. "Thing is, I got somethin' to 'pologize for, too."

"You don't have to, Mama. What you do is your own business."

"Maybe. But what I say 'bout what I do oughta be the truth."

"Huh?"

"I lied when I told you why I done what I did, honey. 'Bout wantin' to be with a man. The truth is, I done it for the money."

"What money?" Jimmy asked, confused.

"'Member how I got promoted right after you was fired? Well, bein' with Waddy was *why* I got promoted." She paused to let this sink in.

"He paid you?"

"Not in money. Just givin' me a better job so's I could make more money. I didn't really think it through, son. You was fired, an' I was worried 'bout how we was gonna pay the bills, an', I don't know, Waddy'd told me I could have this promotion if I, you know...." Thelma stopped. She'd said it.

Jimmy got up from the swing and walked to the other end of the porch. She saw his shoulders rise as he drew a deep breath, then saw them fall when he released it. "You done it 'cause of me?" he asked, not facing her.

She came to him. "It's not your fault, Jimmy. I'm a grown-up woman, I'm responsible for my own decisions. It's nobody's fault. It's just...." Thelma laid her hand on his shoulder. "It's just what happens sometimes when we're tryin' to do right. We maybe end up doin' wrong by mistake. But the important thing is...." She turned him to face her. "To say when we made mistakes an', if we've hurt anybody, to say we're sorry. Now, I'm sorry I lied to you, an' you done said you're sorry to me, so seems like we oughta just let it go at that. Whattaya say?"

Jimmy looked at his mother and took one more deep breath. "I say 'truce'."

Thelma pulled him to her in a deep, strong hug. "There's somethin' I wanna ask you, Mama. Let's set on the swing."

Thelma nodded, sat, and they began swinging back and forth together. "I had this great idea at work, Mama, an' I hope you'll help me with it. Did you know there was a resolution to get Mr. Jackson back into baseball?"

"I heard somethin' 'bout it."

"Well, Rhoda told me yesterday that it's in trouble, that Mr. Dickerson — he's the sponsor — might not be so sure 'bout it now. But I thought of a way to make him more sure. A petition."

"A petition?"

"Yeah. We'd write somethin' up for people to sign. It'd say somethin' 'bout how all these people want to encourage you, Mr. Dickerson, to get this resolution to the governor. Aw, I don't know, not 'encourage.'" Jimmy began pushing the swing higher. "I don't know the right word. I cain't hardly figure out how to put it all together. But, listen, Mama, we could get the whole team to sign it, an' all of us could get our families to sign, an' our friends, an' take it to other mills an' get people to sign it there. Do you think it's a good idea?"

They were swinging higher now. The light breeze was cooling her face, Jimmy's enthusiasm was contagious, and Thelma almost laughed out loud. "I think it's wonderful!"

"Then will you help me figure it all out? Will you help me write the petition, Mama?"

"I'd be honored!" she said fervently, and laughed. Jimmy laughed, too, as they both pushed off to take the swing even higher.

They spent the rest of that morning drafting the petition, but when he raced over to Rhoda's house to tell her about it, she was still asleep. "Rhoda, wake up, wake up!" Jimmy shouted, banging on the door. "I need to talk to you!"

"Just a minute," came a sleepy reply from within. After a few moments, she appeared in the doorway. "What do you want?"

She was dressed in a white, cotton nightgown. Her hair was tousled, falling chaotically over her face. Sleep had softened her features. She looked almost delicate. For a moment, Jimmy nearly forgot his purpose. He strained against his impulse and began.

"I'm sorry, Rhoda." He waited for her to say something, and when she didn't, he went on. "I'm sorry I made you mad, but you were right to get mad. I was selfish, thinkin' only 'bout me. Will you forgive me?"

"Could we talk about this later, Jimmy? I'm tired."

"No, it cain't wait. I've got somethin' I hope you'll help me with, but first, I gotta know you'll forgive me."

"I ain't the one you need to forgive you, Jimmy. You weren't bein' selfish with me."

"I bet I have been, though, haven't I, Rhoda? I bet I've spent a lot of time talkin' 'bout me, an' baseball, an' my dreams, an' my problems, an' not so much talkin' 'bout yours?"

She cocked her head and looked at Jimmy. He seemed different, somehow. "Well, maybe a little."

"So just say you'll forgive me, please? 'Cause I got an idea I think you're really gonna like."

"All right, then, I forgive you." She smiled. The relief he felt when he saw that smile made him almost giddy.

"Thank you, Rhoda," he said gratefully. "Now, lemme tell you 'bout my idea. It come to me last night at work when I was thinkin' 'bout Mr. Jackson an' that resolution. I know how we can make Yancey Dickerson send it to the governor."

"How?"

"We'll start a petition urgin' Mr. Dickerson to get it to the governor for his signature. We'll get lots of signatures. Hundreds!

Thousands!" His excitement grew. "We'll start with my teammates, an' their families, an' their friends in other mill villages, an' all the other teams!"

Rhoda looked at Jimmy, who was pulsing with excitement. "I think that's about the best idea I've ever heard!"

"An' that ain't all. Read this!" He pulled a folded piece of paper from his back pocket and handed it to her. She took it and read:

WE THE UNDERSIGNED BELIEVE THAT JOE JACKSON WAS UNFAIRLY BANISHED FROM BASEBALL. WE URGE SPEAKER DICKERSON TO GET THE RESOLUTION REQUESTING THE COMMISSIONER OF BASEBALL TO REINSTATE JOSEPH JEFFERSON WOFFORD JACKSON INTO PROFESSIONAL BASEBALL TO GOVERNOR BYRNES FOR HIS SIGNATURE. IT IS A TRAVESTY OF JUSTICE THAT THIS SON OF SOUTH CAROLINA, ONE OF THE GREATEST BASEBALL PLAYERS OF ALL TIME, IS INELIGIBLE FOR THE HALL OF FAME. WITH RESPECT FOR OUR HONORED TRADITION OF RESISTING WRONG, LET US STAND FOR THE RIGHT. REINSTATE JOE JACKSON!

"Did you write this?" Rhoda asked.

"Me an' Mama. She came up with that travesty of justice idea. I didn't know what the heck she meant till she explained it."

"What's it mean?"

Jimmy was happy to know something besides baseball that Rhoda didn't. "It means really, really unjust. The worst."

"I like it. I'm proud of you, Jimmy."

"Proud?" Jimmy'd never considered someone his own age bein' proud of him, he thought that was just for grownups.

She came to him and whispered close, "Very proud." She kissed him, then nestled in his arms. Holding her tight, Jimmy felt proud, too.

"All right, then, it's time for your job."

"I got a job?"

"Durn straight. This is a team effort. Your job is to help me make copies for all the players. We'll give 'em out at practice. Okay?"

Rhoda went to the screen door, held it open, and, with a grand wave of her hand, said in her best formal voice, "Kindly step into my office, Mr. Roberts."

Across the village, Katie had a job, too, but of a different nature. Joe had just announced that he saw no point in going to practice that afternoon, he'd work in the liquor store. "What do you mean?" she asked.

"They can get another manager. They're just a bunch of lousy ballplayers anyway!"

"You don't mean that, Joe, an' you know it. You've put up with much worse criticism than a stupid newspaper article an' an awful sermon."

"You're right!" He shouted out some of the insults from his past. "'Back to the sticks, you dumb hick!' 'You're Ty Cobb, Jackson — from the neck down!' "

"Stop it, Joe."

"Why should I sign up for more abuse? I've done enough managin'. Better teams than the Brandon Braves, too. Why should I care?"

"Because you do!"

"What good will it do?"

Pee Wee, hearing an argument, squawked "You're lousy, O'Loughlin!"

"Shut up, Pee Wee!" Joe barked.

"Go to hell!" the parrot squawked.

Frustrated, Joe yanked open a desk drawer, stuffed some tobacco in his mouth, and sat down, chewing vigorously. Katie seized this moment of calm to speak to him quietly.

"What good will it do?" she repeated. "The good it'll do the team is obvious, even to a stubborn ol' goat like you." She smiled at Joe, but he was not to be mollified so easily. "But it's the good it'll do you that I'm interested in." She pulled a chair next to Joe's desk and sat facing him. "Joe, you've been happier these last weeks than I've seen you in years. You don't have to sneak out an' watch games through your binoculars so I won't think you still care about baseball. You can put on spikes an' sit in a dugout, an' teach, an' coach, an' pass on your knowledge to the next generation of ball players. You can give back. Joe, listen to me." She took his face in both hands and turned it towards her. "Baseball took a lot from you, it's true. But it also gave you a lot. It gave you the excitement of a home run an' the thrill of hearing thousands of fans shoutin' 'Give 'em Black Betsy!' An' the friendship of teammates, an' travel to parts of this country that people down here in Greenville can only dream about. Yes, even the money, too, Joe. Enough to keep us comfortable for a long time. You got all this from playin' a game, Joe, a *game!* Do you know how lucky you've been?" She waited a moment, not so Joe could answer, but so what she'd said could sink in.

"An' I've been lucky, too. Baseball gave me a hero, gave me a chance to be married to one of the greatest men I know. Not great for what he could do on a ball field. But great for how he endured what happened to him off it. No one should have to go through what you went through, Joe. You've been so strong through it all. You didn't back down, you sued Comiskey for all the pay he owed you. An' you won. You tried to keep playin' under an assumed name, but you were just so good you couldn't hide your talent an' you were always found out. An', yes, you've managed some, but not for a long time. An' during that time you've grown bitter, Joe." He looked at her, but didn't speak. "The longer you were away from the game, the stronger your anger an' resentment grew. Frankly, Joe, I was worried about you. Until Jimmy."

She paused. Joe stopped chewing, grabbed the wad of tobacco from his mouth, and put it in the trashcan. Katie took her husband's hands, those large hands that could throw a baseball four hundred feet, hands now spotted with age. "A boy has a dream just like yours, Joe, an', like you, he has the courage to try to make it come true. You're a hero to that boy, Joe. An' you're a hero to me. All you need to do is to be a hero to yourself. So go to that practice this afternoon an' become one."

Joe looked at his wife. Emotion swelled inside him, a tear in the corner of his eye. How had he ever been so lucky to have found this woman, who believed in him so much? He felt her boundless faith through the hands that lay warmly on his own. He saw it in the deep wells of her clear, blue eyes. If she had that much faith in him, surely he could have enough in himself, enough to face down the world one more time and say to it, "I am Joe Jackson. I play baseball. An' I play it right."

When the Brandon Braves assembled for practice later that afternoon, the talk was of the "Shoeless Sermon," as people in the mill village had begun calling it. Most of the players were outraged, but a few of them wondered why Rev Bob had said what he did if it wasn't true. Jimmy immediately saw the need to get his team focused and took charge. He quickly handed out the copies of the petition he and Rhoda had made as he explained his idea to his teammates. When nobody spoke for a moment, Jimmy worried that perhaps they didn't like it, or the way he'd written the petition, or both. Then Piggy raised his hand. "What's a 'travesty of justice'?"

"When somethin' really, really ain't fair," answered Jawbreaker. His teammates looked at him, surprised. "When I broke that guy's jaw, they fined me fifty dollars, an' my pa called it a 'travesty of justice'."

Several players laughed. "Okay, then," said Piggy, "I like it."

"Me, too," said Whiff, and the rest of the team nodded their approval.

"Okay, guys, the plan is for all of us to talk to everybody we can, everybody we know. Ya'll get all the signatures you can here in Brandon, my mama an' me'll work on Woodside, an' let's report in every day before practice. Lissen up." Jimmy made sure he had their attention. "Let's keep this a secret, okay? We won't tell Shoeless until we've got tons of signatures, an' ask everybody who signs to keep it a secret, too. All right?"

"This is gonna be so great when we dump all them signatures on Mr. Jackson," Pepper said.

"Yeah, I cain't wait to see his reaction," Petie agreed.

A curious unease suddenly settled on them all. One or two of them peered anxiously at the gate in right field. Wash finally asked the question that was on everybody's mind. "You think he'll show?"

"Sure he will," Jimmy asserted, ignoring his own doubts. "Shoeless ain't the type to run scared. He'll be here."

"Sure he will," Piggy affirmed.

"He believes in us," Murph said. "He wouldn't just cut us loose. Let's play some ball," he continued, but nobody moved. Some pounded a baseball into their mitts, some tapped the end of a bat in the dirt, but not a single Brave felt like playing baseball until they had Shoeless Joe there to coach them. Or not. And even if he did show up, what would practice be like? Loose, like always? Or would Joe be all tense and distracted, and make them that way, too?

"There he is!" Red shouted. They all looked towards the gate in right field, and, sure enough, Joe was ambling through it. As if on cue, they scattered across the diamond, firing the ball to each other, throwing practice ground balls, heaving high fly balls into the air for others to catch — anything to show Joe how hard they were working. As he crossed the foul line at third, he told Jimmy "Call 'em all over." When the team gathered in front of the dugout, Shoeless stood before them, leaning on a baseball bat.

"You boys may have heard some things 'bout me yestiddy," he started. "May have read some things, too — I didn't, 'course, 'cause I cain't read." One or two of them emitted small laughs, the others looked awkwardly at each other. "I'm just funnin', go on, laugh, everybody knows I cain't read, so what?" Shoeless spat some tobacco juice in the dirt. "See that there, that's what you gotta do sometimes when you don't like things but there's nothin' you can do 'bout it. You gotta spit on it!" The Brandon Braves looked at each other, wondering where in the world this was going.

Shoeless reached into his back pocket and brought out a pouch of Redman chewing tobacco. "I need to teach you fellas how to spit. Every man I ever knowed who played ball knew how to spit. There's just somethin 'bout spittin' an' baseball that go together. Take a chew." He handed the pouch to Whiff. "Go on, take some an' pass it around."

Whiff, eyeing the others uneasily, pinched a few shreds of the Red Man leaf between his thumb and forefinger and passed the pouch to Petie, who took some and passed it to Pepper, as Shoeless continued. "Now maybe you boys think all that spittin's just fer nothin', an' maybe most times it is, but I'm here to tell you that sometimes it's got a purpose, leastways for me it does. I'm teachin' you how to spit tobaccy so's you can help me with my purpose, an' maybe it'll come in handy for you, too, some day. Everybody got some?" The Braves all nodded. "All right, in she goes."

They players put the tobacco into their mouths. Jawbreaker stuffed it in confidently, Piggy gently placed it on his tongue, but they all followed Joe's instructions. "Now chew!" he ordered them. They did. "Chew it up till it's good an' soft, kinda juicy."

The Brandon Braves began to chew. Murph made a face. "This tastes awful."

"You'll get used to it," Joe said.

"I like it," Whitey said, as a brown line of juice dribbled out of his mouth.

"Me, too!" added Piggy, surprised, juice squirting out of his mouth as well.

"All right, now, this is where I need y'all's help," Shoeless said, spitting into the dirt again. "I been thinkin 'bout what happened to me yestiddy, it hit me kinda hard, I don't mind sayin'. An' I got to thinkin' 'I need my teammates, I need some help gettin' over all this bull, I need me some spittin' backup'." Jimmy looked at Shoeless. He'd never heard him talk like this, and he couldn't imagine what he was trying to tell them. Spittin' backup?

Shoeless flipped the bat he was holding so the handle faced the ground, and he drew a big "X" in the dirt. "That's the sermon I heard yestiddy." He spat some juice on it. "Nope, that didn't nearly make it disappear. Jimmy, spit on it." Jimmy looked around at his teammates, hesitating. "Come on," Shoeless urged, "Ain't you gon' help me?" Jimmy spat tobacco juice at the "X" as best he could. Most of it got on his shirt, but some of it blotted out a piece of the "X."

"Anybody else?" Jawbreaker stepped forward and spat confidently. "Good, Jawbreaker," Shoeless said. "I 'preciate it. Let me add some words.... 'That was the dumbest sermon I ever heard!' Joe said and spat more juice on the mark.

"Awful!" Piggy shouted and spat. Most of it went on his shoes. "Gimme some more tobacco, Mr. Jackson!" Shoeless pulled out another pouch out and handed it to him.

"It stank to high heaven!" Whitey shouted and spat.

"Bunch of lies!" Petie called out and followed suit.

The craziness of what they were doing began to infect them, and several began giggling. That caused more tobacco juice to dribble out, painting chins, staining shirts, and turning giggles into outright laughter. Players ran up to the "X" and spat on it, then grabbed the pouch for more tobacco. When the "X" had been obliterated, Shoeless drew several parallel lines in the dirt and shouted, "Charlie Deerhart's newspaper article!" This time, they needed no prompting, jostling each other to for position before letting out the best line of tobacco juice they could manage. Then Jawbreaker spat on Whiff's shoes on purpose. "Hey!" Whiff called and returned the favor. Jawbreaker didn't move, as if he wanted the juice all over his shoes. Pepper spat on his own shoes. Piggy astonished them all by taking his tobacco and smearing it on his shirt! Petie did, too. It was as if they wanted to get dirty for Joe, they wanted to help him blot it all out, erase that horrible yesterday, and do it together. After all, they were a team.

"Practice is over!" Shoeless called out suddenly.

"Really?" Jimmy asked.

"We done what was important for today," Joe answered. He looked at them solemnly. "Teammates, I thank you. See you tomorrow." And he walked off towards right field and home.

The Braves dispersed. Piggy and Jimmy walked together towards Piggy's home. "Can you believe what we just did?" Piggy asked

"Not really."

"I never thought playin' ball could be so...." Piggy paused. "I don't even know what to call it. Crazy, I reckon."

"Yeah, crazy. Crazy fun!"

When Shoeless walked into the liquor store, Katie was surprised. "What are you doin' here? Didn' you practice?"

"Yeah, we practiced. We practiced bein' a team." He walked over to the cage. "Sorry I yelled at you, Pee Wee."

"Feed me, you sonofabitch!" Pee Wee squawked.

Joe laughed and pulled Katie to his side. She believed in him. His team believed in him. And, by God, from now on he was going to believe, too.

CHAPTER 16

"We need more." Jimmy and Rhoda were sitting on Rhoda's porch after church, counting the signatures on the petitions he had collected from his teammates, Rhoda, her family, and his mother. "I thought it'd be easier," he confessed. "One man chased me off his property with a hoe, shoutin' 'bout 'God-fearin' folks not supportin' that sinner!' "

"I had a door or two slammed in my face," Rhoda admitted. "Plus, it was hard to get people at the mill 'cause of keepin' it a secret. We couldn't just post it on the board or sumpin'."

"Guess we can try the other mills next week, 'ceptin' I don't know many people in 'em." Jimmy rifled through the pile of petitions again. "We did purty good, it's just I wish we had more."

"We need to reach out more," Rhoda mused. "I got it!"

"What?"

"I know where we can get more signatures, easy. 'Cept we need a car to get there."

"Only person I know with a car is Mr. Jackson."

"Then I guess he's the one who's got to loan it to us. Come on." She started off the porch.

"Where're you goin'?"

"To Mr. Jackson's house," she answered, crossing the yard.

Jimmy had to hurry to catch up with her. "Why would he wanna loan us his car, Rhoda?"

"Kinship," she answered, taking long strides down the street.

"You ain't related to Shoeless!" Jimmy protested, walking fast to catch up with her.

"In a way I am. Can you drive?"

"I got a license, but — "

"Good! Come on!"

It didn't take them long to reach the house on E. Wilburn Avenue. They found Joe and Katie sitting on the porch, enjoying a rare cool breeze on the hot, mid-summer day. Jimmy waved as they crossed the yard. "Hello, Mr. an' Mrs. Jackson. Hope we're not botherin' you."

"Not a'tall," Shoeless replied. "What brings you our way on a Sunday?"

"Well, uh — " Jimmy stammered.

"Hi, Mrs. Jackson," Rhoda called.

"Hello, Rhoda," Katie answered. "Y'all come on up. I been meanin' to introduce you to Joe." Jimmy and Rhoda mounted the steps to the porch. "Joe, this is Rhoda Dawkins. She sits with Thelma an' me at the games."

"Sure, I seen you. I wondered who that purty thing was," he said with a big smile. "How you doin', Rhoda?"

"Fine as frogshair, Mr. Jackson. It's nice to finally meet you," Rhoda said, shaking his hand.

"Y'all sit down, lemme get you some iced tea," Katie offered. Jimmy and Shoeless pulled over two more chairs, while Katie disappeared into the house.

"Don't mind if I do," Rhoda said as she seated herself next to Joe. "It sure is a pea ripper."

"What's that mean?" Jimmy asked.

"Hot enough to bust open peas on the vine," Rhoda explained.

"Rhoda talks kinda funny sometimes," Jimmy said to Joe, "So I gotta get her to explain it."

"Where 'bouts you from, Rhoda?" Shoeless asked.

"Up yonder past Pumpkintown, foot of the mountains."

"You don't say? I'm from up thataway myself, not all the ways to the mountains, but I got kin folks live up that way." Katie returned with glasses and poured tea for Jimmy and Rhoda. "This purty lil' gal's from up my way, Katie," Shoeless said.

"I know. We talked 'bout her folks at the games," Katie smiled to herself. It was nice to see Joe enjoying a pretty girl again.

"What made you leave?" Joe asked.

"Coupla bad crops in a row, barely gettin' by. Pa got so thin he had to stand twice in one place to make a shadow."

Shoeless laughed. "Told you she talked funny," Jimmy said.

"Not to me." Joe turned to Rhoda. "Dawkins, uh? Let's see...." He tilted his glass towards him, swirling the tea while he thought. "You ever heerd tell of a Earle Dawkins?"

"He's my uncle!" Rhoda cried.

"Don't that beat all?" Shoeless said. "I believe Earle's the one who married my great-aunt's second cousin, Betty Lou Bishop."

"He is! Aunt Betty Lou. That makes us kin." Rhoda paused. "She died a few years back."

"I'm so sorry," Joe said. "I ain't seen Earle since I was knee-high to a grasshopper. You tell him I said hello."

"I sure will, Mr. Jackson." Rhoda sipped her tea, then set it down with a sigh. "I wish I could see my kin, I miss 'em so much. But Pa sold the wagon when we come down here an' I ain't got no way to get to 'em. I'd go right this minute, if I could," she said sadly.

"Why cain't you?" Joe sat upright. "I can take us all in my Packard."

"You could?" Rhoda asked hopefully.

"Well, I hate to spoil the party," Katie interrupted. "But you an' I are goin' to see my cousins this afternoon, Joe. We promised we'd bring the devilled eggs, an' I spent all mornin' makin' 'em."

"I forgot about that. I'm sorry, lil' lady," he said to Rhoda.

"Maybe next week," Jimmy offered. At least now he knew where Rhoda was headed.

Rhoda shot him a look before she replied with great disappointment, "I guess so. Darn, I had my hopes up there for a minute." She dropped her eyes and sank her cheeks.

"Well, wait a minute," Shoeless said. "Jimmy, do you drive?"

Jimmy looked startled. "Well, I've got a license, but it's been a long time — "

"Then why don't you take her? Sure. We can walk to your cousins, cain't we, Katie?"

"I don't see why not."

"An' I don't see why Rhoda cain't go see her kin when she's pinin' for 'em like she is. Would you like that, Rhoda?"

"Oh, yes, sir! Thank you!" She jumped out of her seat and hugged Shoeless. Jimmy stared, not exactly sure what had happened. Katie smiled. She knew. Her husband had just had the pants charmed off him.

An hour later, Jimmy and Rhoda were driving up the Geer Highway towards Caesar's Head in Joe's 1940 Packard two door sedan. Or rather, Jimmy was driving and Rhoda was gritting her teeth, as he swerved to miss yet another log truck then swerved again to avoid running off the road. "I thought you said you had a license?" Rhoda asked anxiously.

"I do, I just ain't never had no car. I tried to tell you. I'll get the hang of it."

"If you don't kill us first." For good measure, she placed the picnic basket she'd packed on the floor behind them. "No use ruinin' lunch, in case we make it that far."

"So how'd you know you was related to Mr. Jackson?"

"Me an' Katie had discussed his kin, so I thought Earle might be related. If he wasn't, I got lots of other cousins and such, I was purty sure I'd find kin somewheres."

"An' how'd you know he wouldn't wanna drive us himself?"

"I knew he probly would. But I also knew he was goin' visitin', 'cause Katie was talkin' 'bout it at yesterday's game. She was sayin' how she hated makin' devilled eggs on a Sunday. The rest was just actin' real disappointed an' countin' on his good nature."

"Well, ain't you a regular Vivien Leigh?"

"Am I?" Rhoda looked at him, flashing her dark brown eyes and giving him a coy smile. "Look out!" Jimmy managed to pull the Packard back onto the road in the nick of time. "Will you watch where you're goin'?"

"I will if you'll stop bein' so dad-gum — " He shook his head, unable to think of one word that could possibly describe Rhoda Dawkins. "Whatever you are," he finally said.

"Happy!" she answered and squeezed his thigh.

The Blue Ridge Mountains loomed ahead of them, luxuriantly green, not blue, in the mid-summer heat. Traffic thinned out as they snaked along Highway 276. As they entered a valley, a small waterfall appeared on the right. The road widened a little. "Pull over there," Rhoda instructed, pointing to a hand-written sign marked "Boiled Peanuts" which stretched across the top of a banged-up pickup truck. The tailgate of the truck was lowered and two large tin pots sat cooking on a portable kerosene stove.

As soon as Jimmy had parked the car, Rhoda jumped out and ran up to a middle-aged farmer dressed in overalls and a sleeveless white tee shirt. He had a well-worn straw hat tilted back on his head, and a face tanned a dark brown.

"Well, lookee here!' the farmer called out. "Rhoda Dawkins, I do believe! Where you been, gal?"

"We moved to Greenville to work in the mills, Uncle Earle," Rhoda said, giving him a quick hug.

"That's what I heered. But I didn't wanna believe it. What's this ol' peanut farmer gon' do without his lil' gal to hep him?"

"I didn' help you so much as eat all your peanuts. Uncle Earle, this here's my friend, Jimmy," Rhoda said, turning to Jimmy, who had gotten out of the car.

"How do?" Uncle Earle said, offering his hand.

"Nice to meet you," Jimmy replied, shaking it.

"How 'bout some peanuts?" Uncle Earle asked Rhoda.

"Love some. You like peanuts?" she asked Jimmy.

"Yeah, I do," he said. So Uncle Earle dipped a big slotted spoon into one of the boiling pots, put some peanuts into a paper cup, and handed it to Jimmy. They didn't look like any peanuts Jimmy had ever seen. For one thing, they were warm. For another, they looked gooey.

Rhoda noticed Jimmy's hesitation. "Ain't you never had 'em boiled?"

"No." Jimmy looked suspiciously at the cup.

"Go on. They won't bite you."

Jimmy reached in and withdrew one soggy peanut. He held it between the thumb and first finger of his right hand and began to pull back the shell. The peanut squirted out of his hand onto the ground.

Rhoda laughed. "Don't shell 'em. Like this." She reached in and grabbed a handful of boiled peanuts, popped them in her mouth, and began to chew contentedly.

"With the shell on?" Jimmy asked.

"The shell's salty. That's the best way. You done got too sophisticated growin' up in a mill village, I reckon," she teased.

Jimmy poured a few peanuts into the palm of his hand, examined them closely, then slowly put them into his mouth. They were soft, and he chewed right through the shell. Rhoda was right, they had a gentle salty taste that was quite nice. When he'd swallowed the peanut, he prepared to spit out the chewed-up shell. "Swallow the shell, too," Rhoda demanded. So he did. Surprisingly enough, it went down easily.

They each finished their peanuts, which Earle insisted on giving them for free. Rhoda got him to sign the petition. "Shoeless Joe, huh? Betty Lou mentioned him a time or two, said we might be kin or sumpin'."

"You are," Rhoda told him. "Speakin' of which, how 'bout you get any kin or other folks to sign this, too? We need us a bunch of signatures."

"All right. Hey, why don't I get anybody who stops for peanuts to sign it, too?"

"That's a great idea!" Jimmy said.

"You can mail it to me in a few days, so's I get it by Saturday," Rhoda told her uncle. "My address is on the bottom there."

"Sure thing, Rhoda."

"Well, we gotta get on up the mountain, find us some more signatures." She gave him a hug. "Take care of yourself, Uncle Earle."

"You do the same. Nice to meet ya'," he said to Jimmy.

"You, too, sir," Jimmy responded. They shook hands, and Jimmy and Rhoda got back in the Packard and headed up the mountains. "Next stop, Cleveland," she said.

Cleveland turned out to be nothing more than a grocery store next to where the highway crossed the Saluda River. A smattering of ramshackle houses and shacks nestled on a hillside across from the store. Rhoda thought it would take too long to introduce Jimmy to everyone, so she went into the store alone, emerging with five signatures on one petition, and the promise to have the owners get others to sign the one she left behind and mail it to her. She then knocked door-to-door on the nearby houses, adding at least fifteen more signatures. Jimmy waited in the car, snoozing and daydreaming. Finally, Rhoda showed up holding two Cokes. "Let's go have our picnic," she said, sliding in next to Jimmy. "Take that dirt road off to the right just over the bridge."

Jimmy turned the Packard down the road. It was bumpy with washed-out gullies, so after a few hundred yards they parked the car and began to walk. They went farther back into the woods, following the river. Fields of corn and peanuts spread out from the road on either side. Sometimes a barbed-wire fence sprang up enclosing a few cows or maybe a horse or two. An occasional small cabin with a wooden porch and tin roof tilted silently on bricks or concrete blocks in yards of hard-packed dirt. Small children ran about chasing a dog or each other, while strong-armed women hung out wash or sat in the shade of an oak tree shelling beans. Scrawny chickens moved around listlessly, pecking the hard ground for whatever they could find. Whenever Jimmy or Rhoda spotted a farmer in the field or a woman in the yard, Rhoda would go off to greet them and have them sign the petition. They never said no, and by the time she led Jimmy off the road and back into the woods, they had a dozen more signatures.

At the edge of an old cotton field, they stopped, and Rhoda spread out their picnic on a powder-blue patchwork quilt. They enjoyed fried chicken and potato salad, with pickles and raw carrots, followed by some of the tastiest apple pie Jimmy had ever eaten. After the meal, Jimmy lay down on his back and looked up at the bright, blue sky, his stomach full and his eyes growing heavy. Meanwhile, Rhoda strode into the field, and returned a few minutes later with some reed-like weeds with small, twisted silver-brown leaves. She proceeded to strip the leaves, gathering them into a small pile on the quilt. Jimmy sat up to watch her, as she pulled some cigarette papers from her pocket and rolled the leaves into a cigarette, which she offered to Jimmy.

"You offerin' me some weeds to smoke?" he asked.

"No, tobacco. Rabbit tobacco."

"I didn't know rabbits smoked."

"Funny man," Rhoda said. "You gonna try some? I smoked this all the time as a kid. Cain't beat the price."

Jimmy took the hand rolled cigarette, and Rhoda produced a book of matches and lit it. He puffed the smoke tentatively. "You can inhale it," she told him. Jimmy tried and coughed violently. Rhoda grabbed the cigarette and handed him a glass of water. She took a drag and exhaled the smoke. "Don't take in so much till you get used to it." She handed the cigarette back to Jimmy. He took another puff and managed it better the second time. Then Rhoda rolled one for herself, and they sat there, smoking contentedly, and gazing out across the fallow field at the pine woods on the other side.

"Bet you'll never guess what's back through them woods," Rhoda said after a while.

"What?"

"A still."

"What? A real one?"

"A drop of Billy Jack's white lightnin' an' you'll say it's real."

"I ain't never had corn liquor."

"Well, I'd say it's about time you got educated." Rhoda stood up and stretched her hand down to Jimmy. He took it and hoisted himself to his feet. They rubbed out their cigarettes, put the plates and glasses back into the picnic basket, rolled up the tiny quilt, then set off across the field and into the woods to Billy Jack's still.

If he hadn't had Rhoda to guide him, Jimmy would have been lost in minutes. They squeezed past ancient pines, ducked and twisted through mountain laurel groves, crossed a brook, then followed it down into a small hollow. At one end, a shack nestled next to a slanted sycamore tree. Beside the tree, a large copper barrel, with what looked like a smokestack, sat on rocks over a fire. Another copper pipe funneled down to a smaller copper one, from which several pipes fed into a wooden barrel. Standing beside it and stirring the brown liquid inside was a tall, skinny man in overalls, without a shirt, hatless, a few scraggly gray hairs protruding from his head. Rhoda took Jimmy's hand and hurried him toward the man.

"Hello, Billy Jack," she said. "We come to see you."

Billy Jack looked up. "I know. I seen you a-ways off. Howdy," he said to Jimmy, revealing a mouth missing a few teeth and dark with cavities.

"Hello. I'm Jimmy Roberts."

Billy Jack put aside his stirring pole and took Jimmy's hand. "Billy Jack Barnes," he said. "Ain't seen you in a while, Rhoda."

"Been in Greenville, workin' in the mill."

"Gone to the big city, eh? You can have it."

"I didn't wanna move, but Pa couldn't make it no more as a farmer."

"I told your Pa a hundred times he oughta get into a real business, like mine. Depression proof!" he said proudly to Jimmy.

"Yes, sir," Jimmy smiled back.

"You come for a jug of giggle-juice?"

"Lord, no! Just a drap or two, that's all. Jimmy ain't never had no moonshine."

Billy Jack looked at him. "Is that a fact?" he said, his tone implying that was a pitiful fact. "Well, a drap won't do you much good, but you're welcome to what you want." He turned and led them back towards the shack that tilted precariously towards the ground. He ducked his head, went inside, and returned with a ceramic jug and a tin cup. He put his finger through the small circle at the rim of the jug, swung it around so it lay across his right elbow, and poured a white liquid into the cup. "Some of my best," he said, handing the cup to Jimmy.

Jimmy looked down at the shimmering moonshine. "Ladies first," he said, and handed the cup to Rhoda. She laughed and put it to her lips, taking a small sip. When she swallowed, she shut her eyes and grimaced, then opened them wide. "Oo-eee!"

"Mighty fine, ain't it?" Billy Jack said proudly.

Rhoda nodded her head and handed the cup to Jimmy. He'd heard that moonshine could make you blind, if you drank enough, so he wasn't exactly sure he wanted to try it, but he wasn't about to chicken out in front of Rhoda. He put the cup to his lips and took a small sip. The liquid scalded the roof of his mouth and he immediately spat it out.

"Hey!" shouted Billy Jack. "Don't waste it!"

Jimmy tried to say "sorry," but all that came out was a rush of air and what sounded like "hah-wee."

"Wait a minute," Rhoda said. She went to the wooden table in front of the shack and found a jar full of water. She brought it back and began to pour some into the cup.

"You're ruinin' it!" Billy Jack shouted. "I cain't watch!" he said, turning his head.

The water did the trick, and Jimmy was able to swallow this time. It still burned, especially the inside of his throat, and his stomach screamed "water!" when the white lightning reached it, but at least he didn't spit it back out.

"Let's set a spell," Billy Jack said, pointing to a nearby bench. He plopped down on a wooden crate, wiped his brow with a blue bandanna, and stretched his long legs in front of him. "You two jularkin'?"

"He means, 'courtin'," Rhoda explained. "I don't know, Jimmy, are we jularkin'?"

Whether it was the moonshine in his belly or the beautiful smile Rhoda flashed him, Jimmy instantly sang out, "Yessirree!" Rhoda laughed, and so did Billy Jack.

"Well, that's all right, then," he said amiably. "Believe I might have a pull myself," he said, taking the jug from Jimmy and raising it to his lips. Jimmy could see by the movement of his Adam's apple that, to Billy Jack, a "pull" meant quite a swallow. He shook his head back and forth in admiration.

By the time Jimmy and Rhoda left Billy Jack's still, they had had more than "a drap or two" of his best moonshine. Jimmy found that the more he drank, the less it burned his throat and stomach. After a while, he didn't need to cut it with water any more. As they stumbled together back to the car, it seemed everything they said or saw or did was suddenly tremendously funny. A buzzard circling above? "Drunk!" Rhoda declared, to Jimmy's delight. A field full of corn? "Moonshine to be!" Jimmy said, blessing the field with his hands held high like Rev Bob during the benediction. "Grow in peace!" he shouted and laughed loudly. At one point, they saw a rabbit scamper across their path. Jimmy ran after it, waving his arms and yelling, "Wait, Mr. Rabbit, join us for a smoke!"

Giggling and stumbling, holding each other's hand, they finally reached the Packard. "I could use a cup of coffee," Jimmy said.

"I got a better idea. Think you can drive?"

"I'll try."

"Well, it cain't hardly be worse than the way you drove before. Let's go to my favorite swimmin' hole!"

Twenty minutes up the mountain and down a dirt road through a cathedral of Carolina pines brought them to a large pool at the bottom of a huge slab of rock at least thirty yards long. The Davidson River cascaded down in a steady torrent. Rhoda led the way up a steep path beside the rock until they reached the top. Once there, she took off her shoes and told Jimmy to do the same. Then she took his hand and led him slowly out into the river. It was shallow, and the rock wasn't too slippery, the force of the rushing water preventing slime from building up. The ice-cold water felt good in the summer heat. When they reached the middle of the rock, Rhoda stopped and dropped Jimmy's hand. They looked down at the pool below. "Isn't it nice?" Rhoda asked.

"Beautiful." Jimmy closed his eyes and listened to the crashing of the water tumbling down the rock into the pool. He drew in a breath and smelled the rhododendron blossoms and the fragrant pine needles, felt the water splash around his ankles, and the smooth rock under his feet. He took Rhoda's hand and together they stood still as statues for a moment, silent in wonder.

Suddenly, Rhoda let out a whoop and started running down the rock, pulling Jimmy behind her. She had gone only a few feet when she slipped and fell on her backside, yanking Jimmy down onto the rock beside her. They slid over the lip of the great rock and began to slide down toward the pool, the water deepening and pulling them along with ever-increasing speed. Rhoda kept up a scream the whole way down — "Wooooooooo!" Jimmy was too surprised to do anything but try to sit upright and keep his balance. Rhoda released his hand and he slid into a crevice in the rock, where the water piled upon itself and spun him completely around, so that he was heading towards the pool backwards. Then another rush of water spun him again, a slight rise in the rock shot him upwards through the air, and he splashed feet-first into the pool.

The icy water shocked the breath out of Jimmy as he sank some ten feet down into the pool. He immediately began swimming for the top. When he broke the surface, Rhoda was a few feet away, treading water. "Why'd you do that?"

"Welcome to Slidin' Rock!" Rhoda shouted. She slapped the water with her hand and sent a small wall of it in Jimmy's direction.

He began treading water. "You said we was goin' swimmin'!"

"What do you call this?" Rhoda took a few strokes towards the shore.

"Rhoda, we're in our clothes!" Jimmy began to swim after her.

"It makes it harder, but I couldn't wait." She reached the bank and pulled herself up onto the end of the rock.

Jimmy treaded water just beneath her. "We're supposed to take 'em off *before* we go swimmin', you crazy girl!"

"What's the fun of that? I wasn't sure you'd want to go down slidin' rock, so I thought I'd better make you. Here." She stretched out hand to help Jimmy onto the rock beside her. Instead, he pulled her back into the pool. "Whoo!" she screamed as she landed on top of him, both of them going under and coming back up, sputtering.

"Serves you right," he said. Her answer was to splash him again. He responded in kind, and soon the pool was alive with spraying water. Finally, Jimmy swam to her and pulled her hands behind her back and held them there, forcing her towards the bank until they were both able to stand.

Then, still pinning her arms behind her, he pulled her towards him and kissed her. He could taste the cold water on her mouth, he could feel the whole wetness of her body against his own. He released her arms, and she wrapped them around him, kissing him back, transporting him to that magic place where sensation overwhelms reason. They kissed for a long time, standing in the shallows of the cool mountain pool. When they separated, Jimmy took her face in his hands and said with a huge smile, "Let's go down again!"

Half an hour later they were winding their way along yet another trail on what Rhoda promised would be their last stop on her mountain tour. As the path petered out, she pointed to a large rock with a crevice about fifteen feet long and four feet high, big enough to sit, but not to stand. "That's where we're goin'." She stepped gingerly along the last ten yards to the rock, then crawled on her knees inside the opening. Jimmy followed and sat beside her. Below them stretched the gently rolling foothills of the Piedmont, a large valley spreading to the horizon in all directions. "Guess where we are," Rhoda said. "Stan The Man's mouth!"

"Caesar's Head?"

"Yep." She pointed. "There's Paris Mountain — 'member, we passed that just outside Greenville. Over there's Table Rock reservoir." Jimmy looked in the distance at a large lake beneath the stony face of a huge rock jutting out from the mountain. "I think you can see Brandon village way off yonder-ways."

"It's nice *not* to see it for a change," Jimmy said. They looked down on the beautiful valley below them, a vast sea of dark-green trees, interrupted in places by the light-green rectangles of plowed fields. "I never knowed the world was so big," Jimmy said quietly. An eagle soared above them, banking in circles, looking for prey. An absolute silence engulfed them as they sat, arms around their scrunched-up knees, gazing at the wonder of it all. "Rhoda," Jimmy whispered, his voice trembling with uncertainty, "What if I never make it offa mill hill?"

"Mill hill's just a bunch of dirt, Jimmy. A baseball diamond's a bunch of dirt, too. It's how you live on top of the dirt that counts." She looked at him. "An' who with."

"Who with?"

"One thing you gotta say for mill hill, it's family. People ain't a-feered to live close. They ain't a-feered to touch each other." She reached up and touched his cheek tenderly.

Jimmy put his arm around her and pulled her to him. What a wonderful day it had been. He'd never thought mill life could be anything but drudgery, but with Rhoda...? The wind was strong so high in the mountains, blowing her hair in her face. *But what about my dream? I cain't let that blow away! I've got to hang onto it! If I let another dream creep in....* He looked at the valley, stretching to the horizon. Greenville. Brandon Mill. And beyond the mill? Everything he'd ever dreamed about. Wasn't it?

CHAPTER 17

For Jimmy, the days that next week seemed to go by lickety-split while at the same time passing at a dream-like pace. Work at the mill went more quickly than he had ever imagined it could. On the other hand, everything slowed down at practice. He saw the ball more clearly than he ever had. In the outfield, fly balls seemed to drift slowly into his glove, and he knew effortlessly just where the ball was going to land. At the plate, he was "seeing things true" as never before, hitting hard line drives or slugging deep flies over the outfielders' heads. Shoeless, too, seemed happier, having rebounded from the poundings he'd taken in the paper and from the pulpit. He exhibited a surprising sense of purpose, almost as if he knew the Braves were going to win game after game until the championship was theirs.

The Braves played flawlessly in Saturday's game, crushing Piedmont 10-0 under the two-hit pitching of Red Roe. Piggy had no errors in right field. He made a fine running catch on one ball, but it was always easier for him to catch balls on the run because he didn't have time to think. It was the ones that went high above him, the fly balls for which he hardly had to move an inch that frightened him. He had worked diligently with Jimmy, slowly learning that a batted ball wouldn't really hurt him, using Shoeless's method of intentionally letting a baseball hit him in the head. Jimmy dropped balls on Piggy's head from a ladder. Then they progressed to the middle of the bleachers, Jimmy reaching out over the last seat to drop a ball on Piggy below. Amazingly enough, after enough balls from this height, Piggy started automatically putting up his glove.... to protect himself. Joe's seemingly crazy idea had convinced Piggy that the best way to keep from being hit by a fly ball was to catch it. And that day he had, hauling in no fewer than seven fly balls. And letting fly a stream of tobacco juice after each catch. Piggy had also become the best spitter on the team.

Jawbreaker to Whiff to Wash was no Tinkers to Evers to Chance, but they turned enough double plays to give everybody confidence that, if a man got on first, Murph or Red had a good chance of inducing a grounder which they could turn into two outs. At third, Whitey had become fearless at rushing the bunt and was using his natural athleticism to snag an amazing assortment of ground balls and line drives. Petie behind the plate, Pepper in center, Jimmy in left rounded out a team that had become quite suddenly a fearsome opponent, as Brandon had run up five straight wins. When Woodside lost its second in a row, the Braves found themselves only one game out of first place with two games to play. If they won next Saturday and Woodside lost, they would be tied going into the final game of the season, when the two teams would play each other to decide the championship.

After the game, when everybody had packed his gear and was about to head off, Jimmy said to Shoeless, "Mr. Jackson, the fellas an' me got somethin' we wanna show you, if you don't mind waitin' a minute."

"Sure." He called over to Katie, who was sitting in the stands with Rhoda and Thelma. "Be right with you, hon'."

"Take your time, Joe," Katie replied, a huge smile on her face. The three women looked at each other conspiratorially.

"Mr. Jackson," Jimmy began, then halted. He glanced at Rhoda. He had worked on his speech with her, and he thought he knew it, but now, standing alongside the dugout with his teammates and Shoeless Joe, the words weren't there. Rhoda mouthed "grateful" and Jimmy smiled. "You know how grateful we all are that you've been coachin' us," he began again. "We're probly 'bout the luckiest players in all of baseball. But" — Jimmy hesitated, knowing he was bringing up the unhappy past. He looked at his teammates for encouragement. "We realize you ain't been too lucky in ball, with what happened an' all. An' we know what they said 'bout you in the paper, an' what that preacher done preached." Jimmy noticed Shoeless's face darken, so he hurried on. "We want you to know we think that stinks! Every one of us thinks that's a bunch of baloney!"

A chorus of concurrence issued from his teammates. "That's right, Mr. Jackson!" "They don't know nothing'!" "Idiots!"

Shoeless gave a slight nod of appreciation and Jimmy continued. "So we got together an' decided to do somethin' for you, 'stead of you always doin' for us. We know 'bout that resolution 'bout gettin' you back in baseball, an' we all wanna make sure it passes 'cause there ain't no greater wrong than you bein' banned."

"It's stupid!" shouted Jawbreaker.

"Bunch of ignoramuses!" agreed Petie.

"Here's what I think of that!" Piggy said and spat a stream of Red Man into the dirt.

"Yeah!" his teammates said, laughing.

"That's why, Mr. Jackson...." Jimmy signaled to Piggy, who withdrew dozens of sheets from his duffle bag. "That's why we have created a petition to Governor Byrnes, urging him to sign the resolution an' send it on to Commissioner Chandler, an' get you back in baseball." Piggy handed the papers to Jimmy. "We went out an' collected a bunch of signatures on our petition."

"A thousand and thirty-three!" Whiff yelled out.

"An' here they are." Jimmy gave the pages to Shoeless.

Shoeless Joe Jackson looked down at the sheets of paper in his hands, and then up at his ball players. They awaited his response, a tinge of anxiety on their faces. Would what they had done matter to Joe? Would he be mad that they had stuck their collective noses into his business, and that, by spreading the word, they had brought him more unwanted attention? The pages shook slightly in Joe's hand. He gulped once or twice. Clearly, he was moved. And just as clearly, he didn't know what to say.

Katie filled the void, shouting from the stands, "This calls for a celebration!" Suddenly she, Rhoda, and Thelma stepped onto the field, carrying several bowls filled with watermelon slices, a case of Coca-Cola, and even a cake with thirty-one candles on it. Wash and Petie helped distribute them, and when everyone had a bottle of Coke, Jimmy raised his and toasted, "To the greatest baseball player of all time!"

"Joe Jackson!" everyone shouted and took a swallow. Everyone except Joe. He just stood there, Coke in one hand, signatures in the other, looking at the faces of those who believed him, those who believed *in* him, those who cared about him on the diamond and off. He realized, in that moment, what professional baseball had never given him, what he'd longed for every day of his baseball career: a family.

Somebody brought a chair from the dugout and they placed the cake on it. "Come on, Mr. Jackson, show us your lung power!" Jawbreaker shouted.

As Shoeless approached the cake, Thelma whispered to Katie, "Why thirty-one candles?"

"For the thirty-one years Joe's been banned from baseball," she answered. "Blow 'em out, Joe!" she called to her husband. Joe blew hard, and thirty-one candles flickered out.

The team and the three women circled round Shoeless. "I been given lots of things in my career," he said, his voice choking with emotion "From free haircuts when I'd hit a home run in textile league to a gold watch in the majors. But nothin' beats this. I don't know what to say."

"Don't say nothin'," shouted Piggy. "Let's eat it!"

"You tell 'em, Pig!" Wash shouted. They all laughed.

Katie cut slices and handed them around on napkins. The cake was gone in a flash. Then the players picked up their gear. Each one thanked Thelma, Katie, and Rhoda for the cake and Cokes, and each one shook Joe's hand before heading off to their homes, feeling good about the game they had just won and even better about the surprise they had given their beloved manager. As the celebration broke up, Joe approached Jimmy, who stood talking with Thelma and Rhoda. "'Scuse me," he said, "But I was wonderin' if ya'll would like to come over to the house an' join us for supper."

"Oh, no, we don't wanna be no trouble, Mr. Jackson," Thelma said. "Three mouths is a lot to feed."

"I've already fried the chicken," said Katie, as she joined the group. "If you don't mind eatin' it cold."

Thelma looked at Jimmy, then at Rhoda. "Well, in that case, thank you, we'd love to!" Thelma replied.

"No point goin' all the way back to Woodside, you can wash up at our house. An' please," he continued to Thelma, "Call me Joe."

The house on E. Wilburn Street was nearby, and, after Jimmy had washed off the grime of the game and Katie had served chicken, potato salad, and iced tea, everyone was soon seated on the porch, enjoying an unexpectedly cool summer evening. Rhoda filled Joe in on their trip to the mountains last Sunday and soon had him smiling and saying, "I ain't heered talk like that in a coon's age."

"I'll be glad to come jaw with you anytime, Mr. Jackson," Rhoda said sweetly.

"You just do that, lil' lady, you just do that!"

"You mind if I ask you somethin'?" she asked. "I've heard more 'n once people talk about 'Say it ain't so, Joe,' when they're speakin' of you. What's it mean, anyway?"

Katie sucked in her breath. In all innocence, Rhoda had swung the conversation back to a painful time in her husband's life. Jimmy had also wondered about the phrase, but thought this might not be the time to talk about it. "We've had enough baseball for one day, dontcha think?" he said.

"No, that's all right, I'd like to answer Rhoda's question," Joe said, surprising Katie. "That dang quote'll probably follow me to me grave, an' it ain't even true," Joe began. "Lemme tell you how it was, so at least somebody besides Katie an' me'll know the truth. It all had to do with this newspaperman, Hugh Fullerton, and this story he wrote 'bout what happened when I come out of the courthouse after my grand jury testimony."

"Fullerton's the same man who predicted Joe would fail in baseball 'cause he was ignorant," Katie offered.

"I hope he was a better reporter than he was a baseball predicter," Thelma chimed in.

"Not much of one. He said in this article that Cleveland had to hog tie Joe to get shoes on him 'cause he told 'em he couldn't hit lessen he could get a toe hold," Katie continued.

"How can they just make this stuff up?" Jimmy cried.

"Power. Of. The. Press." Joe enunciated each word with increasing venom. "That's why I never trusted reporters. They just say whatever they want, an' after awhile, people take it for the gospel. Anyway, after sayin' how kids across America idolized me, the 'ignorant mill boy' I believe he called me, he went on to write how I'd sold my honor, gone before the grand jury an' told the story of my own — what was that word he used, Katie?"

"Infamy."

"What's that mean?" Jimmy asked.

"A criminal act that everybody in the world knows about," Katie answered. "An' he wrote this the day after Joe testified! How is everybody in the world gonna know about it in one day!" Her face flushed with anger. "Joe, you cain't just tell 'em what Fullerton wrote, they gotta hear all that hogwash he put into it."

"That's one newspaper article I never saved."

"Well, I did." Joe looked at her in surprise. "Just a minute." She went into the house. An uncomfortable silence settled over the porch.

"I didn't mean to bring up sumpin' I shouldn't-a, Mr. Jackson," Rhoda apologized.

"We ought to be gettin' home anyway," Jimmy added, standing up.

"That's all right," Shoeless said, motioning for Jimmy to sit. "Might as well hear the whole story."

Katie returned with a newspaper clipping, which she proceeded to read in a tight voice. "Here it is.... 'There gathered outside the big stone building a group of boys. Their faces were serious. More serious than those who listened inside to the shame of the nation's sport. There was no shouting, no scuffling. They did not talk of baseball or anything else. A great fear and a great hope fought for mastery within' each kid's heart— ' How does he know what's in their hearts?" Katie interrupted herself, her voice rising.

"It's all right, dear, go on," Joe said.

She picked up the clipping and continued. "'It couldn't be true. After an hour, a man, guarded like a felon by other men, emerged from the door. He did not swagger. He slunk along between his guardians, and the kids, with wide eyes and tightened throats, watched, and one, bolder than the others, pressed forward and said, "It ain't so, Joe, is it?" Jackson gulped back a sob, the shame of utter shame flushed his brown face. He choked an instant. "Yes, Kid, I'm afraid it is," and the world of faith crashed around the heads of the kids. Their idol lay in the dust, their faith destroyed. Nothing was true, nothing was honest. There was no Santa Claus. Then, and not until then, did Jackson, hurrying away to escape the sight of the faces of the kids, understand the enormity of the thing he had done.' "

Katie lowered the clipping, almost shaking with anger. Nearby, her husband's shoulders slumped. He hadn't heard the article in many years. Jimmy looked confused. Thelma's face filled with pity. Only Rhoda seemed sure of her response. "What a load of bull crap!" she shouted. "He don't know pea turkey! You didn' 'slunk,' Mr. Jackson. I wasn't even there an' I know that. You do not slink! You walk tall. An' talkin' 'bout what you did, killin' their faith in Santa Claus! Bull crap, that's all it is, bull *crap*!"

Everyone was stunned by Rhoda's vehemence. But her strong language seemed to perk everyone up. "Of course it is," said Thelma. "There's a lotta words for that, but 'bull crap' will do!"

"How could he write that if it ain't true, Mr. Jackson?" Jimmy asked. "An' that sayin', it idn' even the way it goes. He says that kid asked you, 'It ain't so, Joe, is it?' "

"It got changed somehow," Shoeless offered.

"Even the sayin' is a lie!" Jimmy got up from his chair, too upset to sit. "You told me you played your heart out in that series," he said to Joe. "Isn't that what you told the grand jury? What did you have to be ashamed of?"

Joe glanced at Katie, who sat still, waiting for his answer. Joe took a deep breath. "There were some things to be ashamed of," he answered carefully, "But not the way I played."

"What really happened, Mr. Jackson?" Rhoda asked. "That is, if you want to tell us."

"I will if you promise not to call what *I* say 'bull crap,' " Shoeless smiled. Everyone laughed, calming things down. With the mood lightened, Joe spoke. "I come out of the courthouse, an' there was a bunch of people standin' 'round, photographers' flashbulbs goin' off, reporters shoutin' questions. I just ignored 'em, put my head down, an' plowed through. Maybe that's where he got that slinkin' idea."

"He was just jealous 'cause he'd never had that much attention thrown his way," Thelma declared, to the general consent of the others.

"An' there was a few kids millin' 'bout an' one of 'em did shout somethin.' But you know what he shouted?" Shoeless paused. He had everyone's attention. "He pointed at my feet an' shouted to one of his friends, 'See, I told you the sonofabitch wore shoes!' "

Laughter filled the night air, peals of it, as Thelma, Rhoda, and Jimmy gasped for breath between guffaws. Although she knew the story well, Katie found herself laughing, too. Joe smiled broadly. Jimmy impulsively ran to the porch railing and shouted to the night air, "Say it ain't so, Joe! Tell me you wear shoes!" More laughter tumbled from the porch.

"That's a wonderful story, Joe," said Thelma.

"An' the best part about it, it's true!" smiled Katie.

"Y'all hold on a lil' minute," Joe said, and ducked into the house.

"Thank you for a wonderful dinner, Katie," Thelma said, rising from her chair.

"Yes, Mrs. Jackson, thank you so much for havin' us over," Rhoda added.

"Best night ever!" Jimmy enthused.

Shoeless returned with an envelope in one hand and something wrapped in a towel in the other. He handed the envelope to Jimmy. "Open it."

Jimmy turned the envelope over. "What is it?

"You'll see."

He opened the envelope and pulled out two tickets. "What are these?"

"Train tickets," Shoeless said proudly. "Two tickets from Greenville, South Carolina to New York City! One for me, an' one for you."

Jimmy was shocked. "Me...? New York?"

"I got you a tryout. In Yankee Stadium."

For a moment, nobody spoke. All eyes turned to Jimmy. He blinked a couple of times, trying to focus his thoughts, staring at the tickets in his hand. "A tryout?" he finally mustered. "With the New York Yankees?"

"Got a friend from the old days who ended up in the general manager's office," Shoeless explained. "I thought 'bout writin' him a letter with Katie's help, but I didn't want you to know," he said, turning to her.

"In case things didn' turn out. So, I phoned him. Took me a while, but I finally reached him. An' he agreed we could come up Monday week an' he'd arrange for one of their scouts to try you out. The tickets are to leave next Saturday evenin', after the game, we'll get there Sunday, rest up, see a little of New York, maybe, have the tryout Monday, an' come back home Monday afternoon. You'll be back for your shift Tuesday night, so you'll miss two days of work. Think you can use vacation time or somethin'?"

"He can use some of mine if he needs to," said Rhoda.

"Well?" Shoeless asked.

"I ... I don't know what to say," Jimmy stammered. "Gosh!"

"That'll do," Joe replied, with a chuckle. But he wasn't through. "I figure we can do extra hittin' work all next week to get ready. 'Cause I got you a new bat you need to get used to." He unwrapped the towel and held out an old, black bat that he'd polished to a shiny sheen.

Katie put her hand to her mouth in amazement. Rhoda and Thelma looked puzzled. But Jimmy knew what it was that Shoeless Joe Jackson was offering him. "Black Betsy," he whispered in awe. Shoeless took the fat end of the bat and held the handle out to Jimmy. Jimmy looked at him. "Are you sure?"

"When I used to bat, people would shout, 'Give 'em Black Betsy!' I'm gonna be shoutin' that to you in Yankee Stadium."

Jimmy slowly extended his right hand and took Black Betsy. He was holding the most famous baseball bat in the world, the one that had helped make the man opposite him one of the most feared hitters ever. And this same man was offering him a chance to use that bat in a try-out with the New York Yankees. It was almost too much, and Jimmy dropped the bat to his side in disbelief.

"Charlie Ferguson made me that bat way back in 1903 from the north side of a hickory tree," Joe explained. He knew I liked black bats, so he darkened it with tobacco juice. I added my own over the years."

"It's heavy," Jimmy said, lifting it to his shoulder.

"Thirty-six inches, forty-eight ounces. Never broke in all the years I played. Take a swing or two," Joe instructed.

Jimmy raised the bat, placed his left hand on top of his right, and took his batting stance. The women and Joe backed up a little to give him room, and Jimmy swung Black Betsy, once slowly, to get the feel, then a little harder to build momentum, and, finally, after a waggle or two, with the biggest swing he could muster.

"Home run!" Rhoda shouted, and everybody whooped and clapped, just as if it had really happened.

"Thank you, Mr. Jackson," Jimmy gushed, cradling the bat against his chest. "Thank you so much!"

"My pleasure," Shoeless replied. And Katie smiled, knowing how true it was.

That night, Jimmy slept with Black Betsy in his bed. He didn't want to let go of her. He never wanted to let go of her. He'd give her back to Shoeless, of course. He knew it was just a loan. But what a loan! He felt the bat had magical properties inside her hard, hickory wood, properties that might finally help him start a major league career, just like her owner had done forty-five years ago. As he held the bat and settled in to dream, he whispered, "We'll give 'em hell!"

Across the way, in Brandon, Katie also held something special in her arms: her generous, surprising husband. He had endured so much over the years, but now he was finding a measure of redemption in the simple act of helping fulfill the dreams in a young boy's heart. She nestled close to his ear and whispered, "My hero."

CHAPTER 18

"All aboard!" The conductor's call rang out in the still, humid air of Greenville's Southern Railway station, as Shoeless Joe and Jimmy prepared to say goodbye to Katie, Thelma, and Rhoda and board the Southern Crescent, bound for New York City. It had been a splendid Saturday. The Brandon Braves had defeated Easley earlier in the afternoon, and Woodside had lost their third in a row, so there would be a final game to decide the championship next Saturday. As exciting as that thought was, however, it was the prospect of going to New York that had Jimmy so jumpy that Rhoda had to practically hold onto him to keep him still.

They had worked hard all week with Black Betsy, Jimmy developing a feel for her weight, how fast he could whip her around, how to align the small crook so that it faced the pitcher and let him get the fat part of the bat on the ball. Shoeless had cautioned him about swinging for the fences. "The Yankees got plenty of power hitters comin' up," he said. "What they want is somebody who can get on base. Hit line drives, go with the pitch to the opposite field, show 'em you know how to bunt, that's the way to impress 'em."

Shoeless had insisted that Jimmy "get to know" Black Betsy, not just treat her like a piece of wood. Calling the bat a "her," for starters. Rubbing her, as if she were a pet of some sort. He even encouraged Jimmy to talk to the bat, telling him how he'd always done it, saying she "liked it." At first, Jimmy had felt a little foolish doing that, and his "conversation" with the bat had been half-hearted. Nevertheless, as he held Black Betsy, standing on the train platform, he realized he had developed a sort of relationship with her, and this gave him a different kind of confidence, a confidence not in what he could do alone but in what *they* could do together.

"I hear them New York girls is ugly as sin," Rhoda said.

"Guess I won't do no jularkin', then," Jimmy responded.

"That's the right answer," she said, giving him a quick kiss on the lips.

Thelma gave Jimmy a hug. "I'm so proud of you."

"Let's see how I do, first, Mama."

"I'm proud of you no matter how you do. Now, mind your manners up there, y'hear?"

"Yes, ma'am."

Katie brushed off Joe's coat jacket and straightened his tie. "How're you feelin'?"

"Like I'm not sure I wanna get on that train. I ain't been in a major league ballpark in all these years, Katie. I'm kinda worried 'bout the memories it might stir up."

"You had a lot of good ones, Joe. Think on them."

"But every time I'm with a ball player, I'm always wonderin' what they believe 'bout me, deep down. 'Member that time a few years ago when Ty Cobb came into the liquor store to visit me. I didn't know what to say."

"Joe, this trip's about Jimmy, not you. Think about him an' don't worry 'bout the rest."

"I'll try."

"I'm so proud of you, Joe, doin' this for Jimmy." She gave him a strong hug.

"All aboard! Final call!" the conductor shouted. Joe picked up his suitcase, Jimmy his duffle bag, and they climbed onto the train. As it moved slowly out of the station, they waved through the window at the women, and settled back for the long ride to New York City.

Not far away, in his mansion on a hill, Howard Stone placed a call. He was in a foul mood. His Woodside Wolves had lost three in a row, and, unbelievably, they would now have to play the damn Brandon Braves for the championship. In the Greenville Spinners own Meadowbrook Park, no less, something Toby had arranged with the help of Yancey Dickerson. Toby had called him right after Woodside's loss that afternoon, telling him about the Meadowbrook location and saying he'd just bought a box of Cuban cigars. Howard could practically see him laughing through the phone. He'd also said that Rhoda Dawson would be singing the national anthem, thanks to Shoeless Joe's connections with the Spinners. And Yancey had told him at Saturday's game about the thousand-plus signatures on a petition supporting the resolution that had just been placed on the governor's desk. It was sounding like the whole Brandon family was getting set for a grand celebration next Saturday. *Over my dead body*, Howard thought. *I've still got a few cards left.* And he was playing one now.

"Socks here," Socks Singleton answered the phone in his New York office inside Yankee Stadium.

"Socks, Howie. How are you?"

"Fine, Howie, fine. Wondered when I'd be hearing from you. How's that championship coming?" Socks put down the scouting reports he'd been reading for the last hour, thankful for the break.

"Good, good."

"Glad to hear it. Like I said, you win that thing, I can get you to talk to the right people about purchasing the Triplets. Glad you told me about owning Crusher's contract. If he's as good as you say he is, that'll help."

"Everything's fine, Socks. Only I'm looking for what you might call an insurance run."

"How's that?"

Howard sat forward in his chair. "I hear you're getting a visit from Shoeless Joe Jackson next week."

"Yeah. He's bringing some kid up. Walter over in management asked me to give him a tryout as a favor to Jackson. They played together at Cleveland or something." Socks lit up a Lucky Strike. He had a sudden feeling this was not going to be just a casual conversation.

"That 'kid' happens to be the star player on the main team threatening my championship."

"I see."

"I think you'll like him, Socks. Matter of fact, I think you'd be wise to send him to play in La Grange next spring. But first, I wonder if there might be a little more left of that favor you owe me."

"I'm listening."

"A few days ago I mailed you a copy of the transcript for Jackson's trial in Chicago."

"Yeah, I got it. Why would you do that, Howie?" Socks took a long drag on his Lucky.

"Let me explain." And, while Shoeless Joe and his protégé were traveling to the bit city, Howard laid out his plan for making sure they didn't get the reception they were expecting.

On the train, Jimmy stared out the window, as towns he'd only heard the name of came and went in the approaching twilight. Spartanburg, Gastonia, Charlotte, High Point. A few hours ago, he was a linthead in a textile mill. Now he was on a train to New York City to try out for the New York Yankees organization. With Shoeless Joe Jackson on the opposite seat. He remembered when he'd been fired from Woodside Mill and Shoeless had refused to give him a job and thrown him out of his liquor store. And then Shoeless had shown up in the old barn and started coaching him. And then he got a job at Brandon Mill and started playing for the Braves, then Shoeless started managing them. And Rhoda? Was he in love? Would he marry her some day?

What an unbelievable journey the summer had been, and now he was literally journeying hundreds of miles to try out for the most famous baseball team in the world in the most famous stadium in the world. How had all this happened? The question rocked back and forth in his head to the rhythmic clacking of the tracks underneath the train, lulling him into a deep and peaceful sleep.

He woke a few hours later to find Shoeless looking into the black night outside the train window. "What time is it, Mr. Jackson?"

Joe pulled out his pocket watch. "Near midnight. Have a good nap?"

"Yes, sir. You been sleepin'?"

"Not much. Too excited."

"You?"

"A long time since I've been on a train. Used to take 'em all the time, 'course. I 'member one of the last times I was on one, Ring Lardner was drunk as a skunk. You know that song "I'm Forever Blowin' Bubbles?"

"No, sir."

"Well, Ring was lurchin' down the aisles singin' 'I'm forever throwin' ball games.' He knew I could hear him."

"Who's Ring Lardner?"

"A writer."

"I don't like him."

Joe laughed. "I didn't either, kid! Never got along much with writers no how."

"I don't blame you," Jimmy said strongly.

"Reckon not."

"Mr. Jackson, did you used to read what people wrote 'bout you?" Joe looked at Jimmy for a long second. "Oh, sorry, I forgot."

"That's all right. No, I couldn't read worth shucks. I used to buy magazines before I got on a train, open 'em up, an' pretend to read. Or wait'll a teammate ordered in a restaurant, then tell the waiter I'd have the same." Joe shook his head sadly. "It's amazin' how much time I spent coverin' up who I really was."

"The greatest baseball player who ever lived!"

Joe smiled. "Well, I don't know 'bout that. Ty Cobb was a purty good one in my day. Then Ruth, DiMaggio, there's been a bunch."

"If you couldn't read, how'd you sign your contracts?"

"Katie read 'em for me, an' I could sign 'em by kinda drawin' my name. The one time I didn't let her read my contract, I regretted it."

"When was that?"

"When Comiskey sent his secretary, Harry Grabiner, down to Savannah to sign me, February 1920 it was. Harry lied to me, told me there weren't no ten-day clause in the contract, an' there was."

"What's a ten-day clause?" Jimmy sat forward, sensing that Joe was in a talkative mood. Maybe it was the quiet of the car, with most other passengers sleeping. Maybe it was just being alone with him on a train. Whatever the reason, Jimmy was about to get one of his favorite things: another Shoeless Joe Jackson story.

"That clause said the White Sox had the option to terminate me, I believe that was the phrase, with ten days' notice, without havin' to tell me why. Most teams had 'em, but you could get it waived, an' that's what I'd negotiated for, I thought." Shoeless paused and looked out the window. "Funny thing, though, Jimmy. Signin' that contract probly brought about my last win, if you can call it that." He shifted in his seat. "Did you know I sued Charles Comiskey in a court of law?"

"What?"

"Yep. 1924. In Milwaukee. Sued him for back pay from that contract he tricked me into signin'. Big trial, made all the papers. It always struck me as funny that nobody remembers that trial, only my grand jury testimony an' the trial we won in 1921, when Landis threw us out anyway."

"What happened?" Jimmy's excitement brought him farther forward in his seat, as Joe's memory settled him farther back in his own.

"All the people was there an' they all had to testify. Comiskey, his lawyer Austrian, Grabiner, Happy Felsch, one of the eight players throwed out. Had affidavits from Eddie Cicotte and Lefty Williams, too. Even Hugh Fullerton, that guy who wrote that 'Say it ain't so' crock of crap, he testified, too — for Comiskey's side." Joe snorted derisively.

"'Course."

"An' I won! Eleven out of twelve jurors believed my story. Believed I had played to win in the Series, believed I'd never plotted with the others, believed I didn't know they'd told the gamblers I was in on the fix when I wasn't. They even believed Grabiner had tricked me into signin' that contract an' that I deserved my back pay. $16,704.11! Every penny of it!" Joe's voice took on an edge. "There was just one problem.

See, Austrian had tricked me into signin' that waiver of immunity back in the grand jury testimony, so what I said then was on the record. So there I was, in a pickle, caught in a rundown 'tween second an' third. They had some stuff I'd said in '21 an' it was different from stuff I said in '24.'"

"Why would it be different?"

Shoeless paused. The story of his ultimate victory had somehow twisted back on itself to involve the story of his greatest shame. He looked at Jimmy, the boy he had been grooming all summer for his big try-out on Monday, the boy who just might make it off mill hill like he had, the boy who, it was clear, idolized him. This was not the time to go into the complications of his grand jury testimony. He would explain it all to Jimmy later, after the try-out, after the season, after winning the championship. "It weren't all that different, but, like I say, Austrian had tricked me into thinkin' he was on my side in '21, so I said some things he told me to say. An' when I contradicted them in '24, the judge threw me in jail for perjury."

"You got thrown in jail?" Jimmy asked, incredulous.

Shoeless could see that the story was getting out of hand, the way it always did when he tried to explain what had really happened. It was as if the story had a life of its own, and nothing he could do or say could ever contain it, make it come out right, the way he knew it had been, the simple way: He had known about the fix, he'd tried to tell Comiskey, he'd gone and played his heart out in the Series, and he had the batting average and fielding performances to prove it.

"Just for a few hours, then my friends bailed me out. The point is," Joe went on quickly before Jimmy could ask any more questions, "The jury found in my favor. I won, I beat Comiskey. An' there I was, cheerin', slappin' my attorney's back, huggin' Katie, an' the judge bangs his gavel, an' when we'd all quieted down, he announced he was settin' aside the verdict."

"What's that mean?"

"He started scoldin' the jury for ignorin' 'perjured testimony,' saying he wanted to teach a lesson that nobody could commit perjury in a Milwaukee court an' get away with it. Judge said he was over-rulin' the jury's verdict an' declarin' it void," Joe concluded bitterly.

"How could he do that?" Jimmy shouted.

A few passengers in nearby seats stirred. Shoeless lowered his voice, but still spoke with unchecked vehemence. "Because he's the judge. Two times a jury said I was innocent, an' two times a higher authority threw it out!"

"That's not right!" Jimmy said heatedly. "I'm gonna show those Yankees on Monday. I'm gonna get into professional ball, an' I'm gonna play for you, play for all the years you couldn't, play for you an' me both! An' when I'm famous, I'm gonna make sure the truth comes out, 'bout how Shoeless Joe Jackson was unfairly kicked out of baseball an' denied money he was owed!"

Jimmy's passion stirred Shoeless. He almost believed maybe Jimmy could do it. Maybe the resolution could do it. Maybe he would not die with ignominy and shame following him to the grave. "You do that, boy," he said fiercely. "You just do that."

"It's huge," Jimmy said quietly. He and Joe were standing outside Yankee Stadium, looking up at the massive white façade. They had arrived in New York Sunday afternoon, napped for an hour, then wandered into Times Square in the early evening. Staring up at the neon flashing all around him, hearing the blaring horns of the taxis and other cars dodging in and out of traffic, standing on a corner while hundreds of people jostled past, Jimmy's first taste of big-city life tested his dream of moving off mill hill forever. *Could I bring Rhoda to this?* he wondered. *Would I even like it myself?* "Ain't what you'd expected, is it, boy?" Shoeless had asked.

"It's kinda scary," Jimmy confessed.

"I know. Now you maybe understand why, first time I come north, I got right back on the train an' went back home to Greenville." But Shoeless knew those weren't the kinds of thoughts Jimmy needed to be wrestling with now. "What say let's get us a bite to eat an' go on back to the hotel room an' rest up for tomorrow?" Jimmy had only been too happy to go to bed early. Somehow, with Black Betsy at his side, he had managed sleep well, eat a good breakfast, and make it to his tryout appointment with plenty of time to spare.

"You ever play here?" Jimmy asked, staring up at the silent, stone façade.

"Wadn' built before they...." Shoeless paused. "Anyway, no, never did."

"This'll be a first time for both of us, then."

"Reckon so." Shoeless dug his hands in his pockets.

"Should we go in?"

"Reckon so," Shoeless didn't move. This would be his first trip back inside a major-league ballpark since his ban. He was afraid of what he might feel. He'd spent so much time being angry about what baseball had done to him, there was a good chance being inside the park would bring on more of the corrosive thoughts that had bedeviled him ever since that awful day Kennesaw Mountain Landis had changed his life forever.

"You're a little afraid, too, aren't you, Mr. Jackson?" Jimmy said simply.

Shoeless didn't answer. Then he suddenly shouted, "Hold on!" He bent down and picked something up off the cement. "Well, all right!" he said with a big smile, holding the object up in the sunlight.

"What is it?"

"Good luck for you an' me! Stick out your hand." Jimmy did, and Joe placed the bobby pin in it. Jimmy smiled and tucked the pin into his back pocket. "Now we're ready!" Joe clapped Jimmy on the back, picked up his suitcase, and led the way to the turnstile, Jimmy following with his duffel bag.

The guard was expecting them and let them in. Even though it was morning, the sun was so hot it felt good to be in the cool underside of the stands above. The guard pointed to a ramp. "That'll take you inside, then go straight down towards first base. Mr. Singleton said he'd meet you there."

As they walked up the ramp, the light passing through the opening became brighter and brighter, beckoning them with its promised magic. They walked slowly toward it, drawn to it like a modern-day Mecca, until finally they stepped through the opening onto the walkway surrounding the seats. There it was, the baseball diamond at Yankee Stadium.

They stared. The white-white chalk defining the batter's box, the foul lines in their crisp march to the poles, the incomplete rectangles of the coach's boxes, the chalky bases standing guard in the clean-swept, red-brown earth. And the outfield grass, clipped and manicured, stretching in green perfection to the black cinder track before the outfield wall. Joe inhaled, filling his nostrils with the ballpark's tantalizing scent, a deep relaxation settling over his entire body. He inhaled again, this time closing his eyes. As he breathed deeply in the enormous silence, a thought slammed into his heart with a force that made him ache, and a feeling that almost made him cry. *How I've missed baseball!*

Jimmy pulled up beside him. "It's so beautiful," he whispered.

Shoeless nodded. "Take a breath."

Jimmy did. A warm smile spread across his face. "It's heaven."

A man in a short-sleeved white shirt, tan slacks, and polished, brown shoes, stepped out of the dugout and waved up at them. His bald head shone in the sun, his shirt stretched tight over a tanned body whose firm muscles had lost only a little of their former strength. "That you, Mr. Jackson?" he called out.

"Yeah," Joe shouted back, and walked down the ramp toward the dugout, Jimmy a few steps behind.

The man stuck out his hand. "I'm Socks Singleton, Director of Scouting. It's a real pleasure to meet you."

Joe shook his hand. "Director of Scouting, huh?"

"Walter said to make sure you had the best. And you must be Jimmy Roberts." Socks offered his hand.

"Nice to meet you, Mr. Singleton," Jimmy said, shaking his hand.

"You, too, son," Socks replied. "Why don't you hop over here and I'll take you back to the locker room where you can change. Got your uniform in there?" He pointed to Jimmy's duffel bag.

"Yes, sir." Jimmy handed Shoeless the bag, hopped over the railing, reached back and retrieved it from Joe.

"You coming, Mr. Jackson?" Socks inquired.

"I'll just stay out on the field, if you don't mind. An' please, call me Joe."

"Okay, make yourself at home, Joe. It's a shame you never got to play here." Socks said sympathetically. "Come on, Jimmy." Socks and Jimmy disappeared. Joe placed his suitcase on top of the dugout and hopped over the wall onto the field.

As soon as he touched the ground, his feet seemed drawn like a magnet to his position in left field. In a kind of trance, he walked toward the first-base foul line, but, before he crossed it, he was already jogging towards the outfield. He passed the pitcher's mound and imagined Lefty Williams giving him a wink as he warmed up. He trotted past shortstop and could almost feel Swede Risberg slap him on the butt as he ran by. He picked up speed as he entered the outfield grass, and by the time he'd reached his place in left field, Joe was fully remembering one of the happiest days of his baseball career.

Comiskey Field, Chicago, May 2, 1919. An Opening Day sell-out crowd thundered applause. Shoeless looked up at the stands, where fans had draped a banner over the railing, reading "JACKSON ROOTERS!" He listened to them showering him with shouts of encouragement from the stands above.

"Welcome back, Joe!"

"Have a great year, Shoeless!"

"You're the best, Joe, the best!"

Joe scanned the crowd. Hundreds of open mouths blended into a cacophony of welcome, praise, and thanks — a tsunami of support for their favorite baseball player. He doffed his hat in acknowledgement, which only increased the shouting. A broad smile creased his face. Nothing could be better than this!

Joe turned and settled into position — knees bent, hands on thighs, balanced on toes — as the St. Louis' Browns' first batter came to the plate. He watched as he took a ball, a strike, another ball, then another, then a strike. Count 3 and 2. Looking in at Lefty as he wound up, Joe experienced one of the surprisingly sharpened moments that sometimes swept over him in a game: he knew the ball was going to be hit his way. Sure enough, Lefty's curve hung over the heart of the plate, the batter swung, and the baseball began its long arc towards the left field corner. Anticipating, Joe took off at the crack of the bat. With two strong strides, he was already at full speed as the ball curved away from him. Flying across the grass, he locked his eyes on the small sphere, dazzlingly white against the blue sky. Behind him, the fans rose as one, screaming. But Joe didn't hear them. He heard nothing. He felt nothing. His only conscious thought was, "Catch that baseball!"

Even with all his exertion, Joe felt an inner calm. He knew where he was, he knew what he had to do, and he knew he could do it. As the ball neared the ground, he took a final great stride, then launched his body towards the ball, stretched his gloved left hand, nabbed the ball in the webbing, and skidded to the earth, raising his glove in demonstration of a fair catch. Only with the ball safely in his glove did his senses return to normal and he heard the tremendous roar of the crowd, the wave after wave of noise bouncing around the stadium like a ricocheting rubber ball. He rose and fired the ball back into the infield. As he trotted back to his position, he smiled, remembering the line some sports writer had crafted years ago about his glove: "The place where triples go to die."

In the White Sox half of the first, when Joe came up to bat, the umpire suddenly called time out. A trio of men in blue suits approached home plate. "Mr. Jackson," the one in the middle began. "We are here representing the fans of the Chicago White Sox. On their behalf, we have been authorized to present to you this $200 gold watch as a token of our appreciation for all you have done on behalf of White Sox baseball." Another man pulled a small box from his pocket, opened it, and passed it to Shoeless.

The announcer came on. "Ladies and gentlemen," he said. "Some local businessmen are presenting Shoeless Joe with a gold watch on behalf of the baseball fans of the Chicago White Sox!" A boom of cheers, growing louder and louder, as Joe stood motionless at home plate, Black Betsy dangling at his side. Never had he felt such pride. His whole being glowed with the feeling of being loved by thousands and thousands of people he didn't even know. How could life be this sweet? And all because he could throw a baseball and hit it far.

"Thank you," he managed to mumble.

"You're very welcome, Mr. Jackson," the group leader said and they turned and walked off towards the stands. The batboy came towards Joe.

"I'll take that, Mr. Jackson, if you want me to. Give it to the locker-room man."

Joe handed over the gift, then stepped into the batter's box. The chants began immediately. "Give 'em Black Betsy! Give 'em Black Betsy! Give 'em Black Betsy!" Forty thousand fans urging on their hero. "Give 'em Black Betsy, Joe!" Boy, would he ever!

"Mr. Jackson, Mr. Jackson, whatcha doin'?" Joe came out of his reverie to see Jimmy standing near home plate in his uniform, his hands cupped to his mouth. "Whatcha doin' out there?"

"Ready to start, Joe," Socks shouted.

Shoeless waved and jogged in towards home plate. Jimmy was waiting there with Black Betsy. He looked Jimmy dead in the eye — "Time to show 'em!" — then walked towards the dugout. A catcher and a pitcher in Yankee uniforms trotted past him and assumed their positions on the field.

Jimmy took a few practice swings while the pitcher warmed up. He watched the ball cross over the plate. It had a zip to it he had never seen before. Joe had warned him about that. Jimmy had tried to imagine what he meant, but his imaginings had not come close to the reality that was speeding over the plate right in front of him. And he wasn't even in the batter's box yet.

"Ready?" Socks asked.

Jimmy nodded grimly, took a deep breath, and stepped into the batter's box. Behind him, a major league catcher squatted. On the mound, a major league pitcher went into his windup. Jimmy flexed his knees, placed his little finger around the bat handle, pulled the bat back, and waited to receive his first pitch ever from a professional pitcher. The moment he'd waited for his whole life.

He hardly saw the pitch. He heard the pop of the ball as it slammed into the catcher's mitt. There was no umpire to call balls and strikes, but Jimmy knew it had been a strike, over the outside corner. He stepped out of the box, rolled his shoulders, took a practice swing, and stepped back in. Seconds later, another pop of the catcher's mitt on another ball he hardly saw pierced a moment's doubt into his mind. *What if I cain't do it?*

He stepped out of the box. What was it he and Shoeless had worked on all week? That phrase? Jimmy was having a hard time thinking clearly. How could he forget it, he knew it so well? He bent down, grabbed some dirt, and rubbed it between his palms, stalling for time. They can throw it faster, Shoeless had told him, but they still had to release the ball, same as any other pitcher. There was still that split second when, if you had the discipline, you could see the ball leave the pitcher's hand and get a good idea about what kind of pitch it was. You can hit their pitching, Shoeless had told him, if you ... if you ... if you see things true! That was it! *Relax,* Jimmy told himself. *Remember those dang candles? Just see the pitch true.*

Jimmy watched carefully as the pitcher went into his windup, rolled back his right arm, and thrust it forward, releasing the ball. He saw it begin to spin. A curve ball. He swung. Too soon. He pulled the ball foul past first base. But he had hit it! The sting of ball-on-bat felt good. The strain in his arm muscles pumped him up.

"Attaway, Jimmy!" Shoeless shouted from in front of the dugout. He clapped enthusiastically. Jimmy took off his cap and wiped his forehead with the sleeve of his right arm. *Did it get warm, or is it just me?* He replaced his cap, spit on his hands, rubbed them together, and stood back in the batter's box.

But just seeing the ball true wasn't working. On the next several pitches, Jimmy saw the ball clearly, and he swung well, but he managed only a few weak grounders to the left side, a couple of whiffs, a foul ball behind the plate, and a frozen half-swing on a change-up that had him completely fooled. He looked over at Shoeless, who spat nervously into the dirt. He turned his gaze to Socks. A slight tightening of his lips told Jimmy he had better start hitting the ball soon or his try-out would be over. *No!* They couldn't have traveled all this way, he couldn't have worked so hard, Shoeless couldn't have taught him so much, to fail now. He raised his hand to Socks. "Just a minute," he said, and walked a few feet away.

What was wrong? Why couldn't he make good contact? He was swinging the way Shoeless had taught him, not trying to hit it far, just trying to hit those blue darters Joe had been famous for. He was focused. He was relaxed. He was — *He, he, he ... yes!* Jimmy had forgotten. He was part of a team. There was somebody else that needed to be involved in this. He looked down at Black Betsy. What the hell, he had nothing to lose.

"Okay, Betsy," he said under his breath. "You can do it. You're the greatest baseball bat ever. You've got tons of hits in you, tons!" Jimmy glanced over his shoulder. Socks eyed him curiously. So did the catcher, standing behind the plate, mitt folded on one hip. Jimmy didn't bother looking at the pitcher, who he was sure was staring at him, too. *I don't care.* He'd come this far. He was going all the way.

"Lissen up, Betsy," he said firmly, but quietly. "You're gonna hit this next pitch hard, right back at the pitcher. You're gonna hit it square on the fat part of the bat — " Jimmy smiled to himself. "Square on *your* fat part! You hear me?" He looked down at the black bat in his hands. "Good."

Jimmy walked the several feet back to the batter's box. "Thanks," he called to Socks. He looked over at Joe and gave him a grim smile. Then he stepped back in, dug his left toe into the dirt, waggled the bat behind his left shoulder a few times, and waited for the pitch. When it came, he swung. The ball cracked off the bat straight at the pitcher, who had to duck. A blue darter. "Sorry," Jimmy yelled, then turned away and whispered to his bat, "Attaway, Betsy, do it again!"

His hitting improved dramatically. Not that he didn't swing and miss a couple of times. He did. But he also hit the ball hard, to all fields. He hit long flies, which might have been outs, but which showed he had power. He even laid down two perfect bunts, one down the third base line, one towards first.

Finally, he caught one square and slammed it over the wall in right. "That's enough! Socks called. "Why don't you and me go have a little jaw in my office. Wait here, Joe."

"Sure thing, Socks," Joe said.

"Thanks a lot, fellas!" Socks called to his pitcher and catcher, who walked off the field and disappeared into the dugout.

Jimmy walked over to Joe, filled with nervous excitement. "I think I did okay," he said. He lifted up Black Betsy. "I mean, we did."

Joe could hardly contain himself. "You did great, Jimmy! You powdered that ball!" He punched Jimmy on the arm. Jimmy smiled, and turned to follow Socks through the dugout and into his office.

The office wasn't much. A metal desk, some calendars and schedules tacked to a bulletin board, a couple of wooden chairs, three filing cabinets, one of whose open drawers revealed manila files stuffed with papers and photographs. Socks gestured Jimmy to a chair opposite his desk. Jimmy sat and looked expectantly at Socks, trying to stay calm. But his heart was racing. This was it. A scout — no, the Director of Scouting — was going to tell him how he'd done. Now he'd know whether he ever had a chance of playing major league ball or not.

Instead, Socks slid a pile of papers across the desk to Jimmy. *A contract?* Jimmy thought. *Already?* But upon closer examination, he saw that the first page had typed upon it "Chicago County Grand Jury, Testimony of Joseph Jefferson Jackson, September 28, 1920." Jimmy looked up. "I don't understand."

"It's Joe's testimony before the grand jury in the scandal," Socks said.

"Why are you showin' it to me?" Jimmy asked.

"I think you should read it. Before you and I go any further — if we go any further — I think you should know the truth about Joe Jackson."

"I know the truth," Jimmy said defiantly. "Mr. Jackson didn't do anything wrong."

"Those papers will tell you different. In Joe's own words." Socks leaned forward in his chair. "Look, I can tell you're a nice young man, son. And I like the way you swing the bat. You're at the start of what might be a pretty good career. You don't want to mess things up right off the bat by hanging around the wrong people."

"He is not the wrong people!"

"Loyalty's good, Jimmy. Just make sure it's for the right reason." Socks lit a Lucky. "Go on, have a look. It won't kill you to know what Joe signed his name to all those years ago. I edited it down so you won't have to read the boring part about 'what's your name' and 'where do you live,' stuff like that." Socks took a deep drag on his cigarette, exhaled, and waited.

Jimmy reluctantly picked up the pages. What choice did he have?

Q (District Attorney)   Did anybody pay you any money to help throw that series in favor of Cincinnati?
A (Joe Jackson) They did.

Jimmy drew in a breath. What? He looked at Socks, who gestured for him to continue reading.

Q   How much did they pay you?
A   They promised me $20,000, and paid me five.

Q   Who promised you the twenty thousand?
A   Chick Gandil.

Q   Who is Chick Gandil?
A   He was their first baseman on the White Sox Club.

Q   Who paid you the $5,000?

A   *Lefty Williams brought it in my room and threw it down.*

Q   *Who is Lefty Williams?*
A   *The pitcher on the White Sox Club.*

Q   *Who was in the room at the time?*
A   *Lefty and myself. I was in there, and he came in.*

Q   *Where was Mrs. Jackson?*
A   *Mrs. Jackson — let me see — I think she was in the bathroom. It was a suite; yes, she was in the bathroom, I am pretty sure.*

Jimmy winced. Mrs. Jackson was there? Did she know what happened?

Q   *Does she know that you got $5,000 for helping throw these games?*
A   *She did that night, yes.*

Q   *You say you told Mrs. Jackson that evening?*
A   *Did, yes.*

Q   *What did she say about it?*
A   *She said she thought it was an awful thing to do.*

Q   *Then you talked to Chick Gandil and Claude Williams both about this?*
A   *Talked to Lefty Williams about it, yes, and Gandil more so, because he is the man that promised me this stuff.*

Q   *How much did he promise you?*
A   *$20,000 if I would take part.*

Q   *And you said you would?*
A   *Yes, sir.*

Jimmy paused, beginning to fight back tears. How could Joe be saying this? He forced himself to continue.

Q   *When did he promise you the $20,000?*

A   It was to be paid after each game.

Q   How much?

A   Split it up some way, I don't know just how much it amounts to, but during the series it would amount to $20,000. Finally Williams brought me this $5,000, threw it down.

Q   What did you say?

A   I asked him what the hell had come off here.

Q   What did he say?

A   He said Gandil said we all got a screw through Abe Attel. Gandil said that we got double crossed through Abe Attel, he got the money and refused to turn it over to him. I don't think Gandil was crossed as much as he crossed us.

Q   You think Gandil may have gotten the money and held it from you, is that right?

A   That's what I think, I think he kept the majority of it.

Q   What did you do then?

A   I asked Gandil what is the trouble? He says, "Everything is all right," he had it.

Q   Then you went ahead and threw the second game, thinking you would get it then, is that right?

A   We went ahead and threw the second game, we went after him again. I said to him, "What're you going to do?" "Everything is all right," he says. "What the hell is the matter?"

Jimmy swallowed hard. There it was, right there on the page. *We went ahead and threw the second game....* A tear sneaked into the corner of his right eye.

Q   After the fourth game you went to Cincinnati and you had the $5,000, is that right?

A   Yes, sir.

Q   *Where did you put the $5,000, did you put it in the bank or keep it on your person?*

A   *I put it in my pocket.*

Q   *What denominations, in silver or bills?*

A   *In bills.*

Q   *How big were some of the bills?*

A   *Some hundreds, mostly fifties.*

Q   *What did Mrs. Jackson say about it after she found it out again?*

A   *She felt awful bad about it, cried about it a while.*

Q   *Weren't you very much peeved that you only got $5,000 and you expected to get twenty?*

A   *No, I was ashamed of myself.*

Jimmy stopped. There was more, but he couldn't go on. He wiped his eyes with the back of his baseball uniform sleeve and returned the pile of papers to the desk.

Socks stubbed out his cigarette in the ashtray. "Sorry to have to do that to you, son. You probably idolize Jackson. But if he was telling you getting banned was a great injustice, talking about how baseball done him wrong, well, I just wanted you to know there's another side of the story."

"He signed this?" Socks leaned forward and lifted the papers up, leaving the final page exposed. Right above the typed name "Joseph Jackson," in a painstaking scrawl that was barely legible, Jimmy saw the two words: Joe Jackson.

"Signed in a court of law." Socks paused, shifting gears. "Now, let's talk about you. You swing a good bat, there, son. Considering you're not used to big-league pitching, you did pretty damn good today. I understand you play in the Textile League down in South Carolina?" Socks waited for an answer, but Jimmy was barely listening. "Son?" Jimmy looked up. "I was asking where you play ball."

"South Carolina, yes, sir. Play for Brandon," Jimmy managed. Had the scout said he'd hit the ball well? Jimmy was having a hard time remembering why that mattered. He just wanted out of that office. He wanted to talk to Joe.

"Well, I know the Dodgers got a team in Greenville. Our closest one's in La Grange, Georgia, the Troupers, Class D league. How'd you feel about playing pro ball in the Georgia-Alabama league?"

There they were, the words Jimmy had worked his whole life to hear. They barely registered. "Guess so," he mumbled.

Socks looked at the young man sitting across from him. He'd paid back his debt to Howard Stone, more than paid it back, but he didn't feel good about it. Why had it been necessary to shatter this boy's faith? "Don't be too hard on Joe, son. He's a good man. Plenty of good men do bad things some times. I'm sorry I had to be the one to tell you."

"Yes, sir," Jimmy managed. "Mind if I take this?" he asked, rising and gesturing to the indictment papers.

Socks handed them to him. "Of course. Now, let's talk about — " Jimmy turned and ran out of the office. "Wait a minute, I want to talk to you about a contract!" Socks shouted after him. But Jimmy was gone.

Socks considered going after him, but he needed to finish his favor and get back to work. He dialed Howard's number.

Sitting in the first row of seats, Shoeless saw Jimmy emerge from the dugout. He noticed the papers in Jimmy's hand. "Over here!" he shouted and hopped over the wall to greet him. "How'd it go?"

"He said he liked me," Jimmy said without emotion.

"That's great, Jimmy, great! Congratulations!" Jimmy held out the papers in his hand. "What's this?"

"Your confession."

"Huh?" Shoeless took the papers and looked at the title page.

"It's a copy of your grand jury testimony. I know you cain't read. Do you want me to read it to you, or do you remember what you said?"

Joe's shoulders sagged. "Did Socks give you this?"

"Yeah."

"That son of a bitch!"

"Be careful who you're callin' names!" Jimmy shouted suddenly.

"Jimmy, listen, this ain't the whole story," Joe began urgently, waving the papers. "They tricked me, told me all I had to do was confess an' that'd be that, I could walk away, it was the gamblers they were interested in."

"Why'd you sign it if it wadn' true?" Jimmy cried out, his voice cracking.

Joe spoke rapidly, as if the flow of words could somehow stop the impending wreck of his relationship with the boy he had come to care so much about. "I didn't know what I was sayin'. Cicotte had already named me. I got scared an' I went out and got real drunk. I said what Austrian advised me to say, so's I could get out of there as fast as I could. I also said I played to win, made no errors, turned Gandil down when he asked me — !" Joe began desperately rifling the papers. "Did they show you that part, too, Jimmy? It's in here somewhere — "

Jimmy slammed his hand down on the papers, scattering them out of Shoeless's hand. "You got drunk?" he screamed. "The most important day of your life, an' you got liquored up? You an' my daddy are just alike! Liars an' cheaters an' — !" A sob broke over him, wracking his entire body.

"Jimmy —"

"Shut up! Just shut up!" He reached into his back pocket, pulled out the hairpin, and threw it at him. "Say it ain't so, Joe!"

Jimmy then jumped the wall, grabbed his duffel bag, and ran through the stands out of the stadium.

"Jimmy, come back!" Joe shouted after him. "Jimmy! Wait, I can explain it, gimme a chance to explain it!" Shoeless ran to the dugout steps. "Gimme a chance!" But Jimmy was gone.

Joe grabbed the top of the dugout with both hands and hung his head. After a long while he turned back to the field. The transcript papers lay all about him, scattered at his feet, the words that had haunted him for so long, words, he knew now, would haunt him to his grave. He raised his head and gazed out at the baseball diamond. A little while before it had seemed so promisingly green, so full of possibilities. Instead, it had become, once again, the place of his unceasing nightmare.

CHAPTER 19

It didn't take the three women waiting at the train station Tuesday morning long to realize something had gone terribly wrong in New York. Jimmy exited the train first. Rhoda rushed into his arms to give him a big kiss, only there were no arms to rush into. He didn't even put down his duffle bag and her "I missed you so much!" elicited not so much as a grunt.

Thelma fared little better. "How'd it go, Jimmy?" she asked.

"Fine," Jimmy managed between gritted teeth.

"Where's Joe?" Katie asked and was startled to see Jimmy only shrug. Finally, Shoeless appeared at the top of the train steps, suitcase in one hand, Black Betsy in the other. He limped slowly down the steps. Katie ran to him quickly. "Joe, what's wrong?"

"Nothin'," he mumbled, struggling past her.

The piercing shriek of the train whistle split the air. "All aboard!" the conductor called. Everyone stood uncertainly as the train jerked to life and the engine began to move down the track. They watched in silence as it receded into the distance. Katie pointed, "The car's over there."

"I'll walk," Jimmy said, and started off the platform.

"At least let me take this," Thelma said, wrenching the duffel bag from his hands.

"Wait!" Rhoda called, and started after him.

Joe went straight to the car. Katie approached Thelma. "You're not walkin'," she said, snaking her arm through Thelma's and pulling her towards the car before she could protest.

No one spoke as the Packard lumbered through the streets towards Brandon. Joe stared out the window. Thelma stared at her fingernails. Katie knew better than to try to ask Joe what had happened until they were alone, but no other topic of conversation seemed appropriate, so they drove the few miles to Woodside to drop off Thelma and then on home in absolute silence.

For a while, Rhoda marched quietly beside Jimmy as his quick strides gobbled up the distance to Woodside, but she wasn't a person to walk long in silence. "I take it the try-out didn' go so good."

"It went great," Jimmy replied in a flat voice.

"That why you're actin' like a rooster in an empty hen house?" She waited for Jimmy's answer, but none came. "Ain't you gonna ask me what that means?" Jimmy lowered his head and increased his pace. "It means 'angry,' which is what I'm gonna be if you don't loosen your lips." Rhoda had to jog to keep up with him. "Tell me what happened, dammit!" She grabbed his arm and spun him to look at her. What she saw surprised her. Tears welled in his eyes, his lips quivered, and an expression of infinite sadness drained the color from his cheeks. "Oh, Jimmy!" she exclaimed, pulling him into her arms.

He broke into sobs, small bursts of sorrow that exploded against Rhoda's chest, as she cradled him, murmuring, "Jimmy, Jimmy, Jimmy.... Oh, I'm so sorry.... So sorry...." She caressed the back of his head, as he cried into her neck. "It's okay.... It'll be okay...."

"He cheated, Rhoda!" he spat out between sobs. "That Yankee scout, he handed me a copy of the Grand Jury testimony, an' there it was, in his own words." The memory caused another cascade of tears. When he caught his breath, Jimmy continued. "How he threw the first game, and the second game, too. How upset he was that he hadn't gotten the full payoff. An' Mrs. Jackson knew. She knew, too!"

Rhoda held him. "I'm sure there's an explanation."

"You're right, there is!" Jimmy cried. "He was drunk! The great Shoeless Joe Jackson walked into that courtroom drunk as all get out!"

She waited a moment for his anger to subside. "Is that all he said?"

"He said he was tricked into it by some Chicago lawyer, told him to play dumb. The dumb hick didn' know what he was doin'? Was he too stupid to tell the truth?"

Rhoda realized further conversation was useless at this point. She had learned what she'd needed to know, for now. There was more to the story, she was sure of that, but Jimmy's sense of betrayal by a man he worshipped would not be easy to overcome. And the championship game was just four days away. How would this rift between the manager and the team's best player affect that? There was a lot to be thought through, but first she had to get Jimmy home. He needed sleep for the long night of work ahead. Thank goodness Mr. Gower had cancelled that afternoon's practice to give Joe and Jimmy time to catch up on their sleep and the others time to rest. She slipped her arm around his waist, held him tight, and together they walked the rest of the way in silence.

Jimmy found his work strangely peaceful that night. Watching the empty bobbins fill with the colorful thread, seeing it wind round and round the cone, produced a kind of hypnotic state that shut out all thoughts of baseball and betrayal. Tossing the full bobbin into a bin, putting on an empty one, then hurrying to the next machine before its bobbin overflowed demanded an automatic focus that quieted his nerves and left him exhausted by the end of his shift. Rhoda understood, when she saw him at the exit gate, that it wasn't the time to resume their conversation of the day before. She silently watched him trudge off towards Woodside and home. When he got there, Jimmy went immediately to sleep, not waking until the time he had to put on his uniform, tie his cleats and sling them over his shoulder, tuck his glove under his arm, and set off to Brandon park for practice.

Jimmy worried all the way over about how he should treat Shoeless that afternoon. Should he tell his teammates what had happened? That would only upset them needlessly on the eve of their championship. Should he avoid Joe? But how could he do that without arousing suspicion? *Just act normal,* he concluded. *If I can...*

.He was relieved to find Shoeless had not yet arrived when he reached the ballpark. As expected, his teammates peppered him with questions while he laced up his cleats. "What was Yankee Stadium like?" "Who pitched?" "Who caught?" "Did you play outfield or just hit?" "Why is he called Socks Singleton?" "Did you hit it? How many? How far?" And, most insistently, "What'd he say? What'd he say?" Jimmy answered them all, omitting only two things: Socks' hint that he might be able to play for the La Grange team next spring, and any mention of the transcript of Shoeless's Grand Jury testimony. There would be plenty of time for the former, if it came to pass. As for the latter, Jimmy wasn't sure whether there would ever be time for that. But he was sure that before Saturday's championship game was not the time.

Jimmy was shagging fly balls with the other fielders when Shoeless walked through the outfield gate. He looked, as Rhoda might say, like something the cat dragged in and the dog wouldn't eat. Clearly, Joe had not slept much since arriving home yesterday morning. His white shirt rumpled at the belt, his trousers hung too low, he'd forgotten to wear the straw hat he used to keep the sun off his balding head. He shuffled toward home plate, instead of walking with his usual confident stride. And he was carrying Black Betsy. Ever since Shoeless had loaned it to Jimmy, he always had Betsy with him. Everyone knew he even slept with it, so why was Shoeless carrying the bat? Jimmy's teammates looked at each other, but no one dared ask what was wrong.

Practice went well. They had been at it so long, had sweated through so many hot and muggy afternoons, had shouted and encouraged so many times, that they could perform the routines automatically. Bucket drill, foot drill, batting, pitching, grounders, fungoes, pepper, they moved from one to the other as easily as water over a dam. Shoeless had no more to teach them, and, for now, they had no more to learn. Practice this week would be about remembering the fundamentals, staying loose, keeping focus. Things had gone so well, no one even noticed that when Joe called "That's it!" Jimmy ran quickly off the field instead of helping pack the equipment and walking home with Joe, as he usually did. Joe, too, seemed anxious to get away, mumbling quick good-byes. "Probably still tired," Piggy opined, and they all left it at that.

Jimmy was surprised to see Waddy sitting in his car outside the ballpark. He waved Jimmy over. "Mr. Stone wants to talk to you," he said.

"About what?"

"Didn' say. Just said it concerns your future."

"Why's he interested in my future?"

"What's with the questions?" Waddy barked. "He said to pick you up. I'm here. If you don't wanna talk to him, suit yourself."

Given what had happened, a car ride with Waddy Benson was the last thing Jimmy wanted. His mother had cut off all "unofficial" contact, and, so far, Waddy hadn't retaliated by demoting her. But the way he'd used his position as Thelma's boss still rankled. Jimmy had thought often of retaliation of his own, but so far the opportunity hadn't presented itself.

He climbed into the back seat. "What are you doin' back there?" Waddy asked.

"Makes me feel like you're my chauffeur. To Mr. Stone's!" Jimmy commanded.

Waddy slammed the car into gear, and they headed away toward the north side of town. Jimmy had never been to this part of Greenville before, and the large brick houses, tall columns, and magnolia-shaded lawns amazed him. Would he ever live in a place like this? Probably not. Even a professional ballplayer's salary wouldn't allow that. Would he want to live here? Probably not. He couldn't picture Rhoda in one of these houses, and when Jimmy thought about his future, he increasingly thought about Rhoda as a part of it. Rhoda! She would be expecting to meet him for their usual Coke walk. Well, she'd have to understand. Jimmy wasn't much in the mood for being with her. Too much opportunity to ask more questions about what had happened in New York.

Waddy turned up a long driveway that curved to the top of a hill and pulled to a stop in front of Howard's white-columned house. "He said to take you home. I'll wait down there in the shade."

Jimmy got out and stood for a moment in the driveway. What could Howard Stone possibly want with him? He'd never even spoken to him. Eight weeks ago Mr. Stone had fired him and now he wanted to see him? Jimmy climbed the stairs to the porch and knocked.

Howard opened the door himself. "Come in, Jimmy, come in!" he said in his friendliest voice. "Let's go into my office." He led the way. "Another scorcher. I don't see how you can practice in weather like this."

"You get used to it."

"I'll never get used to it. And I hope to God I don't have to. Have a seat, Jimmy." He gestured to a chair opposite his large mahogany desk. The floor-to-ceiling windows were all the way open and two fans whirred in opposite corners, but it was still stifling.

"It's too hot to beat around the bush, so let me tell you about a little proposition I've got for you." He opened a drawer of his desk and pulled out some papers. "This is a contract for you to play Class D ball for the La Grange Troupers next season. Socks Singleton sent it to me at my request. It's got your name on it."

Jimmy was shocked. "My name?" Jimmy remembered Socks calling after him when he'd bolted the office. Could this have been what he wanted? "Why did he send it to you?"

Howard counted on Jimmy's not knowing that much about baseball contracts. "Socks liked you. But not enough to sign you. But I offered to pay your contract for a year, if you make the team. I'll even pay your expenses to move to La Grange."

"Why would you do that?"

"Because I've got a proposition for you."

"Proposition?"

"Jimmy, I'd like you to emulate your hero, Shoeless Joe Jackson."

"He's not my hero!" Jimmy said bitterly.

"Yes, Socks mentioned that he'd shared a little information with you," Howard said innocently. "Do you know what 'emulate' means?"

"No, sir."

"It means, 'copy.' As in, 'do the same thing as.' As in, do what your hero did in the 1919 World Series in this Saturday's championship game." He looked Jimmy dead in the eye.

Jimmy was shocked again. "Throw the game?"

"That's right. Woodside wins the championship. You get a chance to get out of the mills for good. I get a chance to get out of the mills for good. And Shoeless gets ... what he deserves." He slid the contract across the desk.

Jimmy picked it up. There it was, right on the first page. The logo of the New York Yankees. And his name. Jimmy Roberts. "Mr. Stone, I don't understand. You fired me, an' now you want to give me a contract?"

"Not give, Jimmy. You've got to earn it. I don't want to be two-timed the way Shoeless did, agreeing to cheat and then playing hard. Do we understand each other?" He eyed him carefully.

Jimmy put the contract down on the desk. "I don't know...." He leaned back in his chair and tilted his head up. He closed his eyes. A dozen thoughts zinged around his brain. *How could I do this? Is this my only chance to play professional ball? What about my teammates? What would people think if they found out? What would Rhoda think?*

Finally, he sat up. "Can I think about it?"

"Till Friday morning. But then I've got to know. Got a few bets to lay down," Howard said with a smile.

Jimmy picked up the contract and moved silently toward the door. "Jimmy!" Howard called. Jimmy turned to face him. "It's just a game."

Jimmy looked at him for a moment, then walked out of the office. Howard followed him to the porch and watched him get into Waddy's car and drive away. He looked skyward. *Isn't that what you always told me, Daddy? It's just a game? Well, I didn't believe it then, and I don't believe it now. No, it's* the *game, the game that's going to break the grip of this mill you've shackled me with and set me free. Of it, and, by God, of you.*

If work Tuesday night had almost been restful, work that Wednesday was a torment. Try as he might, Jimmy couldn't keep the questions from exploding in his brain. *Could I really do this? To Petie an' Whiff an' Pepper? An' Steve? 'Course, they'd never know, they'd just think we'd lost, fair an' square.... An' maybe we wouldn't lose. I'm just one man, who knows, everybody else might win it for us. That'd show Stone...! But what about my contract? I won't get it if we win, I bet.... Do I really want to play professional baseball that bad? Yes, anything to get me out of this damn mill! If I have to doff another bobbin I'll puke! How about doffin' another million...? An' Rhoda? Would she come to Georgia with me? How could she, she'd have to work here? But not if we was married. Could I support us both? I gotta read that contract again, I don't even remember how much it was I'd get paid. More'n I make here, that's for sure. An' I'd be doin' what I love, what I always dreamed of doin'.... But be a cheater? Like my daddy? At least I wouldn't be hurtin' anybody. Not really. It's just a game, it's just a game.*

"Ten Jim Beam's!" Joe called out to Katie in their liquor store late Thursday morning. They were doing inventory. They'd started the day before, but Joe had been so distracted that they hadn't been able to finish, worried about his first practice with the Braves since his return from New York. Just showing up had been one of the hardest moments of his life.

Had Jimmy told his teammates what happened? Would the whole team turn against him? After he'd overcome his pride, put aside his bitterness, and gotten back into ball? After he'd worked so hard to create a team? Was it now all to fall apart, the way his White Sox had disintegrated after the 1919 World Series? If Jimmy had told them, how could he endure the cold stares of the young boys he had grown to care about so deeply? And Jimmy? How could he possibly step on a baseball diamond with him again?

But nothing had happened. The Braves had gone about their practice with carefree commitment. Jimmy had avoided any closeness, to be sure. They had hardly exchanged a word, but Jimmy had done nothing to attract attention to the rift between them. Rift? *More like over with.* Somehow Joe had survived practice. *Yeah, that's the word for it, survived.*

But now another day had come and he'd have to survive it again.

"How many pints?" Katie asked. She'd watched her husband pace around the store all day yesterday, jittery as a spooked horse, smoking cigarette after cigarette. It had been painful for her to watch. She could only imagine how painful it had been for Joe.

Joe stared at the shelf of Jim Beam and counted. "Eight."

Katie, seated at the desk, wrote it down. "We'll have to order more."

"Lemme check what's out back first." He moved to the next shelf and counted. "Six fifths of Old Grand Dad."

She wrote it down. Joe went to the desk, opened a drawer, got out the birdfeed, and went to fill Pee Wee's cup. "Joe, you just did that," Katie reminded him. He opened the cage door and saw that she was right.

"Fill 'er up!" Pee Wee squawked.

He shut the cage door and put the food away. "Dumb bird," he muttered. He reached into his pocket, pulled out the packet of Red Man, and stuffed in a chew.

Katie pondered what to do. Joe had told her what had happened in New York in staggered sentences, words she had worked hard to pull from him. She had never known him to be so silent, so pent up. If he would just talk about it. "Looks like you'll have beautiful weather for practice today."

"Same weather as always," Joe grumbled. He returned to the shelves of liquor. "Only four pints of Old Crow."

"How'd yesterday go?" She took the plunge. "With Jimmy, I mean?"

"Fine. Seven fifths of Jack on the shelf, five pints, plus whatever you got behind the counter."

"Good." She wrote it down. "Maybe he's forgiven you." The minute it left her lips, Katie knew she'd chosen the wrong word.

"What's to forgive?" he asked sharply. "You know I didn't cheat. I know I didn't cheat. Jimmy knows I didn't cheat. That is, if he takes my word for it. If he dudn', nothin' I can do about it."

"I'm sorry, Joe. You know what I mean. I just wish we'd explained more about the confession, that's all."

"None of his damn business!" Joe shouted. "Eight fifths of Southern Comfort, six pints, five half pints!"

Joe's loud voice stirred Pee Wee. "You're lousy, O'Laughlin," he squawked.

"Shut up, Pee Wee!" Joe yelled. "I'm goin' out back!" He shook a cigarette from the pack and slammed the door on his way out.

Katie started to go after him, but thought better of it. "That didn't go so well," she said to Pee Wee. She sat on the edge of the desk, thinking. If Joe could just make it through today's practice, then tomorrow's, then the game Saturday. What if they won it? It had been a wonderful summer. Joe had been so happy, coaching and teaching. Surely there'd be time to straighten everything out after Saturday. They could invite Jimmy over, Rhoda and Thelma, too. Tell them the whole story, all of it, including what they had decided to do with the $5,000, how they'd put it in a bank, hadn't touched it until they'd used it for Joe's sister's illness. And the resolution, if the governor signed it! If the Commissioner agreed! It could all work out fine.

Out in the shed, Joe stared at a crate of Jim Beam. *Why'd she have to go pryin'?* He'd managed to get through yesterday's practice, why hadn't she just left well enough alone? He checked his watch. Another practice to get through started in a few hours. He raised his head, looked around the shed. Crates and crates of alcohol. He'd seen its effects on others. Lefty had been a pretty good drinker. Swede, too. Happy drunks. Happy…. A nip or two… He reached into the crate of bourbon. *Hell, it's just a practice.*

"I got it!" Piggy called out, as he settled under a fly ball and easily snatched it from the air.

"You really aren't afraid any more, are you, Steve?" Jimmy smiled, as Piggy fired the ball back to Petie at home.

"Nope, thanks to you an' Joe. Where do you think he is, anyway?"

"No idea," Jimmy answered. They had waited half an hour for Shoeless to show up, then had begun practice on their own. Jimmy trotted a few paces and hauled in his own fly ball. "Steve, you ever think what might happen if we lost?"

"Shut up, you'll jinx us! Whattaya wanna ask a question like that for?"

"I was just wonderin'. I mean, nothin'll really change, will it? You'll still go to church on Sunday, work on Monday. We'll still be friends. I'll still come over from Woodside for pickup games. What's the difference?"

"This difference is, I'll feel a heckuva lot better at church on Sunday an' work on Monday if we win. I ain't never heard you talk like that. You sure nothin' went on in New York?"

"I done told you. Mr. Singleton liked my hitting, said I might hear from him next spring. But don't tell the others, like I said. Let's just see what happens."

"Then how come you ain't takin' Black Betsy home with you after practice?"

"Just think Shoeless'll take good care of her, that's all," Jimmy dodged. He still used Betsy in practice, but he wanted as little to do with anything involving Shoeless Joe Jackson as possible. "Speak of the devil."

Piggy looked where Jimmy had nodded. Shoeless had entered through the right field fence. "He looks a little better than yesterday," Piggy observed. Shoeless had his Panama on and was walking briskly towards home plate, Black Betsy slung over his shoulder.

"Everybody come on in!" he yelled.

Piggy, Jimmy, and the other outfielders jogged in and joined the rest of their teammates. "Boys," Shoeless said, "I've decided to cancel practice." The players were shocked. "Now, hold on, lemme explain. There's such a thing as too much practicin', 'specially when you're about to play a big game. I don't want you to get all tired out."

"We ain't tired, Mr. Jackson," Whiff said. Several of his teammates voiced their agreement.

"I don't mean physically, I mean mentally."

"You gon' cancel tomorrow's, too?" asked Pepper.

"No, it's important for us to get together, stay connected. But I probably won't work you hard."

"We like workin' hard!" Wash shouted out.

"I know you do." Joe reached into his pocket for a cigarette. The truth was, he didn't feel up to practicing. Not having drunk in a long while had made him woozier than he'd expected. "But you're ready, fellas, an' a dozen more ground balls or pop flies or times at the plate ain't gon' make you any readier." He shook out a cigarette and was putting it to his lips when he noticed Jimmy looking at him. *What am I doin', I don't smoke in front of them!* He quickly put back the cigarette. "So what say let's gather up the equipment, you boys go on off an' enjoy the rest of the afternoon. An' stay outta the sun, that's the best thing you can do. I b'lieve we got us a heat wave comin'."

Grumbling a little, the players began to pack up the equipment. Shoeless approached Jimmy. The alcohol gave him courage. He held out Black Betsy. "You sure you don't wanna take this home with you? For luck?"

Jimmy was untying his cleats. "I don't need no bobby pins." He stood up, next to Joe.

"Suit yourself."

Jimmy paused. What was that he'd just smelled? He peered more closely at Shoeless. Joe averted his eyes. Jimmy leaned in for a harsh whisper. "So that's why you wanted to cancel practice!"

He bent down, picked up his shoes, and marched away in his stocking feet, leaving Joe alone at the plate, eyes downcast, Black Betsy dangling from a listless hand.

At work that night, Jimmy found his anger mounting, and, with it, his answer. *Why would I want to play for a man like that? Why would I want to win a championship for him?* He looked around him. Spinning machines spat out the yarn, yard after yard after yard. Fill a bobbin, chuck it in the bin, ram on another, move to the next spot, repeat, repeat, repeat. The floor beneath him shook with the rumble of fifty carding machines, whose steel teeth tore apart the cotton fiber. Above him, the ceiling shook with the sound of dozens of weaving machines — warp, weft, warp, weft, on and on. Rhoda was up there somewhere. Shouldn't he save her from all this? And the noise! Why had he never noticed how absolutely unbearable it was? *I'll go deaf if I stay here!* He wiped his brow in the 100-degree heat. Lint stuck to the back of his hand when he pulled it away. It clung to his clothes. It filled the air. *Lint, lint, lint, now and forever!* And the solution was right there, right at home under his pillow. Sign his name. Shoeless Joe Jackson had done it. *Why shouldn't I?*

"What happened to you yesterday?" Rhoda asked Jimmy on their way out the gate Friday morning.

"Shoeless cancelled practice. Told us to go home an' rest, so I did."

"An' the day before?"

"Had somethin' I needed to do."

"Musta been pretty important to make you pass up a walk with me!" Rhoda smiled.

"It was."

"Ain't you gon' tell me what it was?"

"I cain't." Jimmy increased his speed, and turned towards the street to Woodside.

"Secret, huh?"

"Yeah."

"Slow up, will you?" Rhoda ran beside him. "You got somewhere you're off to again?"

"No, just home." Home, and then to Howard Stone's.

"I've got some news for you. Been meanin' to tell you, but you've been kinda hard to pin down. Guess who'll be singin' the National Anthem at tomorrow's ball game."

"Who?"

"The   Carolina   Songbird   herself,   Miss   Rhodaaaaaa Dawsonnnnnnnnnn!" She drawled out the words like an announcer.

"That's good."

"Good? Hey, lissen up, linthead!" She grabbed Jimmy's arm and forced him to stop walking. "I know what happened to you an' Mr. Jackson is hard, but you cain't let it dry you up like a prune. When your cup runs dry, the best medicine is to partake of the joy of others. So lemme hear a proper response for my good news, like 'Yee-haw!' or some such!"

"Rhoda," Jimmy suddenly said urgently. "What do you think 'bout Mrs. Jackson stickin' by Shoeless all these years, when she knew what he'd done?"

"First of all, I ain't so sure everybody's agreed on what he done."

"All right, then, what he *testified* he done. Would you stick by me like that?"

"Why? You done somethin'?"

"Just answer the question!"

Rhoda saw the urgency in his eyes. "Well, that'd depend on what you'd done," she said slowly. "You got somethin' you're tryin' to tell me, Jimmy?"

"No. Never mind." He started walking again.

"Hold on, hold on!" Rhoda said. He stopped. She came close to him and spoke with quiet purpose. "I think if somebody I love's done a bad thing, even if it's a really bad thing, I'd stick by him on one condition. He's got to ask forgiveness. I believe like Jesus: forgivin' people's what God wants us to do."

Jimmy gave a small nod. His shoulders relaxed. For the first time all week, a smile creased his face. *She'll forgive me.* "Thanks," he said.

Rhoda undid her bun and shook lint out of her hair. *Someday, someday*, Jimmy thought. *No more lint!* "Jimmy, are you gonna miss playin' ball every day, when the season's over?"

He thought about it. Every other year, the season's end had caused an empty ache in his soul. But this year would be different, and the difference was standing there right in front of him, clothes full of lint, face smudged with sweat, eyes warm as melted chocolate. He put his arms around her. "No, I won't miss it at all." He kissed her. "Gotta go."

"You cain't just kiss a girl like that an' run off like a jackrabbit!" She drew him to her and they kissed again. "What's your all-fire hurry?"

"Just wanna rest up before practice. I'll see you later."

Jimmy gave her one more quick peck and headed off towards Woodside. Rhoda called after him.

"I'll collect my 'yee-haw' then!"

Jimmy hurried home. Now that he'd decided what to do, he wanted to get it over with. Sign the contract and get it to Mr. Stone. Then one more practice. He could handle that. Who knew, maybe Shoeless would make it a short one, like yesterday. The less time he had to spend with his teammates, the better. Same for Shoeless Joe. Then a Coke walk with Rhoda. He'd enjoy that. More kissing. More dreaming of what they'd do when baseball season was over. Then work. The monotony would be a distraction. He wouldn't think, just do. As much sleep as possible. Then the game. How would he do it? How would he not try? Make errors? Strike out? He'd think about that later. He'd do it, somehow. Then it would be over and his new life could begin.

He pulled the contract from under his pillow, holding it in his hands like a sacred book. He carried it across the room and placed it in the middle of his shrine to Shoeless Joe. He knelt down and opened the two sides of the folded cardboard. There it was, his crude drawing of the outfield bleachers at Comiskey Park. With the headlines taped over them. "The Carolina Confection." "356" — Joe's lifetime batting average, still third best behind Ty Cobb and Rogers Hornsby. *Local Greenville Boy Making Good.* Jimmy had taped that one back up when Shoeless had begun managing them. He slipped his thumb and forefinger around the headline, yanked it off, placed it on the floor in front of him. He smoothed it out, put the contract on top of it, and picked up a pen. *Yeah, local boy making good. I don't need any heroes any more. I'll be my own hero.* He flipped to the last page of the contract, poised pen-in-hand above the line with "The Player" typed underneath, lowered his hand and scrawled his future.

CHAPTER 20

As Jimmy looked out across the professionally manicured diamond at Meadowbrook Park, he thought about how his baseball season would be ending here, where he had come three short months ago to try out for the Greenville *Spinners*. That day had ended in a fiasco, Jimmy using the knothole in right to launch himself out of reach of Smitty and the *Spinners'* screaming manager. *I wonder how this day will end. Will I be chased from the park again, this time by my own teammates?*

He stood in front of the dugout between home plate and third base, waiting for the National Anthem. He looked up at the stands, where thousands of Greenvillians had turned out to see whether the Brandon Braves or the Woodside Wolves would become the Western Carolina League Champion. His glance fell on Howard Stone, sitting a few rows up behind home plate with Yancey Dickerson and Toby Gower. Howard smiled at Jimmy, a smile Jimmy chose not return. Toby clapped his hands and called out, "Go get 'em, Jimmy!" Jimmy chose to ignore that, too. He'd decided that the best way to do what he was going to do was to shut out everything but the moment before him, to build a wall of silence around him that would protect his fragile nerves and help him stay focused. *Don't think about anything but baseball* was his game plan.

"Ladies an' gentlemen, our National Anthem," Dixie Dawkins announced over the loudspeaker. Jimmy looked towards the backstop where Rhoda had been awaiting her cue. She was wearing a simple blue dress decorated with tiny white flowers. It pinched her waist and gently snugged her breasts. She had used a curling iron to add a few curls to her blonde hair, which hung gently down to her shoulders. Catching Jimmy's look, Rhoda gave him a dazzling smile. She had never looked so beautiful.

As Rhoda made her way towards the microphone that had been placed in front of the pitcher's mound, the Woodside players filed into place along the first-base line. Jimmy took his place alongside his teammates on the third-base side. He looked down the line. Petie, Whiff, Pepper, Wash, Murph, Jawbreaker, Red, Whitey, Steve. They had come a long way that summer. They were a team. But as he stood there waiting for the bands to begin and for Rhoda to sing, Jimmy couldn't help but ask himself the question he knew everybody was asking: where was Shoeless Joe?

The team had met at Brandon Park earlier that morning, but Shoeless hadn't shown. Assuming he'd meet them at Meadowbrook, the Braves had taken the bus Toby Gower had provided to the park, but Joe wasn't there, either. They'd gone through their practice routine, anxiously looking about, certain that he would appear any minute, but the minutes marched by and there was still no sign of their manager. "Maybe's he's sick," Piggy had suggested, but a quick conference with Katie had revealed that Joe had been fine when he'd left home earlier. Toby Gower had no clue as to Joe's whereabouts either. And now here they were, on the eve of the biggest game of their lives, and there was no one to guide them.

Rhoda finished her singing to generous applause. She had sung beautifully, but Jimmy had only half heard her. Much as he'd tried, he couldn't stop thinking about Joe. He'd seemed fine at yesterday's practice. Quieter, maybe, than usual, but he'd put them through their paces. Jimmy had stayed clear of him, not wanting to know if he'd been drinking again. Even if he had, and even given all that had happened that week, it had never occurred to him that Shoeless would simply abandon them. But apparently he had. Jimmy allowed himself a grim smile. It'd be easier to do what he had to do without Shoeless around. *It's better this way.*

Rhoda walked past Jimmy after the Anthem. "How'd you like it?" she whispered.

"It was great." Jimmy tried to muster as much enthusiasm as possible, but Rhoda wasn't fooled.

She stopped. "You hardly heard it, didn' ya? That's all right. I know you were thinkin' 'bout Mr. Jackson. It'll be terrible if he dudn' show up an' ya'll lose."

"It's just a game," Jimmy said, scuffing the dirt with his shoe.

Rhoda looked at him sharply. "You never said — "

"Hey, Jimmy, come over here, we got to decide somethin'!" Jawbreaker yelled. The Braves were gathered in front of their dugout.

"See ya'," Jimmy said quickly, and trotted away to join his teammates. Rhoda watched him go. Something was wrong, she thought. She expected him to be nervous, of course, but this was different. He was acting so strange. When she'd shouted out to him during warm-ups, showing him where she, Thelma, and Katie would be sitting behind third base, he hadn't even looked over. They had planned for him to escort her onto the field for the National Anthem, but, apparently, he had forgotten so she got an usher to do it. And now it seemed he couldn't get away from her fast enough. She thought back to the conversation they'd had when Jimmy asked her if she'd stand by him no matter what. Had he done something? Was he responsible for Shoeless not coming to the game?

"The ump says we got to have an official manager," Jawbreaker said when Jimmy had joined them, "An' I nominate you."

"I don't want to be manager," Jimmy protested.

"Second!" said Piggy. "All in favor?" The whole team raised their hands.

"Here's the line-up card for Frankie." Jawbreaker held it out for Jimmy.

He looked it over. "Piggy's battin' third?"

"He wanted to. I said I didn' mind," Petie said.

"I got a feelin', Jimmy," Piggy said. "I wanna hit in front of you. I been buildin' my muscles all summer, been swingin' the bat good."

Jimmy shrugged. If nobody else cared, why should he? He looked at his teammates. They had their game faces on. They were behind him. They expected him to lead them. If they only knew where he was planning to take them.

"Wait a minute," Murph said. "If Shoeless was here, you know what he'd want us to do." He stuck out his hand, palm down. The others piled their hands on top of his. "One, two, three," he counted, and they all shouted "Failure!"

"Did they just shout 'failure'?" Yancey asked Toby in the stands behind home plate. Howard had once again bought up a few surrounding seats to pretend he had a box.

"Somethin' Shoeless taught them, don't ask me why," Toby responded.

"Speaking of which, where do you think he is?" Howard asked.

"I wish I knew," Toby replied, shaking his head glumly.

"Hope you didn't put too much down with Jellycakes," Howard teased. "Well, if you did, that'll help him cover my bet. Cigar, Yancey?" He pulled out his case and opened it.

"Thank you, Howard, don't mind if I do. I take it you placed your usual big bet."

"Even bigger. I got a strong feeling this is a sure thing. And Shoeless not showing makes it even surer. Now, *that* I didn't plan on."

"Plan?" Toby asked. "What do you mean?"

"Just a figure of speech, Toby. Cigar?" He paused. "Oh, that's right, you brought your own. Better light it now so's to make sure you get to smoke it!"

"Howard," Toby said, "I'm sorry there's this netting behind home plate, otherwise there might be a chance for a foul ball to smack you in the head!"

Yancey laughed. "I'm glad I'm sittin' between you boys!"

At home plate, Jimmy and Crusher had given Frankie their line-up cards. "Thank God this is the last time I'll have to look at your ugly mug, linthead," Crusher said.

"Oh, might see you in the big leagues someday, Crusher" Jimmy answered, "If you make it."

"Only way you'll be there is sellin' hot dogs."

"We'll see." Jimmy stuck out his hand, which Crusher took and squeezed harder than necessary. "Save your strength, Crusher, you'll need it. " Jimmy smiled, and headed back towards his dugout.

"Where's your no-brain manager, Roberts?" Brownell shouted from his front-row seat near third base. "Never mind, he couldn' manage his way out of an outhouse!"

"I wish somebody'd shut him up," Piggy said, when Jimmy had reached the dugout steps. He spat expertly. "Maybe I could drown him in juice."

"Play ball!" Frankie cried.

"Let's get 'em!" Jawbreaker shouted and the Brandon Braves sprinted onto the field.

"I love you!" Jimmy heard Rhoda yell.

I hope so, he thought.

Jimmy had no plan for how he would throw the game. If he'd been a pitcher, it would have been easy, as it had been for Lefty Williams back in 1919. But he was a fielder, so he had less control over how the game would go. His only plan was to take each opportunity as it occurred, and simply not play his best. Make a mistake that anyone could make. Know the situation, as Shoeless had taught him.

The first situation occurred right away. Murph set down the Woodside lineup in order, one, two, three. In the bottom of the inning, Brandon's first two batters made outs, but Piggy, batting third, lined a double to left. Jimmy, batting cleanup, worked the Woodside pitcher into a two-balls, two-strike count. A hit would score Piggy. If he hit the ball, even if it wasn't hard, a player might make an error. The safest thing was to strike out, if the pitcher would throw something that was close enough to a strike to swing at. It would be too obvious to lunge at a pitch that was an obvious ball. Fortunately, the pitcher threw a fastball over the heart of the plate, a pitch Jimmy would normally have crushed. This time he swung and missed. "Strike three, you're out!" called Frankie Thompson. Brownell filled his leather lungs. "Swingin' like a rusty gate, Roberts!"

As Jimmy walked back towards the dugout, Pepper tossed him his glove. "You'll get him next time!" he said and patted him on the butt as he ran out to center field. Jimmy slipped the glove on his hand and followed him to the outfield. *This might be easier than I thought.*

In the bleachers for the colored fans, Jellycakes was worried. He didn't like surprises. If anything out of the ordinary occurred, the betting line he had set might work badly against him. And Brandon's not having Shoeless to manage was definitely out of the ordinary. Howard's heavy bet wasn't the only one on Woodside; most of his clients had put their money there, too. What he wanted was bets on both sides, then he'd take his cut both ways. If Brandon lost, Jellycakes wasn't sure he could cover all the bets.

And where the heck was Willie? That was another thing out of the ordinary. Willie never missed a game. He was there early, when the teams were warming up. *An' now he's gone? An' Shoeless not here neither? Somethin' ain't right.* A loud "crack!" brought his attention back to the game. He watched Crusher Goodlett's leadoff home run clear the center field fence. *Now somethin' really ain't right!*

"Hey, Daddy!"

Jellycakes looked down to see his son standing next to him. "Where the heck you been?"

"Findin' Mr. Jackson."

"You found 'im?"

"Yeah, but you ain't gonna like the condition he's in."

"The hell with his condition, get him here!"

"I cain't, Daddy. He cain't walk. You gon' have to drive him."

"I ain't got no car, boy, you know that!"

"You got to borrow one," Willie said urgently.

"You mean, hot-wire it? I ain't got time for this foolishness, boy!" A "whack" sounded from home plate. Jellycakes watched the next Woodside batter round first base and dig for second, as the crowd's noise rose. Jimmy Roberts fielded the hit, bobbled the ball, then fired it to second. The runner beat the throw by a second. "Let's go!" Jellycakes said.

Outside the ballpark, Willie led his father up to Howard Stone's Cadillac. "I like your taste in cars, son." Jellycakes applied the skills he'd learned in his former profession before turning to bookmaking as a safer occupation. He climbed into the front seat on the passenger side and ducked his head under the dash, near the steering column, finding the wires he was looking for. "Uh-huh," he muttered, as he ripped them loose with a quick jerk. Reaching into his pocket, he pulled out a penknife and expertly stripped three of them. As he touched the bare wires together, he stretched up his hand and pushed in the starter button. The engine coughed for a moment, then sprang to life. He peeked his head up and smiled at Willie. "Where to, son?"

"Brandon field."

Jellycakes sat up, scooted behind the wheel, and Willie jumped into the passenger seat. As Jellycakes maneuvered the car out of the parking lot and onto the city streets, Willie turned on the radio and found the game. Dixie Dawkins' voice came through the static. "And the runner scores! Woodside leads two-to-nothin'. It's only the second inning, but the momentum seems to be goin' their way." Jellycakes slammed his palm onto the steering wheel and stepped harder on the gas.

Ten minutes later the car screeched to a stop near Brandon field. "There he is!" Willie pointed towards home plate. They both jumped out of the car and ran towards Shoeless Joe, who was stumbling around with Black Betsy in his hands.

"All right, Betsy" Joe said to the bat, words slurring. "Outta the park. Way outta the park!" He banged the bat on home plate a couple of times, took his stance, and swung. His follow-through caused him to stumble, and he hit the ground. Jellycakes and Willie ran to help him up.

"That's all right, Mr. Shoeless, we gotcha," Jellycakes said, as they strained to hoist Joe to his feet.

"Who's that?" demanded Joe.

"Jellycakes an' Willie."

"I ain't sellin' you no booze!" Joe shouted at Willie.

"That's okay, Mr. Shoeless, I don't want no booze today." Willie tried to take Black Betsy out of Joe's hands.

"Let go my bat!" Joe shouted, and yanked the bat away, causing him to stumble to the ground again, taking Jellycakes with him.

"Goddammit!" yelled Jellycakes. "Help me out here, Willie!" He pushed Shoeless off him.

"Get me up to the plate," Joe slurred. "Throw me a pitch!"

"Yessuh, Mr. Shoeless, we'll do that." Jellycakes and Willie managed to get Joe upright.

Joe staggered toward home plate. "I'll show you the swing Babe Ruth copied."

"Now what, Daddy?" Willie asked.

Jellycakes thought for a minute. "Mr. Shoeless," he said. "We got to take you to your wife."

"Katie?" Joe asked. He leaned on his bat.

"Yessuh. She's awful worried. Nobody knew where you'd run off to."

"I didn' run off. Came here to practice my swing. 'Ja know this where I started out?"

Jellycakes began easing Joe towards the car, with Willie's help. "Yessuh. But we got to get you home now, home to your wife. She'll take care of you."

"She always took good care of me, Katie," Shoeless said. "Wonnerful woman, jus' wonnerful."

"Yessuh. An' she misses you, wants to see you again, real soon." They had reached the car. "Now just get on in here." Willie opened the door.

"Why idn' she at the game?" Shoeless asked suddenly.

"She didn' wanna be there without you."

"I didn' go," Shoeless informed them. "Thought they'd be better off without me. 'Specially Jimmy."

"Yessuh, Mr. Shoeless." They maneuvered Joe into the front seat.

"Jimmy hates me," Shoeless said sadly.

"No, he dudn!" Willie said, slipping into the back seat while his father went around to the driver's side. "You his hero. Mine, too!"

"Don't wanna be nobody's hero!" Joe shouted.

"That's all right, now, Mr. Shoeless." Jellycakes gave his son a look in the rearview mirror, then stepped on the gas.

A short time later, they had Shoeless sitting in his favorite armchair in the small brick house on E. Wilburn Avenue. While Willie pulled Joe's shoes off, Jellycakes banged around in the kitchen, getting coffee started. "Where's Katie?" Shoeless shouted.

"Musta gone out for groceries or somethin'," Jellycakes called back. He turned on the radio in the kitchen. The voice of Dixie Dawkins came on immediately. "...line drive to Roberts in left. This'll score the runner from third an' — Roberts throws the ball to the plate! No way he can get the runner at home. Merritt short-hops the throw an' fires to second. Safe! Why in the world would Roberts throw home? He must have forgotten the situation."

"Turn that damn thing off!" Shoeless shouted from the living room.

Jellycakes turned it down and entered the living room. "I got to get back to the park, son," he said to Willie. "There's coffee brewin'. I'll take the Caddy, so if you can get him sober, maybe he can drive his car. But he's probly too damn drunk to do anybody any good, no how." Jellycakes couldn't control himself. "What'd you wanna go an' do that for?" he shouted at Joe.

"Wha'?" Joe asked.

"Let yo' team down!" Jellycakes shouted again.

"I didn't let my team down!" Joe shouted back. "I never let my team down!"

"Oh, shut up!" Jellycakes walked quickly out the door. Willie went into the kitchen to wait for the coffee. He heard a door open and the Caddy speed off. Now he was alone with Shoeless Joe Jackson, something he'd always dreamed about. But not like this.

By the time Jellycakes reached his seat, the game was in the fifth inning. He glanced at the scoreboard. Brandon had managed to score a run, but Woodside had scored four. A shout pulled Jellycakes' attention back to the game. Jimmy was racing towards a ball hit down the line in left. He dove for the ball, missed, and it rolled all the way to the wall. Pepper ran over and managed to get the ball back into the infield to hold the runner to a triple. Fortunately for Brandon, the next batter popped up for the third out. "Dumb-ass play, Roberts!" Jerry Brownell yelled at him as Jimmy ran in from the outfield.

Pepper was trotting beside Jimmy. "Why didn't you just play it for a single? We had two outs."

"Thought I could catch it!" Jimmy said sharply.

Pepper was surprised by his tone. "You all right?"

Jimmy realized the pressure was beginning to affect him. He gathered himself. "'Course I am, Pep. Come on, let's go get some runs."

Back in Joe's kitchen, Willie listened intently to the radio. "Simpson's walk puts a man on first base," Dixie Dawkins announced, "An' brings Roberts to the plate."

"More coffee!" Willie looked up, surprised to see Shoeless standing in the doorway to the kitchen. "An' turn it up. That announcer says Jimmy dove for a ball he shouldn't have?"

"Yessuh," Willie answered.

"Sit with me, Willie." Joe sat down heavily. His was still woozy. Willie turned up the radio, filled Joe's cup, and sat, too.

"This might be a good hit-and-run situation," Dixie continued through the radio. "Roberts could advance the runner into scoring position, a single might help get Brandon back in the game."

"Come on, Mr. Jimmy," Willie whispered.

"Here comes the pitch, there goes the runner...." Dixie said. "An' Roberts doesn't swing! The throw down to second — got him by a mile! The runner at second shouts somethin' to Roberts as he heads back to the dugout. First base coach yells at him, too. My-oh-my, what a turnaround! Must have missed the sign or somethin'."

"Or somethin'...." Shoeless muttered. He took a long gulp of coffee and stared at the radio, thinking hard.

"Roberts steps back in, the pitcher winds an' throws.... A swing an' a miss an' the inning's over! A lost opportunity for Brandon, I'd say."

Joe held out his cup. His hand shook a little. "More."

At Meadowbrook Park, the bands played "Dixie" as the fans stood for the seventh inning stretch. Jimmy trotted past the seats behind third base. Rhoda waved at him, but he just kept on running. "What's wrong with Jimmy?" she asked Thelma.

"He seemed all right this mornin'. Maybe a little nervous."

"He say anything to you?"

"Well, when I wished him good luck before he took off, he did say 'It's only a game, Mama.' "

"He said that to me, too! That's not Jimmy, is it?"

Thelma shook her head. Katie started for the aisle. "Hey, where're you goin,'?"

"Joe always made me leave in the seventh inning. For luck. Said he'd play better."

"But, Joe isn't — " Thelma began, then stopped.

Katie's eyes welled up. She had borne her anxiety well until now, certain that Joe would show up soon. But after seven innings, still no Joe. "Maybe he's home," Katie said, hopefully.

"An' if he is, he's safe."

"He was so upset this week. About Jimmy."

Thelma nodded sympathetically. "He probably just didn' wanna be here, that's all. I'm sure he'll be home after the game."

"Stay with us, Mrs. Jackson," Rhoda pleaded. "We need you to help us pull for Brandon."

Katie hesitated. Thelma put her arm around her and gently guided her back to her seat. "Come on. Let's focus on the game."

In his "box," Howard pulled out a cigar. "Ain't that a little early?" Toby inquired.

"Just smellin' it." Howard ran the cigar under his nose. "Anticipation is three-fourths of the fun of winning."

"An' one hundred per cent of the pain, if you lose!" Toby shot back.

Yancey laughed. "Since it doesn't matter to me one way or the other.... Howard, how 'bout I relieve you of another of those fine cigars?"

"My pleasure, Mr. Speaker." Howard handed Yancey a cigar and brought out his lighter. He snapped open the top, rubbed his thumb down the small wheel, and a large flame sprang to life.

"That's quite the torch you got there!" Yancey exclaimed.

"I like to make sure I'm lit," said Howard.

"What do you think's wrong with Roberts?" Yancey asked.

"What do you mean?" Howard replied, a slight edge to his voice.

"He's not havin' a very good game, far's I can tell."

"He's havin' a terrible game!" Toby added. "Never seen the likes of it from Jimmy."

"Jackson's absence is probably affecting him," Howard offered.

"The rest of the team's playin' good," Toby said doubtfully.

"The game's not over yet, Toby," Yancey replied.

"I just hate to give this Yankee a reason for bringin' out that damn lighter again!"

"Play ball!" Frankie Thompson shouted from behind home plate.

Two and a half miles away, Shoeless and Willie were glued to the radio as Dixie Dawkins talked them through the bottom on the seventh and one out into the top of the eighth. He kept thinking about how Jimmy was playing, and the more he thought about it, the more an idea settled into his mind. At first, he couldn't believe it, refused to believe it. But why else, after all these years, had Socks had a copy of that transcript? If Howard Stone would go that far, then why wouldn't he go one step farther? Shoeless began gulping the fresh coffee as fast as he could.

"Murphy looks in for the sign...." Dixie announced. "Goodlett dances off first base ... The pitch.... Line drive to left, Roberts fields it, the runner rounds second, fakes goin' to third.... The throw goes over the shortstop's head! Wofford can't handle the short hop at second, Washington chases the ball into shallow right, and Goodlett cruises into third without a throw. Another error on Roberts!"

Shoeless stood up abruptly. "Come on!" Standing so fast caused him to wobble, and he had to lean against the wall for support.

"Where you goin'?" Willie asked worriedly.

"We got to get to Meadowbrook fast!"

"Can you drive, Mr. Shoeless?"

"I don't think so. But you can."

"Me? I cain't drive!" Willie started backing away.

"It's easy." Joe took Willie's arm. "If I can teach Whiff to hit, I can teach you to drive."

"But I cain't hardly see over the steerin' wheel!"

"We'll fix that. Wait a minute! Where's Black Betsy?"

"In the livin' room."

"You get the bat, I'll get the pillows." Joe headed towards the bedroom. "Car's out back."

Even sitting on three pillows, Willie could barely see over the steering wheel. Shoeless started the engine. "Just steer, Willie, I'll work the pedals." Joe sat next to Willie, put the car in first, and off they went, radio blaring to let them know the score.

Willie had never been so scared in his life. The first car he approached frightened him so much he jerked the wheel to the right. The Packard bumped over a curb and Willie pulled the wheel back to the left just in time to avoid a telephone pole. "Woo-eee!" he yelled.

"Less shoutin', more concentratin'!" Shoeless commanded. He reached into the glove compartment, took out some Red Man, and stuffed tobacco in his mouth.

Reaching Augusta Road, Shoeless spotted a large oil truck coming towards them. "Now just relax, Willie. You got plenty of room."

"I don't know, Mr. Shoeless," Willie said, beginning to tug the steering wheel both left and right. Shoeless grabbed the wheel to steady it, and, for a moment, they both wrestled to steer the car.

"Help!" Willie shouted, and yanked the wheel hard. Shoeless countered with a yank of his own, which sent the Packard careening towards the big truck. The truck driver leaned on his horn. Willie shouted, "I'm dyin'!" released the wheel, and covered his head with his arms. Shoeless pulled the car out of the truck's lane, yelling "Whoa!" The shout caused him to swallow his tobacco. He began coughing furiously, spitting whatever he could out the side window. He managed to pull the car onto a side road. When he'd caught his breath, he shouted at Willie. "Switch places! I'm sober as hell now!"

Shoeless drove as fast as he dared, the radio letting them know they still weren't too late. "An' Brandon's down to its final out," Dixie was saying as they pulled into Meadowbrook's parking lot. Joe grabbed Black Betsy and they jumped out and ran to the gate. They heard a cheer from the crowd inside the stadium.

An usher tried to grab Willie, shouting "That nigger cain't come in this way!"

"The hell you say!" Shoeless barreled him aside and he and Willie crashed through the turnstile and ran up the ramp to the seats. "I'll go on down to the colored section, Mr. Shoeless," Willie said. "You take care of business." He sprinted off towards the left-field bleachers, and Shoeless ran down to the third-base dugout, jumped the wall, and stood on the field.

"Shoeless!" Jawbreaker yelled, forgetting how Joe hated the name.

"What's the situation?" Shoeless gasped.

"We're down 4-2, but Piggy just walked an' Jimmy's up. Two outs."

Shoeless looked toward home plate. Jimmy stood outside the batter's box, taking a few practice swings, his back to Shoeless. Joe walked towards the umpire. "Time, Frankie!"

Frankie looked up, startled. "Hello, Joe. I, uh...." He looked confused for a minute. "I don't think you can call time, Joe. The manager's gotta do it."

"Who's the manager?"

Jimmy had turned around. Frankie nodded towards him. Joe walked over to Jimmy. "I need to talk to you," he said calmly.

Jimmy hesitated. He'd come this far. One more out and he'd be home free. One more out and he'd have that contract. One more out and he'd be able to leave mill hill, maybe forever. Why should he talk to the man who betrayed him, who betrayed all of baseball?

"Jimmy!" Joe said forcefully, staring at him.

"Time," Jimmy said softly.

Shoeless motioned for him to step away from the plate a little. "Did Stone offer you a contract?"

"How'd you know?"

"Been doin' some thinkin'. I remembered Socks knew Stone, too, from way back. Didn't see why he'd bring out that confession, unless somebody put him up to it. Stone seemed a likely candidate." Joe paused, then said evenly with the greatest conviction he could muster. "Don't do it, Jimmy."

Jimmy eyed Shoeless. The look in Joe's eyes told him he knew. "It's a little late."

"You still got one more at-bat. Sometimes that's all it takes."

"It's just a game," Jimmy said, and started towards home plate.

Shoeless stopped him with a hand to his chest. "No, it's not!" He looked at the sky for a moment. He'd never been much for words. He prayed he could find the right ones now.

"I want to thank you for all you taught me this summer," Joe continued. "Rather, what you reminded me of, things I knew but had lost along the way. You taught me it ain't what you hit on the outside that counts, it ain't your average with a bat. It's what you hit on the inside, it's your average with yourself." Joe took a moment to gather his thoughts. "Before you came along, I'd been battin' zero on the inside for too long. But seein' the way you loved playin' baseball, seein' how hard you worked at gettin' better, reminded me how much I loved it, too." Shoeless paused. He kicked at the dirt with his feet, then smiled. He'd rushed out of his house so fast he'd forgotten his shoes.

"I didn' cheat in 1919, Jimmy," he said firmly, looking Jimmy straight in the eye. "Not in the game, anyway. That confession was a lie, plain and simple, somethin' I said 'cause that lawyer told me to. But I did cheat myself. I cheated myself because I played my heart out on the field, but I didn' do it off the field. I shouldn'a let Harry Grabiner shut that office door on me, I shoulda pounded on that door till he opened it an' let me in to see Comiskey. An' that $5,000 Lefty throwed on my hotel room floor? I shoulda crammed it down his pants. Or taken the train from Greenville to Chicago an' throwed that money on Comiskey's floor. I shoulda never stopped tryin' to clear my name, *never*!"

"Get the cheater off the field, ump!" the leather-lunger yelled. Frankie took a step towards Shoeless, but Joe held up a hand. Frankie backed off.

"You don' wanna be called that, Jimmy," Shoeless continued. "Even if nobody knows you cheated but you. Believe me, you do not want to be haunted for the rest of your life for the things you didn' do. You want to be remembered for the things you did." Shoeless took a moment to look deep into Jimmy's eyes. "It's not just a game, Jimmy, an' you know it."

He pointed Betsy towards the diamond, the brown-red clay of the infield, the emerald lake of the outfield grass, the cloudless blue sky. "There it is, Jimmy. It's all before you." He turned back. "So, here's the situation: man on, Roberts up, game on the line." He pulled Jimmy's bat from his hand and held out Black Betsy instead. "The *real* game."

"Batter up!" Frankie yelled. Jimmy took Black Betsy and Shoeless walked back to the dugout. Slowly, reluctantly, Jimmy moved back to the batter's box. He took a few practice swings, trying to clear his head, trying to think. *What did Shoeless say? Somethin' 'bout battin' averages. Inside an' outside. What'd he mean?*

"Get on in there, Roberts," Frankie said. Jimmy stepped in to bat. He saw Piggy take his lead off first base. "Come on, Jimbo, little bingle, little bingle!" he called down to Jimmy. *Yeah, that's right, just a single, that's all. Let somebody else lose the game. Or win it! That would cost me my contract!*

Jimmy heard the pop of the ball in the catcher's mitt. "Strike one!" Frankie called. He hadn't even realized he was batting! Jimmy stepped out of the box, tapped Black Betsy on his cleats, right foot, left foot, stalling for time. He looked towards the seats where his mother, Rhoda, and Katie were standing, yelling at him, but he couldn't hear the words. *Rhoda said she'd stand by me. She wouldn' even have to know. Nobody'd have to know. But what did Joe say about* me *knowin'?* "Roberts!" Frankie gestured for Jimmy to get back in the box.

He stepped in, banged Black Betsy on the plate, cocked her back behind his ear. "No hitter, Randy, no hitter!" Crusher shouted from shortstop. "Blow it by him!" *Crusher. Look at him. So sure's he's gonna beat me. Do I want a guy like him to be holdin' the trophy, lordin' it over me?*

"Stee-rike two!" Jimmy looked back at Frankie whose right fist was raised in the air. *Focus, Roberts, for God's sake! At least know what you're doin'!*

He stepped out, picked up some dirt, rubbed it between his hands. "One more strike an' it's back to the mills, Roberts!" Brownell yelled from his seat behind third. *Oh, yeah? One more strike, an' next spring I'm not pickin' up bobbins at Brandon, I'm pullin' in fly balls in Georgia. That's what this is all about.* He stepped back in the box. The pitcher wound and threw. *That's what this is about!*

"Ball!" Frankie called.

"Attayway, Jimmy, be a hitter, be a hitter!" Jawbreaker called from the dugout. Jimmy looked over. Shoeless stood on the top step, staring back at him. *Did he cheat? He said he didn'. But others say...? Aw, what's it matter now, today? It's just a game, just one lousy game.*

Jimmy held up his hand to call time out. He looked up behind home plate. There was Mr. Stone. Everybody else was yelling and cheering, and there he was calm as could be. Jimmy could see the fat cigar in his hand, the big smile on his face. The game was in the bag. One more strike and he'd be lighting up. He'd played to win, and soon victory was gonna be his. *Jimmy* was gonna be his. *Is that what I want, for the Howard Stones of the world to win? Is that the real game Joe was talkin' 'bout? The one that goes on your whole life long?*

Jimmy shook his head, trying to understand, trying to decide what to do. *I just don' know.* He stepped back in to hit. *I'm gonna let the game decide.* He took his stance, the one he had copied from Joe. Weight back, right toe balancing him, bat higher than shoulders, pinky finger around the handle. A couple of waggles, not too many. *I'll see the pitch an' my body will decide, my mind will decide. The real me, or somethin', I don't know, whatever my real instincts are, they'll take over, an' I'll swing or I won't swing. The real me....*

He saw the pitcher get set. Piggy had his lead at first. Crusher crouched at short. The game was on. *Steady... Good eye.... Here it comes....*

He picked up the baseball as soon as it left the pitcher's hand. A curve ball. He saw the spin, right to left, round and round, round and round. He saw the ball start to arc as it neared the plate. And he saw it get bigger, and fatter, and slower, and slower, until it seemed like it stopped right over the heart of the plate, daring Jimmy to hit it. Or miss it.

He swung. The sting of contact, bat on ball, felt fine as it rippled up his arms. The *whop!* of wood on horsehide sounded loud and clear as a bell in the woods. The crescendo of cheers from the crowd, as it rose to its feet, seemed to push the baseball into the blue sky and towards the Burma-Shave sign in deepest center field. Jimmy watched it go and began to run. But he didn't run hard. He knew it was gone. He knew he'd hit it out of the park. He knew he'd won the game. Not the outside game, like Shoeless said. That would only be tied after the two runs crossed the plate. No, the inside game, the game in his heart, the game where, at that precise moment, Jimmy Roberts was batting 1.000.

By the time Jimmy rounded first base, he saw the centerfielder stop and look up as the baseball sailed over the fence. By the time he rounded second, he saw Petie Merritt outside the third-base coach's box jumping up and down like a maniac on a pogo stick. By the time he rounded third, he saw Rhoda and his mother and Mrs. Jackson hugging each other and screaming. And by the time he touched home plate, he couldn't see anything but the flannel of uniforms, as his whole team smothered him on the ground. But he could hear, oh, yes, he could hear! The screams and shouts and cheers and laughs and whistles and whoops and hollers, a cacophony of overwhelming joy.

"Put away that cigar!" Toby Gower shouted above the din.

"The game's still tied," a stunned Howard choked out.

"Not for long!" Toby yelled, then joined the noise with a long "Whoooooo-eeeeee!"

After a few minutes, Frankie starting pulling players off the pile. "Batter up, let's go!" The Braves got off Jimmy, and each other, and headed back to the dugout. Somebody put a bat in Jack Washington's hands and pushed him to the plate. Wash had a grin as wide as the sky as he watched the first pitch go by him for a strike. The grin only got wider as he looked over at his teammates jabbering in the dugout while the next pitch whizzed by for the second strike. Then Wash started laughing, and on the next pitch, which was clearly a ball way outside, he swung anyway and ran giddily back to his teammates.

"I struck out!" he shouted happily. His teammates were so ecstatic over Jimmy's homerun they started laughing, too. Who cared, the game was tied!

Jimmy saw Shoeless, looking as happy as he'd ever seen him.

"Got somethin' for ya'."

Shoeless reached in his back pocket and pulled out a bobby pin.

"You gave it to me up in New York, if throwin' it at me is called givin'," he smiled. "Thought you might want to keep it."

Jimmy took the bobby pin from Joe's hand and smiled back.

"Always," he said.

"Let's go win us a championship!" Piggy yelled. His teammates grabbed their gloves, gave a loud *whoop!* and took the field for what they thought would now be a sure win.

But victory did not come. After nine innings, Murph was tired, so Jimmy substituted Red, who shut down the side in the tenth. But so did Woodside's pitcher. No runs scored in the eleventh. Nothing happened in the twelfth, either, except for a little payback. On a pop foul down the third base line, Jimmy came barreling in from left field. Whitey moved over to catch it. "I got it! I got it! Move, Whitey!" Whitey was confused — clearly this was his ball. A quick glance over his shoulder told him Jimmy was coming full-speed, so Whitey moved out of the way. The ball descended just inside the stands, where Jerry Brownell reached up his hands to gather in the souvenir. He never touched the ball, however. Neither did Jimmy. Pretending to try for it, Jimmy launched himself straight at Brownell, smashing into him hard and knocking him back into the row of seats behind him. Seeing him sprawled across the seats, gasping for air, Jimmy smiled and said, "How're your lungs now, Mr. Brownell!"

As he trotted back to his position in left field, Jimmy heard a loud shout from right. "Thanks!" Piggy called, and when Jimmy looked his way, Piggy pumped his hand in the air.

And then the baseball gods turned their faces from Brandon and smiled on Woodside. In the top of the thirteenth, Crusher Goodlett lived up to his name with a long drive over the fence in left field, scoring the runner before him. Jimmy made a play for it, but the ball dropped just over his glove, giving Woodside a two-run lead. Crusher yelled out as he ran the bases, "Stick to makin' towels, Roberts!"

As the Braves came into the dugout for what could be their final at-bat, they were discouraged. It had been a long, draining game. And now it seemed as if all their hard work — all the wind sprints and fungo-catching and practice sliding and double-play workouts, all the time training eyes and bodies to work together to produce that exquisite timing that meant solid contact with the bat, the long, humid summer of slowly getting better and better until they'd found themselves in the championship game — might not be enough.

Joe tried to put the game in perspective. "Remember Babe Ruth: every strikeout brings me closer to the next home run." But this time he had a group of rebels on his hands.

"But I don't wanna lose!" Piggy Simpson said.

"Failure *ain't* fun!" Pepper Forrester howled.

"Not this time!" Whiff Wofford cried out.

"Winnin's funner!" shouted Jack Washington.

"The next home run is *now*!" Jawbreaker Johnson yelled.

"Yeah!"

"Let's do it!"

"We're the Brandon Braves!"

"We're gonna be champs!"

"Let's win! Win! Win! Win!"

The shouts renewed their spirits. And the baseball gods seemed once again to rotate their heads. The Woodside pitcher walked Petie. Red struck out, but that was expected. The top of the order came up. Whiff couldn't connect, but Jawbreaker got a single. Two on, two out. Piggy came to the plate. He'd gone hitless all game. So much for that feeling of his. But maybe this was the time. *Save me a bat, Steve!* Jimmy was in the on-deck circle. Piggy fouled one off. *You can do it!* Piggy took a strike. *Just put it in play!* Piggy did. A slow roller to Goodlett. Jawbreaker took off for second. Petie broke for third, jumping over the ball. That distraction caused Goodlett's throw to be a step late. Piggy crossed the bag, safe! All of a sudden, Brandon had the bases full.

This time it was Toby Gower who pulled out a cigar. "And you thought *I* was over-confident!" said Howard.

"Roberts did it the last time."

"Maybe he's had time to reconsider his decision."

"What decision, Howard?" Yancey asked.

"Nothing, Yancey. Let's watch the game."

"With pleasure," Toby replied. He lit his Havana and exhaled luxuriously. "Ahhhhh!"

Jimmy started toward the plate. "Your time again, Jimmy!" Shoeless called from the dugout steps. Jimmy looked down at Black Betsy in his hands. *My time?* He looked back at Shoeless. A thought popped into his head, a thought so good, so right, so perfect for the situation that it made Jimmy smile and jump in the air. He ran to Frankie and spoke to him urgently.

"What's goin' on?" Shoeless asked Murph, standing next to him on the dugout steps.

"No idea."

"We're about to find out." Whitey nodded towards Jimmy, who was coming back to the bench.

"What're doin'?" Shoeless asked.

"Made a line-up change," Jimmy answered.

"Who can you put in? We've used up everybody on the bench."

"Not everybody. We haven't used you."

"Me?" Shoeless said. "I cain't play, I'm not on the team."

"Sure you are. Frankie just confirmed it. You're listed as the manager on the official score-card, an' in this league, managers can bat."

"That's ridiculous. Get up there an' hit!"

"Whattaya think?" Jimmy turned to his teammates. "Does this situation call for Shoeless Joe Jackson, the greatest natural hitter of all time, to bat?"

His teammates didn't hesitate. "You bet!" shouted Whitey.

"Great idea!" cried Pepper.

"Give him Black Betsy!" yelled Wash.

Jimmy grabbed the fat part of the bat and held the handle towards Shoeless. "Your teammates want you to hit."

"No!" Joe shouted.

"Then I guess we'll forfeit the game." He walked past Joe and sat down on the bench. Then Wash sat down, then Pepper, Murph, Red, Whiff. "This is the situation," Jimmy said.

"The situation is, you're a bunch of idiots!" Shoeless yelled. He kicked at the dirt. "I ain't got any shoes!"

"Ain't your name Shoeless Joe?" smiled Jimmy, prompting laughter all around.

"Shut up! All right, goddammit, guess I'll have to make a fool out of myself an' you, too! Gimme some tobacco somebody."

Whiff gave him the Red Man pouch and Joe jammed some in his mouth. He yanked Black Betsy out of Jimmy's hands. "Don't forget to talk to her," Jimmy said with a wink. Joe spat and walked to the plate.

"Ladies an' gentlemen, I don't believe my eyes!" Dixie said into the microphone. "I do believe I see Shoeless Joe Jackson comin' to the plate. That must've been what Roberts was doin', talkin' to the umpire, makin' a battin' change. Well, this is one helluva change! I apologize for my French, but I think the occasion calls for it!"

The hushed murmur that had spread through the crowd as they'd watched the conference between Jimmy and Shoeless now changed to applause and cheers, as Joe approached the plate. He was in a daze. It was as if he'd gone back forty years and the Chicago fans were cheering for him again. He stopped outside the batter's box. "Gimme a minute here, Frankie."

"Take your time, Joe," Frankie said, with a chuckle. "I'd say, after all these years, folks'll wait another minute or two for you to hit again."

Joe grunted and swung the bat back and forth a few times to loosen up. *Not that it matters.* Oh, sure, he'd hit lots of balls in practice, but he knew there was a big difference between tossing a ball up in the air and facing a ball thrown by a pitcher trying to make you swing and miss.

In his box, Howard said delightedly, "Well, well, well, look who's coming to the plate! Still confident, Toby? Or does the prospect of a sixty-something year old batter who's been off the field for decades fill your heart with dread?" Howard raised his cigar and passed it back and forth under his nose.

"Here's some history for you!" Yancey said, somewhat awed. "The last at-bat of Shoeless Joe!"

Toby let his cigar drop to his side. He was conflicted. On one hand, he was thrilled to be at this historic occasion. On the other, he wished he could have been more of a bystander, less of a man with a lot of bragging rights on the line and even more money. "Once a hitter always a hitter," he said weakly.

"Yeah, and once a loser, always a loser," Howard laughed.

In the colored bleachers, Jellycakes was doing a brisk business. "Two-to-one he hits it out," one fan said, proffering money. "Ten-to-one he whiffs it," said another. "I got fifty dollars says he'll never even get the bat on the ball," said a third. Jellycakes happily accepted all bets. "Kill it, Mr. Shoeless, kill it!" screamed Willie.

Rusty Peters stepped out of the Woodside dugout and took a few steps toward his fielders. What should he tell them to do? Back up? Come in? How do you manage a situation where the greatest natural hitter of all time, who hasn't swung a bat in forty-odd years, comes to the plate? He raised both hands over his head and pushed them forward. The Woodside players backed up. Crusher snarled "No way!" and took a few steps in. On the mound, Randy Ross was nervous. Never in his life had he imagined he'd be pitching to Shoeless Joe Jackson, much less with the bases loaded and a championship on the line. But nobody on either team was more nervous than Joe. He spat some tobacco juice in the dirt, hitched up his pants, and stepped, shoeless, into the batter's box.

The Woodside catcher decided to call for nothing but fastballs. This wasn't a time to get cute, this was a time to get this old man out, win the game, and get on with the celebration. He squatted down, flipped down the "1" sign, and got set for the pitch. Randy reared back and fired. Shoeless barely saw the ball, it came so fast. "Strike!" yelled Frankie, and the crowd erupted.

Joe stepped out of the box. *Dang, never even saw it!* He blinked a few times and rubbed his eyes. "You can do it!" Jimmy called from the dugout. *Not if I cain't see it.* He sighed. *Got no choice.* He stepped into the box, tapped his bat against the plate a couple of times, and crouched.

Randy fired again and again Joe barely saw the pitch. "Stee-rike two!" called Frankie. Joe backed out of the box. *Ain't never been in such a fix in my life!* He scuffed the dirt with his foot. *No damn shoes, cain't even dig in. Lotta good it'd do me anyway.*

He looked at the Woodside defense. Goodlett had come in even closer at shortstop. "Come on, Shoeless, hit it to me, hit it to me!" he yelled, slapping his fist in his glove. "If you *can* hit it! Right here, right here!" *Like I could get it that far!* Joe thought. He looked around. The outfielders were back, the infielders were back, except for Goodlett. He managed a smile. *Just like the old days, playin' me deep. Well, this ain't the old days, boys!*

"Might as well do it now," Howard said, pulling his lighter from his pocket. "You're looking a little glum, Toby."

"He hasn't struck out yet," Toby managed.

"No, but assuming he does…." Howard flicked the lighter and the huge flame sprang to life.

At home plate, Joe turned and spat some tobacco juice just in time to see the flame from Howard's lighter. *Doggone, that's big,* he thought. *Wait a minute!* He quickly covered one eye with his hand, staring at the flame. Howard put it to the cigar, and Joe switched eyes, staring harder. Howard puffed the cigar to life and pocketed the lighter. *Maybe that'll help.*

Back in the box, Joe looked out at the pitcher. *This is it. What the heck am I gonna do?* He looked down at the bat in his hands. *Got one left in ya', Betsy?* Then Joe gasped. He'd had an idea. *That's it! Of course! That's the situation!*

A huge smile spread across his face as he raised Black Betsy. He slammed the bat on the plate a few times and glared at the pitcher, menacingly. He got set, put his weight back, put the little finger around the handle, and waggled the bat threateningly. *Come on, come on, bring it to me! You have no idea what I'm gonna do to your pitch!*

And the pitch came. The Woodside players tensed in anticipation. Petie, Jawbreaker, and Piggy danced off the bases. The rest of the Braves crowded the dugout steps. The crowd at Meadowbrook Park stood and waited in eerie silence. And Shoeless Joe Jackson, perhaps the greatest hitter in baseball history, The Carolina Confection, The Carolina Crashsmith, Homerun Joe, squared around... and bunted the ball.

For a split second, nobody moved. The defenders seemed frozen in place, shocked. The Brandon runners looked at each other, as if they'd never considered what to do when a teammate bunted. The crowd gave a collective gasp that rose in the air like a rocket. It was if the cosmos itself stopped for a nanosecond, stunned in incredulity. *The bases are loaded, the game's on the line, and Shoeless Joe Jackson bunts???*

Then the earth started spinning on its axis again. "Run you shoeless son of a gun!" yelled Rhoda. And Joe did. Petie took off for home, Jawbreaker flew towards third, and Piggy broke for second. Randy sprinted off the mound, fielded the bunt, and turned to throw to first. But the first baseman had been playing so far back in right field, Randy doubted he could get there in time. So he turned to throw to third. The Woodside third baseman, running in from his spot at the edge of the outfield grass, didn't have time to get set, and Randy's throw pulled him just enough off the bag for Jawbreaker's slide to beat it. Safe at third, and Petie had crossed the plate. Brandon was one run behind.

"Second! Second! Second!" Crusher yelled at the third baseman, who threw it as hard as he could. But Piggy Simpson was not about to be the last out in this game. "Crusher!" he screamed, flung himself at the bag, and, legs flailing wildly, kicked Crusher's foot off to avoid the force-out. As he did so, Jawbreaker, who had immediately jumped up from his slide at third, ran for home. Crusher thought about a throw, but held up. "Folks, this game is tied up!" Dixie Dawkins shouted into his microphone as Jawbreaker crossed the plate. "But Jackson's gotta make it to first for the runs to count."

Joe was trying. He hadn't run this hard in years, and his age was showing. And it didn't help that he'd drunk all that bourbon. From the corner of his eye, he saw Goodlett cock and fire. *Gotta beat it!* Joe stumbled. *Dive!* The first baseman stretched for the throw. Joe saw the white base. He never wanted to touch anything so desperately in his life, but he was going to be too late! He saw the first baseman's feet, one on the bag, one stretched out to snag Goodlett's throw. *Dammit!*

Then the feet moved. They rose in the air! Goodlett had hurried the throw, and now it was sailing over the first baseman's head. Joe dived forward on his elbows, dirt kicking into his face, and hugged the bag. Safe! The crowd roared.

But the roar didn't diminish, it increased. Joe turned his head and saw the second baseman, backing up the play at first, run towards the stands, chasing Goodlett's wild throw. *No need to worry*, thought Joe. *If you think I'm tryin' for second, you're nuts!* But the player fielded the ball and started to throw, not towards second base, but towards home. *What the heck?* And then he saw. *Piggy! He's tryin' to score!*

Joe scrambled up on the bag and looked towards home plate. Piggy was churning down the line from third, pumping those fat legs like pistons in a racecar. The Woodside catcher was blocking the plate. Jimmy and the rest of the team were standing nearby, screaming. "Run, Piggy, run! Run! Run! Run!" The crowd's noise was deafening. *Run!* The ball came in, popping into the catcher's mitt. In time. Piggy was going to be out.

But not Piggy, not this time. He wasn't called Piggy for nothing. He lowered his shoulder and hurtled into the catcher with a force that sent him flying backwards like he'd been shot from a cannon. The ball popped out of his mitt and rolled away. Piggy, tumbling through the air, managed to reach back and touch the plate with his foot before he slammed to the ground. The run had scored! "Brandon wins the championship!" Dixie wailed. "Brandon wins the championship!"

Poor Piggy. He never had a chance to get up. Petie jumped on him, then Whiff, then Wash, Jimmy, Jawbreaker, the whole team piled on top, a jangle of arms and legs, a chorus of hollers, hoots, and hoorays. In the stands, Thelma and Rhoda and Katie danced up and down, screaming "We won!" "We won!" "We won!" in ecstatic rhythm. Toby slapped Howard on the back. "Too soon on the celebration, Howard!" he yelled, then threw his arm around Yancey and they both jumped up and down. Willie and Jellycakes ran onto the field, and, when a guard tried to steer them back into the stands, scooted around him and raced about the outfield, punching the air with pure-fire joy, hollering "Shoeless Joe! Shoeless Joe! Shoeless Joe!" Others joined them, white and black together, reveling in the pandemonium.

On first base, Shoeless Joe Jackson stood and watched it all, smiling to himself. How proud he was! Of himself. Of Jimmy. Of the team. Proud of the whole dang world! And grateful. Grateful he was here again, standing on top of a base. On top of the world. Baseball had always been his world, now it was again. He looked down at his stockinged feet, smiled even more, and straightened to his full height. No doubt about it. Shoeless Joe was safe!

CHAPTER 21

The weeks after the championship game went by quickly, the days as sweet as the scent of fall that began to perfume the air. Jimmy settled into a new routine, one that didn't include baseball practice, but did include his daily Coke walks with Rhoda, interspersed with treats of ice cream sodas at Tucker's. Life inside the mill was as monotonous as ever, but, even there, the bobbins seemed to fly through Jimmy's hands and into the bins almost by themselves. His thoughts often drifted to Rhoda in the room on the floor above. He never tired of imagining her soft hair and laughing eyes, and sometimes he had to shake his head at the realization that he had the love of a girl like her.

There was still baseball, the players getting together some afternoons during the week, maybe a pick-up game on Saturday in the twilight, with only crickets and birds for fans. They'd remember highlights of the season, a nifty double-play Jawbreaker, Whiff, and Wash had turned, the one-hitter Murph had thrown, Jimmy's amazing "train home run," they began to call it. "Piggy, show us how you took out that catcher," one of them might say, but Piggy would answer, "I ain't riskin' my neck just for fun!" The play they never tired of recalling, however, was the final at-bat of the season.

"Did you see the look on Crusher's face when Shoeless bunted?" Pepper said. "Thought he'd seen a ghost."

"You shoulda seen the look on yours, Pep," Red rejoined. "Thought you'd seen a nekkid lady!"

"Heck, I knew he was gonna bunt," offered Petie.

"That why you forgot to run?" taunted Wash.

And the joshing would continue until one of them said, "Seriously, though, wadn' that the best dang time you ever had?" And they'd fall silent a minute, basking in remembered glory.

Though they asked him to, Shoeless never came to Brandon Park to be with them. He'd had enough baseball for one summer, and plenty enough for one life. He was happy going to work, jawing with customers, returning home to sip sweet tea or lemonade with Katie on their porch, and enjoying a few memories himself. "I fooled 'em, didn' I, Katie?"

"You did, Joe." What a thrill it was to see her husband enjoying success again after all these years.

"Wonder who ol' Stone'll bring in next season?"

"Don't know."

"Won't make no never mind, we'll whip 'em again!"

In his mansion on West Avondale several miles away, Howard Stone wasn't thinking about next season. He was having a hard time thinking past next week. When all his plans and schemes had come to naught, he had never felt so depressed. He hadn't even bothered to make a bid for the Binghamton team. What would have been the point? He spent a lot of time sitting behind his desk, staring out the window. *Stuck!* was all he could think. *In a damn textile mill! I've got to sell. But, then, what will I do? And how will I get into professional baseball? Maybe next season, if I can produce a winner. Could be other teams I could bid on. But how will I find out, stuck in this sinkhole? Socks isn't going to help again.* Howard leaned back in his chair and closed his eyes. *Cotton, yarn, cloth.... Lintheads, rednecks, hicks....* Words and images plagued him like locusts. And there was one word he could never drive away, no matter how much Scotch he drank, a word he always heard in his daddy's distinctive growl: *Loser.*

At his "office" at the Riverside, Jellycakes felt anything but a loser. The championship game had been very good to him, and now football season had started. The Furman Purple Paladins were looking pretty good, they'd surely garner some bets. And the Clemson Tigers, those fans were rabid. True, Howard Stone didn't drop by any more, and he was a big bettor, but there were always plenty of bettors, big and small. *An' I get my piece of the pie no matter what.*

He looked over at his son, tossing a brand-new baseball up and catching it with his new glove. Joe Jackson had come by one afternoon and picked up Willie in his Packard, jokingly asking him, "You wanna drive, Willie?"

"No, suh!"

"Well, all right, I'll drive, then."

Joe had taken Willie downtown and bought him a baseball glove. And Jellycakes had bought him a baseball, with a promise that he'd replenish Willie's supply instead of making him play with a taped ball. *Gotta do somethin' with my money!* his father had told Willie with a laugh.

One afternoon in November, Joe and Katie were working in their liquor store when the phone rang. "Hello," Katie answered.

"Is this Jackson's Liquor Store?" a man's voice asked. He had a northern accent.

"Yes."

"Can I speak to Joe Jackson?"

"Who's calling, please?"

"Name's George Winston, but he doesn't know me."

"Just a minute." Katie put down the phone. "Somebody for you, Joe."

"Who is it?"

"A Mr. Winston, but you don't know him."

"He could have given the order to you as well as me," Joe grumbled as he took the receiver from her. "Hello."

"Hello. Is this Joe Jackson, the baseball player, the one they call Shoeless Joe?" George Winston asked.

"This is Joe Jackson."

"Mr. Jackson, my name is George Winston and I have great news for you. I'm the booking agent for 'The Toast of the Town.'"

"Never heard of it. An' we don't want no books."

George laughed. "No, I'm not calling about books, Mr. Jackson. 'The Toast of the Town,' you know, Ed Sullivan's television program on CBS."

"Don't watch it," Joe said. "Look, what can we do for you?"

"It's what we can do for you, Mr. Jackson. Mr. Sullivan wants to put you on the show, on December 16, in New York City. He heard how you were inducted into the Cleveland Baseball Hall of Fame in September but couldn't make the ceremony. I'm sorry you were ill. Well, we've decided to hold another ceremony on television! There'll be over 4 million viewers, more than everyone who ever saw you play. We'll have Tris Speaker present you with the gold clock, just like he was supposed to do in Cleveland. What do you think of that?"

Joe hesitated. Television? New York? "Would I be havin' to sign anything?"

"Just the standard release form." George was a little nonplussed. He'd booked hundreds of people. Most were a little more enthusiastic.

"Then you'd better talk to my wife." Joe handed the phone to his wife. "They want to put me on TV."

Katie took the receiver. "This is Mrs. Jackson."

"Mrs. Jackson," George began. "As I was telling your husband, we would like him to appear on Ed Sullivan's 'Toast of the Town' in New York this December."

Katie looked at her husband. He hadn't been in the best of health recently, that's why they had decided not to attend the ceremony in Cleveland. The summer had taken its toll on him. Another trip to New York would be hard. But to appear on national television being inducted into the Cleveland Hall of Fame. And the resolution, signed by the governor, was already sitting on the Commissioner's desk. Maybe this was Joe's moment at last. "Tell me more, Mr. Winston."

The news quickly spread all over Greenville. Jimmy and his teammates began planning a big send-off party. Toby Gower promised to host it in his own home. Charlie Deerhart of *The Greenville News* started looking through his files, jotting notes for a big article. "Local Boy Makes Good.... Again!" seemed like a good headline.

"I'm so excited I cain't hardly sleep," Jimmy said to Rhoda. They were sitting in a booth at Tucker's Soda Shop. Thanksgiving had come and gone, December had arrived, the date was getting closer.

"An' I cain't hardly wait for the party. It'll be our first." They smiled at each other. They had begun memorializing things they did together, the mere fact of naming something a "first" implying with sweet anticipation that there would be more to come. "You gonna dance with me?"

"Dance? What?"

"Square dance."

"I don't know how."

"Lord, I got lots to teach you, don't I?" Rhoda feigned exasperation.

"I'll be a good student." The thought of Rhoda teaching him made him smile.

"Durn straight!"

"An' I got to teach you how to throw a baseball."

"Looks like we got lots to learn from each other." Rhoda snuck a hand under the table. Jimmy reached his under to meet it.

"I got a present for Joe."

"What is it?"

"It's a secret. But he's gonna love it!"

"You gonna have secrets from me?" Rhoda demanded.

"Durn straight!" They laughed the carefree laugh of people in love. And Jimmy thought of the other present he was going to buy down at Hale's Jewelers, the one he was going to give to Rhoda on Christmas Eve.

The shop door opened and Thelma walked in. Jimmy looked up. "Mama! Why aren't you at work?"

Thelma looked grim. "Waddy let me off to come find you."

"What's wrong?" Jimmy asked.

"Oh, Jimmy!" Thelma took a deep breath, steeling herself. She was about to hurt her child deeply and there was nothing she could do about it. "There ain't no easy way to say this, Jimmy. But Katie came to find me at work this mornin'. Joe died last night from a heart attack."

"No! Mama!" he cried out, the joy of a few moments before replaced in an instant with inconsolable sorrow. Rhoda squeezed his hand hard. Jimmy closed his eyes and began to sob. A familiar phrase screamed unspoken from deep inside. *Say it ain't so!*

The funeral was that Sunday at the Brandon Baptist Church, exactly one week before Joe's scheduled appearance on Ed Sullivan's show, an appearance that might have paved the way for the greatest natural hitter of all time to take his rightful place in the Baseball Hall of Fame. The church was so crowded, loudspeakers had to be set up outside for the people who could not get in. There were so many flowers, the local florists had completely sold out. Jimmy and his teammates pitched in and bought a floral wreath shaped like a baseball diamond.

Reverend Manning gave the eulogy. He'd felt a little guilty about having invited Reverend Nally as a guest preacher when he'd delivered the infamous "Shoeless Sermon" earlier that summer, so he was glad to be able to use his pulpit to praise Joe this time. He used the analogy of another Joseph, this one the favorite son of Jacob, whose coat of many colors so infuriated his brothers. "They threw him in the pit," he intoned, "But the Lord brought him forth. Potiphar sent him to prison, but the Lord brought him forth. And placed him at the right hand of the Pharaoh, where his wisdom during the seven years of famine led the people to salvation." Reverend Manning looked down from the pulpit to Jimmy sitting with Rhoda and Thelma in the second pew, directly behind Katie, his Brandon teammates behind them. "I know some people Joseph Jackson led to salvation, not on as grand a scale as his namesake, perhaps, but salvation nonetheless. A young man sought him out, an' he led him an' his teammates to victory. An' by leadin' them, he led himself to victory, too."

Reverend Manning paused. "Victory! That's what we're celebratin' here today, my brothers an' sisters, victory! Just like Joseph, Joe Jackson faced times of trouble, faced times when he was in the pit, in the pit of despair. Just like Joseph, Joe Jackson was thrown in jail. An' just like Joseph, Joe Jackson overcame his despair, Joe Jackson walked out of that prison, Joe Jackson went on to live a good life, lovin' his wife, helpin' his neighbors, servin' his God."

Jimmy looked at the coffin, thought about the man inside, the man he had idolized, then hated, and then had come to love. *I'm not worried 'bout Joe an' God,* he thought. *I know Joe. When he gets to that diamond in the sky, he'll knock it out of the park.*

It was as if the Reverend had heard his thoughts. "Victory, that's what I said, victory! All you people here to celebrate Joe's life, that's victory! All you people outside, too many for a church to contain, that's victory! The Brandon Braves with that championship trophy in their mill, that's victory!" He gathered himself for the final crescendo. "Life's full of wins an' losses, my friends. Nobody knew that better'n Joe Jackson. But I'm here to tell you, I can feel victory in this room! I can sense it in the air, surely as the sun shines bright outside, even in December! I can hear it in the hearts of all of you who knew Joe Jackson, who lived with Joe Jackson, who loved Joe Jackson. He will have the final victory, the greatest victory, the victory that seals away all loss! Victory over death! That's your victory, Joseph Jefferson Wofford Jackson, now go forth an' claim it!"

The congregation sang the final hymn, "Abide With Me," the pallbearers came forth, and the funeral procession made its way to Woodlawn Memorial Cemetery on the north side of Greenville. Only Jimmy, Rhoda, Thelma, and the family were gathered round as Joe's coffin was laid in the ground. Katie had held her tears throughout the service, but now she let them flow. She gathered some dirt in her hand and threw it on the coffin. She had no final words, at least none to speak out loud. Whatever words she said, she said them in her heart. Thelma put her arm around her and led her away.

One by one, the mourners tossed in some dirt and paid their final respects, until only Jimmy was left standing at the gravesite in the bright, cold light. He picked up a handful of dirt, and, following a sudden impulse, rubbed it together in his hands, as if he were standing at home plate, roughening his hands for a better grip on the bat. The dirt fell out from his hands onto the copper coffin. He slapped his hands together, dispensing the final grains.

"A little baseball dirt for ya'." Jimmy paused. All the things he'd wanted to say to Shoeless but never had a chance to, all the words that had poured out of him during the preceding nights, during the agonizing walks he'd taken with Rhoda over the past few days, were gone. All the things he'd planned to say in this good-bye suddenly seemed not to matter. "You're finally at rest, Shoeless. Always wanted to call you that, hope you don't mind now. But don't worry, I ordered your headstone for Mrs. Jackson, an' I made sure it don't say 'Shoeless' on it." Jimmy smiled. He always liked the name, but he could understand why Shoeless didn't.

He stared at the coffin. It was time to go, time to let the gravediggers finish their job, time to move on to whatever victories and defeats awaited him on this baseball-diamond of a life. "I left a little somethin' with ya'. I was gonna give it to you at your party, but maybe this is better. I think you'll like it." He thought of the final gift he was giving to the man who had given him so much. "I think you'll like it a lot."

There was just one more thing to say, something he'd missed saying to a man ever since his father had left, something he was so grateful to be able to say now. "I love you, Joe."

Jimmy waited for the tears, but none came. Instead, he felt a kind of comfort, a small delight that brought the tiniest of smiles to his lips. For he knew the secret that was being buried with his hero. He knew what would go with Joe Jackson into eternity. Something he had sneaked into Joe's coffin during the public viewing when no one was looking. It was a baseball — the one he'd saved from the championship game — the bunted ball from the last at-bat of Shoeless Joe.

THE END
of
THE LAST AT-BAT OF SHOELESS JOE

AUTHOR'S NOTE

Growing up in Greenville, South Carolina in the early 1950's, I played Little League baseball for the Lions Club. Second base — it was the shortest throw to first. I actually led off for a time because I didn't usually strike out. I also didn't usually get a hit, but the coach hoped I might at least get a walk. Such was the strategy of Little League ball, circa 1956.

In all the years I played, I never heard the name of Shoeless Joe Jackson. It was as if he didn't exist. Joe had died by the time I started playing ball, but, still, one might have expected that the greatest natural hitter of all time would have deserved some recognition. After all, he began his baseball career in the Textile Baseball League playing for Brandon Mill, and he ended his life as a liquor store owner in West Greenville. But Joe had been involved in the infamous Black Sox Scandal of 1919, banned from playing professional baseball and from ever being in the Hall of Fame. He was considered a cheater by some-- certainly not someone to be held up as a model for young boys just learning the game. All my research, however, convinced me that, while Joe knew about the "fix," he did not participate in it. How else can anyone explain his outstanding play in the Series? I wrote this novel partly to say to those who still believe Joe should be kept out of the Hall of Fame: "Say it ain't so!"

Later, I did learn that Shoeless had lived and died in my hometown. I was amazed—and a little mad. Guilty or not, it didn't seem right that Joe's hometown refused to claim him. So I set out to claim him. I wrote a screenplay about him and then turned the screenplay into a novel. Of course, it's usually the other way around!

Writing *The Last At-Bat of Shoeless Joe* has been one of the happiest writing experiences of my career. It is an homage to my hometown, and I delighted in putting in the novel many of the places that have remained dear to my heart. The mountains, where my siblings and I still have a home—very close to Caesar's Head! The mill villages, whose houses still remain even though the mills have closed. During the writing of the screenplay and then the novel, I had wonderful times driving around these villages with my mother, carefully noting their cookie-cutter designs, sometimes-slanted porches, and barren yards with wash hanging on the line. I would get out and walk a street or two, imagining myself a young Jimmy Roberts on his way to the mill. And, yes, looking up, there was the mill, empty then, but still looming massively above me. I even went inside a textile mill that was still running, the noise unbelievably loud—and I was wearing earmuffs. To this day I cannot imagine enduring that noise, and the heat and cotton lint that accompanied it, day after dreary day. So I wrote this novel also partly to pay tribute to the men and women who did their job, clothed their children, loved their neighbors, and somehow carved out a meaningful existence on mill hill.

No novel is entirely the work of one person, and this novel is no exception. Thanks are owed to my brother, Frank, and his wife, Diana Martin, for their careful reading and helpful insights. Fellow author Brooke Stoddard also gave valuable input. I want to thank Ed Rucker for his thorough perusal and challenging questions and Donna Levin for the scrutiny of a final read-through. And, of course, my wife and steadfast supporter, Reba. But most of all I wish to give great thanks to my friend Charlie McCormack. Charlie is a long-time baseball fan and Red Sox fanatic, and he brought that same passion to his work on this book. He started by simply asking if he could read it, then volunteered to fact-check, and soon I was asking him to research which minor-league teams were relevant to the story and what kind of contract they might offer and a hundred other details, not all of them baseball-related, that helped flesh out my story and make it real. Most writers need a sounding board, someone who knows the story almost as well as they do, someone you can talk to about every single problem and decision that arises in the course of completing a novel. Charlie was that person for me, and I am eternally grateful.

I am happy to note that today Greenville has completely embraced its hometown hero. There is a statue of Shoeless Joe downtown. Brandon Field has been restored and one can, as I have, stand at home plate and imagine young Shoeless Joe Jackson looking out at that same outfield and that same mill on the hill. The city has even moved Shoeless's actual house next door to its minor-league ballpark and made it into a museum, full of pictures and memorabilia and over 2000 books related to baseball. Imagine: sitting in Joe's chair in his living room in the home where he lived and died. It's as if the great Shoeless Joe Jackson never had a last at-bat at all, but comes to the plate every day, finally celebrated in his hometown. Here's hoping one day he will be rightfully celebrated in the Baseball Hall of Fame as well.

Granville Wyche Burgess,
Greenwich, Connecticut, November 2018

OTHER BOOKS FROM
CHICKADEE PRINCE YOU WILL ENOY

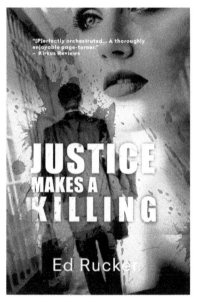

Justice Makes a Killing: *A Bobby Earle Novel*, by Ed Rucker –
ISBN 978-1732913905

"A thoroughly enjoyable page-turner.... The classic courtroom drama at the heart of this story is perfectly orchestrated, and the seemingly impossible odds make Earl's masterful handling of evidence, witnesses, opposing counsel, the jury, and the judge wonderfully satisfying to read. Rucker has a knack for explaining the minutiae of legal procedure clearly as he weaves them into the story." — Kirkus Reviews

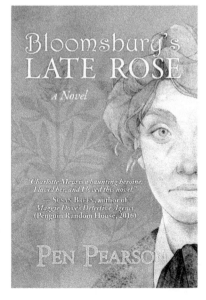

Bloomsbury's Late Rose, by Pen Pearson – ISBN 978-1-7329139-4-3

"Charlotte Mew is a haunting heroine: brave, talented and tormented. I loved her, and I loved this novel." — Susan Breen, author of *Maggie Dove's Detective Agency* (Penguin Random House, 2016)

"Written with such skill that I found myself walking the Edwardian London streets alongside Mew, this novel does what great historical fiction should: it brilliantly illuminates the past." — Tracey Iceton, author of *Herself Alone in Orange Rain* (Cinnamon Press, 2017)

CPSIA information can be obtained
at www.ICGtesting.com
Printed in the USA
LVHW041156030320
648828LV00004B/183